FARSEEKER

JOANNA STARR

StarFire

ACKNOWLEDGEMENTS

Thank you to Jon for his unending support and patience. Thanks to Jill for her excellent editorial work, and to the Deranged Doctor Design team for their wonderful cover art.

A special thank you to Ian, my precious Reader Team, my subscribers, and to all the great people on my FaceBook group who never fail to make my day. Thanks to the Cosmos for making this work possible.

I would also like to thank you, the reader, for joining us on this epic adventure.

FARSEEKER

JOANNA STARR

For Urtha

1

THAYA

It wasn't human.

Thaya's blood ran cold, her breath catching in her throat as she stared at the skeleton lying in the dirt of the cavern fifteen feet below. Its lower half was crushed beneath a fallen megalith, a great slab of smoothed and polished rock twice the height of a man. She leaned further into the hole, angling to get a better look, but the earth crumbled beneath her palms. Screaming, she plunged into the darkness, the light of day disappearing as she tumbled along with the dirt and scree.

She hit the ground, the breath exploding from her lungs as soil and stones rained down. The earthy shower abated and she groaned as every muscle complained.

Something moved by the wall.

She clawed the earth from her eyes. The something was merely dust motes circling in a shaft of sunlight. Nothing sinister lurked here, unless you counted the skeleton. She relaxed. *No, I haven't awoken the dead,* but still, she took several breaths in the deepening silence to still her nerves.

The dust ceased billowing and settled in a strange

brown mist on the floor of the, of the...*What exactly is this place?*

Above ground lay a jumble of enormous, pale yellow megaliths; some stacked, most fallen, and each stone larger than a cart. The Old Temple, as it was called by the people of Havendell, although no one knew if it was a temple, or to which god it belonged, stood out peculiarly at the base of the White Mountains on the most perfect plain of grasses and wildflowers bordering the edge of the North Forest. Only a couple of miles from her village of Brightwater, it was a place she'd come to for quiet and solitude. To her, it didn't look like a temple. Instead, she thought of it as a place of power, perhaps where Ley Lines met. Her ancient ancestors had been deeply learned in those things.

There were no other yellow stones to be found anywhere in Havendell—so where had these come from? Over the years, she'd inspected them meticulously, and those still standing had been cut to fit against each other so perfectly there was no need for mortar. There were no tool marks upon them either, so what fine machinery had cut them to ensure that not even the wind could find a gap? *Clearly built by master stonemasons and architects to some long-forgotten power. The recent heavy rains have done this; caused land subsidence and potholes to appear everywhere, but they've also revealed wonders from our ancient past just for me, for who else comes here? Who else cares about our past?*

Eyes adjusting to the dim light, she took in the small cavern of earthen walls and ancient megaliths. Above, daylight spilled through the hole, and she could see thick roots knotted the walls. Thank the gods, she could climb up them and get out. She rubbed her sprained neck. The knees of her trousers were torn which was a shame as they were only a few months old—and just look at her shirt, all muddy and grass-stained!

The skeleton stole her gaze, sending a chill down her spine. She pulled herself up, and sidled towards it, her hands clammy. She didn't believe in many things, but she *did* believe in ghosts, and right now she hoped they didn't believe in her. *It's just a skeleton; probably the previous idiot who decided to explore this temple... or is it a tomb?*

Her heart raced as she expected the skeleton to spring to life, but it lay silently, vacantly, in the earth. It was *similar* to a human's; its height, the size and shape of its bones, its pale white femurs and gently curving spine, but it was the skull that caused her to inhale sharply. It wasn't the normal smooth and round affair, neither did it have flat orbitals, or an angular jaw, or rows of blunt teeth. *This* skull protruded forwards with a heavy snout; its lower jaw was extremely slender; and those teeth? Well, she could try to deny it, but they *were* canines—long ones, *real* ones.

She'd seen a lion's cranium before. There was one in a glass cabinet in her old school, casually left on display to give children nightmares. This skull was identical to it.

Dear gods, there's another one beside it!

This neighbouring skeleton was buried deeper into the mud, obscuring it from her view when she'd first peered down into the cavern. It was definitely human, like any other she had seen in the Ancestral Vaults. Both were of a similar height, bipedal, and each had two arms, normal ribs and hips. Which meant the strange skeleton could only be one thing; *a human cat-person! A real-life—or real-dead—lion-man-woman!*

She let go of her breath. What did it mean? Had she missed something in History? She'd spent her childhood in the library, how could she have overlooked any mention of cat-people? For all her studies, she felt remarkably ignorant.

Standing beside the skeletons, the weight of aeons pressed down. It was sad, seeing their demise beneath the impossibly large stones, their final resting place. *Imagine dying here and being forgotten.* They reminded her of human-kinds' tenuous hold on life.

She laid a hand on the cold stone pressing upon them. It had to be several tonnes in weight, so what on earth could have toppled it? The stone was broken on one end too, snapped by some great force. There had been cataclysms in the past, world-shattering earthquakes, sky-splitting storms, and floods that had ravaged the entire surface of the planet —was that what had happened?

She bent down beside the skeletons. *Hmm, the human skull is more peculiar than I thought. It's longer towards the back, larger brained, more sophisticated,* she mused. She looked at its hands. *And what's this?* Clutched in its metatarsals was a thin tube, dull with grime. Holding her breath, she reached over the lion-person and gripped it. No longer held by flesh and blood, a gentle pull caused the tube to slide from its grasp, but the end caught on a bone and the finger snapped off.

She stared at it rolling on the ground. "Urgh! Sorry," she whispered.

She brushed the dirt off and inspected the tube praying it wasn't a curse. It looked to be made of gold, and the complete lack of rust suggested it was. Apart from a slight dent on one side, it had miraculously survived its owner's demise and the collapse of the temple. It was too light to be solid and something rustled inside. Carefully, she tried twisting one end. It squeaked and, slowly she unscrewed the end off. A roll of parchment slid out, perfectly clean and crisp with no signs of mould or age. Either a spell or the gold tube had protected it.

Thaya swallowed. It was clearly important to the person who had gripped it even in death. What if it was a spell that had caused the collapse of the stones? Spells or curses would have long worn off, wouldn't they? Surely time expired all things? She licked her lips—it didn't matter, there was no way she *wasn't* going to look at the scroll.

She unravelled it, wincing at every protesting crackle as the paper yawned awake between her fingers. There were no balls of fire or crashing thunder, only a deafening silence. Black ink inscribed the parchment, and in the dim light, Thaya scrutinised the exquisite lettering. It was unlike any she had seen, even stranger than the whirling script of Adansk, a land as far to the east as one could go. This writing consisted of square-like letters with long curling ends, but no amount of squinting revealed the meaning of the words. She unravelled the scroll further and a different language began. To her shock, she found she could read the rounded, simpler lettering.

"Lonohassan!"

She'd grown up in Havendell but had been born in Lonohassa. Her native tongue might be Havendellian, but the ancient language of Lonohassan was her first. She sat in the dirt and traced the words. It was hard work. The words didn't immediately make sense as it was written in a very old form of Lonohassan, but with growing excitement, she picked them out and read the script.

———

We are not the First Peoples of Urtha, we are the Third. The First and the Second were destroyed by the Fallen. And now they have returned.

Mighty beings from utter darkness came as beings of light to Lonohassa the Beautiful. The Pretenders came with promises, bearing gifts of power and magnitude. Naked, innocent, pure, we were awed by their astonishing technologies and embraced them as brothers. We let them come, and then they turned on us.

With their powers from the darkness they unleashed the Age of Cataclysms. The seas rose, great storms ravaged, disease spread as fast as the wild fires torching the land. Our history they destroyed, the old temples, palaces and palisades, the ancient forests and lush gardens, the crystal monuments reaching unto the clouds...all these are gone. They turned to ruin our high culture and wit. Laughter and joy left our lips and hearts. Everything we once were, they plundered... And bright Lonohassa was no more.

Let this be a warning, for we have foreseen a future when beloved Urtha and her people are no more. Before the End, the Hidden Darkness will move amongst us pretending to be as us, infiltrating in silence, dominating from the shadows, twisting and destroying all things holy and human to an agenda that is evil utterly. We will be their slaves, and all humanity will fall as they have fallen.

Recognise the evil in our midst, the only cause of disaster, war and hatred—for the nature of humans is not these. Awaken, arise! Set yourselves free from their reign. Rekindle your innocence, rediscover your power, remember, We Are All One. Remember.

They came and conquered, destroyed, burned, raped, and killed, but the blame is ours. For it is we who let them...we let the gods in, and they destroyed us.

"We let the gods in, and they destroyed us." Thaya shivered.

Lonohassa had long ago been hit hard by a cataclysm that destroyed much of its landmass, causing it to sink or simply vanish—the myths and legends could never quite agree.

She took a deep, steadying breath. The dim cavern, the skeletons, the stones, the scroll in her hand...it was too much, she had to get outside into the daylight. Hastily, she unravelled the last few inches of the scroll. There were no more words only a peculiar coin-sized seal affixed to the bottom. It was paper thin, flexible as foil, and just as shiny. The swirls and straight lines were unlike any seal or coat of arms she had ever seen.

She touched it.

A spark of blue light burst from the symbol and she dropped the parchment with a jump. The light grew fast until it filled the cavern and the air shivered with energy. Thaya stepped back until her shoulders pressed against the fallen monolith. Had she foolishly activated a curse?

Beyond the din of her pounding heart, voices echoed. A vision appeared before her, engulfing her current world as clear as day. The dark cavern disappeared and sunlight shone down as if she'd been transported to another world. Beside her was the magnificent temple, but as it once had been thousands of years ago. Shaking with fear, she stood, both spectator and hostage in someone else's body, as unimaginable events unfolded.

Junis held his breath as the long, slender Nuakki ship landed on the plain of grass a hundred yards ahead, sending dirt and leaves swirling into the air. Despite its enormous size, it touched down gracefully beside their own small bronze vessel. The brief silence shattered as an orange phaser beam burst from the Nuakki ship and slammed with a spray of sparks into their own.

"No!" Junis screamed as their ship blazed orange in the immense heat. The craft wobbled, then melted into nothing. The beam vanished, leaving a blackened scorched circle on the ground where their craft had been only moments before.

"How did they find us?" He spun to face Hothermae.

A faint smile formed on the tall, Illuminated Nuakki's perfectly chiselled face. His dark eyes sparkled as he raised a hand to smooth his hair back over his elongated skull. All Nuakki had large brains and elongated skulls; they were exceedingly intelligent.

Hothermae's given us away, betrayed us to his own kind and led the Nuakki all the way here! It was obvious, however desperately Junis wanted to believe in his trusted friend, his instincts told him otherwise. The implications were so monumental he could barely grasp them, and he had so very little time. Hothermae had switched sides, and in doing so stepped away from the Path of Light, forgoing it and condemning himself and all Nuakki to an immortal life, trapped in time. He was throwing the hope of his entire race away.

"Why?" he gasped, but Hothermae's smile deepened and his eyes darkened. Junis carried on, his voice thick with disbelief. "You alone of the Nuakki have found the light, found the path to freedom! Through you alone, all Nuakki can find it too; that which you have sought for millennia. We, your friends, have stood by you for aeons, why would you betray us now and throw it all away? Why forgo the light and remain trapped here?"

Junis struggled to breathe. For ten thousand years, Hothermae had worked with them, the Azuri—or the Blue Ones as they were known to other races on account of their skin colour—to grow within him the power to reach the light, and enable others of his race to reach it too. For the Nuakki were born in darkness, created by their gods, the Nuakkine, to destroy humans wherever they found them. Doomed forever to be trapped in the Lower Worlds, some Nuakki wanted freedom from their Overlords, and thus freedom from the worlds of time. These Nuakki yearned for the light the Azuri and countless other ascended races held naturally within them.

Such yearning came as a surprise even to the ancient and learned Azuri, for no one thought a race born without the light would ever seek to find it. And so, willingly, many ascended races came to help the Nuakki. Hothermae was the first of his kind to touch the light, if only for a short time, and he had worked hard to bring that light to his people. In so doing, he held the hope of millions.

Junis looked back at the ship as a door slid open on the hull, and tall, heavily muscled Nuakki warriors spilled out. They wore their warped death masks of black, white and red, and carried raystaves of destruction—short thin staves made of the purest gold or silver, commanding devastating power. They had come here to kill, and now, without their ship, Junis and his entourage had no way of escape.

He laid a firm hand on the Nuakki's forearm. "Please, I beg you, don't give up the light, not for this. There is always forgive—"

Hothermae moved in a blur, grabbing Junis by the neck and hurling him against the temple wall.

Junis slammed against it, felt ribs crack, and fell to the

ground. Stunned and winded, he sprawled on the floor, blinking through the blue blood dripping into his eyes.

"Weak," Hothermae sneered, the rage and arrogance he had never quite been able to heal, unfettered and vivid on his face.

His old nature revealed, thought Junis. Perhaps there never really was any hope.

Hothermae marched triumphantly towards the approaching warriors, hands opened wide in friendly greeting.

Thunder peeled across the cloudless sky and a thick bolt of lightning exploded into the earth, shaking the ground. The Nuakki stumbled and looked up, weapons ready. Junis got onto his knees staring skyward as a new monstrosity revealed itself. A black and grey Ordac ship moved slowly into the visible spectrum, a terrifying predator stalking its now cornered prey: the Nuakki ship and its occupants.

His shoulders slumped, the reptilians were here. Had every Fallen One in the solar system followed Junis and his party? Did everyone know what they were looking for in the few remaining temples built by exiled Lonohassans? *No, Hothermae brought the Nuakki here, the Ordacs simply followed for they're always hunting their most hated enemy.*

The Nuakki warriors shouted and ran back towards their vessel, but a thick phaser beam of dark red burst down from the underside of the Ordac ship, instantly turning the Nuakki craft vermilion.

Junis's skin tingled with the immense heat.

The ship exploded in a startling spray of debris, the almighty boom shaking the earth and shuddering through him. It would have knocked him over had he not been on the ground already. The Nuakki fell to the ground as thousands of fragments of their ship rained down, burning wherever they struck.

Junis flinched as a piece struck him on the shoulder, flaring straight through his shirt and singeing his skin. Ordac technology was not as advanced as that of the Nuakki; it lacked a lot of finesse, but although the reptilians were not as clever and cunning, they were just as deadly. He staggered up and leant against the wall, cradling his ringing head.

Hothermae glanced at him and Junis couldn't help but grin. "I guess you won't be leaving either, then," he said.

Hothermae glowered, but Junis was already running to the others inside the temple.

Nusa paused as the explosion vibrated through the temple and shook the ground. Junis's mind telepathically touched both his and the minds of all those beside him, filling them with vivid imagery. The Fallen Ones had arrived and brought their toys of destruction with them. Sadness, rather than fear, rippled through his body, and he glanced at the others. Even stoic Ashemi's feline face frowned in worry. The Leonite's blue eyes widened and her pupils narrowed into slits as she looked at her brother, Heelio. He laid his ears back, his whiskers twitching. The Azuris; Vayen, Onico and Ushay, also shared Nusa's sorrow, their emotions amplifying his own.

"The Nuakki have come. Hothermae has betrayed us." Nusa said aloud what they all knew.

"Hope fades for the Nuakki." Ushay shook her head, and dropped her gaze, her pure white hair falling forwards over her shoulders.

Nusa turned back to the ornate stone he had just been about to lift from the floor and began to work quickly. They had already removed the protective seals placed upon the pavings by the Lonohassan humans of old, all of whom had long since been destroyed or enslaved by the Nuakki. They had hidden important artefacts from the Fallen Ones, and now the Azuris and Leonites were here to retrieve them for protection.

Nusa splayed his hands over the stone and hummed softly, magnetising his palms and the stone beneath. The stone lifted, grinding on the surrounding slabs as it drew upwards towards his hands. It was heavy, several tonnes in weight, and Nusa tired quickly. Breathing hard, he set the stone aside, and looked at the beautiful silver box nestled in the earth beneath. It was two hand spans in width and length and shone as if recently polished. Beside it lay a golden scroll-holder of human design. There were no enchantments on the scroll-holder, and like all holders, Nusa knew it contained human-written accounts of important events or findings.

He reached down, immediately feeling the seals of protection upon the silver box as he lifted it from its resting place. Only the Azuri, the Leonites, and certain humans had the innate power to open the box, and only then if they had been entrusted with the commands to unlock it.

In a quiet yet commanding voice, Nusa spoke aloud the tones and the others joined in, their voices resonating throughout the chamber. The final twelfth word of power sent a vibration through the entire room. The smooth, rose crystal walls shimmered as the air became charged with fluorescence. The silver box made no sound as it unlocked, and Nusa gently lifted the lid.

Inside, surrounded by white satin, shone an Urthan

object of power; a quartz crystal disc the size of his splayed hand with a silver rim and centre. He smiled and tears filled his eyes as he looked up at the others. Equal wonderment reflected back at him.

"It's here," whispered Nusa. "That which our races created long ago for the human guardians of Planet Urtha."

The disc contained the History of Records from the time Urtha was created. It contained the truth about the First, Second and Third Peoples of Urtha, and how they were invaded and destroyed. It contained the truth of what happened to Lonohassa, and Viamu long before her. The invaders knew its worth, for if they could control a people's history, they would forever control the people.

A second, larger explosion rocked the chamber, cracking walls and showering them in shards of crystal.

"The Ordacs!" Heelio shouted, stumbling.

"They, too, must have discovered we're searching for the crystal disc," said Onico. He smoothed back his white hair, his bright blue eyes looking to the door where at any moment a Nuakki or Ordac might appear. "We always knew coming here would be dangerous, but we cannot, we absolutely *cannot* let them capture this—they will destroy it to stop the truth from ever being known. Our plans remain unchanged, we must take it and hide it, and pray for the time when humans will be ready to take care of it again. But that time is not now."

Nusa sighed. "If only we could take it off Urtha's surface, all would be well." Removing the disc from the planet's surface would cause it to lose the planet's encryption and thus wipe all information upon it.

"That's if we still had a ship!" Junis gasped as he fell through the doorway.

Vayen leapt forwards to support him.

"Thank you, brother," whispered Junis, blood still dripping down his face. "I fear our time is done here. Hothermae..." His voice broke.

The pain of betrayal twisted Nusa's insides, and he struggled against overwhelming emotions. The crystal disc of truth was all that mattered; whilst humans still lived, there was hope. The Nuakki or Ordacs might be fighting over the planet, but the humans were still here. The place was not a wasteland...*not yet*. With no ship, there was only one way out, and not everybody would be able to go. Nusa knew the sacrifice he must make, but who of the women would stay with him? It took a male and female body to hold open a portal for others to pass, but this terrible day a normally beautiful action had become a terrible thing to ask.

Standing straight, he said, "Then the path is clear, who will stand by my side?"

Nusa's partner and his family awaited him beyond Urtha, as was the case for every one of them here; no one was a better choice than another.

They all knew what he asked. They all understood the sacrifice, and their hearts grew heavy.

"I do."

All the women spoke in unison. Nusa closed his eyes and sighed, feeling tears trickle down his cheeks. No one wanted this, no one could choose, everyone had a reason to live, a hundred reasons to live.

A warm furry hand took his and he looked into Ashemi's shinning blue eyes. Heelio's face was a mask of woe, everyone's was.

"Sister," Nusa whispered and pulled her close into an embrace. Heelio stepped forward and embraced them both, then all the others stepped forwards and surrounded them with their arms.

Shouting scoured their ears and pounding feet echoed closer, sullying the beauty of the moment. The people parted.

Still embracing Ashemi, Nusa began the Song of Arising, toning the spell and creating a spark of light above them. The others joined him, and the light grew fast, reaching down to engulf them in a roar of cool yellow flames. The power gathered, the crystal walls glowed, adding more energy to their own as they quickly became beings of pure light.

Through the brightness, Nusa saw Hothermae burst into the room. The Illuminated Nuakki's face twisted in rage, a heart-breaking thing to see on one who had striven so long to embrace the light. Nusa smiled sadly at him, Hothermae had hurt himself the most.

The Nuakki roared and began shouting, lifting his staff and causing it to flicker with power. Other Nuakki burst into the chamber and beyond them could be heard the roars of approaching Ordacs, their clawed feet scraping the floor.

"Go now, my brothers and sisters," said Nusa, in a calm and soothing tone.

They melted into pure light and became a singular orb shooting above him and Ashemi, passing unhindered through the stone roof and into Urtha's Upper Dimensions.

Nusa smiled at Ashemi, and she smiled back. The others were now free, and the disc was safe. The staves of the Nuakki flared into him, but he refused to cry out in pain. The Ordacs did something then although Nusa was in too much pain to know what, but the whole temple shook and cracked as if someone was shaking a giant rug beneath it. The pink crystal walls exploded.

2

ALIEN CAT PEOPLE

THE VISION RELEASED ITS GRIP.

Thaya slid down the stone to the ground, sweat covering her face and sticking her shirt uncomfortably to her body. What had just happened? The air tasted thin as if the vision had exhausted it. She sat in the cold and damp, long moments ticking by as the light falling through the hole turned dim. Everything was darker now the vivid imagery had passed.

Her gaze fell on the skeletons. Now they had faces and voices, personalities which had long since left this life. Beneath the human-written script, Nusa and Ashemi had sealed their last moments forever in the scroll. *A magic spell crafted and executed by a Master so anyone who found them would know,* she thought. Her eyes drifted to the scroll lying flaccid on the ground. It had changed her life. She wanted to wish she had never touched it, but how could she not want to know even a smattering of the truth of their past? And what in all the heavens was on that crystal disc?

She got onto her knees and inched up the wall, placing her hands against it and breathing heavily. *I should go home, and not tell anyone about this or they'll send me to the Illumined Acolytes for "Readjusting."*

She looked up at the thick roots hanging down from the ceiling around the hole she'd fallen through. Luckily, she was good at climbing, thanks to growing up with two older brothers. With a steadying sigh, she pushed herself off the stone she had been leaning on and then paused, noticing it for the first time. The stone had been shaped, a definitive curve disappearing into the dirt and roots.

Pushing the tangle of vegetation away, she brushed the dirt off to reveal the whole structure. A perfect oval had been carved in the stone, roughly three feet wide and four feet tall, and jutting out several inches from the stone behind it. Two smaller ovals only the width of her hand decorated either side. The pale stone was completely smooth with no hint of any inscription. *Peculiar, going to the trouble of carving out the structure, and then not decorating it further.*

She laid a hand on a smaller oval, her hand fitting over it perfectly as if it were made to be touched. An odd tingle tickled her palm. *Strange.* She placed her left palm on the other one and a tremor shook her so hard she had to lean against the stone to stop herself from falling. Like plunging into the ocean, the air became as thick as water and everything turned dark and cold. The large oval stone wobbled like liquid in her vision.

What on Urtha is happening?

The tremors intensified and heat warmed her forehead where the third eye sat. Her palms became hot, and liquid light burst within the smaller ovals she touched, then sprayed within the stone across to the larger oval nestled between them. It was as if her touch had activated them in some way. She stared at the two streams of light flowing like golden ink from the small ovals into the large one. The two streams met in the centre with a flare, then filled the central oval with glowing honeyed splendour.

Thaya sucked in greedy breaths of air as images formed within the light-filled stone. The tremors calmed and the golden light dimmed to pale, revealing three indistinct figures in the fog. She felt eyes watching her. Sweat beaded her forehead and her palms pulsed and burned, but she clung to the stone as if it was the only thing anchoring her to the present.

The figures moved closer, becoming more distinct. She could see the faint shape of eyes peering at her just as she stared back at them. They had large, bulbous white heads, completely bald and etched with dark throbbing veins. Their chins were tiny and their necks impossibly thin to support such huge craniums. Tiny black pupils were lost in large, red-rimmed and watery, white eyes. Their noses were barely a bump with two slits, and they had no mouths at all —perhaps the most horrifying thing about them. *Urgh, they're revolting!*

Thaya became distinctly aware of another being just beyond them. This one was not repulsive but as close as her own soul, and she had the strangest feeling that a part of her was on the other side of this stone mirror, just beyond the three creatures. She tried to see it but could only pick up a faint light.

The ugly creatures lifted their hands and long, spindly fingers akin to spider's legs reached for her. *Bloody hell, they can see me!* Their eyes widened curiously, and their fingers touched the blur in the window between them. Thaya's vision wavered from between her own and the part of her that was on the other side of the window with the ugly beings. She recoiled as their cold caress covered her nose and cheeks. So icy was their touch, it burned and leeched the warmth out of her.

A scream not her own tore through her mind and a struggle of wills ensued. Thaya shut her eyes and tossed her head as the being to which she was somehow joined tossed its own, but she couldn't break the creatures' grasp.

"Gah!" Pain burst in the centre of her forehead.

A light flared and a force flung her from the stone window, slamming her backwards into the earthen wall. She flopped onto the ground, shaking. Her forehead burned and ice-pick pains shot through her head. Something kept deep and forgotten within her soul stirred and awoke. When she opened her eyes, she looked upon a different, dream-like world.

Gone was the cavern, the earth, the fallen stones, and the darkness. Instead, a bright world of rivers and pools and grassy banks appeared. Perfect white clouds hung in an azure sky, and the warmth that enveloped her told her it must be summer. A wide, shallow river rushed over pebbles and tickled her bare feet. She looked at her throbbing palms and stared at the golden light pulsing in her baby, podgy pink, hands.

In shock, she wobbled and lost her balance, falling on her bottom with a splash. She giggled as the water flowed over her plump little legs and she stared at her hands. Her tiny palms were the hands of a toddler, a baby!

Light appeared to her right and she turned to look. Beautiful creatures walked towards her and she giggled again. Their shining horns twirled out from their foreheads, and their gilded hooves sploshed in the river, making the air and water sparkle around them. Silver-white manes and tails wavered in the warm breeze, and whatever was wrong or dark in the world fled. Between the large ones, a little one danced, his topaz eyes watching her all the while as if daring her to join him. A baby, just like her, and he wanted to play. She *had* to go to him, and all the world would be perfect.

Thaya pushed her hair back from her face, her palm connecting with her forehead in an explosion of light and pressure. The bright, warm world and the beautiful creatures vanished, and the cold dark cavern enclosed her again.

"What in the world is happening?" she whispered and stared at the rapidly fading light in her palms. The heat upon her forehead faded and she shivered. Daring to look, she inched her gaze up. The carved oval was once more an empty blank stone as if nothing had ever been there.

I'm out of here! She leapt up, grabbed a hold of the dangling roots and hauled and clawed herself out of the hole.

Thaya pelted through the tall grasses towards the oak and evergreen forest, stumbling onto the rough path that led home. The trees thickened and hugged around her, and only then did she slow, her breath ragged and her head light. *Calm, calm,* she told herself, fighting the panic and the need to get away as fast as possible, but she didn't stop running. *Thank the angry gods the journey home is downhill.* At this pace, her legs soon ate up the miles.

The Old Temple, I'll never go back there! The folklore was the giants had built it because only giants could lift such massive stones. This had angered the gods, so they sent an earthquake and destroyed it with the giants inside. It was fear of the giants' ghosts that scared everyone away apart from her. Either her idea of a giant was too small, or the stories were wrong, for the stones were too large even for a giant to lift. Besides, giants were notoriously dim-witted, and the stones whispered of sophistication and devotion. And who were these angry, destructive gods? Were they the same gods the Illumined Acolytes forced upon the people?

She had never cared for such gods and preferred not to believe in them at all if they were so inclined—but she'd learned to keep her thoughts to herself. Questioning anything was frowned upon by the people of Havendell. Questions came from enquiring minds and enquiring minds caused trouble, or brought trouble—either way, they weren't good. Havendell was the safest place in all the world, and that's because the people didn't question anything, or so they said. But Thaya didn't believe that and she thought the people afraid and weak, though she kept *that* to herself, as well.

Well, she'd proven herself correct now, there were no giants at all. *The Old Temple was built by humans and aliens, alien cat people!*

She should tell everyone what had happened; it would prove her right, but they'd probably get angry with her like they always did. She could see their pinched faces and hear their cursing even now, if she brought into question anything they believed. Things were the way they were and were done the way they were done, and nothing had changed for hundreds of years—and that's why they lived in peace and harmony! Or so the discussion always went.

Despite everything she'd been taught at school and after, she keenly felt their history didn't add up. And now she'd just discovered strange humans and cat people not mentioned in any of the history books—and powerful magic was abundant once; at least, it had been in Lonohassa, she'd just witnessed it.

Her incessant querying set her mind afire and herself apart from everyone else in Brightwater, and probably the whole of Havendell. No one in Havendell cared for the truth. Perhaps beyond its borders there were people who questioned. Her community were good people, the best, but they did not look beyond the confines of their village, and they did not want to. With an aching heart she realised that for all her efforts she could never be like them. Something drove her to reach for more.

When she looked up at the night sky and saw the stars so very far away, she wondered how they came to be. Who had put them there, and why? Were they really suns? What about the people who could use magic? Were there really witches and wizards and animals who could speak, or were they just children's stories? And where had the people gone who'd built the Old Temple?

Now she knew, and yet their mystery deepened with their words written upon the scroll. It was the gods themselves who had destroyed them, and they weren't giants, but ancient humans with powers she could only dream of. Exiled Lonohassans. Did any remain or were they all destroyed? What did it matter anyway? She'd never go back to her sacred place of solace and introspection ever again.

Her parents had come from Lonohassa before the war to the north took them away and left her, little more than a baby, with her adopted grandparents; Yenna and Fi. The great lake continent lay many leagues to the west, across the vast Emerald Ocean. Legend said it had once been a land of warmth and plenty—a bit like Havendell, she supposed. The people there had been tall and regal, beautiful in body and in mind, and all could command powerful magic, even children. Their way of life was extremely advanced; they had complex mechanisms to work the fields and lived in houses built of stone and crystal that shone in the sun and moonlight. They could make it rain when they needed it and sunny thereafter. Wondrous things they were said to be able to do.

Those were the people of antiquity, for her parents hadn't been especially tall, or able to command powerful magic. Still, she had tried to keep the language alive within her through books, but it was hard when no one spoke it. Havendellian was a dialect of Familiar, the common tongue spread by merchants and traders from Central Sian—the massive continent of which Havendell was part. It was considered the Trading Tongue, but she loved the language of Lonohassa, it felt so sophisticated. Speaking it was one of the few skills she had—that and her uncanny knack of being able to tell the truth of things or when someone was lying, but there her talents, as she saw them, stopped. Neither were very useful, which was why she hadn't tried for work in Havendell Harbour...*Yet. I can read and write and speak eloquently. I should probably try for a job in the library or in the guesthouses.*

Thatched roofs and chimney smoke welcomed her through the trees, and she rolled her shoulders back with a sigh, finally allowing her feet to slow. Smoothing her shirt was useless and wiping the muddy patches only made them worse. She looked like a feral child covered in grass stains and dirt, not a fully grown, dignified woman.

I'll tell them I fell over. But anything she told her grandparents wouldn't stop them worrying. Fi and Yenna worried incessantly about her since Eddo had left without a goodbye six months ago. They said she'd never been the same since.

But her fiancé wasn't lost at sea, nor had he been killed by brigands—she'd be able to forgive him for that—no, he'd shacked up with some wench in Aspsfield, and that was pretty much the end of her love-life for this lifetime.

'*Love me forever,*' he'd said. She pulled a face. Thank the gods for Rayanne. The number of nights she'd spent sobbing around at her best friend's house didn't bear thinking about, but her friend had since married a sailor and that was the last she'd seen of her too. She'd been left to rot in Brightwater all alone. Well, no one could really rot in the most beautiful, warm, tranquil, and *boring* place on Urtha.

She was no longer upset about Eddo, just furious, and the fury would come out at times, which was why she went to the Old Temple so often since he'd been gone. But now her place of respite was gone from her too.

The path joined a wide earthen road lined on either side with quaint thatched houses stretching like open arms welcoming her home.

"What the hell happened to you?" A tall, broad man suddenly appeared from the other side of a garden fence, startling her. He had dark hair and a beard, and a wriggling toddler firmly clasped against his side.

She gasped. "Bron, you made me jump!"

"Come here, Sis." He embraced her in a bear hug.

She returned her brother's rough hug and squeezed the toddler's cheek. The boy scowled and howled. He hated it when she did that, which is why she did it. The boy was a terror, which was probably why Bron had the squirming oik in an iron grip.

She shook her head. "I fell down a hole up by the Old Temple, can you believe it? The heavy rains have loosened the earth. Luckily I've only got bruises."

Bron shook his head. "Trust you to find them. Dan fell in one too. Well, half of him did. Sprained his leg badly and the Doc says he was lucky he didn't break it. Be careful going up there alone, I don't want to have to find and haul out your broken body. Better get yourself inside and changed, Fi'll think you've tried to top yourself." He winked.

Thaya laughed. "Too right. Maybe one day I'll grow up! See you later."

She hurried home thinking about her brothers and their families. *It's over for me, I'll never have kids, not now.* This thought came with its usual defiance, but she couldn't admit to herself that it wasn't what she truly wanted. *Stupid world and all the nonsense I have to deal with.* No, she'd never marry nor have kids—forget all those heart-breaking, unfulfilling relationships! *I'll be old and lonely like poor old Toothless Betty! Well, she isn't poor, in fact, she must be quite rich with her fresh thatching and garden full of Emeny Roses. And she seems quite happy to boot, perhaps a life of singledom won't be so bad!*

She was too drained to feel her usual 'Eddo fury,' and a dull headache was nestling itself nicely behind her eyes. The village clock chimed five, it's doleful bonging echoing around Brightwater. Fi and Yenna would still be working the fields—it had been her afternoon off, and now the Old Temple was off limits she'd have to think of somewhere else to go on her break.

She turned down an alley, startling a ginger tom and a black cat who were both hunched and wailing at each other, and emerged the other end opposite her house. *Not my house, Fi and Yenna's.* Her brow furrowed, increasing the dull ache behind it. *I had my own house once, a nice one! Albeit briefly.* It had been on the southern edge of Brightwater, tiny, but it had everything she and Eddo needed. When he ran off, she could no longer afford it and ended up back at her grandparents. Going back to them had been a good thing, they needed the extra help around the farm, and it stopped her from fading away or exploding in a fit of rage.

I'm no silly girl, I should have a family by now like everyone else. Thaya ground her teeth. *Self-sufficiency, that's what I need, not a grumpy husband and wailing kids. I'll get a job in Havendell Harbour and buy a fine house there.* One thing's for sure, she couldn't stay in Brightwater like her brothers. No! She'd suffocate. Even Havendell Harbour was claustrophobic, but the sea gave the illusion of freedom. *Is this all I've got to look forward to? Everything is so boring, or at least it was, until...*Her throat constricted as she recalled Ashemi and Nusa.

She lifted the latch to the back door, peeked inside to see a large, blessedly empty kitchen, and slithered silently through. Kicking off her boots she rushed to her bedroom and shut the door firmly. Leaning back against it, she let out a long sigh.

Her headache worsened exponentially as the silent minutes ticked by. *Dear gods,* she prayed, *I hope I'm not coming down with a fever or a curse!* She managed to slip off her clothes and washed herself in the basin, but by the time she was dry and dressed in lounge pants and a jumper, she could barely see through the pain. The only place to go was bed.

3

MAGGY

MAGGY KNEW IT WOULD HAPPEN, SHE JUST DIDN'T KNOW when.

As the years turned into decades, she began to doubt her own prophecy, but that night her dream ended abruptly, and she sat up as wide awake and sprightly as a girl. She stared at the golden orb glowing in the centre of her otherwise dark bedroom. Her palms and third eye grew warm and glowed with a similar light.

"Ahhh, it's happened," she said, relief but also fear washing over her.

The child had begun her awakening and the spells of concealing—Maggy's own spells—were now falling away. Soon she would remember all that had happened. Maggy closed her eyes and saw for the hundredth time the chained Saphira-elaysa screaming. Her throat constricted painfully around the lump in it.

The screams faded and in the remaining light she saw a woman, her hair bronzed waves, and her unmistakable tanned, almost golden skin. *The child has grown up. Little*

Thayannon Farseeker is a woman. The woman faded and a much larger shimmering being appeared in her place.

Maggy stared at the image of the magnificent being before her; the Saphira-elaysa Thaya had touched all those years ago. Whether it had happened by divine providence or a terrible curse, only the future would reveal. He was no longer small but huge, a fully grown male, and his coat no longer shimmered white like all other Saphira-elaysa, but deep purple and silver. Seeing him transported Maggy back to the time it had all begun, and she indulged in all its vivid re-remembered glory.

I remember, I remember, such a beautiful wondrous day!

The star burst into the atmosphere, shining bright in all its grandeur against a flawless deep blue sky. Maggy panted and dragged her aching body forwards, leaning heavily on her walking stick. She was going to miss it! The one thing she'd waited for all her life, and she was going to be bloody late!

"Curse those sodding Dryads!" she wheezed. *Always playing tricks, always taunting humans. Annoying imps could have told her they were coming sooner.* 'They' were the shining ones, the Pure Ones, the bringers of joy and beauty—just thinking about them brought tears to Maggy's eyes.

The star flared and arced gently down over the lake and into the trees beyond.

Curse this damn old body, why'd they have to come now? Why not come when I was young and pretty and full of joys and foolish dreams? Now my mind is sore, and my experiences may have made me wise, but they've made me suspicious and bloody grouchy too!

"Hmph!" Maggy waved her stick and swatted at the butterflies flapping in her face. She reached the top of the hill, sweating and panting, and fell to her knees as her old heart lurched at the sight. 'They' were here, after six long decades waiting and watching, she'd finally found them.

Sunlight danced on shimmering white fur; silver manes shone with all the lustre of the stars within which they travelled. Tears rolled down Maggy's wrinkled cheeks and her heart fluttered with joy and awe.

"Saphira-elaysa," she whispered, her voice breaking with emotion. The Dryad name for these beings from heaven fitted so much better than the human one. *No, these are not unicorns. They are most certainly Saphira-elaysa!*

Hearing their name spoken, even from far away, one turned his elegant head towards her. His single golden horn shining brighter and more beautiful than the sun, his supremely intelligent topaz eyes beheld her.

Maggy looked down at her ragged skirt and socks more woven of mud than cotton. One had stayed up to her knee, but the other had given up ages ago and flopped limply around her ankle. Strands of long white hair had run for freedom from her bun and languished in draggles around her shoulders, and her old, old hands were gnarled and wrinkled like the bark of an oak. To say she felt ugly didn't capture it. She felt truly lesser, unquestionably unclean, and in all ways primitive—a savage in every instance when compared to *them*.

But those topaz eyes shone with only compassion, and they understood her better than she did herself for they could read her every thought, intention, and emotion. They *knew* she had searched for them her whole life. Was that why they had come? She liked to believe it was all for her. She liked to believe a lot of foolish things.

Maggy wanted to run to them, to touch them, to bathe in their light, but she was frozen on her feet and shivering in awe. There were six of them, and a tiny one shying between their legs, *and they are all looking at me!*

The large unicorn flicked his head and with his horn beckoned to her, suggesting she come closer. Maggy inhaled sharply, and then, like a girl, she was running towards them hands flailing, all aches and pains forgotten from her body.

The Saphira-elaysa waited for her, *they're actually waiting for me!*

She skidded to a stop two yards away, her feet unable to take her closer—she was too in awe, too afraid of being dirty and ugly.

The unicorn smiled. "Join us, for a time," he said, his voice very low, almost a whisper, and holding all the wisdom of the world within it. Maggy nodded vigorously, grinning foolishly. *Of course he can speak, all magical creatures can speak!*

The Saphira-elaysa did not walk like horses or deer, they appeared to glide without making a sound, every silver-hoofed step gently placed. Fine silver-white hair, which started a third way down their tails, swayed and floated from side to side. Where they passed, the flowers turned towards them and opened their petals wider. The butterflies Maggy had swatted earlier, danced merrily above them, their amethyst and vermilion colours shimmering even brighter, and the grass at the unicorns' feet sprung up stronger and richer wherever they stepped.

All Maggy's worries and fears, her anger and bitterness, melted away in the presence of the Pure Ones. Why had they come here? Why now? What were they looking for? Maggy had a hundred questions, but she could not ask even one of them for the lump that stuck in her throat.

But the unicorn heard her thoughts, and he chose to answer. "Great change is coming, and we bring a gift to Urtha's waters so it and she will remember the Eternal Spirit in the times to come. All those who drink of the pure waters will remember also."

Maggy nodded, understanding the words but not the implications.

They came to a stream which fed into a shallow pool, surrounded by a grassy bank. Beyond the pool stretched a wide plane to the Village Green, and beyond it stood rows of little thatched houses. Maggy didn't know the name of the village; she had travelled here a hundred leagues from the mid-south of Lonohassa. *All that way to meet these beings of light.*

The unicorns stepped into the water, causing it to sparkle and shimmer around their cloven hooves. In unison, they dipped their horns into the pond and the water glimmered a beautiful aqua. A golden fish leapt into the air, falling back with a joyful splash, and a child giggled, startling Maggy.

She bent down and peered through the unicorns' legs. A few yards away, a little girl, surely no more than two years old, sat quite happily in the shallows, splashing and soaking her dress. She pointed a stubby pink finger at the little unicorn and laughed when he sprung into the air and landed with a torrential splash.

Maggy didn't know what to make of the little brat. Where were her parents? These country folk let their feral offspring roam the place without a care in the world. Didn't they know there were trolls and bears and all sorts of hungry creatures just waiting to take a bite out of a human? And that's not to mention the Others, the Fallen Ones who came from beyond the stars and preyed upon the weak. In spite of the unicorns, Maggy shivered. She'd been young and naive once, but not now, oh no. Now she knew the world was violent and unjust, and she was old and wise and intolerant. Her innocence had long since left her.

The child was slow and ungainly compared to the young, nymph-quick Saphira-elaysa, but Maggy found herself smiling at their playful innocence, and her bitterness dissolved.

The elder Saphira-elaysa who had spoken lifted his head and became still. The others followed. Maggy clasped her hands together, uneasy as the whole world fell to silence.

"Danger," said the unicorn, and yet there was no fear in his countenance.

Maggy looked around; the tinkling river, the blue skies... she could see nothing wrong but she could *feel* the growing tension. She picked up a noise beyond the silence, a strange ringing sound that grew louder.

The ship appeared in the sky. It hadn't flown there, it just appeared out of nowhere, a round, metal, disc-shaped vehicle, perfectly smooth and shining in the sunshine.

Maggy's blood ran cold. "Vormae," she whispered. "Run, Bright Ones. Run!"

A red beam blasted down from the ship with a vibrating hum. She screamed. Twice before she'd witnessed such ships and had screamed then too, but this time she was the closest she had ever been to the Vormae's craft. She could feel the heat, the red light burning into her eyes, the noise an unforgettable din that she would hear forever.

The horns of the Saphira-elaysa glowed, and white light burst upwards from them to meet the red.

Crack!

The two beams hit and flared against each other, hissing

and crackling.

"No you don't, you bastards!" Maggy screamed and waved her stick menacingly at the ship.

There were no windows. The disc appeared to be made of a single sheet of metal folded perfectly into shape. Inside, she knew, there were three or more of the Ugly Ones from beyond the stars. *Unicorn hunters, abductors of humans, destroyers. And to think some called them gods, pah!* Maggy spat upon the ground and screamed at the disc some more, wishing she had all the powers of the Magi at her command.

Instead, all she managed were terrible curses. "You'll burn forever in the fires of Degenna. You'll reincarnate as worms for humans to crush in the mud under their feet. Corvids will rip out your eyes and spray their contents into the dirt. Maggots will devour your rotting, stinking flesh."

She rolled her curses out one after the other, pouring her fury through her stick, but all she managed were small licks of flame that flew at the ship and bounced harmlessly off its surface.

The red light intensified and the Saphira-elaysa struggled. One screeched as their white light became tinged with magenta. They tossed their magnificent heads and shut their eyes under the strain but for all their resistance, they began to fade from the world.

Tears blurred Maggy's vision, unable to bear witness to their suffering. *Oh dear God of Light, why did they dare come to this cursed planet?* The struggle became chaotic as the forces battled. Light flared erratically as electricity crackled, and somewhere a child screamed.

The young unicorn darted out from under the legs of his parents.

Maggy held her breath. Was the little one bolting? He'd

be captured easily if he left the safety and light of his elders. She stumbled closer, shielding her eyes against the light. The human child now stood dangerously close to the struggling unicorns; her eyes wide with terror. She reached a tiny grasping hand out to the little Saphira-elaysa. He stuffed his horn into her grasp, and she hung on to it.

A flash of light blinded everything and the ground trembled. The ship's beam weakened and flickered.

A brief moment of silence stilled the raging powers. The little unicorn staggered back into the light of his parents and the red beam intensified. The Vormae would never give up their prey.

The Saphira-elaysa fell to their knees.

A great wind gusted, bending over trees, sending dust and leaves billowing into the air, and knocking Maggy to the ground. Darkness fell upon them as something enormous covered the sun. She squinted up, shielding her eyes from the flying debris, and stared at the new disc-like craft three times the size of the other. She gasped in each breath, tears streaming from her eyes. A strange humming howl emitted from the new ship and the hairs on Maggy's arms rose as the air became charged. The white and red lights vanished, along with the Saphira-elaysa and the smaller craft.

The gasp of people captured Maggy's attention, and on the far bank, villagers gathered, bracing themselves against the wind. The entire village stood there, men with arms around their wives, women holding babies, all pointing and staring at the huge silver ship in awe and terror. The ship moved slowly and silently towards them, more horrifying than if it had been a screaming, wailing demon stampeding out of hell, and the people just stood there rooted to the spot.

The Saphira-elaysa were gone. Maggy cared nothing for

her own life any more. The loss wedged itself darkly into her soul.

There came a snivelling sob, and her eyes were drawn to the soaking, mud-covered wretch curled up in the shallows. The child shivered and shook, her red face scrunched up and acting out all the emotions Maggy felt raging within her at the loss of the Pure Ones. A rare and overwhelming sense of pity came over her. She forced her shaking legs forwards and waded towards the girl. Curling her hand under the child, she held the sobbing urchin against her chest.

Light blazed from the ship, drenching everything, blinding everyone, and a sonic wave assaulted Maggy's ears, vibrating through the very ground. The tremors drove Maggy to her knees and screams erupted from the crowd.

Squinting into the glare, she watched the people scatter as a thin orange beam burst from the ship. It struck a young man and he howled as it lifted him several feet into the air. Then he shivered and simply turned into dust, his howls cut short as all that he was, was blown away by the wind. A woman ran, dragging her toddler behind her, another babe wrapped in her arms. Neither of them screamed when the orange beam hit them, they simply disappeared and turned to powder that scattered over the grass.

The bundle in her arms trembled and bleated. Maggy sobbed and held her closer, hiding the child's face against her bony shoulder. "Don't look, Pumpkin," she rasped.

She had to get this child away! She got up and in a stumbling run made it across the river in the opposite direction to the fleeing villagers. She clambered up the bank and through the bushes and brambles. Shaking and unable to go further, she collapsed amongst the branches, hugging the child against her, praying for the blinding flashes of light and the screaming to end.

4

DESTROY THE DESTROYERS

THE HOWLS AND FLASHES STOPPED SIMULTANEOUSLY AND abruptly.

How long had passed since they'd started, Maggy didn't know. Even now, she didn't move, and the child in her arms was so quiet she wondered if it was still alive. *Curse the Others, curse them!* Had they taken the Saphira-elaysa, or did she dare believe they'd escaped? Of one thing she was certain, no human had escaped.

These attacks by the Vormae were rare but they were always devastating, and there was little humans could do against them. The Ancient Lonohassans would have known what to do and how to protect themselves, but they were long gone. The Vormae came at random from the sky—how could anyone defend themselves against them? What had these village-folk ever done to them? The world was evil to allow this to happen, no wonder she had turned away from the gods so long ago. *It's all wrong, wrong, wrong!*

Maggy lifted her gaze from the ground to find herself surrounded by a dark mist. The bushes, and the trees beyond them were all grey and faded. In the mist appeared people. They walked towards her and she saw that they didn't really look like humans, not normal ones anyway.

A cold hand gripped her shoulder from behind and she screamed, making the child wail. She looked back, her heart in her throat as her eyes travelled from the deathly white hand with its contrasting black fingernails, over the silver rings on every finger, and up the dark sleeve to the paper-white face of a man. He looked to be in his thirties and his long black hair was combed neatly about his shoulders. Black eyes beheld hers and his grey lips turned down in a grimace.

"We are too late," he said, in a soft, low voice.

The emotion in his tone immediately moved Maggy and she found her fears running away. Whoever these people were, they had not come to harm her.

The man let go of her shoulder and stood. He was very tall and dressed in black from his boots to his coat. Silver chains tinkled about his neck as he folded his arms. His face was very long and angular, handsome but not human, and his eyes were deeply sad as he stared ahead. He was probably looking at the destruction Maggy could not and did not want to see, from her position behind the bushes.

The other people came closer. Men and women who looked and dressed as he; tall, black hair, nails and clothing, and extremely pale-skinned. All adorned themselves with silver rings, bracelets and necklaces—worn as if they had power or a purpose.

Maggy stared at each of them in turn while they looked ahead. Sadness emanated from them, so deep and poignant, her breath caught at the pain. Who were these people and where had they come from? She wanted to understand them but knew they were beyond her reach.

"I followed the Saphira-elaysa," Maggy said, her voice a rasp. "And, it seems, so did the Vormae. Wh-who are you?"

"We hunt the hunters," said a woman. Her long black hair was tied up in a messy fashion that became her, and her skin was completely smooth and unblemished, much like marble.

Her black eyes were penetrating and Maggy dropped her gaze, feeling naked and weak. She'd felt the same meekness when she'd once spoken to a High Magi, so these strange people were probably also magicians of the highest order.

The woman continued. "And we destroy the destroyers of Light Bearers. We come from Arothia, a world beyond your furthest star, but always we remain hidden in the shadows."

"We knew the Vormae were up to something, but what happened here it...it shook the ethers," said the man, frowning. "We followed them, as we always do, but then we lost them in the chaotic energy. Something happened, something very important." He turned his questioning gaze onto Maggy, and she looked from him to the child squirming in her arms. The brat had been remarkably quiet. The tear stains on her grubby face had dried, and she stared unabashedly up at the man with her large hazel eyes.

"She's not my child. She belongs to..." Maggy trailed off, knowing the whole village was dead and the child now an orphan. "Everyone is gone."

No one spoke. The man and child stared at each other, and his eyes widened as if in surprise. He knelt and pressed his large palm against the child's forehead, and both closed their eyes. The man inhaled sharply and let go his touch, his brows knitting together with worry. "I don't know what this means; I don't understand. The child, she's human but...*changed.* She's no longer purely human."

Maggy thought back over the events, the little unicorn running out to her and the child reaching out to touch him. "It shouldn't have happened...Sacrilege to touch one of the Pure Ones. She must be cursed!" She grimaced and started to push the child away, but the man shushed her.

"No, she is not! Be still."

Maggy stopped and he became still himself.

He looked far away then spoke in wonder and mysterious lights danced in his eyes. "Through her eyes I saw what happened, but I can't explain it...it's as if their souls melded and became one. When they separated, they were as twins, their powers shared, their futures forever entwined —neither are the same as they were before. Ahhh, what can it mean? This occurred through joy and innocence, the hallmarks of perfection in the eyes of the Infinite One. Thus, it was *meant* to be. The Saphira-elaysa are fading from the mortal worlds, hunted to extinction by the Vormae. Could this be a way they might be saved?"

"If that's so, then why are you afraid?" asked Maggy.

The man looked at her sharply. "Very perceptive, Amaggena Evergreen. Indeed, I feel the cold touch of fear wrap around me, for now, this child will be hunted by them until the end of her days, just as they hunt the Saphira-elaysa. And a human's life is short compared to those who are immortal."

Maggy's mouth fell open. How on all Urtha could he know her full name? No one alive knew her full name. She looked from the man to the woman, and then the other three standing in the mist. All looked to be around the same age, and the peculiar air they held about them...Maggy just

knew. "You're immortal aren't you, like the Saphira-elaysa."
It was a statement, not a question.

The corner of the man's lips curled up ever so slightly—
she got the feeling he didn't smile very often—and he said,
"Again, very perceptive. The Saphira-elaysa have endowed
you with gifts even you are not yet aware of. Yes, we are
immortal, sadly. And before you ask, I say alas for we are
immortal, *not* eternal."

The others murmured in agreement, their gazes settling on
the ground, and the sadness around them deepened as the man
continued. "The child is not alone in being fundamentally
changed, for none can walk beside that which is pure and not
be affected by it. You will discover in the long years left of your
life, that which really has unfolded this day. As you meditate on
all that has occurred, you will begin to understand many things.
Seek, Amaggena Evergreen, seek that which you most desire."

Maggy chuckled at the man's grandiose manner. "Seek?
Me? I'm in my sunset years, young man. You might be ten
thousand years old but by my measures you're still a whip-
persnapper, and I'm far older than you. I've got at best ten
years so don't you fool with me." She waggled a finger
at him.

The man took no offence and instead his smile deepened, and his eyes sparkled. "I see hope in you," he said
softly. And then he spoke as clear as day and yet his lips did
not move. *"Forget the gods they make you pray to. Follow your
heart to that pure and singular source that illuminates all and
you will find the Eternal Spirit beating hard within you. You and
I and all are One."*

The spell broke when he lifted his eyes and gazed into
the distance. Maggy blinked, what had just happened? The
man continued speaking, his lips moving this time. "Well, it

looks like you have a child to care for, and she is cold, hungry and exhausted."

Maggy looked at the child and grimaced, but the girl only giggled at her funny face. "Bah," said Maggy. "Why'd you think I never had kids? I don't rightly want them now, now of all times!"

But there was no one else here, everyone was likely dead, and these strange Others didn't look like they were going to take her, not that they'd done much here to help at all anyway. Could she knowingly abandon the brat on the side of the road? As she thought about it, her grimace softened, and she felt again that rare pang of empathy. "All right, I'll take her, but only for a month or so until I find someone more suitable."

The man nodded approvingly, "We do our work in the shadows of your world. At this moment it won't seem like much but you'll notice no Shades appeared this day."

Maggy shivered at the mention of the shadowy ghosts that always appeared before the Vormae attacked. He was right, there hadn't even been one Shade. Perhaps if there had, she would have had more warning.

"There is never enough warning when the Vormae come," said the woman at the man's side.

"Will you stop reading my thoughts?" Maggy frowned, but the woman just looked at her with those unblinking black eyes. Maggy sighed. "I guess you must be the Watchers the Magi and the Acolytes talk about. I hadn't thought it 'til now, but I guess it makes sense. Do you have a real name?"

"The Watchers? Interesting..." The man stroked his chin. "Wherever you find the Fallen Ones, you'll find us. For we are ever watching and hunting down those who destroy those of the light, for it is the Fallen who made us fall, and we *cannot* forget."

Maggy shivered against the chill in the man's words. They might be watching, they might be helping, but whatever they did was not enough to save the Saphira-elaysa or the village people this day. And, like it or not, she now had a child on her hands.

"But you, what is your name, or don't you have names?" Maggy pressed. "I'm not privy to mind-reading, and I don't think it's proper to look inside someone's head. Or at least it's not fair when I can't do the same."

The woman smiled this time, the subtle curve of her lips softening her handsome but hard face. Maggy began to think she was amusing to these Others.

The man spoke. "Indeed, Amaggena Evergreen, it is not polite or fair, please forgive us."

Before she could flinch away, he laid his cold palm on her forehead. Pressure grew fast in her head as some kind of power flooded from him into her. It didn't hurt but felt weird, heavy, making her instantly sleepy, then sparks flashed in her mind and behind her eyes. Her thoughts twisted, then became ordered as if he were rearranging a portion of her brain. The fog that clouded her mind, which had grown ever worse with age, suddenly lifted, and all the little things that caused confusion now made sense.

She blinked in shock at the sudden knowledge that filled her head. "My tomatoes! Of course! They never failed because of Giffrey's Curse but as a result of Soil Blight rising from the bedrock. The key to my jewellery box, it's in my old shoe where I'd hidden it safely, how could I forget? And those bastards, I always knew it... the Illumined Acolytes' gods are fake! Weak, angry charlatans and nothing at all compared to the Grand Creator of All. Hah!" Why on Urtha had she not spent more time thinking on these important matters?

A hundred other little things became clear in her mind. She needed another lifetime just to rethink everything, *and to refind everything I've lost!* The pathways of her thoughts and her reasoning were crystal clear, as if she were a teenager again, and her mind became sharp and keen as the bitterness within her, acquired over the long hard years, melted away.

"Now you are as all humans should be, and like your race of old, you can once again hear our thoughts," he said, his voice appearing directly into her head, bypassing his mouth.

She understood how he did it; it was purely by intention. He spoke in his mind the words he wanted to say and placed them into hers simply by willing it.

"I understand," she replied with her mind, copying his technique.

"Only a properly functioning, perceptive and willing mind will you be able to speak to in this manner, and there are few of your race capable now," he said aloud. "We have spent too long here already. I feel the madness of this place creeping closer. We'll meet again, Amaggena Evergreen, but not for a long time in your Urtha years. Take the child, keep her safe. We are not sure why and to what end the events of today have occurred, but in the child's soul burns a fire that cannot be extinguished even in death. And one day, when she is full-grown, the loneliness and hunger will drive her to her soul mate, and nothing will be able to stop it."

The dark fog drew together and the strange Others became indistinct. "My name is Arendor." A voice whispered, as the fog vanished and the people along with it.

Night had fallen in the time that had passed since they'd

arrived. Now it was cold and clear, and the stars twinkled above. "Arendor," Maggy whispered, and the child giggled.

"Right, best get you dry, watered and fed," Maggy said, daunted by the huge responsibility that lay ahead looking after herself *and* the child. "I'll get a dog to look after you, something for you to play with too."

The child pointed towards the village. "No," said Maggy, pursing her lips. "We're never going back there." She lifted the child, puffing as she did so. "Gosh, you're heavier now!"

Hugging her to her side, she started walking, resisting the urge to look back at the destroyed village. The smoke and smell of death in her nostrils was enough.

"Hmm." The world as she'd known it for seventy years of her eventful life had been utterly changed in a day.

Picking up her walking stick, she started back along the path she had trodden in the warm sunlight with the Pure Ones. The way home was long, especially for her tired old legs, and it could take months.

5

AGAROTHS

Thaya tried to sleep, but her throbbing head relentlessly hammered her brain.

In the periods where she managed to drift, the faces of Ashemi, Junis, and Nusa swam before her, burning themselves into her mind so that she could not forget them.

When they faded away, she drifted back to the sparkling river and the summer sunlight dancing on the silver-white coats of the Saphira-elaysa. The little one threw his head back and cried out a sound so human and plaintive it made her heart tremble. Was he calling for her? A desperate need to go to him filled her now as it had then. Through sheer exhaustion, she slipped into a deeper sleep, where memories and faces of the far distant past could not haunt her.

She did not wake easily, and a fever descended, keeping her bedbound for the next two days.

During Thaya's hazy, headache-filled stupor, Yenna's kindly face creased into a thousand worried wrinkles as she placed a cool compress on her forehead. Sometimes Fi would be with her, her grandfather's heavy brows knitting together as he looked on.

.   .   .

On the third day, the fever lifted.

She threw off the sheets and leapt out of bed with ravenous hunger. Thank the gods, the curse had passed. She had beaten it and was keen to get back to work but Fi and Yenna refused, telling her to rest and eat.

Come the fourth day, nothing could stop her from getting outside. Their farm was small, just a simple holding of a few fields beside the house, a coop of chickens, three cows and a couple of horses, but it was a lot for her ageing grandparents to manage on their own.

Thaya struck her hoe into the earth, working to break up the clods, then stood and straightened her aching back. Her new-found enthusiasm for work had worn off by midday. Nusa and Ashemi's faces lurked in the background of her mind and every now and then she looked north to where the Old Temple stood. She could still hear the plaintive call of the Saphira-elaysa, and each time her insides tightened.

She hadn't known it until now, but there was a gaping hole within her, and if she dared to focus on it a desperate longing to fill it overcame her with such force it took her breath away. Not only was there something incredibly important that had happened in their history which had been forgotten, there were also huge gaps in her own history that had been forgotten.

She hadn't told anyone what had happened, she just couldn't find the right words. *And what would I tell them? That alien cat people once existed here?* They'd think her mad, and the Illumined Acolytes wouldn't hesitate to take her away. Until she worked out the right approach, the best thing to do would be to keep silent.

As she worked the field, a slow realisation dawned on

her. Knowing what she knew, and feeling that empty hole inside her, set her even more apart and estranged from everyone else. She never really fitted in, and now all of this would make it harder. *That, and...something calls to me from far, far away. Is it really the Saphira-elaysa? The strength of it...I doubt I'll be able to withstand it forever. One day I'll have to leave here, and somehow I've always known that; only now it's more pertinent.*

Wiping the sweat from her face, she glanced at their house on the edge of the field, noting the grey flint bricks that made up the walls disappearing into the thatch. Each brick varied from the size of her hand to the length of her forearm, small and without uniformity. Compared to the perfect alignment and cut of the yellow stones, the grey ones were shoddy, amateur, and all stuck together with mortar that constantly fell out when it rained and needed repairing. No, the yellow stones were far superior in every way, and they were beyond ancient.

"Fi, those old myths say giants are stupid, they can't have made the Old Temple," she said, smoothing back her hair and tightening her bun.

Fi grunted as he broke apart a particularly dense and stony clod. The heavy rain these past few days had virtually turned their rich soil to clay, and it was proving hard work getting the first crops in.

She caught the scowl on his red, usually jovial, face and swallowed. Oops, she'd done it again and spoken about things that couldn't be known, especially about the Old Temple.

"You and those bloody stones..." he grumbled. "Isn't it enough to know that we'll never know?" He stood and stretched with a groan. He was old now and his thinning hair all white under his straw hat, but though he was short and plump, he was still straight and mobile. All the old people here in Brightwater—and indeed Havendell—lived to ripe old ages and remained fit and active until they died. Sickness and disease were rare; something to do with the good soil, the sunshine, and the lack of strife or interference from the meddling warlords beyond the White Mountains.

Those mountains kept everything out, even the wars, and that's the way the people wanted it. The latest distant bloodshed appeared to be about an invading army, a King, and the land in between, and that was as much as she knew about it. Questions threatened their peace, and deep down she knew the people were worried that they could lose their beloved Havendell at any moment.

"But it's not just that," she continued, her voice less certain than before. If only she could get these people to think about their mysterious past. "The stones are yellow; no mountain or even pebble is remotely yellow in the whole of Havendell."

She realised as she said it that this was not what anyone wanted to hear. The stones clearly came from somewhere else beyond Havendell—and that meant other things could come too. After all, hadn't *she* come here with her parents? She, herself, was a reminder that though few things came over the mountains or across the seas, *some* things came. There were ancient, little-used passes through the mountains—and that meant one day the war might reach them.

Fi growled and struck at the clod until it broke apart completely. Thaya sighed silently.

When his irritation had abated, he said, "You must remember, Thayannon Farseeker, you were brought here, but not born here. You are *not* from here, but you must follow our ways or nothing good will come of it. You're a fine young woman, but your crazy thoughts drive the lads away. If you carry on scaring 'em like that, you'll end up alone like Toothless Betty." Fi sucked in his lips, squinted his eyes and opened and closed his mouth with a smacking noise.

Thaya laughed. "Poor Betty, she has a heart of gold."

"Aye, but she's been alone most her life, and you don't want that now, do you?"

Thaya imagined it, a whole life alone, and shivered. "No, I s'pose not."

"So stop filling your head with pointless questions and work the field. Goodness knows what the bloody Acolytes will think or do if they ever hear you talking." He shook his head and bent his back to his hoeing.

Defeated, Thaya did the same. *Fear keeps them trapped,* she thought, and when she thought about being alone forever, the fear kept her trapped too. She glanced over the thatched roofs of the village to the meadows and lush green trees, beyond which the yellow stones lay. If a people much more advanced than they could be destroyed, what was the point of anything?

Her eyes travelled up the nearest mountain to its snowy peak and followed the jagged range all the way along as it curved around Havendell. The range only stopped when it hit the ocean, the last mountain faint and blue in the distance, it didn't even taper into foothills. The whole of Havendell was encircled, safe and protected from evil and the war beyond it. But more and more she felt that those mountains were her walls, a fence that kept her in rather than anything out. Whatever called to her soul and filled it with longing came from beyond them. *But if I left, I'd never find anywhere as peaceful and beautiful as Brightwater...*Could she really leave it all behind? And yet she was unfulfilled—content, maybe, but without purpose. There was nothing for

her here and, more than that, there was something she had
to do.

The headache began again, a painful dull thump in the
centre of her brain, and the empty hole grew, and the call
sounded stronger.

Her eyes drifted down to the forest of oaks and
sycamores just beyond the meadow, their canopies laden
with the bounty of spring. There, in the darkness of the
forest, shimmering ghost-like, emerged the silver-white
form of a Saphira-elaysa, golden horn gleaming, topaz eyes
staring right at her.

Her heart lurched and her breath caught in her throat,
the Saphira-elaysa wobbled as her vision misted over. She
blinked, casting tears down her cheeks and the beautiful
creature was gone, leaving her world cold and empty. No
leaf moved to show its passing. *It was a vision, a mirage. I'm
going mad!*

"Are you all right?" Yenna came over, her basket filled
with weeds—strangle nettle mostly—and mud smearing
her reddened cheeks.

The last thing she wanted was for her grandparents to
worry. "Yes, I'm fine," Thaya replied strongly. "Damn mud in
my eye is all." She rubbed away the tears and bent to her
work with vigour, which appeared to satisfy Yenna who
continued weeding. Now and then, Thaya glanced back to
where the image of the Saphira-elaysa had been but there
was nothing there, if there ever had been.

'Brought here, not born here,' she muttered to herself. It
would have been harsh had she not known how much Fi
loved her. To her adopted grandparents, she was the little
girl they had always wanted and was brought up as such.
Their two, much older, sons became her benefactors and
torturers, getting her into and out of trouble as any siblings

would. She grew up with the people of Brightwater, but not everyone belonged where they were born, and for all Brightwater's homeliness, Lonohassa's mysteriousness drew her to it more.

Thaya caught Yenna's gaze. Her grandmother had paused, her basket now brimming with weeds but her eyes sad, worried almost. Then she simply smiled and turned away. Thaya bit her lip, she didn't want to cause her family strife. She shoved all her questions aside and forced herself to think only upon her work and the trip to the market she'd be making in the afternoon.

"She's not a child anymore, far from it. She's restless," said Yenna.

Thaya, unable to sleep, crept out of bed to listen to her grandparents more clearly. She opened her bedroom door a little wider, letting candlelight and their voices spill into the room.

"Havendell is too small for her. You know she'll want to go, and when that time comes, we cannot stop her. Even her name speaks of one who never settles," Yenna continued.

"No, she must be as one of us," said Fi. "If she leaves, she'll die a terrible death, whether on someone's sword or through sickness and disease. She'll never return to us. You know how it is beyond Havendell, the stories are enough."

"You can't let your love for her keep her from her soul's desires," said Yenna.

Tears prickled Thaya's eyes at their concern.

Fi sighed heavily. "I know I can't. I just always felt sorry for the gal when her parents never returned and wanted to keep her safe. I suppose we can't stop her if her questioning mind takes her away—but even so, you shouldn't listen to Toothless Betty's ramblings. We can't know another's future, or even our own, nor even hint at it. But you're right in that we should talk to Thaya. We should at least give her that much."

Thaya tiptoed back to bed feeling bad for eavesdropping. What had Toothless Betty said about her? Had the old soothsayer seen she would leave? Her heart lurched with excitement, it had always been just a dream, seeing the world for real and discovering what might be out there. Were there really great cities larger than all of Havendell? She'd sure find out where those ancient yellow stones had come from, and did she dare believe she'd meet a cat person? She loved Brightwater and Havendell and all the people here—could she ever leave? She clenched her eyes shut and tried to think of nothing, hoping it would get her to sleep, but if anything, now Fi and Yenna had mentioned her leaving, she only thought more about the world beyond the sea and the White Mountains, and the emptiness within her grew at the thought of remaining here.

She listened to Yenna and Fi going to bed and the house fall silent and dark. After an hour and still no sleep, Thaya threw off the covers. She pulled on her boots and the clothes she'd worn earlier, though dirty, she didn't want to open her creaky wardrobe and wake up everyone. She just needed to get outside, to see the stars, to smell the air and the freedom in it.

Slipping out the backdoor, she sidled out of the gate and onto the path leading towards the copse of birch trees. The moon came out then, just a half, and lit up the trees. It was a chilly spring night, but the air was fresh and pure. She crossed Littlewater Spring using the wooden bridge and sat on the bench the other side.

Frogs croaked in the reeds and an owl hooted in the distance. If she were a bird she could fly far away over the mountains, and still be back for breakfast. If only she had wings. She watched the water glisten in the light as it trickled over the pebbles and into the pools. If she were a fish, she could follow the river downstream all the way to the sea, exploring all the other streams along the way. If only she had fins.

She thought about what Fi and Yenna had said and made a mental note to seek out Toothless Betty herself. The woman had 'powers', so people said, but she'd never mentioned anything unusual to Thaya. She was just an old woman nearing her hundredth year and had a cat and fed the birds. But if she had powers, no wonder Betty'd lived alone all her life, Brightwater would never accept strange abilities.

Would that be my fate? It's lucky I don't have any powers... Sitting here wondering at things all night was no good. She had to get up at dawn and work the fields, but sleep still felt far away, and the more she tried to dampen her yearning to explore the world, the more it burned within her.

A cloud covered the moon and the forest turned very dark. Thaya shivered and got up to go, but the shadows thickened, becoming so dense she could no longer see the wooden rail of the bridge. Even the trickling stream had fallen silent. Her heart began to pound in the growing cold.

"Hello?" Her voice echoed oddly and as it faded a deeper silence fell.

She felt, rather than saw, something move, and she inhaled sharply. The shadows coalesced and lunged at her. Cold black engulfed her face, wrapping around her neck, liquid-like and with a tangible evil intent. The animated liquid tightened, and she choked and struggled against the smothering black. A strange whooshing sound grew, and the ground melted beneath her feet.

Sinking, she thrashed her arms in wild panic, but they couldn't find her face or the thing that was smothering her. She tried to scream but she couldn't inhale. Strange sharp whispers hissed around her, and her body sagged as the energy was sucked out of it.

"Help me!" She screamed, but only a rasp came out.

A giant crack like thunder jolted everything, then a flash of light. Something else grabbed her neck, even colder than the black liquid, but her throat opened a little and she managed to gasp a breath. The smothering black liquid was wrenched painfully from her face, and numerous tiny claws dragged along her cheeks and jaw drawing blood.

She gulped in air, and the blackness receded. She stared up at the silhouette of a man grasping her loosely but firmly around her neck. Bright moonlight shone behind him, making her eyes smart. As a thin cloud dimmed the moon, she saw the man had the palest face she'd ever seen, and his corneas were black onyxes in the pure whites of his eyes. His lips were grey and drawn down, and his face was long, framed by slick-black hair that hung to his chest. He did not look human—not ugly, he was handsome in a way, just not *human!* Silver earrings pierced his ears and around his neck lay a heavy silver chain and pendant with a symbol on it that was half concealed by the folds of his black robes. He wore silver rings on every one of his fingers, each engraved with an interesting symbol, or maybe words in a language she did not recognise.

In his other hand he gripped the writhing mass of black slime. It shimmered greasily, and a screaming wail came from it. A thin tendril whipped out and lassoed her neck.

Her heart thundered as the world wobbled, and she would have collapsed had he not held her. The man gripped her tighter and yanked the black slime back with his other hand. The tendril snapped and fizzled into smoke, causing the thing to scream.

He threw the writhing mass on the ground, where it howled and turned into a gaseous cloud. Swiftly the man drew a device from his clothing—a silver tube with a handle that looked like a small version of Fi's shotgun, only different enough so as she didn't quite know what it was. An orange fireball exploded from the device and hurtled straight into the black gas. It screeched and thrashed and turned into a human-like form, but long and thin and on all fours. It turned a faceless head to look at the man and growled in utter hatred before dragging itself away and vanishing.

Thaya stared from where the thing had been, back to the man. He replaced the weapon in the folds of his robes and looked at her. Slowly, he released his deathly cold grip and she sunk to her knees, shaking and rubbing her bruised neck. She wanted to run, but her body was shaking too much. When the man did not speak, she looked up at him. He was very tall, and his clothing moved around him as though he stood in a breeze. He didn't smile or blink and she felt as afraid of him as the thing that had attacked her.

"What was that? Who are you?" Her voice trembled.

Light glowed in his eyes and she felt him looking right into her mind. It was the strangest feeling; she knew he could read her thoughts.

"Your mind is...*empty*, and you are shieldless. I pass through you without resistance." He spoke Familiar in a deep voice with a sharp accent she had never heard before. There was a sense of wonder in his voice—and she felt it wasn't a good wonder, more like one analysing a strange specimen. "It is no surprise I had trouble finding you."

"Finding me?" she asked. *Why would he be looking for me?*

He ignored the question and answered the first, lifting his gaze to the darkness of the forest. "They were Shades, sent by the Vormae. They'll be back. Never killed, just... stalled. You can't kill that which isn't alive."

He turned his dark gaze onto her and she felt cold again. "You're weak, you cannot survive, and there's so little time. Get yourself ready, much time has been wasted."

"What do you mean? And ready for what?" Thaya attempted to get to her feet, expecting a helping hand from the strange man but none came. Instead, she gripped the railing of the footbridge she'd not been able to find before, and heaved herself up, leaning weakly against it.

He shook his head, pursed his lips and spoke as if answering his own questions. "Pah, there is no time, they must already know, no time at all. Look, find the Old One who found you, learn what you need to know. Leave and go now, we can't protect you."

"Who's the Old One?" Thaya frowned. "And who are you? What's going on?"

He eyed her up and down, then frowned as if finding her lacking. He pulled a ring off his little finger. "Take this, it might help us find you again. Our work is, as you might say...cut out."

She took the silver ring he shoved into her hands, and he whirled away, his cloak swirling.

"Wait!" she cried.

He paused and looked back, his white face the only discernible thing in the darkness.

"Where...Who is this Old One? You mean Toothless Betty?"

He frowned. "Toothless who? What? No!" He sighed. "Look."

An image forced into her mind, a map, and a picture of a round house surrounded by water. There was no time to analyse it.

"How did you...?" But the exasperated look on his face paused further questions. "Okay already, I'll get my things and—"

"No, do not return to your home. Not if you want anyone to live," he said, turning fully to face her.

She couldn't return home? Thaya felt the blood drain from her face.

"They are following you. Run, now, run far away."

"But who are you?" she asked, desperately wanting some answers.

To her astonishment, the man began to fade and disappear, just like the Shade had done but slower. His white features became indistinct, but before he disappeared completely his voice echoed, low and whispery, "Agaroths."

Thaya stared at the space where he had been. The stream gushed as noisily as before and the half-moon had moved across the sky. Frogs croaked and the owl hooted again. *Agaroths. Was that his name or his people?* She looked at the silver ring in her hand. It had symbols etched into it, mostly circles, some touching, others overlapping and some separate. She sensed they held meaning but had no idea what. The only finger it fitted was her thumb, and she dubiously slipped it on, expecting something strange to happen or to feel weird—but nothing changed.

Had all this really occurred? Were these 'Shades' really

hunting her? She shivered, imagining another jumping out
of the trees, and started back across the bridge. *I'll get my
things. I'll tell Fi and Yenna, and draw out the map Agaroths put
in my mind. I don't want anyone to get hurt because of me!*

She glanced back into the woods. The world was
suddenly a frightening place and she no longer desired to
explore any of it. All she wanted was to wake up in her
warm bed with the sunlight spilling through her
window. *Forget about it all,* she nodded as she hurried. *I don't
ever want to see those Shades again nor leave blessed Brightwater. It's a good life, a peaceful life, and I'll find none better!*

She stumbled to a stop at the edge of the village and
gasped. "Who turned off the lights?" All the streetlamps
were out, and no light shone in any window, not even in
Geoffrey's house and he always left one burning to keep out
the wood sprites. She had always made Fi turn every light
out at night wishing the wood sprites *would* come and make
things interesting.

The entire village was dark, lit only by the stars and half-
moon. She took a few hesitant steps towards the last tree,
and hid behind it. The shadows cast by the houses were
moving. Her hand flew to her mouth, stifling a yelp as the
shady patches drew together, all grainy and unnatural as
they clustered around the dark window of Jenny and Flynn's
house.

Shades!

A Shade separated from the mass and went right
through the glass window into the house. Thaya's heart
leapt into her throat. Another shadow emerged out of the
front door of Geoffrey's house whilst another flew out of the
top window. There were many shadows, conjoining and
then separating as they moved unhindered through doors,

windows and chimneys. The whole village was being smothered by Shades—*Shades hunting for me!*

"*...do not return to your home...*" Agaroths' voice echoed in her mind, sending a shiver down her spine.

Yenna and Fi! She cried out in her mind. Her eyes began searching for a way to get to them without the Shades seeing her.

All at once the shadows ceased moving, as if her very thoughts had alerted them. She heard voices whispering, sharp yet indecipherable. Unseen eyes hunted for her presence making the hairs on the back of her neck stand up. The whole village darkened further until she could barely make out her own house. She sidled silently backwards, cold sweat covering her face, and then she was running.

6

HUNTED

THAYA TORE THROUGH THE FOREST HEARING ONLY HER pounding heart and gasping breath.

She startled a fox and it hurtled into the bushes. Branches caught her hair and thorns scraped her face as she clawed through the foliage, but she dared not use the path, instead keeping it to her right, just out of sight. The river turned in front of her and she splashed through it without pause, soaking her trousers. Her legs burned and feet ached, but she could not stop.

She prayed to angels, to the Cleric of Brightwater, even to the gods, to see her plight and send her help but, as usual, nothing came. She fell over a rock and scraped her hands bloody but rolled to her feet and pelted on, leaping over logs and tearing through bushes, which fast became exhausting. Fatigue bore down, forcing her to clamber back onto the path. She was making so much noise anyway, it was silly to avoid the easier, faster ground.

A tiny golden lantern appeared in the distance through the trees; a beautiful glinting light of hope. *Havendell Glen, thank the angels!*

The streetlamps were lit; Brightwater's closest neighbour didn't seem to be suffering the same fate, and no Shades smothered it...*yet!* Thaya's smile faded. What if they hunted her here? She couldn't risk their lives as well!

The welcoming lights of Havendell Glen grew brighter, but rather than take the path left towards the village, Thaya forced herself on, her aching legs making her slow to a jog. She longed to see another face, a Night Hunter or someone, anyone, to dampen the fear and loneliness. With a painful swallow, she watched the lights of Havendell Glen pass her by.

Clouds darkened the sky and the path became harder to see, forcing her to slow even more. Her legs and body now trembled with fatigue and she imagined stopping to rest, if only for half an hour. She dared to glance behind her. There was nothing but the path, the forest, and a brief ray of moonlight between the clouds.

It usually took a good hour and a half to walk to Havendell Glen, so she must have been running for at least half of that. The Shades were surely far enough behind. She crossed over a bridge and made her way down to a small shingled shore on the riverbank. Crouching, she dipped her hands into the water and drank the cold clear liquid. The shore continued narrowly under the bridge where it was pitch black—perhaps a safe place to hide? She shivered. Trolls lived under bridges, but Shades were worse!

She slipped down the bank and under the bridge and collapsed against the cold stones. Hugging her knees against her chest she sunk her head on to them. *Fi and Yenna, were they all right?* She stifled a sob. How long until dawn? She longed for the sun to rise and had no intention of sleeping. With her heart racing like this, it probably wasn't possible—

but the fatigue was stronger than she thought, and she began to drift.

The close darkness of her dream opened up into an enormous space where she hung suspended, as if in the night sky. Light shone, the pure white of a single star, and she longed to be with that star with all her heart. Responding to her desire, it moved towards her.

The light became very bright as it neared, and something moved within it; the lifting of a limb, the curve of a being, nothing distinct enough that she could make out. There came a sound, a soft whispering or blowing of wind, and beautiful tones sang all around. The light held truth, something she should know, something she should be, and as it neared the strangest feeling came over her; she felt as if a great part of her had been missing her entire life and now she was becoming whole. Love, a pure love, nothing like that which she'd experienced in the waking world, engulfed her. This love was broader, all-encompassing - the feeling of home - her true home rather than what she had known in Brightwater.

Needing more, desiring more with a thirst she could not quench, she reached for the light and the light reached for her. Her outstretched fingers strained towards it as tears filled her eyes. *I've been empty my whole life!* She squinted into the brightness, willing the being to reveal itself. A long, straight shard of glowing golden silver light formed. A vivid indigo eye opened, too large and luminous to be human.

Thaya's heart lurched and a great, roaring, howling gale tore around her. The light and the enormous space compacted, the sudden pressure crushing. Shadows filled the space between her and the light, and the light screamed in anguish. Pain throbbed through Thaya and she screamed too.

The light fled and she fell.

———————

Thaya jerked awake, her heart hammering. An owl hooted loudly in the darkness. Her eyes darted left and right; she was still under the bridge and there were no Shades. She sighed and laid her head against the wall, *what a strange dream!* And now it was gone she felt completely empty. She closed her eyes and recalled the light, trying to make it fill her again like it had moments ago, but it wasn't the same. She gave up and touched the bruises made by the Shade on her neck. They were painful and tender and very much not a figment of her imagination. How long had she been asleep? She still felt exhausted, but there was no way in hell she was staying here any longer.

She heaved herself up. *I'll get to Havendell Harbour,* perhaps hiding amongst the many people there would throw the Shades off of her scent. What they were and why they hunted her remained a mystery. It was a day's ride from Brightwater to the harbour, she had no idea how long it would take on foot from where she was.

She drank from the river and set off at a swift pace along the path. Blisters that had formed upon her feet earlier now burst painfully, but she couldn't stop, she could only ignore them. At least the pace she set kept her warm.

As the sky brightened, her fears lessened, but she didn't slow, not even when her stomach growled. Perhaps Brightwater was normal now and everyone was going about their business, or perhaps they were all dead, murdered like that thing had tried to murder her. Her mind flip-flopped between the two scenarios, but her feet carried her onward, she couldn't go back.

The day wore on, her stomach growled louder, and the sun soon made her sweat. A loud crack echoed through the forest behind her making her jump. It was followed by the sound of wood splintering and a man cursing.

She spun around. A carriage, tilted awkwardly and half off the road, was behind a panting and sweating bay horse. A man with a rotund belly grabbed hold of the side where a wheel had splintered on a rock. Both horse and man struggled to keep the cart from rolling.

Ecstatic to see another living being, Thaya swiftly retraced her steps.

"Hey, Miss," called the man, his round red face shiny with sweat under his hat, "grab that wrench there at the front, would you? If I let go, this thing'll tip and injure my horse."

The stumpy bay whinnied.

"Sure!" replied Thaya and scrambled up the steps to grab the wrench from the driver's seat.

"This is the second damn wheel in a month, curse that carpenter. If you look there," he nodded to the back of the cart, sweating profusely as he held it from rolling, "there'll be a spare strapped to the back. Bring it to me would ya, kind gal?"

She unstrapped the wheel from the back and rolled it to the man. With him using the wrench and her guiding the horse, they lurched the cart forwards and got it balanced on a rock to support the underside. He removed the wheel and together they fought to attach the new one.

With the wheel finally on, the man bent over and leant on his knees, wheezing laughter. "Thank the gods someone was there to help - should the gods even exist, of course. Don't tell the clerics," he hushed under his breath with a chuckle.

Thaya laughed, and the cold fear that had hung over her all this time lifted a little.

"Anyway, Miss, I'm Brennan, pleased to meet you. And this is my mare, Pixie." Thaya took his outstretched hand and tried not to wince in his hearty grip. "And what's a fine young gal doing out here at dawn in the middle of nowhere? I've got two daughters half your age and I'd never let them go a wanderin' all alone. There's wolves and Gryphons and all sorts out there—and that's if the Acolytes don't find you first!" He chuckled again and she found herself grinning.

She looked back along the path, but even thinking about Brightwater made her shiver. Should she say something? Would he try to go back there if she did?

"I'm Thaya, and I—I'm on my way to Havendell Harbour, but I took a wrong turn and got lost," she said. *Weak, very weak.*

"Bloody gods, no wonder you look bedraggled and half-starved. Well, I'm on my way there to deliver these..." He indicated with his thumb towards the jumble of boxes over-loading the cart and nearly spilling over the sides. No wonder a wheel had broken, and poor Pixie. "Jump in, it's the least I can do for your help."

Thaya wilted in relief. Surely Pixie wouldn't mind a little bit more? The man seemed honest enough and she was too tired to care. "Thank you so much."

She took her seat beside him and they rolled along the road to Havendell Harbour. He shared his flagon of water and pointed out a bag of green apples under the seat.

She hungrily bit into her apple, savouring the tart juici-ness, and wondered whether the man had witnessed anything unusual. She couldn't just ask him about Shades, he'd think her mad or cursed and take her to the Illumined Acolytes no matter what he thought about the gods.

"Where have you come from?" she tentatively asked.

"Far West Havendell. It's been a long journey, but the pay's good this year and I'd happily do it again tomorrow."

Thaya's heart sank. The road would not have taken him through Brightwater and he wouldn't know anything about it.

"Then I swung by Brightwater to drop off a few deliveries."

Her pulse quickened. "You've been to Brightwater? When did you leave?"

"Just this morning, early—Gal, what's got you so worked up?" He frowned.

"Well, I come from there and...and...is everything all right?"

"Aye, and why shouldn't it be?"

Thaya paused, her mouth opening and closing, her mind whirring. "Oh good," she said, her voice strained. "Of course, why wouldn't it be? I meant, is everyone all right? I always worry about my grandparents when I journey away from home."

"Aye, Miss, don't you worry, they were all tilling the fields before even I was up. Nice peaceful place it is. I'll bet no nonsense or anything much happens there. Say, why are you going to Havendell Harbour? The weekend markets are two days away, and you don't look like you've much to sell. Or are you sneaking away to meet a lover?"

Thaya reddened with indignation "No of course not! And I'd never be the type of woman to *sneak* around." Who did he think she was? Sheesh, he was nosey. Thaya dropped her gaze from his. "I'm running an errand, a delivery such as yourself." She fumbled for an excuse whilst her mind whirred on other matters. She couldn't just return to Brightwater, but why was no one looking for her? Everything was normal, but how could it be after the Shades, and that she was clearly missing?

He held up his hands. "Okay, okay, no need to get wound up. You look all faint; I hope you're not sick. I don't want to catch it. There's all sorts spreading from the war-front. Here, have another apple." He reached into the sack.

She took it with a nod, but didn't feel like eating any more. Her brothers, Finly and Bron, would be hunting for her this very moment. *Did I dream it all up? Is this all one stupid nightmare?* If she went back, would the Shades return?

"Yes," a voice said loudly. Agaroths' voice.

Thaya sat upright and stared at Brennan, but the man hadn't spoken, his eyes were fixed on the road and he was lost in his own thoughts. He clearly hadn't heard the voice.

She stared at the silver ring on her finger. *No, it wasn't a dream!*

In complete confusion, Thaya sat silently for the next few hours. Nothing that had happened made any sense. It was as if her family and Brightwater had utterly forgotten her existence. Had the Shades done something to them? If she endangered their lives simply by being there, there was no way she could return. Now that she was out here exploring the world beyond Brightwater, she just wanted to go home and for everything to be like it was yesterday.

Something else gnawed at her; that empty, lonely feeling within was driving her, urging her to seek for that which called to her. It only served to unsettle her further.

Clouds covered the sun and a chill wind blew, carrying upon it the scent of the sea. Brennan wrapped his cloak around him and began to grumble to anyone who'd listen.

"The pay could be better, given how dangerous the roads are. War displaces all sorts and soaks up everyone's money. Now I'll have to fork out for another spare wheel, and I doubt Geff's gonna help pay for it. And look at those clouds, it'll probably start raining before we get there."

He clearly didn't expect her to answer as he droned on about the weather, his old cart, his weary horse, and anything else that came to mind. He liked to grumble, Thaya decided, and looked forward to getting off this jolting, jarring cart.

"Wolves I've seen and they've never really bothered us, but there aren't really Gryphons, are there?" she asked, attempting to take his mind off his troubles.

Brennan snorted. "Hah, of course there are. Well, I've never seen one, but my uncle's friend, now he knew someone who'd been on the road like you and me are now, and his horse was ripped right from the cart and carried away, talons so sharp they sliced through the bridle and harness as if they were butter. He was lucky to survive, especially when the bandits came and sacked the remains of his grounded cart."

Thaya remained sceptical. "I thought they were noble, magical beasts?"

"That's what the fairy tales will have you believe, but the real world is a far uglier place, young lady." The man sniffed.

Thaya still didn't quite believe him, but she kept glancing up at the sky none-the-less. Compared to Shades, a Gryphon would surely be better.

Brennan took out a pasty wrapped in paper from his pack and began munching on it, making her stomach rumble. He side-glanced her. She could tell he didn't want to share it, but, with a sigh, he reached back into his pack and shoved one her way.

"You look like a strong gal, the farming sort," he said, squinting at her. "If you help me deliver this stuff, I'll get you a hot meal and maybe you can sleep in the cart for tonight – but I'll be off at first light. Gotta make it to the border before the close of day, and passing through those border patrols takes hours."

"I can do that." Thaya nodded eagerly. She hadn't even thought about dinner, let alone where she might sleep. She wanted only to get as far away from Brightwater as she could. Those Shades could be hunting her in the forest right now. Maybe they could smell her scent like a fox. Getting a lift on a cart was the best thing that could have happened.

There were cleric houses at the harbour, initially created by clerics for the poor and homeless to sleep and shelter, but the reality was they were nothing more than shack-like hovels inhabited by thieves, murderers and beggars. She'd be safer sleeping out in the open. And what would she do in Havendell Harbour when she got there? She had a purse in her trouser pocket with four silvers. Things were expensive in the harbour and she didn't know how far it would go, but there was always work available and usually food and board.

She travelled to Havendell Harbour once a month with her brothers to peruse the markets and buy supplies, mainly seeds, clothes and food, and to sell their surplus crops. It was the furthest she had ever travelled from home, and she loved looking out over the endless blue ocean that sparkled in the sun, wondering how far it stretched and what was out there on the other side. People would recognise her, especially Pete who ran the Old Tavern where her brothers liked to drink. Her hand stroked her bruised neck. She longed to see a familiar friendly face, but what if the whole harbour was engulfed with Shades?

"Someone been hittin' ya? You been gettin' into fights?" Brennan nodded to her neck, his brown eyes hard. She wondered how bad the bruises looked.

She swallowed. "No, I—well, I guess I've always been a bit of tomboy and I fell into the river. Luckily my brothers got me out before I got washed away." She hated lying, but she couldn't tell the truth. Besides, it was a good idea to mention her big strong older brothers in case this man had any nefarious thoughts towards her, not that she thought him dangerous, but she was on her own and every bit of protection helped. She forced a smile, but he seemed unconvinced and turned back to watching the road.

"See that old dead tree in the distance?"

Thaya looked at the gnarled trunk of an ancient, long-dead oak. Lightning had split the poor thing down the middle, but it had become such a prominent marker for travellers, the mayor had decided not to cut it down. It stood on a hill surrounded by greenery.

She nodded, "Havendell Harbour is only an hour's ride once we reach Dead Tree."

"Indeed, though more like an hour and a half with this load." He tutted.

They took the left turn at Dead Tree where the road split.

A line of four clerics walked silently along the side of the road, their hoods drawn up. Their rich red and yellow robes made of expensive material such as royalty might wear, swished around them. The clerics' simple old rope girdles showed they were not quite Illumined Acolytes—otherwise, their girdles would be red or orange—but they still asserted a feeling of power and arrogance around them, or perhaps it was just arrogance and they had no real power.

Their hands were clasped inside their robes and they stared hard at Thaya and Brennan as their cart jostled past. For all acolytes, smiling was forbidden, and so was music, alcohol, feasting, celebrating, and all manner of normal human enjoyments. Self-flagellation was positively encouraged, as well as flagellating anyone else, especially the blasphemers. Thaya didn't like them and she didn't much like the angry gods they worshipped either. The gods were more like myths than Gryphons were. The gods were definitely absent, but Gryphons, apparently, were real.

She shivered under their gaze. It was almost as if they knew something evil had touched her, had left its mark, and for some reason she covered up Agaroth's ring with her other hand, forcing her gaze to the road ahead.

"Bloody clerics," Brennan grumbled under his breath, clearly keen to avoid said flagellations. They took his attention off other things, however, and he grumbled about them instead as they rocked all the way to the edges of Havendell Harbour.

The harbour walls and buildings were made out of pale grey stone, and they reached from the sea all the way back up the long sloping hill. The larger, plush mansions of the rich stood on the top of the hill, along with the mayor's austere Manor House and the overly fancy Illumined Acolytes' House of God with its garish orange domes.

Compared to Brightwater, Havendell Harbour was enormous, heavily populated, and chaotic. It was always busy, and when they reached the main road leading towards the harbour gates, people and merchants filled every space, milling amongst horses and mules pulling carts and carriages, and poorer people and labourers pushing wheel-

barrows. Every day appeared to be market day, and through
the gates, she could see the bright colours of the many stalls
and marquees.

"Get out of the way!" Brennan shouted at the people, but
no one paid him much notice. For the first time since she'd
left Brightwater, Thaya felt able to relax. There were no
Shades here and they'd never find her amongst all these
people. She was safe, at least for now. Perhaps she should
simply wait it out here for a few days and then go home, but
another part of her felt uneasy at the thought, and that
strange lonely emptiness pulled her on.

Brennan guided his horse and cart through the crowds and
along the wider cobbled streets, pulling up outside a store
selling ribbons and cloth.

"Right, let's offload these." He motioned for her to help,
then stacked her arms with two heavy crates and took two
for himself. She followed him down a side alley to the backdoor, where he rapped loudly.

The door creaked open and a stocky man with a long
black moustache stood there. "Ah, Mister Brennan, about
time we saw you and you've come not a moment too soon, as
always."

Brennan scowled. "I do my best, Mister Harbon. Broke a
wheel on the way, but this 'ere gal saved the day." He
slapped her heartily on the back nearly knocking her over,
and she grinned foolishly.

Too busy to chat, Mister Harbon nodded at her and
ferried them inside to drop their crates in the storage room.
Brennan and Thaya jumped back on the cart and delivered

six more crates around the town, leaving just four in the cart.

Brennan stretched his arms above his head and sighed. "That's it for now, Miss, the rest are for further afield. I can't be thanking you enough. We'll park the cart around the back of World's End Tavern and get a hot meal there."

Thaya had heard of the tavern but never been. She rarely explored Havendell Harbour east of the market.

The sky had turned crimson and a chill wind blew off the sea. She'd only managed to glimpse the ocean between the crowded houses. Harbour-folk hurried past, keen to get home for dinner after a long day at work. The less salubrious types didn't hurry and were pulling down their dark hoods or hats and looking suspicious. Usually in the protection of her brothers, Thaya felt nervous as it grew darker and wished Finly and Bron were here. The horse's hooves and the cartwheels clopped and clattered on the cobbles, and the city guards took to lighting the street lanterns.

Brennan pulled through two knackered wooden gates half hanging off their hinges, and into a yard ringed with stables and filled with carriages and traps. It was almost full save for one stable, and just enough room for his cart between a row of wheelbarrows and a rickety-looking trap. With her help, he bedded the horse down fast and grabbed his bag.

"Right, let's get some ale and some of Peggy's grub." He rubbed his round belly, his eyes shining.

Thaya followed Brennan closely into The Old Tavern where warmth, firelight and the smell of sweat and hops engulfed her. Beyond the fug, the tavern was full of people all shouting to be heard, and awful music came from somewhere towards the back. They squeezed past patrons both standing and seated. Two men argued over a board game and, glimpsing the board, she guessed it to be Checkers. One of them had a thick brush of a moustache, the other was clean-shaven and waving his fist. She lost sight of them in the press of bodies.

The music, or disharmonious warbling, grew louder as they neared the back. That had to be a flute, but in the rising din, she could barely hear the airy notes and doubted the person playing it could either. She caught sight of the musician, a small thin man flopping on a stool, every now and then pushing back his thin, limp hair. A half-eaten tomato suddenly splattered over his shoulder. He paused and looked balefully out across the crowd then down at the mess on the floor. Shoulders slumping, he hunted through his music book for something to entice the mob.

She lost sight of him as Brennan grabbed hold of her arm and dragged her through the patrons. Two people, a man and woman, well-dressed in silks and velvets, were just vacating their stools around a beer barrel, and her benefactor hauled her in for the kill.

He slumped himself down and without asking her what she wanted, ordered loudly, "Two ales and two plates please, Miss Peggy!" easily drowning out the rest of the patrons, most of whom flinched and stared their way. Thaya swallowed guiltily and looked down at her hands.

A pink-cheeked woman burst forwards to remove the empty glasses and nodded at him, her mass of red curls bouncing as she deftly grasped tankards in one hand and dirty crockery in the other. She whirled away, her ample bosom jiggling and straining against the snares of her blouse as she swung back through the kitchen doors.

A young serving girl, her thin arms bending from the weight of tankards of golden ale, slammed the pints down and Brennan grabbed his thirstily.

Thaya lifted the bitter drink to her lips. No one paid them any attention, so she dared to let herself relax. Brennan didn't talk much, seeming content to place all his attention on his rapidly disappearing pint. She was too tired to speak anyway, and instead enjoyed watching the people as they laughed and shouted.

The food arrived; a bowl of steaming stew, a hunk of bread and a wedge of cheese. They both devoured it and meticulously mopped up the sides with their bread. Brennan finished his third pint whilst she still nursed her first, then disappeared off to the privy, leaving her to defend his empty stool for a good while.

She enjoyed the rest of her pint and the crowd began to thin as people left for home. The flute player had given up and now sat dozing in his chair, flute grasped like a weapon, a selection of empty glasses and tankards rolling beneath his stool. Thaya yawned. How comfortable was her straw bed on the cart going to be? She could ask for a room here in the tavern, but without knowing how long she'd be away from home, saving her money would be wise. She had a free bed so she should take it.

Agaroths' ring caught the lantern light and she inspected it. If it was made of silver, how come it was bright, clean and completely unscratched? She wondered at the symbols upon it, they surely meant something or said something in a language she didn't know. She put it back on as Brennan returned.

"Right then, Gal," he said, then belched. "I'm getting myself another pint, but you'd best get yerself some sleep before the drunks start bothering ye'. I'll pay for this as thanks for your help today, and then we're square."

"Thanks Brennan." She smiled and got up. Not wanting an excuse to stay, she made her way to the door. A couple of men cast her drunken glances, but rather than admire her honey brown locks, saw only her torn muddy clothes and grubby state. Losing interest, they turned back to their drinks.

She stepped out of the warmth into the cool night and yelped, falling back from the road just in time to avoid a cart clattering past.

"Get out the way, wench!" shouted the driver, as the wheels splashed dirty puddle water all over her already soiled attire.

"Thanks a lot!" she cried, stepping into the road and waving her fist at the driver. This only made him laugh and he wafted a dismissive hand before careening around the corner.

"Just great! Now I'll have to sleep damp." She sighed, looking at the mess on her trousers.

Loping across the road, she dared any other cart to come her way. None did, and the night fell to silence and the lonely streetlight glistening off the cobbles. She walked the short distance to the cart and looked balefully at the clumps of straw and horsehair blankets. It was a far cry from her own solid oak bed with its warm mattress and soft covers.

She pulled herself into the cart and fluffed up the straw. She wrapped herself in the rough, pungent blankets and lay down beside the remaining crates. There wasn't enough room to stretch out fully, but it was better than being under the bridge, or out there with those *things* hunting her.

7

SOLIA

"Remember."

The bright living light grew in the darkness, pulsing and radiant, lifting her from her dream and filling her up with its wholeness.

"Remember," a voice whispered, soothing yet loud, and neither male nor female.

"Remember what?" Thaya asked, her own voice coarse compared to the other.

"Remember," the voice simply repeated and faded away, along with the light.

Thaya fell into the heavy darkness of dreamless sleep.

The shaking carriage jerked her awake. She sat up and scratched at the straw sticking into her hair. It wasn't yet dawn and the night sky was barely brightening.

"Right then, Gal," Brennan said, adjusting Pixie's bridle, then slapping his wide rump down in the driver's seat. She hadn't even awoken whilst he attached the horse to the cart.

The man was remarkably perky for one who'd drunk a gallon the night before. "I'm late, and it's time for us to part ways. All the best!" He whipped his reins and the cart jolted forwards.

Thaya yelped and rolled off the back, barely catching her balance. He waved goodbye and clattered through the gates.

"Good morning to you, too," she muttered, pulling straw out of her clothing.

What do I do now? She looked around and spied an open barrel filled with water and a tin mug hanging from a string. Water for the stableboys, *and me.*

She drank and watched the sky slowly turn pink as she thought about her next steps. After a proper night's sleep, the Shades no longer seemed so fearsome, and the whole thing was taking on the feel of a peculiar nightmare. But no matter how she worked it through, the thought of returning home filled her with a sense of foreboding and she dropped the matter.

She was here for a few days at least, and her stomach was grumbling. Perhaps her brothers would come looking for her in a day or two. She could find work and sleep in someone's barn if necessary. It would only be for a couple of days. Down at the docks, there was always work, and if she was lucky, she'd find work aboard a ship and thus a bed *and* meals.

She finished the water and with determined steps made her way through alleys and roads towards the shipyard.

A hive of activity hummed at the docks, though the sun was only just rising. Sailors worked the decks and set sails as the first ships began to leave port. Dockworkers scurried everywhere, loading ships, unloading others, and in the distance, the clanging of metal and sawing of wood filled the air. Somewhere, a donkey brayed.

Thaya approached the nearest worker. "Excuse—" she began.

"Not now, Miss." The dockworker shook his head and stalked on, hefting a barrel on his shoulders.

"Mmm." Thaya pursed her lips and tried another person, but he shook his head apologetically and carried on across a gangplank.

She paced the wooden walkway, marvelling at the enormous ships. Their mahogany wood polished and shining, their names carved ornately on their bows; *Seabound, Firefish, Windward...* their plumb lines all freshly painted in red, yellow or blue. She tried to catch a few more people, but they all shook their heads and hurried on.

She spotted a woman a little way ahead and dressed unlike any other in her royal blue velvet robes detailed with orange satin borders and swirls of thread. Her hood was pulled up against the chill morning sea breeze, and she had an air of authority, her long sleeves swinging as she pointed left and right, directing dock workers and sailors. Surely, she needed her help, didn't she? Thaya smoothed her grubby trousers and looked ready for business, her growling stomach making her bold.

"Excuse me, Miss, I mean, Lady," Thaya bumbled out and didn't wait to be told 'no.' "I'm looking for work, er, just for a day or two. I don't need money, only food and a bed."

The woman turned to her. Her deep blue eyes blazed with intelligence and something else Thaya couldn't quite decipher. They appeared to glow briefly and then were normal. Her hair was dark mahogany and braided down over one shoulder. She looked to be in her thirties or forties, though it wasn't easy to tell. Thaya had the strangest feeling that this woman was looking right through her. She couldn't see the Shades in her memory, could she? She tried to hide her alarm but sensed even this the woman could detect. She looked her up and down, a frown knitting her brows, although not one of disgust.

"Hmm, I don't hire runaways," she said in a voice that was deep and rich. "And don't look at me like that, a runaway doesn't have to be a child. It could be a woman forced into an ungodly marriage to a fiend!"

Thaya checked herself, "Oh, I see, um, I'm not that, either of those. Actually, I'm the opposite, Lady, er." She stumbled, this woman's confident and commanding presence tied her tongue. "I'm actually trying to get home! Although I just need a bit more time away...Uh, it's complicated." She slumped.

The woman laughed. "Well, I see you don't lie, and though I need no more hands, I also see one in need. A wise woman helped me once, so I shall help you. Hmm, can you cook? Hmm, never mind that, our cook won't have another work beside him. Perhaps you can clean up after meals, yes? He could certainly do with that kind of help. However, there'll be no pay, there's none to spare and the ship's full as it is, only meals and board like you asked for. Although you'll be alone in a hammock with the cargo, I'm afraid, as there are no more beds. Still, that might be better for you, an attractive woman alone, yes? Good. We set sail today, it's only a short trip, three days there, three days back, and afterwards you'll have to make your own way I'm afraid."

Thaya quickly thought about it, a week was a long time away. Yenna and Fi would be worried sick, and she'd never been at sea before. She'd heard that people got ill the entire time until they set foot on land again, and there were enormous beasts out there lurking under the waves. She thought about the Shades choking the village and shivered. Surely after a week, the Shades would all be gone, and everything would blessedly be back to normal?

"A week is perfect." Thaya beamed.

The woman pursed her lips then smiled knowingly as if she had seen something of Thaya's thoughts. "All right then! Now get yourself some decent clothes, you can't work aboard like that, you'll make everything dirty!" She lifted a pale hand and pointed to the closest ship. "Mid-deck you'll find baskets of clothes, gloves, and boots for the deckhands. You won't look pretty, but you'll look better than you do now." She winked.

"Thank you, Lady, er, Ma'am." Thaya nodded gratefully and started towards the ship.

"It's Solia Penumbrow. And use the washroom! You stink of horses," the woman shouted after her, then turned back to directing the dockworkers as if she were a choral conductor.

Thaya climbed the steps and sidled nervously across the gangplank. It was a long drop to the sea below, and midden floated beneath. She even spotted a dead rat, all bloated and ready to burst. '*Solia Penumbrow*' she said, over and over in her mind, making sure she wouldn't forget it. That had gone easier than she'd thought, or had the woman taken pity on her? She'd seen something in her mind, somehow, otherwise she would have asked for references, or made a note of employment for assurance. Still, better thank the gods for this one.

"'Scuse me, Miss." A sailor swung deftly past her when she hesitated on the gangplank's midpoint. It wobbled violently under his steps as he all but danced along it with a barrel on his shoulders. Thaya swayed for balance. Holding her breath, she rushed after him and did not look down again. Stepping onto the deck, she fell against the handrail. Her neck hairs prickled, and she caught the gaze of the woman looking her way.

Urgh, she'll know I've never even been aboard a ship before! Thaya politely tipped an imaginary hat then turned towards the nearest door. Though the ship was docked, the way it shifted under her feet was quite unsettling. She also had no idea where the mid-deck was but took the stairs down into a wooden corridor and pushed through the only door.

Sailors brushed past her along the narrow hallway, frowning and making it clear she shouldn't be there. Later, when the rum came out, they'd probably see her rather differently. She came to a wide, empty room that had small round portholes along the side to let in thick shards of sunlight. Baskets, filled with clothes and shoes, lined the walls, and she got busy digging around them. Marked as small, medium and large, she pulled out a pair of breeches, a white shirt, a tan jerkin, boots and gloves. They were nothing special, but a sniff of her own clothes had her rushing to the changing room. She paused before four doors in a row, and peering into each revealed buckets of water and a simple drain running across the floor and out of the ship.

She entered one, wedged the door shut, undressed and washed with a bucket of cold water and hard soap. Using the cleanest item of her old clothes, she dried herself and dressed in her new attire. It wasn't as good as a bath, but she was no longer smelly and grimy.

Feeling refreshed, she stepped out of the washroom. Much to her disappointment, the hat basket was empty, but there were a few red kerchiefs remaining. She grabbed one, smoothed back her hair and wrapped it around her head.

Rather than reporting back to her mistress, Thaya took the initiative and went looking for the kitchen. It took a whole hour of searching through dozens of doors, stairways and corridors until she found it on the lower decks. She pushed through the swinging doors and tripped straight over a scuttling rat. It squeaked, glared at her, then disappeared down a hole in the floorboards. *Rats love ships,* she thought, hoping not to see any more.

The kitchen was large and warm and occupied by a fat man in greasy whites bent over a giant pot on a monstrous stove, stirring and muttering to himself.

Thaya composed herself. "Good morning, Sir. Lady Solia employed me to help you clean."

"What?" the man bellowed. He straightened, his piggy eyes squinting at her, and blew out his thick grey moustache. He looked very much like a walrus and Thaya hid a grin. "Curse that woman, she knows I hate useless oiks getting under my feet!" He shook his dripping spoon at her. "And she's no 'Lady!' That woman there is a wizard, a Magi, a sorceress, and don't you forget it or you'll end up for the worse."

"A Magi?" Thaya's eyes widened. "You mean, they're real? And magic's real?"

"What?" The cook bellowed again. He stood tall and wide and growing redder. "Are you a half-wit?"

"What? No, Sir, uh, we don't have those things where I'm from." She stared at the floor.

"Ah, I see," he said, looking her up and down as if checking to see she was all there. "A country bumpkin— about as close to a half-wit as you can get. Now stop wasting my time and clean up those tables." He nodded his head towards the door.

"Yes, Sir." Thaya darted away, leaving the angry cook to his pot. *I'm not stupid, child!*

In the large, functional dining room, or mess as it might aptly be called, long rows of tables and stools lay covered with dirty bowls, spoons, crumbs and slops of porridge—the remnants of a hastily eaten breakfast. At the end of a table stood a large serving pot and she scraped out what remained with the serving spoon. Though it was long cold, her stomach didn't care, and the porridge was creamy and filling. The squeak of a rat told her she wasn't the first to get here and she hoped it hadn't made it inside the pot. She stacked the bowls, as many as she could carry, and headed to the massive ceramic sinks on one side where she got to work.

Eyes settled on her again, this time more than one pair. When she looked up, something scurried in the darkest corner. At least the rats would help her clean up the floor, she thought. An hour passed before she was done, there were so many bowls and cutlery she wondered how many sailors worked the ship. It wasn't the largest boat in the harbour, but neither was it the smallest.

She finished wiping the tables and went back to the cook, only to find him gone. So, he'd snuck off and left her to clean up—fine. There was no point in her hanging around waiting for more work, so she thought she may as well go back upstairs for some fresh air.

Warm sunlight greeted her and the sight of sailors scrubbing the decks. Solia was talking to a tall, well-built man who had hazelnut hair and stubble. His thick arms were folded across his chest and curious faint blue lines swirled over his forearms. An air of authority hung about him too, but despite his handsome face, her eyes were drawn to the enigmatic Magi, Solia. Was the cook just playing her or could this woman really use magic? What kind of things could she do? Thaya imagined her sprouting wings and flying, or fire bursting from her fingertips.

The woman caught her stare and Thaya found herself walking over.

"The cook needs an assistant, someone to help clean up," Solia explained when the man raised an eyebrow at her.

"An attractive one with honey tresses? That'll keep the sailors happy or distracted, I can't decide which." The man's voice was deep, and she couldn't tell if he was jesting or not.

"Thaya," said Thaya, holding out her hand.

The man's clear green eyes scrutinised her, but his frown softened as he shook it. "The fewer women we have aboard the better. They tend to cause havoc with my crew."

"What, by working them harder and instilling civility and better manners?" Solia retorted, her eyes glittering humorously.

The man snorted.

"You'll get no trouble from me, Sir," said Thaya, standing tall. "And I can look after myself, thanks to my older brothers."

"I don't know, Captain Arto, the men don't pay me much attention at all," chuckled Solia. "If anything, they run away from me."

Thaya was surprised the man was a captain, he could only be five, certainly no more than ten, years older than she.

"No wonder." He frowned. "They've seen you turn rats into pumpkins and vice versa!"

Thaya imagined the kitchen rats turning into all manner of vegetables with a click of Solia's fingers.

"Bah, merely illusions, and not real magic at all." Solia

waved dismissively, but her mischievous grin remained. She laid a companionable hand on Arto's arm and turned to Thaya. "Don't let my good friend scare you, I rarely do magic tricks, and only to alarm his superstitious crew."

"I can see that you're fit and strong with no sign of the fevers, but what are you really, a runaway? Thief? Up-to-no-gooder?" asked Arto, his eyes narrowing.

The questions caught her off guard. "Neither, Captain, I'm a farmer, though just urgently needing time away from..." She struggled for the words, failed and shrugged. It had to be enough, didn't it? Why did they have to question her?

She felt Solia searching her with her eyes again, a strange feeling as if she were being read like a book. The sorceress's eyes widened imperceptibly, as if she'd seen something. Was it the Shades? Was it Agaroths or whatever his name was? Thaya chewed her lip.

Arto nodded. "I understand. An argument perhaps? Hmm, time away, usually from family, often from partners, always helps. A lithe young woman like you shouldn't be wandering the streets alone. Bad things happen to good people, then get worse when your husband comes looking for you.

"Well, if you work hard and don't get in the way, I see no harm in it. There are only a couple of hammocks spare, not the best, mind, but it's better than sleeping rough. For now, get ready to sail, there are reports of a storm headed our way and I want to be well away before it hits."

Already, sailors were loosening the mooring ropes and readying the sails. Nervous excitement stole over Thaya; she really was heading out to sea and leaving Havendell! She'd dreamed of this moment her whole life, if only it didn't have to be under these circumstances.

The gangplank lifted and the last of the mooring lines released them from the land. The sails dropped and suddenly the wind pulled them away from the dock.

We're free! Thaya almost cheered.

She waved at the crowd of townsfolk and dockworkers watching them depart. Her eyes fell upon the lone old woman waving back. She straightened. "Toothless Betty?" There, amongst the fishmongers wheelbarrowing their wares, stood the old woman in her unmistakable red skirt and bright green shawl gazing at her. She smiled a toothless grin, visible even at this distance, and lifted her walking stick in farewell. *She's alive, she'd know everything that happened!*

"Wait, I've got to talk to her!" Thaya panicked and ran to where the gangplank had been.

A strong hand grabbed her arm and pulled her back from the edge. "You can't leave now Miss, we've left port!" Arto said. "Just relax and enjoy the journey."

He placed her hand firmly on the rail and went back to yelling at his crew. Thaya spun back to stare at Toothless Betty who was fast disappearing into the distance.

"Who did you see?" Solia came up beside her and squinted into the crowd. Her hood was pushed back and her freshly oiled brown sable hair was smoothed back into a silver clasp.

"Toothless Betty. She's from my village. From Brightwater. I, I have to talk with her, it's a matter of life and death," Thaya insisted, but there was no way of stopping the ship and returning to dock. Already wind was filling the sails and the ship turned swiftly seaward.

"The old soothsayer with the walking stick? Yes, she spoke to me not an hour before you arrived. That's how I knew to expect you," Solia replied, unasked questions in her eyes.

"What? You spoke to her? You were expecting me? How, why? What did she say?" Thaya suddenly felt afraid.

"I think you'd better tell me everything that happened since you left your home, Thayannon Farseeker," Solia said, in a manner she could not disobey. The Magi knew her name—she really *had* spoken to Toothless Betty. "Come to the stern, there's a quiet corner behind the helm where we can talk in private."

Solia turned away, but Thaya lingered. She waved back at Toothless Betty, though it was doubtful the old woman could see her anymore. Her eyes travelled over the port town to the clock tower and then to the green forest beyond. Over the hills and far away lay Brightwater, her home. She glimpsed the dusty curve of the road she and Brennan had travelled earlier, and something moved. She stared, her mouth going dry as the road darkened, becoming hazy and indistinct as if shadows collected upon it. She glanced up, but no cloud had passed across the sun, the sky was clear. The shadows moved into the forest and the road returned to its greyish brown colour.

Thaya whirled after Solia. She *had* to tell someone what had happened, and the sorceress was the only person who would understand.

Hot sunlight spilled down upon them in the relatively quiet corner of the otherwise manic ship. White water frothed at the stern below them, and all around swirled endless blue.

"She came to me with a sooth," began Solia. Thaya searched her face for ridicule but found only seriousness. "And it was this, 'Today, one will arrive fleeing the shadows sent to find her. She will not understand why she is hunted, and neither do I.' She said to tell you to run and not look back. She said the people of your home are alive and well, but all memory of you has been erased by the darkness that came upon them."

Thaya inhaled sharply and gripped the rails, her mind spinning. So, Toothless Betty knew. How had she come to Havendell Harbour so quickly, and why? Had she been looking for her? In the face of everything, it mattered little. Everyone was alive, alive!

Solia continued. "This might sound crazy to you, though I suspect that it doesn't, but I'm trained in truth seeking and the old woman did not lie. So tell me, Miss Thaya, what it is that happened to you."

"They're alive, can it be true?" Thaya whispered.

"If she said it, then it is so. Soothsayers cannot lie." Solia's eyes were penetrating.

Relief flooded over Thaya. Toothless Betty was eccentric, but she was not mad, and had she ever lied, Thaya would have felt it too.

"Here, look into this." Solia drew a pouch out of her pocket, inside which was a glass disc about the size of her palm. "Pass your hand over it like so." Solia slowly waved her hand over the glass and Thaya followed suit.

The glass clouded instantly, and an image formed; a field and people working it.

"Yenna and Fi?" Thaya grabbed the glass from Solia and stared into it. Clear as day, she saw Fi hoeing the field. He paused and stretched his back, and for a moment looked right at her. Beyond him, Yenna smoothed her hair back into a bun. "How can I see them? Is this a trick?" Thaya glared at Solia. Could Magi be trusted?

"No trick," Solia shook her head and took the glass from Thaya. "The Looking Glass is a magical device, and what you see within it, is what is so right now, for the ones you love. So tell me, Thaya, why are you here?"

Thaya glanced at the Magi then looked away, wondering at the marvellous things this woman—this sorceress—knew about the world with a pang of envy. She took a deep breath. "I went for a walk, to look at the stars, I guess, and wonder who else is up there, but also because I couldn't sleep. Anyway, I was about to return home when the shadows came alive and this, this *thing* tried to choke me!"

"A Shade, I can see it in your mind," breathed Solia. She too turned and gripped the rails, the colour draining from her face.

"Yes, a Shade," echoed Thaya. "But then a man came out of nowhere; he just materialised. I don't know how, but he wasn't quite human. He was terribly pale with a long face and black hair. And he wore silver jewellery, everywhere. The jewellery felt odd, maybe magical like your device."

"So you can feel magic, meaning you have some ability?" said Solia.

"I guess, I wouldn't know. But this man helped me."

Thaya told her about Agaroths and what happened. Solia frowned and said nothing as she stared at the white wash churning below. Only after Thaya had finished, did she stare out to sea and speak.

"The Agaroths. Ancient texts call them The Watchers, but they are rarely seen. I've not seen this man before, nor any of his race. What can it mean? Hmm. I must report back to my order at once. Perhaps you should come with me; it seems like you could learn a thing or two to protect yourself. You're not young—positively old for a novice Magi—but anyone can learn the basics, especially if you have an enquiring mind like you clearly have and a little natural magical ability. You can tell your story to my superiors yourself; it's always better coming from the source."

"I would be honoured!" Thaya jumped at the thought. *Imagine speaking to an order of magicians and learning to hurl fire from my fingertips!* Most importantly she needed to defend herself against the Shades. Thank the gods Solia believed her and didn't think she was crazy, but that only made everything more frightening and real. She took a deep breath. "So I'm running from them, as he told me to do. And what's more, I think I saw one just a moment ago in the harbour. It may be nothing but...on the road I travelled yesterday, the one leading into the port, a large shadow grew then moved and disappeared into the forest."

"Hunting, yes, that's what Shades do, and they never tire or give up." Solia shook her head. "Oh dear, this isn't good, not good at all. Where Shades are, their masters aren't far away. The Vormae are relentless."

"The Vormae?" A strange fuzzy feeling entered her mind and in her minds' eye, Thaya witnessed tall thin beings draped in black and red. Their large bulbous heads were greyish-white and covered in veins. Long, watery eyes were slanted and half-closed, and their mouths—dear gods, they had none! Thaya gasped at the smooth skin extending from their nasal slits to their necks. She felt sick.

"You see them?" Solia asked. "Good, I placed that image there to test you. You have a mind that can see, a mind that is open, even after all this time amongst the ignorant—not their fault, of course, it's just the manner of our world. People prefer not to question, for the truth is as hard to find as it is to take. Yes, you will learn our teachings well, my order will be most pleased to meet you.

"What you see are the Vormae, and they send their Shades to do their bidding—hapless souls of the lost;

enslaved, tortured, and twisted with rage through their masters. The Vormae are aliens who do not live among humans, but upon a dark world far beyond our sun. Wherever they go, they seek dominion over all others, but upon our planet Urtha, they are unseen and unknown to all but a few. They are a most ancient enemy to the peoples of this planet."

Thaya listened, enraptured, a fear growing inside of all the things she did not know. What did these Vormae want with her? What were her strange dreams of the light and of remembering about? Were they put there by the Vormae? *No, that didn't feel true.* She chewed a fingernail; her life was spiralling out of control.

An odd feeling came over her, like a cold wet blanket slithering over her skin. Everything became heavy and her head ached dully with the sudden pressure. The strangest noise grew in her ears, like a great swarm of wasps approaching. Thaya winced.

"What is it?" Solia began, then she too smarted and covered her ears against the growing, maddening sound.

In the sky, three metallic discs appeared out of nowhere and hovered above them motionless. They shone like silver in the sunlight, were bulbous in the middle and tapered out towards the ends, incredibly smooth and perfectly shaped. Lights shone from under them, a ring of round yellow lamps that did not flicker like fire but were still and constant. The lights turned green and then orange then back to yellow, as the strange metal discs hung in the sky like squashed baubles. They looked small, but the distance was deceptive, and how exactly *did* metal fly?

The noise coming from them made it impossible to think straight, Thaya could only gawp. Everyone on deck now had their hands clasped over their ears; no one could move, not even the captain.

Suddenly, the discs shot closer, moving faster than a falcon and in a completely straight line. They stopped abruptly, barely yards above their ship, hanging in a perfect chevron alignment, impervious to the wind or gravity or any of the natural laws that should have bound them.

The wind vanished from the sails and their ship abandoned its course, bobbing purposelessly as Arto swore and spun the now useless wheel. The sea became flat and still. The noise coming from the discs stopped abruptly. Silence clamped upon the world.

Thaya felt sick—something terrible was about to happen. The lights of the discs flared angry red, and the chaos began.

8

CAPTURED

A THICK BEAM OF RED LIGHT BURST FROM THE BOTTOM OF THE hovering disc.

It crashed into the ship. Smouldering splinters erupted into the air. The beam moved, slicing right through the hull, disintegrating masts and rigging and anyone who got caught in the deadly ray. They didn't have time to scream, they just turned black and vanished into smoke and dust. The ship groaned under the assault before cracking into two wildly unstable halves.

Thaya's half of the ship bucked, hurling her screaming into the air. Solia was yelling something and suddenly a golden bubble surrounded Thaya, slowing her ascent, and causing her to float rather than fall back towards the ocean.

The bubble remained, even when she plunged into the cold, dark sea. White froth and sea salt assaulted her eyes, yet she found she could breathe, even underwater. But the bubble couldn't protect her from the cold, or physical objects, and a barrel smacked into her head, spinning her over. Her back slammed into something hard, exploding the breath from her lungs. She gasped in the maelstrom and the bubble shivered then vanished.

Rising flotsam shunted her upwards and she found herself above the surface, gasping and grappling for anything floating. Her hands grabbed onto a large piece of the hull as it rolled before her. Slipping and clinging, she blinked through the stinging seawater. On the surface, amongst the debris of barrels and splintered wood, Solia bobbed, face down, her robes splayed out around her floating in a sheen of crimson.

Thaya gasped for breath as other bodies floated to the surface. She swallowed a shuddering sob. A glint of metal came from the sky; the silver discs were flying towards Havendell Harbour. A red beam burst from one and the others followed suit. Smoke billowed where they hit as they destroyed everything in their path. The wreckage she clung to rolled again and she lost her grip and yelped as she plunged back into the ocean. She shouldn't scream—they would hear her.

Thaya gulped a breath and thrashed to stay at the surface, but something thumped into her and knocked her under again. Her vision darkened in warning and her body trembled with fatigue; for a moment she couldn't tell which way was up. She felt herself drifting and becoming numb to the frigid water.

"Remember," a voice whispered, the same voice from her dream, but her mind was foggy.

In the darkness, a light appeared, right there in the sea, and within the light, a being. An eye blinked, a deep indigo eye, and its pupil widened. Pain racked Thaya's whole body and she cried out. It cried with her. She had to go to that being, through life, even through death, it mattered not.

The darkness deepened, serving only to make the light

brighter, and now her body felt very numb and far away. The light vanished and with it, her hopes dissipated.

A large hand grabbed her jerkin and wrenched upwards. Her shaking, spent body rushed back to her, and she forgot about the light and the being, and clasped at the hand viciously, begging for it to not let her go. Air filled her lungs in splutters, and she blinked away the stinging salty water. Faint blue tattoos swirled up the well-muscled arm that gripped her, and Arto's face appeared, furrowed deep with worry before softening as he gazed down at her.

"Thank the gods, you're alive." He dragged her onto a floating section of hull more stable than the one she had previously clung to.

She just couldn't stop shaking. "What ha-happened? What are they?"

Arto's voice was low, breathless. "We've seen them before. They always bring death, nothing can escape. Solia said the Magi call them the Vormae; they come from a different place. Now stay low." He flattened himself beside her. Unable to see anything as they were shielded by the upwards curve of the hull, she listened to the enormous explosions and her nostrils flared at the stench of burning flesh and wood. Clouds of smoke rose into the blue sky. Thaya found herself thankful she couldn't hear the screams of the people.

All she could do was lay there shaking, too frightened to speak. Vormae, the ones who sent the Shades. Were they looking for her? Arto said they had attacked other places, so it couldn't just be about her. But how could they hope to fight something in the sky that killed them with red beams of light? These beings were more advanced than them—there was nothing they could do.

They lay there for hours, unmoving. The sun burned into her bare flesh through the tears of her clothing, and the sea lapped over her legs, slowly freezing her lower half. The banging and explosions subsided, but even then, they didn't move. How long would they have to lie here? How long before it was safe? They could be drifting out to sea, or about to be smashed onto rocks.

As new fears arose, Thaya dared to turn and glance at Arto. He looked at her and lifted his head. She did the same and then a shadow cast over them, making them freeze. A strange hum came from above, and the shadow stayed—a perfect round shadow engulfing her and Arto. Unable to stop herself, she found her gaze lifting upwards. A whimper escaped her throat. Barely ten yards above them hovered a silver disc, and it was not moving. Sweat covered her face and she trembled. Arto's eyes were clenched shut.

A beam burst from the bottom of the ship, but not a red one—this beam was white. With a scream, Thaya leapt up, and Arto rolled. She got nowhere. The white beam engulfed her and then she was lifted bodily so fast her head spun. She could hear Arto yelling and wondered if he'd been captured into the beam along with her. The upward movement stopped, and she found herself on solid ground, probably inside the craft but strapped and held erect.

It was so bright she could barely see, and found herself incapable of proper thought. All impulse to fight vanished and her limbs wouldn't respond to her brain's command to move. Faces crowded into the light, all looking down at her; hideous faces she'd seen before. Balloon-like pale heads cracked with dark veins, mouthless, and large red-rimmed eyes. *Vormae.*

"Dear gods, you are ugly!" she gasped.

A strange sound emitted from them. It came directly from their heads and into hers, making her feel dizzy and even weaker. She sagged against the straps that held her upright. The Vormae clustered closer and she gagged from the smell of them, a mix of sulphur and rotting vegetables.

The nearest raised a hand. Three long white fingers with yellowish claws wrapped around her forehead. Terrible pain exploded in her mind and she screamed.

Thaya felt like she was fighting a battle in her head, pushing against an invading force she didn't quite know how to fight. Through will alone she withheld them, but they were more numerous. Shades appeared, some taking basic humanoid shapes, others remaining formless shadows; predators, slinking around her.

"No!" Thaya cried and forced them back, shunting them out of her mind.

She glared at the Vormae. They stepped back, eyes wide, and looked at each other, hands flaccid in front of their thin chests then, as one, they lifted their fingers and lunged towards her, all trying to clasp her head. Their cold flesh touched hers and the pain tripled. She couldn't fight it. But through the agony, as they looked into her mind, she also saw into theirs.

Strange images appeared. From inside a craft, she saw many flying discs like the one she was in, hundreds of them, and they battled in a hazy pink sky against other impossible flying crafts. These others were dull and dark and angled. Below them lay the blackened and broken remains of great buildings, temples and fallen ships.

The battle swept away, and she again looked down from a high place, everything hazy and light. Below were many beautiful beings, horse-like, deer-like creatures with glimmering silver-white coats, and more noble than any beast she had ever seen. *Saphira-elaysa!* It felt deeply wrong to call them beasts or animals, the Dryad name for them fitted perfectly. They were being pulled down and made to kneel on their forelegs by chains, forcing their long, golden horns to dip into a strange pool of pulsing blue liquid. Shackles clamped around them, holding them in this uncomfortable position. Their eyes were shut and they shivered in pain.

"Help us!" one screamed. Had it sensed her presence?

Her heart leapt into her throat. She tried to move nearer, wanting to free them but she couldn't. She saw then, something hanging above the pool.

"Remember," the voice whispered.

Thaya's breath caught as immense pain waved through her, the same agony the entrapped beings felt. Above the pool, hanging by chains, another being tossed his head and screamed in pain. It ripped right through her and she cried with it, their voices and their pain becoming one. The being shook his head. He was not like the others but darker; his coat shimmering between silver, black and purple, his long golden horn mixed with silver, and his mane and tail pure white. His eyes were not sparkling topazes like the others but the deepest indigo.

He ceased prancing and looked at her. Their gazes met. Memory unlocked. The world fell away and the Vormae cried out triumphant.

Thaya ran through tall blades of the richest green grass, the warm sun hugging her. She stumbled into golden buttercups, sending a cloud of tiny white butterflies fluttering into the blue sky. She giggled and lifted a small pudgy hand towards them, a baby's hand. Wobbling on stumpy legs, she stared at the wondrous sight before her. Standing placidly beneath the tinkling leaves of the old oak and chestnut trees, were six of the most beautiful creatures alive.

Spiralling golden horns captured the sunlight making it glow all around their tall sleek bodies. Their coats shimmered white and silver and their gentle eyes sparkled as they watched her. Long tails of soft white hair drifted gently in the breeze and their silver hooves gleamed in the sunlit pool in which they languished.

Laughing, Thaya stumbled forwards, little fingers outstretched ready to touch these pure beings of light. Between long sculpted legs, a smaller one emerged, flicking his white tail playfully, his shining eyes mischievous and showing nothing of his elders' reserve.

An adult stepped between Thaya and him, but the little one snorted and pranced around its legs towards her, and she squealed in joy. She splashed into the pool and slipped, landing with a bump on her bottom. The little one raised his nose, horn gleaming, and he laughed, creating the sound of tinkling bells. Thaya laughed with him and the world shivered with joy.

She splashed at him, and he dipped his horn and flicked water at her. Awkwardly, she got onto her feet and he danced away. She ran after him, darting between the legs of the elders, who now looked on with amusement. She was far too slow for him, and he darted behind her, his soft nose nudging her forward. She sploshed onto her knees, turned and splashed him back. She tried to catch him, but her hands found only air.

A cold wind blew and shadows fell.

Darkness entered the world and joy became tainted. Thaya looked up at the silver disc blocking the sun and trembled. The beings reared and the little one ran into the centre of them, afraid. Their horns glowed brightly and from them spread a growing field of protective light.

Someone, a human, shouted a warning. Thaya glimpsed a very old woman on the opposite bank beyond the beings.

A beam of white light burst from the flying disc and plummeted ferociously towards them. Golden light burst up from the creatures to meet it. The lights crashed together in a spray of sparks and crackling lightning. *They don't want angry light,* Thaya thought, a whimper escaping her lips as the struggling beings faded. What happened when they were gone? Who would protect her from the angry light?

Out of the good light, the little one burst. She reached for him; would he take her with them? He thrust his horn into her outstretched hand, and she gripped it tightly.

Immense power filled Thaya, too much for her tiny body to hold and understand let alone harness. It trembled through her, filling her with strength, warmth, and peace. The beam of golden light pulsed strongly forcing the angry light of the disc back into its underside and shunting the ship into a spin.

The hand that grasped the horn throbbed and a glow spread over her whole body. The little one's body pulsed and shone too, and they both rose into the air, the light lifting them up. The river, the pond, the ships, and the sky all vanished in the power of the pure light. Just she and he remained. She stared at her fingers and then at him; they were both turning into pure light too. The light that was his and the light that was hers reached out for each other, touching, melding and becoming one.

An immense feeling of absolute freedom and awe washed over her. She was pure, she was free, and she understood all that he was, and all that he could be—and she knew in her heart that he understood her in the same way. His power became hers, and hers became his, and both knew the purest joy of a thing truly shared. They had become one.

The light dimmed and her physical body returned. The skin on her hands gleamed almost golden, and her hair captured the light in golden copper hues. The beautiful being before her was no longer white and silver, but a shimmering of dark silver, purple and black, and his eyes shone a fathomless indigo.

They separated further, wrenching apart their bodies, minds, and souls. She cried out along with him, not wanting to be apart, separate and alone. But the light faded, the ground appeared and the little being of purity was gone, along with the others, leaving her world dark and empty. Thaya fell to the ground and lay sobbing.

Saphira-elaysa! Thaya's soul screamed as if doing so would bring them back. She had a name for them in her adult life. That terrible emptiness filled Thaya now as it had all those forgotten years ago. Since that day, a part of her soul had been missing, and now she knew where it was. These hateful beings had wrenched her soul in two when they'd taken the Saphira-elaysa, destroyed her home, and turned her life upside down. They'd terrorised her village, and murdered Solia and countless other people of Havendell and beyond. They had entrapped those creatures of light—and thus a part of her soul—and by the gods, she'd find and release them.

"Saphira-elaysa." She growled aloud the name the Dryads gave to the creatures of light she had seen and touched and become inextricably part of. The name rang within her, giving her power and strength, for it was their true name, the true sound tone of the vibration of light out of which they came. 'Unicorn' as they were called in Familiar, did not do them justice, did not express the purity that they were.

The need to speak the name again arose like a tide within her soul and exploded in a scream. "Saphira-elaysa!"

The Vormae released her and stepped back, hands clasping their heads.

Somewhere to her left, someone groaned. Arto lay curled up in a foetal position on the metal floor, his bloodied hands clasping his head. She had forgotten about him. What had the Vormae done to him?

She closed her eyes. Could they hear her call? They must! She could feel the dark unicorn out there, reaching for her, screaming her name, 'Thaya!' The pain of their separation coursed through her soul, filling her body. There was another name, she knew the sound-tone of it intimately, but her human mouth could not express it. How could she speak it? How could she call him?

In the darkness, a light, and the light was akin to a star, her lode star. Like the pure horn of light upon his head, illuminating the darkness of his body.

She cried out, seeing him prance and buck, demeaning himself like a beast, fighting to be free of the Vormae chains that bound him.

The flying disc began to shake under the power and

emotion of her words. The Vormae stumbled away, eyes wide in fear. For all their power, they did not know what to do or how to control this chaotic human before them. Her bleeding, rent soul had found its other, and nothing could stop them reaching to be whole again.

Mechanical blue lightning flared over the walls and between the peculiar mechanisms as the ship went haywire. The closest Vormae raised its hands and shadows emerged from its fingertips. Small at first, the shadows grew and separated, swiftly becoming numerous.

"Shades!" she gasped.

They flew at her, engulfing her in darkness and seeping into her mind, trying to block out the light of her lode star, trying to choke the memory of what had happened to her so many years ago. Beyond them, she felt the ship spinning and falling uncontrollably. Whatever she had done had sent the craft out of control. She clenched her eyes shut, feeling sick from the Shades' touches and the erratic plummeting ship.

Another presence appeared in the chaos. He was surrounded in smoke, barely an apparition dressed in black clothes and a cloak, and followed by two other men and a woman.

"Agaroths!" Thaya rasped and tried to focus on the tall, thin blurs of white skin and black hair.

Silver flashed on their hands as they reached for the Vormae.

The Shades vanished along with her bindings, and a great pressure sucked her forwards into a flash of light. Cool clean air blasted her face and she plunged into cold water, barely glimpsing Arto fall beside her. Thrashing to the surface, she grabbed hold of the wreckage and Arto at the same time. The man hardly moved as she heaved and struggled just to get his heavy arms onto the wood. She clawed herself out then dragged him up and flopped onto her back, shaking with the effort.

The flying discs were gone, along with Agaroths and his friends, and the sun had moved much closer to the horizon. Night would fall soon, but she was too exhausted to move.

9

ARTO

"Thaya? I think she's coming around now. No, I don't know how long I was out, either."

Arto's worried voice echoed loudly in her head as he spoke.

"Is she alive?" another male voice asked dubiously.

"Yes, just."

Hands lifted her and delicious cool water touched her lips. Her mouth responded and she swallowed it down.

She opened her eyes only to smart at the bright light. Her body ached as if she had hoed every field in Havendell.

"Dear gods, what the hell happened?" Her cracked and rasping voice didn't sound like her own.

She closed one eye and Arto's face came into focus.

He pursed his lips then grinned. "Everything! I saved you, you saved me, twice, then I saved you. Now we're equal."

"Oh." Thaya grimaced and tried to sit up. Even muscles she didn't know she had protested. "I remember it slightly differently." She frowned, taking in the sides of the small boat. It had a single red sail and was half-filled with six other sailors alongside her and Arto, all sporting various injuries and bloodied bandages. The least injured managed the tiller, and the filled sails gave her a sense of relief; they were moving, hopefully away from where it had all happened.

Arto lifted a none-too-steady hand, started to speak, then gave up and chuckled to himself, shaking his head. "I think we died about three times."

"Solia's gone," Thaya whispered.

Arto stopped laughing. He didn't say anything, but his cheek muscles clenched.

"Trust me, from the stories we've heard, she was lucky compared to those who were taken," said the sailor whose voice she'd heard when she was coming around. He swallowed, took off his white hat and smoothed back his dark hair.

Arto looked skyward, then spoke his orders. "Tighten the sails and let's get out of here, quick-smart! They could return at any time."

Despite his ordeal and pallid complexion, he assumed command, and for that, Thaya was grateful. She felt that the Vormae wouldn't return so soon, but she didn't want to be out at night on the pitch-black ocean in this tiny vessel. There were other monsters lurking in the depths; krakens, sea wyrms, and sirens, not to mention sharks and giant octopi. Thaya shivered. Why had she ever wanted to leave Brightwater?

Arto helped angle the sail to catch the wind and they moved fast through the waves. It wasn't long before land was visible again, and Thaya breathed deeply as her eyes followed densely forested hills—but the mountains ringing Havendell were nowhere to be seen. Despite the comfort of seeing land, and even though she was surrounded by sailors and Arto, Thaya did not feel safe. Even Agaroths and his friends could not stop the Vormae from taking her. She hugged her knees and watched the sea darken in the deepening dusk.

"We'll make it to Little Bree before full dark—there, you see that spit of land ending in a hill?" Arto said to her, pointing over the bow. He smiled as if trying to offer comfort. "Lost Sea Tavern will give us a meal and a barn to sleep in if they don't have a bed. The next morning, perhaps, would be a good time for you to head back home?"

Under his warm gaze, Thaya self-consciously smoothed back her dishevelled hair, feeling more than a little ragged. "Right now, I want nothing more than to return home, but Solia showed me something right before we were attacked, and things are not what they were." Her voice dropped to a whisper. "No one at home remembers me anymore."

"Rocks ahead!" shouted a sailor, and Arto's attention was taken to navigating them.

A thick mist gathered on the shore and the wind dropped, slowing their progress as they approached the spit. The moon was already in the sky and, though not full, offered enough brightness to see. The lights of a small village nestled on the shore glowed welcomingly and Thaya longed to sit before a warm fire.

The sailors docked the boat between fishing vessels and Arto helped her disembark. She swayed on solid land still feeling the sea beneath her.

"You'll get used to that." Arto winked. A keen glow grew in his eyes, "Now let's get a drink!"

The sailors cheered and, for all their weariness, virtually skipped along the cobbled stones towards the low roofed tavern. Its bright golden lights spilled out of every window, and the sign hanging above the front door was of an ocean with curling white horses.

"The Lost Sea," Thaya mouthed and followed Arto inside.

Warmth, smoke, and a drunken, raucous wailing scoured her ears. The blazing hearth melted the chill from her bones, but everything else caused a headache. A woman in a low-cut bodice and with bright red lips danced on a small rickety stage, striking a tambourine and squawking. Beside her sat a man furiously torturing a fiddle, and around them rolled empty mugs and glasses. The noise they made might have passed as music to the drunken patrons swaying before them, but Thaya gladly pushed through the crowd away from them and followed Arto's broad back.

Finally, the bar appeared, behind which a tall bald man peered at them through a monocle, hands splayed wide on the bar. He scowled. "No sailors, and certainly not eight!"

"I'm not a sailor," said Thaya hopefully.

The sailors shot her looks and she stared at the floor.

Arto leaned forwards. "Good Sir, a terrible thing has befallen us, and we are in sore need of food, drink and a place to stay. You have all of these things to offer, and I shan't be paying for them either—"

The owner glared, but Arto carried on in a storytelling voice, intriguing even Thaya "—but this terrible tale is like no other you'll ever hear for the rest of your long life. You cannot yet know this night what befell the people of Havendell Harbour this day." A slow hush fell upon those nearest as people pricked their ears for gossip. Arto raised his voice and spread his arms melodramatically. "All who remain of that once-prosperous port are dead and the place ravaged. Dead! For the metal ships came in the sky and the evil Vormae descended upon us. Would you like to know more?"

"Yes," people shouted, nodding their heads.

The barkeeper's eyes widened so much his monocle fell off and swung on its chain. He battled with himself, his mouth opening and closing. "I had heard something...Quit stirring up the crowd. All right! You can stay, but all that you request is half price with your story and not free, and you can wash up too."

"A quarter price and no washing up!" Arto countered, leaning forwards.

"A quarter price and you can all stay in the barn!" growled the barkeeper.

"Done!" said Arto, smacking the bar top and grinning widely. "Now bring us drink, man."

In a whirl of activity, patrons eager for gossip gave up their tables and chairs for them, whilst barmaids delivered ale, cider and steaming plates of food fresh from the kitchen; stew, cheeses, pickles and thick hunks of bread. Thaya's mouth watered and she tucked in like a sailor. The barkeeper might run a tight bargain, but he was generous with his portions, and she fell back against her seat stuffed full.

Arto, unperturbed by the crowd closely watching his every mouthful, swallowed his last, swigged his ale, and pushed back his chair to stand.

"Here, now, ladies and gentlemen," he hollered.

The musicians glared at him—tambourine raised, fiddle still cocked as the last notes faded away. The swaying drunks stilled, somebody belched, and somewhere a plate smashed on the floor.

"I bring news most dreadful of what befell my crew and

I, and all of Harbour Havendell this most evil day." Arto began in a storytelling voice that made Thaya grin. Raised eyebrows replaced scowls and those not already close, shuffled nearer. "Listen close, people of Little Bree, and listen well, for what befell us might befall you too—this very night should the Vormae strike again."

People paled at the name, and a handful of men rushed to the bar for a drink, fearful it would be their last.

Arto continued his tale in the silence that fell. Thaya looked at the floor, not really wanting to relive it even in a storytelling fashion. Perhaps it was wrong of him to make light work of what had happened today, or perhaps it was his way of coping. She couldn't begrudge him getting them all a meal and a place to sleep. Pain passed over his face when he spoke of Solia and his fallen sailors, but he did not alter pitch. *He's being strong for his men,* Thaya thought.

With a face splitting yawn, she was gratefully too exhausted to think about those lost, and she was thankful for Arto's strength, as he must be as tired as she was. Right now, she had nowhere to go, and no idea what to do. If she stayed with Arto and his crew at least it would be safer than being alone. It didn't matter if Fi and Yenna, her brothers and the whole village had forgotten who she was, as long as they were alive and well, that's all she could hope for.

"Here, take this." Arto pulled a knife from his belt as they left the tavern. "It's dangerous out there, as you've seen, and this may help." He shoved the hilt into her hands.

She looked at it and thought about giving it back—it wasn't like it would be much use against Shades or the

Vormae—but decided against it. It offered some protection, nonetheless. "Thank you, really. Is everything all right?"

Arto looked pale, his hair a mess. He'd fallen into brooding quietness after telling his tale. "I'll be all right, eventually. I just need some rest."

"Me too. Let's go."

The noise of the tavern faded as they made their way to the nearby barn; a low squat building that hopefully housed bountiful fresh hay to sleep on.

"I've lost everything; my ship, my goods, my contract, and thus my job and wages." He ran a hand through his tangled hair.

"Sorry, it was a stupid question." Thaya stared at the ground, trying not to think that this was her fault. "What will you do now?"

"I don't know, drink?" He grinned at her, he'd already had quite a few, and so had she if she were honest. It had helped enormously to still the nerves though. "I think we should get you to safety, a large town like Geldayo or even a city would be good. Kiln is the closest from here. Places like that have plenty of work, especially since you don't want to go home yet. Maybe I'll find work too and go back to my old job."

When he didn't say more and fell into brooding again, she asked, "What did you do?"

He took a deep breath. "I was a knight."

"Really? I expected a knight to be, well, older. A retired knight, that is. Not that I know any."

"Not retired. I guess you could say I'm disgraced, although I regret nothing. My lord and I fell out, and I didn't agree with his orders. He asked too much of us and paid too little, and his morals were... questionable. He was not someone I wanted to work with. It was to his father I was loyal, but when his son, the Duke of Aremoth, took over, everything changed for the worst. Of course, as with all these things, there was also a woman involved, a former lover I suppose you could say. I swear he wooed her to get at me. In the end, I had to leave before I throttled the bastard." Arto took a deep breath and slowly relaxed his clenched fist.

"It was several years ago, so forget her, but I had trouble finding work with that stain upon me. When my uncle fell sick and became land-bound, I took on his job as a Captain and sent my earnings back to assist him. That was his ship, you see, and now it's floating in pieces in the ocean. Everything I touch turns to shit."

"That sounds like really bad luck, and I'm sorry, again. Then I turned up to make it worse." She laughed.

He shook his head with a half-smile. "It's not your doing."

She smiled. "It's not all lost, I'm sure someone like you will find work easily. For me, I, hmm, Solia mentioned her Order of Magi before she...well, she's at peace now. She wanted to take me to them, and perhaps I should go anyway, alone if I have to. Maybe they can help me discover why the Vormae and their Shades are hunting me."

"Well, I can see why they would with your mysterious eyes and shining amber locks," Arto teased, smiling.

She blushed and lowered her gaze, his words worryingly pleasing.

He continued speaking. "Solia belonged to one of the highest Order of Magi, The Loji. They are very secretive, and for the first two decades of their training cloister themselves high up in the Western Mountains of Creeth some one hundred leagues to the east. If that is where you're headed, I don't envy your journey." He shook his head and her heart sank. It sounded like it would take a lifetime to reach them.

He heaved back the sliding door of the barn. Inside, a lamp burned low, softly illuminating the curled-up figures of a few sailors who had gone to bed early. The barn was long and wide and filled from floor to ceiling with mounds of hay. There were no blankets, but it wasn't too cold, and even a mound of hay looked enticing to her aching body.

In silence, Arto and Thaya made their beds by fluffing up the hay. She lay down, but Arto sat, pulled out a hip flask and took a dram. He passed it to her, and she sipped the sweet rum, watching him staring at the floor, lost in his own thoughts.

"Have you seen them before, the Vormae?" she whispered.

"I've seen those flying ships and the destruction they always bring, but never the captains, those ugly bastards inside. Others have told me about them and there are myths and legends about their torture."

"Why have I never heard of them?" asked Thaya. "No one speaks of them where I come from."

"They mostly attack along the coasts, and people are afraid, particularly in these parts. Nobody wants any trouble, least of all the wrath of the gods those damned acolytes always preach about. Fearful people ask no questions. Besides, most don't believe they exist. They say none escape, but I've heard some have, I don't know how. They found themselves sick and alone in the middle of nowhere, unable to remember who they are or were or what happened to them. They relive the torture in nightmares, no one believes them, and communities shun them. It's all so wrong." Arto shook his head and took another dram.

"But you believe them, even though you've never seen the Vormae," said Thaya.

"Yes, because I can tell when someone is telling the truth, and I'm sick of ignorant people."

"I can tell when someone's telling the truth, too," said Thaya.

Arto smiled at her, his green eyes dark in the low light. "I guess we have something in common, then. Truth Sight. It's a rare thing though, and it can be a curse. Well, Thaya Farseeker, you look exhausted so let's get some rest." He put his flask away and lay down.

With a long, weary sigh, she did the same and watched the flickering lantern.

10

DRYADS & SPIRIT WOLVES

THAYA AWOKE WELL BEFORE DAWN.

The lantern must have died for it was dark save for the white moonlight creeping through a crack in the door. Needing the toilet, she heaved herself out of bed and tiptoed past the sleeping sailors. The door creaked as she opened it, but only Arto stirred. Squeezing through the gap, she stepped into a night hazy with mist and searched for a suitable bush to squat behind. Beyond the barn to the left stretched a long shore and an inlet, and ahead, across the dirt road, a dense forest clustered. Gingerly pushing through ferns to avoid nettles, she squatted behind a hornberry bush.

So, reaching Solia's Order of Magi would be a long journey, but what choice did she have? A deep hunger burned within her, not one for food, but for the light she had felt when she'd touched the Saphira-elaysa's horn. The events within the flying ship felt like a crazy dream, but this new yearning burned within her, a yearning she had no idea how to quench. Find the Saphira-elaysa, but where? How?

Maybe, if she stayed with Arto and his men for a little longer, she'd figure something out.

A wolf howled in the distance, its call long and mournful. Thaya shivered, glad for Arto's knife at her side. A ghostly, bluish-white light flashed between the trees in the distance. She stood up swiftly, gripping the knife hilt—but knives couldn't harm ghosts.

I'm being a coward, let's just get back to the others. Rolling back her shoulders, she pushed through the ferns. The light appeared again between the trees beyond the brambles. It wasn't ghostly and immaterial at all but glowing. Intrigued, she peered at it and crept silently forwards, but a bramble snagged her ankle and she fell into the bushes, cracking twigs and crushing ferns.

Disentangling herself, she clawed her way back up on to her feet, shaking leaves and mud out of her hair and clothes. She froze as the light moved towards her. Barely breathing, she watched as it came closer. It didn't glide but loped, like an animal, *like a wolf!* Dear gods, it *was* a wolf; large and fluffy, but made of pale bluish light as if it were pure spirit.

Eyes wide and bright, its tongue lolled out and the ghost-wolf panted, making it appear to be grinning at her. The wolf lifted its snout and let out a long, lonesome howl. Thaya stepped back, was that the noise it made before it fed?

Through the bushes, another ghostly wolf bounded to join the first, and nuzzled against it. The first licked it back affectionately. They were cute, the opposite of threatening, but still, her heart hammered.

Her eyes darted to the tree beside them. The thick trunk of the old oak had begun to move! Thaya yelped as a greenish-brown hand, seemingly made of bark, lifted from the tree itself. A long slender leg emerged from the tree and a face materialised out of the bark and moss, the gnarled wood softening into smooth green flesh.

Thaya couldn't move an inch as the Dryad appeared. She was shorter than Thaya by a foot or so and had young, almost child-like features. Her face was beautiful, in a non-human, fairy way, with her smooth green skin, huge emerald eyes and mass of earth-brown locks. She grinned at Thaya, her numerous small white teeth gleaming like pearls.

She appeared to be clothed in rags of varying shades of bronze, moss and sage, worn as a dress that barely covered her chest and floated down to her upper thighs, leaving her long smooth legs exposed. When she moved, her attire shifted and Thaya saw they weren't rags at all but leaves and ferns held around her with twine.

Thaya had seen a Dryad before, but never this close, never this real. The first one she'd glimpsed had been from afar, nothing more than the outline of a man within the trunk of a chestnut tree, deep in the woods east of Bright-water where humans rarely went. She'd felt his eyes watching her every move as she ran away.

The Dryad reached a delicate hand towards the wolves and they licked her fingers, then rubbed against her thigh. The Dryad giggled and extended her translucent dragonfly wings causing them to shimmer through the full spectrum of the rainbow as they fluttered on her back. The wolves' and Dryad stared at each other; their eyes glowing brighter as something passed between them.

The Dryad turned to Thaya, her eyes dimming. "They come for you," she said in Familiar, her voice low and whispering but child-like.

"Me, why? I don't have any b-b-bacon," Thaya's voice was barely a squeak. It was a ridiculous thing to say, but she couldn't think past her pounding heart, and Fi had always said wolves couldn't resist bacon.

The Dryad entrapped her in an emerald gaze. "Because the time has come. That which should have happened long ago has finally occurred. You have re-found the light of which you are part, and now that light needs you. It calls to you and you must go to it."

"The Saphira-elaysa," Thaya whispered, seeing in her mind the unicorn made of pure light and innocence.

"Yes," said the Dryad, walking silently closer, hips swaying, eyes wide and glowing. "You have seen him, and I can see them all enslaved in your eyes. They are hunted, trapped —only you can free them, and this the Fallen Ones know. Either they or the light will find you, it is only a question of which will find you first. Set them free. You must!" She shoved her face an inch from Thaya's, green eyes menacing.

"I will, I-I know I must," Thaya stammered, "but I don't know how. I, uh...Agaroths gave me a map in my mind, but I don't recognise where it is."

The Dryad pointed at the wolves made of spirit. They wagged their tails and panted at Thaya. They had come for her?

"Pathetic! Humans always deny the truth screaming in their hearts," the Dryad snarled. "Always they delay what they know must be done, and the whole world burns around them. You're no better than all the others; ignorant, weak and afraid. The Saphira-elaysas' very survival depends on what you will or will not do! Do not ignore that which you know you must face. Follow your feelings with all that you are, for *they* are all that you are."

The wolves stood up, expectant. She looked from them to the Dryad and back again. Were these wolves really going to lead her somewhere? Could they understand what was being said? One of them howled, then the other followed, and together they bounded away through the ferns.

Thaya looked back at the barn beyond the trees where Arto and his crew slept. "What about them?" She turned back to the Dryad, but the Dryad was gone, and apart from the glow of the wolves disappearing into the distance, she was alone. In her heart something cried out—perhaps the light calling to her—and she felt again the terrible pain of separation as if she were just half a being. It didn't matter about Arto, he'd be more than all right, and she had nowhere else to go.

The Dryad is right, I know what I should do, I should follow the wolves but I'm afraid, weak. Making up her mind, she took a deep breath then scrambled through the ferns after the wolves, suddenly desperate to not lose sight of them. She glimpsed their glow ahead of her, and every now and then they paused briefly to look back. They followed no path through the forest—there was no path to follow—and it quickly became hard work pushing through the bushes and clambering over boughs. *If I lose them, I'll be lost in this forest forever, or until bears or trolls get me!* She paused to wipe the sweat from her face and was surprised to see the wolves waiting patiently. She focused on quickening her pace.

The denser the trees became, the less ground foliage she had to push through, and the easier it was to move between tree trunks. The tinkling sound of flowing water grew until it was quite loud. The wolves finally slowed when they emerged into an opening. Enormous sheets of grey rock held back the forest and a waterfall gushed between them; a white, frothing, vertical stream tumbling into a deep pool several yards below. The wolves sniffed the air and padded a little way ahead. They stopped at the rock's edge and sat on their haunches, waiting.

She approached them slowly. "Are we here?" There was nothing particularly special about this place other than its natural beauty. The wolves looked at her then into the space between them.

The hairs on her arms rose, flattened, and rose again as Thaya felt the air become charged like during a thunderstorm. The wolves stood, threw back their heads, and howled. A rush of wind swirled old leaves and dirt up from the floor and in the dust eddies, lightning flickered. Thaya stared as the air in front of the wolves began to swirl and spin, flashes of light flaring and then sizzling away within its six-foot circumference. Nothing beyond the miniature storm was affected; the small maelstrom swirled only in that area and didn't wander as wind eddies do.

The wolves looked at her, barked, then jumped into the swirl of light and vanished.

Thaya gasped and blinked in disbelief. What the hell was going on? She darted around the maelstrom, but the wolves had really vanished. *Into it!* This close, the vortex pulled upon her, whooshing, crackling, and causing the hairs on her arms and neck to rise.

She lifted a hand towards it. The pull of the maelstrom intensified, magnetising her entire body and strongly pulling on her. She tried to step back but couldn't. The forces quickly overcame her and, with a shriek, she hurtled into it, the forest and the waterfall vanishing.

The maelstrom whipped all around her; a spinning tunnel of wind, light and sound hurling her forwards at a phenomenal pace as her screams tried to catch up. She tumbled helplessly over and over as the tunnel stretched on, seemingly, forever.

Far ahead, she glimpsed two glowing shapes. The wolves of light weren't spinning out of control like she, but were running and jumping, thoroughly enjoying themselves in this hellish chaos. *Stupid mutts!* Why couldn't they help her? Trying to control herself, she splayed her arms and legs, but that only made her spin faster. Now she felt sick and faint. Shutting her eyes, she focused on catching her breath, but it was impossible to keep hold of her consciousness and she passed out.

Cold air brought her back to her senses and she found herself clawing frantically as she sprawled headfirst into a cold muddy puddle. Gasping, she writhed and flopped like a fish onto her back, blinking dirty water out of her eyes. *What in the cursed darkness just happened?*

The maelstrom hanging in the air before her quickly lost its gusto and swirled away into nothing. A hot, wet tongue licked her cheek and she stared up into the golden eyes of a salt and pepper coloured wolf, its ghostly glow fast receding as it materialised into solidity. Thaya lay, stricken with fear and confusion, but the wolf wagged its tail. Its mate stood beside it, also real and solid.

Her awe ended when the world lurched sickeningly. She rolled onto her hands and knees and her stomach clenched, powerfully emptying its meagre contents. The maelstrom felt like it was in her stomach, spinning, churning and flaring. She heaved violently again, and then again, until she could heave no more.

It was surely hours later when the spinning in her

stomach subsided, and she sat back on her haunches, exhausted.

A wolf nuzzled her arm, and the other licked her forehead.

"Ugh," she grimaced. She went to push it away, but hadn't the strength and ended up stroking it. Her mind still spun and the sick feeling remained, but thankfully her stomach had ceased heaving. The wolves remained at her side, golden eyes looking left and right, noses scenting the air for danger.

Any evidence of the maelstrom had vanished, apart from the pile of vomit marking where it had been. Disgusted, she pulled herself onto shaky legs. She was standing on the banks of a very wide, very slow-moving, river. Behind her was nothing but trees, and ahead, a vast stretch of dark water, reeds and an endless bank of more trees. It was cool and overcast, the heavy grey clouds making it particularly dark. High-pitched caws announced the presence of birds, and now and again she heard the bark of a fox. She appreciated the calm vista even if it was a bit dark and heavy.

The wolves began pacing the bank, keen to get moving. Thaya started wringing the muddy water from her shirt but soon gave up. What was the point when she was already soaked through? *May as well run with the wolves to keep warm. If I stand still too long, I'll catch a cold!*

She trotted after them, her sodden boots splashing through the swamp. It didn't matter where they were going as long as there was a fire to dry her clothes and warm her bones. But as she walked something about the terrain impressed upon her, and she found herself focusing on the mental map Agaroths had given to her.

There in the distance, a hill rose just as she saw it

marked upon the map. With each step, this place felt uncannily familiar, and the map became more and more recognisable. This wide river was marked out clearly and even the tiny streams she had to jump over. Ahead, they would eventually come to open swampland, and in the middle of that swamp, she would find that which she sought...*A dwelling. And within the dwelling? Someone I once knew.*

Thaya quickened her pace.

11

THE OLD ONE

THAYA AND THE WOLVES ROUNDED A BANK OF TREES AND paused.

Here, the river became a wide shallow swamp dotted with clumps of reeds, and between the reeds, white, long-legged water birds waded gracefully. Far across the dark water rose a grassy hillock, and perched upon the hillock was a small round house with a conical thatched roof. Within the centre of the neat roof rose a stone chimney, and from it trailed a thick line of wood smoke.

The wolves looked back at her as Thaya held her breath, something about the place was familiar, although she couldn't place it.

Disturbing the peace and quiet came the distant sound of a latch being drawn. The door of the house opened, and a thin, old woman stepped out. The wolves wagged their tails, then bounded through the shallows towards the old woman, sending the long-legged birds squawking into the air. Smiling, the old woman bent down and hugged both of them. She was tiny compared to the wolves, making Thaya realise just how big they were.

Thaya followed slowly, her eyes transfixed on the woman in the doorway, deep memories and feelings unfurling within her. She *knew* this woman and had called her 'Grandmother' once. Apart from a few defiant straggles, her long white hair was tied up into a loose bun, and with every step, the woman's face became clearer. Memory told her this woman had not aged a moment in the intervening decades since she had last seen her—but when had that been, and what was the woman's name? Thaya could not remember.

Moving almost in a trance, she reached the hillock, walked up the steps and stood at the edge of the porch, hand gripping the rail as she stared up at the old woman's face. She spoke in a hushed voice. "I had forgotten you all my life, but now you're before me I remember you once more. Your name I can't recall, and who you are to me, I don't know, but how could I forget?"

The woman's face broke into a warm smile and a hundred wrinkles appeared. Her eyes were an uncanny blue that could have belonged to a young woman, so clear and bright were they. "Dear, little Thayannon Farseeker, I don't think you were ever meant for this world. It has been better and safer for you that you do not remember, but now you're grown up, the time for remembering is upon you. I am Amaggena Evergreen, but you'll remember me as Maggy. When the Saphira-elaysa came, the whole world was turned upside down and our lives changed forever. Look at you now, all tall and grown-up, and yet I'd recognise you even if you were my age!"

Strange, overwhelming emotions flowed through Thaya; grandmotherly love, fear of what she'd forgotten...the realisation that a far different world existed to the one she had lived all her life in Brightwater. She didn't come from

Havendell and her parents were gone, never to return—she'd long made peace with that, but now it seemed to matter. "I know you from so long ago I can barely remember. When the Saphira-elaysa came, something happened... is that why I'm here? And I know in my heart of hearts that you haven't even aged a day." Thaya stared at the old woman, remembering every line of her face. Perhaps her eyes were even bluer now.

Maggy chuckled like a little girl. "Indeed, it is the truth. At first, I wished their presence, their touch, had reversed my age, not kept me old, for who wants to live forever in an old body? But I've had many decades to forgive them for that."

Emotions rose uncontrollably. "Dear Maggy, what's happening to me?" Thaya broke into a sob.

"Ahh, shh, shh, little one." The older woman dragged her into an embrace and rocked her back and forth as she had done so long ago. The wolves came close, one licking the hand clasped around Maggy's shoulder, and the other nuzzling her thigh.

Rain began to fall, a soft light mist settling gently over everything.

"Come inside for some hot cocoa," said Maggy. "Stay with us, for as long as you wish. I missed you so much after you were gone."

In a daze, Thaya let Maggy lead her through the creaking door and into a warm, fire-lit home. It was all one room sectioned off with long curtains, and with a central, large round fireplace and chimney reaching up through the thatch. The living area surrounded the blazing fire; an oven, hob, kitchen table and chair to her right. To her left lay thick red rugs and large deep cushions appropriating a lounging area. The corner of a wooden bed was just visible between the curtains on the far side of the hearth.

The wolves quickly made themselves comfortable on the rug by the fire and panted at Thaya, their unblinking golden eyes following her every move. Maggy sat her down on the largest cushion beside them and busied herself with a teapot upon the hob.

"I remember this place, just," said Thaya, reaching back into her memories so far it hurt. "Like you, it's unchanged— even that wooden lintel above the fire and your ceramic songbird upon it, for some reason I remember them clearly."

She examined the stones of the fireplace, perfectly smooth and curved and glistening silver-grey. They weren't uniformly made but interlocking like the pieces of a puzzle. Whoever had built the fireplace was a master stonemason. Where had the pretty stones come from? There was nothing but water and trees for miles.

"I built it, such was my profession in the past, and the stones came from Itana," said Maggy, smiling at Thaya's shocked expression. "Yes, I *can* hear your thoughts. Ever since that day the Saphira-elaysa came, they unlocked the power within me. It's not a new power but an old one that humans have lost, having been forced to lose it—though that's a story for another day."

"Itana?" asked Thaya. "Where are we? And the wolves, they came to me as spirits, ghosts, and led me here through a strange storm—"

Maggy held up her hands. "One thing at a time, there is much to talk about. I didn't think you'd remembered where we are. Itana is the capital of this region, or was, it's all destroyed now. This is Lonohassa, a part of what remains, in the southern half and far to the east."

Lonohassa, Thaya mouthed the name of her home continent. Was she really here? Was she really home? It was dark
and swampy, and she'd seen none of the advanced civilisations and beautiful lands the myths and legends spoke
about.

"No," said Maggy, giving a deep sigh as she tilted her
head and looked up into the rafters. "Whatever it once was,
whatever we once were, it's all gone. Lonohassa the Beautiful fell thousands of years ago to the same ones who
returned recently. The Nuakki are here again, and that's why
I had to get you to safety all those years ago. They were
hunting for all the first newborns—they felt entitled to
them, as it is so done on their own planet Rubini—and since
I had no other child, I knew they would take you."

One of the wolves whined softly.

"How could I have forgotten the wolves?" Thaya looked
at them trying to remember. She closed her eyes and
reached far back into the past until she winced. Deep in the
fog of her memories, she glimpsed soft muzzles and small
balls of fur she always loved to stroke.

"They were your playmates and your protectors," said
Maggy, smiling.

She put a glove on, lifted the kettle, and poured thick,
dark cocoa into an earthenware mug. The cup was coated in
beautiful turquoise ceramic—far prettier than the chipped,
unadorned brown mugs Thaya had at home. She took the
steaming cup—surprised to find it still cool on the outside
—and looked hungrily into the thick dark liquid. The
merest taste of the stuff instantly told her it was the best
cocoa she'd ever had, the perfect balance of bitter, sweet and
richness. She took a few more sips, feeling increasingly
warm and relaxed with each one. "Mmm, this is good, I've
tasted none better. So, was it you who sent the wolves? How

did they find me, and what was that thing they led me through? It's beyond magic."

Maggy seated herself on the adjacent cushion, sitting cross-legged with an ease even the old people of Brightwater could not match. "Yes, I sent them, but before anything else, let me tell you the story of my pups."

Maggy stroked the nearest wolf. He looked up at her adoringly.

"A month before I decided it was too dangerous for you to stay here, I'd gone to the city to find a dog, something to keep you entertained and out of my way. Oh my, I really didn't like children at all." She chuckled and sipped her cocoa. "I never made it to the city, for in the woods a Dryad accosted me, all tall and green and threatening. 'There's a fallen she-wolf and her pups are starving,' he shouted and aimed his bow at me. I was a little frightened for sure, but since the Saphira-elaysa came, fear for myself and all that might be has diminished. Still, I did not fight him with my fire as I would have done in the past, but let him steer me with his arrow in my back to a shallow den.

"Well, it was a sad sight. Three of the pups were already gone and two barely moved at all. 'You take them, and you care for them, human, for it was your kind who killed the she-wolf,' warned the Dryad, his eyes fierce with green fury. 'These wolves are special; they have the power of old, the power to become one with the Spirit World,' he said, and I knew then I couldn't just leave them.

"So, these are the two I saved that day, Teo and Tess. I brought them home, and when they could walk, they never left your side. I swear they were so weak they wouldn't have survived even in our care had the Saphira-elaysa not blessed us both. How we all missed you when you were gone." Maggy shook her head, gaze cast at the floor. "So I knew they would find you if I sent them, and they did."

"But how?" It still didn't make sense to Thaya. "This place lies beyond a vast ocean, how did I come here? I saw them as ghosts, only more glowing, and they brought me through this swirling energy *thing*, uh, I don't know what it was, a doorway or something, a vortex that sucked me in. I was falling and spinning and there was all this *energy*, and then we were on the other side and the wolves were no longer ghosts."

Maggy had an enigmatic look in her eyes. "These wolves are not just any wolves, they are Lonohassan Spirit Wolves blessed with a power of their own, and they brought you through a moving Vortex, literally an energy portal to another place...I can see this is new to you, let me explain as simply as I can.

"Ley Lines of energy crisscross the entire planet as they do on all planets and stars. The larger, more powerful ones are called Portals, and these are fixed in a particular place. Here, continuous lines of Urtha's energy meet and connect to several different places. The smallest ones are called Vortices, and these are where only two lines meet, and only two places are connected. The other Vortices are moving vortices; these are not fixed and thus terribly difficult to locate. Advanced Diviners were able to detect them once.

"There are many lines of energy that move according to the seasons, the cycles of the moon, even through the passage of a day. Everything is energy, moving all around us at all times. These Portals are sacred places where the energies of our planet Urtha meet and entwine and enable rapid transportation across her surface to another portal."

Thaya didn't dare breathe as she considered what Maggy was saying. The ability to move from one side of the planet to the other in the same day, was it really possible?

Maggy lifted a hand in wonder. "Humans once had the power to harness this energy, to combine it with their own will and spirit and create their own Portals to move through, but we are now far less than we used to be. The people of Lonohassa—our ancient Lonohassan ancestors—were the last able to command fragments of such power. Spirit Wolves can find Portals, even moving Vortices, sniffing them out much like they can their prey, and they can move through them. No animal, other than magical animals like Gryphons, Dragons and Saphira-elaysa, are able to do such things. This makes Spirit Wolves—as they are called by us educated Lonohassans—distinct from all other wolves for they've been gifted the ability to use Urtha's Portals. This places them somewhere beyond animals and closer to magical creatures, and they thrive only on Lonohassa, but their numbers have dwindled alarmingly.

"Many standing Portals exist, and our ancient ancestors used to mark such places of power by placing great Portal Stones for all to see. The truly powerful ones were able to harness great energies and anchor them to the earth to create their own Portals.

"You were able to pass through one because you have ability to do so. A bit like owning the key to a door only the keys are in your blood—codes, as they were called. Just like some can use magic, and others cannot. Those who retain the old codes, and only a small percentage of Lonohassan do, have the power in their blood to use these passageways. Most animals cannot, unless in the presence of a human or magical creature with the correct keys, or coding."

Thaya frowned, "What's special about Lonohassans? Are

we aliens? If I'm from Lonohassa, why haven't I done anything interesting..." No one had ever mentioned these strange energy gates to her, and she'd certainly never seen one until today. The people of Lonohassa were said to be advanced in every way, but she didn't feel advanced, not in any way.

"It's all about what's inside, and no, we're not aliens, far from it," Maggy chuckled. "The people of Lonohassa are the oldest upon Urtha, and yet we only retain a fraction of the powers we once had. It's a long sad story, covering thousands, possibly millions of years. I shan't talk much on this now, another time perhaps, but let's just say we agreed to help another species—for that is why we were created, to help others—and they turned on us and are now taking over."

"The Vormae?" Thaya asked.

Maggy shook her head. "Not so much, but they are sometimes in league with the other Fallen Ones." She hushed her voice then. "Some say the Illumined Acolytes were created and are directed by the Fallen Ones, and it would be no surprise to me. It was the Nuakki who came and infiltrated the Lonohassan High Priesthood, and then they destroyed us. The Ordacs also came and fought them and us. That was the Time of Cataclysms; a long time ago. Many things were lost and destroyed. The Agaroths have told me—"

Thaya sat up, excited. "You've met him? Them?"

"Yes, and therein lies the reason why I sent the wolves," said Maggy. "The Agaroths are not Urtharian, they come from far beyond our nearest stars. Their world is...broken, crippled by the same Fallen Ones who are trying to destroy ours. In their time, the Agaroths managed to expel the Invaders, but in the process caused themselves to fall. Now they cling to the fading light and have taken an eternal vow to assist all those still within the light who are persecuted by the fallen. Driven by revenge, which is itself a fallen trait, they are a devastating match for the Nuakki, the Ordacs, and the Vormae.

"Among those they assist are the Saphira-elaysa who are being ensnared by the Vormae in their thousands and will soon be extinct from the mortal planes. That fateful day that brought you into my life, the Agaroths were here when the bright ones came and witnessed all that took place."

Maggy fell silent and Thaya joined her brooding, memory of that day strong in her mind. The hearth crackled and they sipped their cocoa. Maggy eventually continued.

"The Agaroths gifted me with the power of telepathy to make our conversing easier, for human languages are not advanced enough to articulate their concepts. They told me many things; that the Nuakki were coming and would take you away, that more of Lonohassa would fall until it was no more. Ahh, they told me of the future, past and present; the history of Lonohassa...not even those who remain remember. We are savages compared to how we once were. Can you believe that it's unnatural for any being not to remember its own species' history?

"They told me that humans are the third seeding on planet Urtha—placed here by the Divine Ones; those who would seem as gods to us—and that our races were utterly wiped off the face of our beloved planet two times previously. Can you imagine it? In a way, the Agaroths are the Keepers of Records of the history of Urtha and the other planets they are able to assist. They see themselves in divine service to the Eternal Spirit and of all creation."

Thaya couldn't believe it, yet she felt Maggy spoke the truth, the *real*, incontrovertible truth, and it filled her with awe. "I *knew* the stars were other places, and that other beings inhabited them, but no one else did." She tried to fathom Urtha millions of years ago, and the annihilation of humans twice over. It was beyond her. Cold crept down her spine. " 'We let the gods in, and they destroyed us.' "

12

STAR PORTALS

Maggy looked at her.

"What did you say?"

Thaya shrugged. "I don't know what it means, but I found an old scroll in the hands of an ancient *almost* human skeleton. It was inscribed in Lonohassan. There's this old temple in Havendell, massive stones blocks not even a giant could lift, though it's all destroyed and broken now."

Maggy nodded. "Indeed, in the lands surrounding Lonohassa, you will find many such temples. When the deluge came long ago, people fled to other continents and tried to rebuild what once they had. The deluge was no natural event, far from it. Urtha herself would never torment her people so. No, the catastrophe was caused by *them,* the Invaders, and their fallen gods. In fear, some people even worship those gods now—many are forced to, but I *never* will." Maggy scowled fiercely then looked away. "Anyway, I've learned to put my anger aside..."

Thaya nodded, finally she'd met someone who agreed with her about the violent gods they were forced to serve, and who wasn't afraid to speak her mind.

Maggy's fierceness softened. "But my wolves, yes, they travelled to you in spirit using a portal, and it seems they returned with you through a Vortex—which says something about the power, or the codes, you carry within your blood. Navigating a Vortex is harder than a portal." She eyed Thaya with intrigue before continuing.

"I must add that Dryads may also use these Portals, but they prefer to remain in their own domain just beyond ours. True magical creatures use Portals to travel anywhere, even between times and dimensions, as Dragons are wont to do, whilst Gryphons seem to prefer abiding upon their home planets, choosing only to move backwards and forwards in time within the same space.

Thaya nodded. It all made *logical* sense, but it was far beyond her realm of comfort and she struggled to fully comprehend it all.

Maggy continued without pausing. "And here a distinction must be made: the Saphira-elaysa travelled through something much larger than a portal, and it's called a Star Portal. That's how they arrived on Urtha that wonderful, dreadful day so long ago and changed our lives forever. For, little Thaya, it was not just me who remained unchanged, but something far greater happened to you and I still have not fathomed what. Perhaps you can tell me?"

Thaya remembered the ethereal light that had surrounded the Saphira-elaysa, and stood and went to the fire, leaning her hands upon the wooden lintel. What had happened back then, could she even decipher it herself? Her mind settled upon those terrifying moments in the clutches of the Vormae and cold shivered down her spine.

"The Vormae came just a day ago. Back then I'd never seen them before or heard of them...I guess we were all lucky to survive." She could barely think of it let alone speak of it. When Maggy nodded she was glad she didn't have to describe anymore. Tears blurred her vision and she looked down into the flames.

"I saw them, the Saphira-elaysa, so...beautiful. But now they are trapped. In my heart I hear him calling to me, I can't ignore it. I don't understand, and it's hard to explain. Somehow the Vormae taking me...it flared alive our connection that I had long ago forgotten. I *know* that he felt it too, and I felt his thoughts and his feelings as my own, as if we shared the same soul. I reached for him and *memory* returned to me."

Thaya closed her eyes and felt tears trickle down her cheeks at the beauty of the pure ones. That feeling of wholeness in his company she could almost rekindle through memory alone, so powerful was it. She smiled, remembering playing with the little one as he shied behind the adults, and beyond them all had stood Maggy. "I didn't know who you were then, but now I do."

"So you know, then, what happened next." The older woman stared down into her cup. "They came, they destroyed, and I've prayed since that day that the Saphira-elaysa escaped."

Thaya chewed her fingernail. "I have to find them; I have to find *him*. I've seen him, he's an adult now, but somehow not like the others, he's darker, like aged silver and violet. Mark my words, if they weren't trapped that day, they're trapped now, and they're calling for help. He's calling for me." Thaya paused as a stab of pain took her breath away. Nothing else mattered compared to finding that to which her soul was joined, not Lonohassa, not the Agaroths, not the Vormae who had nearly killed her, or any of the other Fallen Ones Maggy had mentioned. Even sitting here talking was wasting valuable time—time which could be spent searching for him. *But where do I even begin looking?*

"Yes, you're right, every moment spent waiting is wasting time," said Maggy, reminding her she could hear her thoughts. "But I must finish the rest of this story so you know, at least in part, who and what you are, and for my own peace of mind for I feel as though I abandoned you to a world in which you did not belong."

Thaya worried her lip as Maggy continued. For all her impatience, she needed to hear what the old woman had to say.

"As I said, the Agaroths told me the Nuakki were coming and taking every firstborn girl under three years old. They were to be taken to the Nuakki's home planet, Rubini, a far distant star, and there trained to become slave-wives to that despicable fallen race. No one returned. Nowhere was safe to hide from the slavers.

"I, an old woman, was no good for you, just a babe. How could I possibly be the mother that you needed? How could I ever protect you from them? I had to do something before they came so I took you to the closest port and there, aboard the ships, I found a couple; soldiers from the West Lands travelling east. I made them take you—and before you judge me, your life depended on it, and I was not alone in giving you away. So many parents lined the decks that day, trying to save their children from the Nuakki. I can hear their wails and see their parents' sorrow." Maggy blinked away tears.

Thaya stared into the fire, her life unravelling before her eyes. So, her parents who had left her with Fi and Yenna weren't her parents after all, and they, like Maggy, simply found a safe place to leave her. The war may have taken them, but the Vormae had killed her real parents. She was too stunned to feel anger, everything she'd thought of as true just wasn't so. Maggy's voice pierced through her thoughts, recapturing her attention.

"Aw, who could deny you? You were so cute with your fair curls and bright eyes. They took you willingly, and that's the last I saw of you. But I was relieved for at least I knew you would be safe. There was no hope if you remained. What happened next, well, that's for you to tell me. How I missed you...the way you smiled made even the air shimmer golden around you. If you were sad, the shadows gathered close—for you were always between the two, day and night, light and dark.

"On the outside, you were like any other little girl, but inside I knew you were broken. You would stare at the stars, the moon, even the sun you stared at like *they* do, like the Pure Ones. You were waiting for them to return. It was because of what happened, that day you touched the little Saphira-elaysa your souls melded and became one. Without him, you were broken and could never be whole again. I can't say there is anything good about it, but the Eternal Spirit has allowed it, so what can an old woman know?"

Thaya breathed deeply against another stab of pain. Maggy spoke deep truths and the jagged edges of her broken soul cut painfully.

Maggy rubbed her temples, staring at the fire licking hungrily against a log until it cracked in a spray of sparks. "Well, two days ago the Agaroths came to me and I had not seen them for nearly a decade. They said they had finally 'found you' and begun the 'awakening', for you remembered nothing of your life before reaching Havendell. They reached you only because the Vormae found you, but why the Fallen Ones hunted you, they didn't know. The Agaroths were very unsettled about this.

"You see, the Vormae feed off the Soullight of others like vampires, and nothing has more light than the Saphira-elaysa. They hunger after them like no other; moths to a flame, some might say. They're ruthless hunters who know their prey well and, having unlocked their weaknesses, they can capture even the most resilient unicorn. Once entrapped, there is no escape. No one knows what happens to them, but it can't be good; the Vormae have no regard for life and are able to do the most horrific things."

In her mind's eye, Thaya saw darkness and fear became a physical presence. The light of a shining horn flashed, an indigo eye opened wide, staring wildly, and all-around muttered distorted noises from the mouthless Vormae. She blinked the images away and focused on Maggy's words.

"When the Vormae attacked Havendell Harbour, the Agaroths thought they'd taken you, and that's why they came to me, asking if I could find you. And I did, or rather, my Spirit Wolves did." She chuckled and ruffled the male wolf's thick mane. He grinned and rolled over. "Now you're here, and the world for us is whole again. I'll admit, I did doubt. I didn't think you'd have the power, the coding in your blood to travel through Portals like our ancestors of old did. Our powers are weak, and our connection to the planet is nothing like it used to be." Maggy sighed and looked far away.

Thaya considered Maggy's words after she'd finished speaking. "Will I find him using the Portals? There are others trapped, he's not alone."

"Yes, but not through any ordinary portal, for the trapped Saphira-elaysa are not upon Urtha. You will need to locate a Star Portal and to do that, you'll need to find the

Book of Maps—and this is where the trail runs cold. Star Portals are much more powerful than planetary Portals, and far rarer because they don't just lead to other gates upon Urtha, but to other worlds.

"Our ancestors knew the locations of all the Portals and Star Portals before the Nuakki came. It was sacred common knowledge upon Lonohassa. Now that knowledge is lost to the Four Winds, and you must find the Agaroths for they are the current keepers of the Book of Maps and they will be able to tell you how you can find the trapped Saphira-elaysa. The Agaroths have shown me that the Vormae keep them trapped upon their world, Geshol, but how you get there, I do not know."

Maggy wrung her hands. "I've been trying to find ways to reach them, to help them, all my life, but what can I possibly do?"

"Find the Book of Maps," Thaya echoed. "Find the Agaroths... Won't they just come to us? Can't you call them in some manner?"

Maggy shook her head. "They come when they will, or more accurately when they can. They're forever fighting the Fallen Ones for control of the Portals, not just on Urtha but on other places. A Star Portal existed on Lonohassa once, but it was destroyed when the Nuakki shattered the land.

"The Fallen Ones frequently swarm the Portals to take control of them and enslave the people living there. Such swarming destabilises the Portals and shuts the gate, as it were. Fallen Ones cannot access Portals directly, only the indigenous peoples of a planet have the coding to access the gates and Portals of their home planet—which is why they force hybridisation with humans. They want those codes in their offspring, their future little foot soldiers."

Thaya was aghast. "A sort of rape? That's terrible." She thought of the Vormae and felt sick.

Maggy nodded, her eyes wide. "It's a dirty, evil, insidious takeover of an entire planet, and the devastating enslavement and destruction of an entire guardian species. Humans were created as the guardians of Urtha and it's a crime that we've been forced to forget our job. But Urtha has not forgotten and she waits patiently for us to remember again who we once were. The Book of Maps details all the Portals, Star Portals, and Vortices of any planet, and the Fallen Ones are always trying to steal it, relentlessly so. Thus, the Agaroths' work is cut out, for all their problems, I envy their stamina and resolve.

"I pray that they will come to us soon, but we're running out of time. Rumours are the Nuakki are marauding the countryside again, forcing the poor who remain from their lands. But I'll do the same as I've always done and stay put. I'll not leave this land, no matter how much it's changed."

Thaya glanced at the door, half expecting a Nuakki marauder to burst through, but there was only the sound of the rain pattering on the darkening window. She frowned. "I remember this place being different. I remember lush glens, meadow flowers, and blue skies. Wasn't there a farm nearby?"

"Yes," Maggy nodded. "There was a place, decades ago, but the waters rose. Some say the whole land is sinking. Well, the farm's foundations are still there. If you walk due north, you'll see the structures just beneath the surface of the water."

"And the home of my parents?" Thaya dared to ask. Try as she might, she could remember nothing of them, not even a feeling. It was as if she just suddenly existed, and her memory began with the little Saphira-elaysa. Not many remembered their very early childhood, so perhaps it was normal. After all, who could forget that moment with him?

"A village far to the north that the Vormae destroyed in their fury," said Maggy. "I did not return, and there would be no point, the place was flattened. It would take days to get there, even on horseback, and I don't recommend it, there's nothing there for you."

"There's nothing for me anywhere any more, only you, and...*him*, my lode star," said Thaya. She had nothing apart from the clothes on her back. Even her past was empty. *There is only forwards, there is only what happens next.* Despite her lack of roots and lack of belonging, an enormous sense of freedom washed over her.

"Who is 'him'?" Maggy frowned.

"The little Saphira-elaysa you call my soulmate. I see him in my mind, a shining light in a sea of darkness." Thaya stared into the middle distance, her heart thumping hard. "My guiding star, leading me on."

"Well, you can dream all you want, girl, but flights of fancy never got stuff done." Maggy sniffed and sat up straight, suddenly all business-like. "Somehow we have to reach the Agaroths."

Thaya clasped her hands together. "I forgot, the Agaroth, he gave me a ring." She showed Maggy the silver ring on her thumb. "I thought his name was Agaroths, not the name of his race, for he didn't tell me his real name. He said this ring would help them find me."

"That's no good, we need to find *them*," said Maggy and she tutted. "Maybe we can wait a little longer... Either way it's getting late, and my little chicken has finally come home to roost."

To Thaya's surprise, Maggy reached over and squeezed her chin between finger and thumb like any grandmother might. "Let's have something to eat and get to bed. You look as exhausted as I feel."

Maggy busied herself in the kitchen pulling out potatoes and spices from her cupboards—cupboards made of cherry wood, beautifully decorated with carved leaves and flowers. Not wanting to be left with her thoughts, Thaya got up to help her.

For all that there was to say, neither spoke much as they sat beside the fire after dinner cupping their drinks, each content to lose themselves in their own thoughts. Thaya's mind drifted back to Arto. Why hadn't she left him a note or something? There just hadn't been any time, the wolves had already bounded off. She deliberately tried not to think of Fi, Yenna and her brothers, but homesickness settled like a hole in her stomach.

The hours passed but still, no Agaroths showed. With a deep sigh, Maggy got up. "I don't think they're coming this evening. Make yourself comfortable here by the fire and I'll bring you some blankets. Don't worry about a thing, the wolves will alert and protect us should anyone unwanted arrive."

Thaya took a soft blue blanket and lay on cushions beside the wolves. Warm and comfortable, an exhausted sleep swallowed her.

13

AN ADVENTURE

Dawn came, awakening Thaya with an unbearable sense of urgency to find the Saphira-elaysa.

She jumped up to find Maggy already dressed and busy in the kitchen. A cool breeze came in through the open door and the wolves stood in the doorway facing outward, noses lifted to the air.

"Here," said the older woman, passing her a rough woven backpack and a pile of clothes. "They might not be fashionable anymore, but you're slim like me, so some should fit you well enough. Just choose what you want."

Thaya washed with a cloth, soap, and a pail of hot water Maggy had warmed for her, then selected from the pile; fresh linen underclothes, a shirt, thick woven leggings, and a toughened pale green jerkin. The style was strange with the jerkin being long and fitted rather than cropped and loose, as was the current fashion in Havendell. It covered even below her hips and the long tails reached almost down to the backs of her knees. The shirt was plain and simple, but all of the materials were superior to anything she had seen at home and expertly stitched. There was even a long thin pocket on the side of the jerkin into which Arto's knife fit perfectly. She kept her sailor's boots on for they were tough and warm but took some thicker socks from Maggy's collection.

"Right then," said Thaya standing straight, "I take it we're going somewhere?"

Maggy chuckled. She wore a long woollen cloak over a faded red tunic, thick evergreen leggings and heavy boots. Leaning on her stave-like walking stick, her eyes gleamed with excitement. "We're going on an adventure! I haven't been on an adventure in years."

Thaya smothered a grin and followed her out of the door, the wolves pushing impatiently past them, yelping and nipping at each other like pups.

"We'll head along the water's edge until we reach the broken barge, then we'll turn into the forest toward the base of Coldheart Mountain." Maggy swung her stick in the direction of travel as she spoke, then set off at a pace no old person should be able to manage.

Thaya ran to catch up, splashing noisily through the water. "What's at the base of Coldheart Mountain?"

"The start of your path up it," said Maggy, "and the end of my journey."

"Oh, I'm going up to the top? On my own? What for? What's up there?"

"Well, you don't expect an old woman to carry on climbing mountains, do you?"

"No, of course not..."

"There you'll find a Gryphon, and not just *any* old Gryphon, this one's exceptionally grumpy. However, he is learned and will know where the Agaroths guard their Star Portal. He'll take you there if you can pay him in some manner and, of course, depending upon how silver-tongued you are. In saying that, the beast owes me one heck of a favour, so maybe just mention my name.

"The Agaroth's Star Portal leads to Arothia, the home of the Agaroths, but they will already be there guarding it. Now, you must remember that some Portals stay, some Vortices move. I was never one to portal travel, all the nasty sickness it causes, and I could never find them like my friend could, but you can learn the skill. It will be enough for you just to find it."

"I'm really going to meet a Gryphon?" Thaya ran a hand through her hair. A part of her always disbelieved the ancient books depicting magical creatures, but now she was about to meet one in the flesh. What if it had a sharp beak and long, knife-like talons? It could be violent. She swallowed her excitement.

Maggy raised an eyebrow. "How else do you think you can travel hundreds of leagues to the Arothian Star Portal? Flying is the only way unless you can find a local portal to get you there, and I'm done with looking. Portals are remarkably complex, and a real art to navigate in themselves. Our ancestors spent their whole lives studying them and still couldn't use them predictably. I'd be surprised if any Lonohassan still studied this ancient art, certainly not with the Nuakki in control. We're a fragmented and scattered people." Maggy fell into a brooding silence.

These invader Nuakki would be more of a problem than the Gryphon, Thaya thought as she navigated a deep bog of mud. She glanced at Maggy. "Will we encounter the Nuakki?"

The woman pursed her lips and frowned. "You hide and run if it comes to it. I'll stay and...talk. They have little interest in old women, though I'm worried for my wolves, they don't like the invaders, and invaders care nothing for the creatures of this world, preferring to eat and wear them. They're not dogs, I can't control their behaviour, and neither would I want to. Like Portals, wolves are unpredictable."

Thaya trudged along the muddy bank behind Maggy, the swamp stretching out before them under a heavy grey sky. The wolves were somewhere in the forest scouting ahead, and only the calls of water birds accompanied the sound of their squelching boots. Maybe that's why Maggy began to sing, if that's what it could be called. To Thaya it sounded more like wailing. It echoed through the quiet marshland alerting anyone near and far to their presence. First, Maggy sang in Familiar, swishing her free hand to and fro with gusto as Thaya winced. Then she sang in Lonohassan, which was more bearable to Thaya's ears.

When she thankfully paused, Thaya quickly spoke to stop her singing again, "Can you speak only in Lonohassan with me? I'd like to remember and relearn it."

"Indeed, for it is the richest language in all the world," exclaimed Maggy, and with abandon launched into Lonohassan lessons with barely a breath. "Now, vowels are slightly different to how they are pronounced in Familiar, I'm sure you've already noticed. And when writing them be sure to remove those silly accents the Acolytes added to Familiar."

Thaya tried not to lose track as Maggy schooled her. At least she no longer sang, but the rate at which she spoke, Thaya wished she'd brought her notepaper and pencil. Still, she was heartened by the words she *did* know, she just needed to work on her pronunciation.

. . .

After half an hour she stifled a yawn and Maggy must have grown tired too for she stopped speaking and paused to check their surroundings. Nothing had changed, it was still the same endless marshland and heavy slate sky.

"Does the sun ever come out in this cursed place?" Thaya threw up her hands, bored with the endless grey.

Maggy shook her head. "Not much anymore. Once we only had rain at night when it was needed, thanks to the network of crystals that used to control our climate. That all changed when they were destroyed, and now ancient diseases like rickets have arisen. My childhood was filled with sunlight, now it's only rain. Look over there by that dead old tree, see the barge?" Thaya followed where Maggy pointed her stick and noted the decaying old boat with holes all along its hull. "There's a rough road just past it leading through the forest. Another day, and we'll reach Coldheart Mountain."

They rounded the bank past the wrecked boat and came to a tiny track leading away from the marsh. Thaya stepped onto the drier ground with relief, thankful her boots no longer squelched with every step. Trees crowded their passage and the gloom increased. Oaks and birch jostled against pine, creating canopies so thick no sunlight could reach them even on a clear day.

They stopped on a damp log for a brief lunch of dried apricots, cheese and water biscuits, then Maggy was up again and ready to go, seemingly feeling none of the aches and pains plaguing Thaya. She dragged herself up, her legs groaning, painfully letting her know she'd never walked this far in her life. Immediately she fought to keep pace with the spritely old woman. Again, the wolves avoided the path and made their own way through the forest, sometimes disappearing, but mostly just visible through the trees.

Was Maggy moving faster than before? And why wasn't she singing? Was she worried about Nuakki patrols? Thaya was too out of breath to ask.

It was eerily quiet. Thaya scanned the empty path ahead. What did they look like, the Nuakki? Were they uglier than the Vormae? She felt inferior to them, unable to fly, stuck on only one planet when there were so many up in the heavens to explore.

A few smaller tracks veered off theirs, causing Maggy to pause and allowing Thaya some rest. Hopefully, there was a settlement nearby, some people to talk to. "So, where's the nearest village?" Thaya asked.

"Yes, indeed you might ask." Maggy indicated to their right. "There used to be many where now the marshes have grown. Between my house and the barge, there used to be two small villages in lush green grassland. The people were forced off by the Nuakki and there was no point returning when the land sank, and the water rose.

"We all fled to the coast and there I stayed for many years. Those not enslaved tried to find peace and work with the invaders, some have even joined them, though they are treated like second class citizens at best, and often working in slave-like conditions. I refused any of that and so I returned to my ancestral home, what's left of it. Most think this is a wasteland, even Nuakki rarely come here. But the rumours speak of ploughing the land, of mining for gold."

"Didn't they fight? Surely there must have been a great war." Nobody simply just lay down and got trampled, especially not an advanced civilisation, Thaya thought.

"Oh yes, many, many died—most, probably. But even the Lonohassan army, such as it was, cannot withstand the might of those coming from the very stars. Besides, war and fighting are not natural reactions for those who have lived in peace and harmony for thousands of years. Yes, we were advanced in every manner, but we're not skilled warriors like the invaders, it simply isn't in our blood."

Thaya imagined fighting and killing to survive and shivered. "No, I suppose not."

When the sky darkened even more, Maggy veered off the path towards a hollow surrounded by oaks where she stopped and inspected the place, nodding with satisfaction. "We should be safe to camp here, as long as the wolves keep watch."

They made a simple camp with a sheet of fabric from Maggy's backpack draped over two thick branches.

"Let's hope it doesn't rain," muttered Thaya as she ducked inside.

"You won't need to worry about that. Look, can you feel the wind?"

Thaya held her cheek close to the fabric and raised her eyebrows. "No, I can't, is it enchanted?"

"Nope. Thin, light, yet strong, waterproof and windproof. Ah, that's Lonohassan technology." Maggy winked and set about building a small fire just outside their makeshift tent.

"Lonohassan wonders." Thaya shook her head. What Fi and Yenna could do with this material... "Do you know how the rest of the world lives?"

"I do, my dear, and I'd prefer their way of life with all its hardships and strife than to see my beloved homeland destroyed by those thugs."

Thaya considered this as Maggy set a ring of pebbles around the campfire. She was right. Having fancy things and controlling the rain was nothing compared to having the people you loved around you.

A steaming pot soon hung above the fire and Thaya settled down beside it as Maggy continued her story.

"Seventy years ago this road shone like quartz, though it's all broken and overgrown now." She pushed at the grass growing in clumps over very pale rock. "A busy road it was, leading to the city. Safe too, unlike those beyond Lonohassa, plagued with bandits and those hideous Illumined Acolytes —now that's another story I don't need to get started on. Thank our Creator *they* never managed to get a foothold in Lonohassa, and that's only because the Nuakki kicked them out. One thing we can be grateful for from our enslavers, I guess. They say you can only have one infectious malady at a time, and the first will always kick the second out. Hah!

"Ahh, but we shouldn't just cry for Lonohassa, poor Urtha is being torn apart between these invading outsiders. And don't you look at me like that, I know what you're thinking. Yes, we did let them in. Or, rather, the Magi Priesthood who had been corrupted a long time ago, aeons some might say, did, but always they were kept in check by the opposing Guardian Magi.

"I left the city a long time ago, but even then, the increasing corruption was plain to see. Ancient pristine roads turning to potholes and rubble, poverty, increasing crime, grisly rapes and murders that were simply unheard of before, as if darkness had infected the land and was spreading. Once, there was no word for 'theft'—it just didn't happen. And murder...well, what can I say?

"Darkness always follows where the dark ones tread. Since the last cataclysm, evil embedded itself and grew in the minds of the rulers and the Magi. Once guardians of the people, these now became elite rulers of the people—our own appointed leaders had become our slavers. And, yes, it was they in their greed for power, and in the trickery of the off-worlders who let them in, who did terrible deals, and let them live amongst us." Maggy shivered and fell silent. Teo and Tess padded silently into the firelight, tongues lolling, golden eyes wide. Maggy brightened and stroked Tess. "We should settle down and get some rest. I'd like to be off before dawn."

Thaya agreed and tried to get comfortable on the cold hard ground with just her cloak for cushioning. It wasn't easy, but staring into the fire had a soothing, mesmerising effect that soon sent her to sleep.

A soft muzzle butted her face, followed by a hot tongue dragging over her forehead. Thaya sat bolt upright and stared into the gloom trying to gather where she was.

Borienna, the brightest star, shone down and the embers of the campfire glowed orange. The male wolf, Teo, sat grinning at her, panting.

Maggy was already up, sitting on her skinny haunches, wrinkled hand resting lightly on Tess. "Shh," hushed Maggy pressing a finger to her lips. "They say danger draws near. Dawn is an hour away still."

Silently Maggy stood, kicked soil onto the embers and began packing their things. Senses heightened, Thaya pulled on her cloak and helped. They were done in moments, and Maggy led her away from the track and deeper into the forest. It was slow going, especially when trying to be quiet. Twigs snapped underfoot, and branches and blackberry bushes snagged clothing and hair. The wolves proved much better at it, leaping silently through the foliage.

"What did they see?" Thaya whispered.

"Nuakki," hissed Maggy.

A chill went down her spine and she moved even more stealthily.

Slowly, the sky brightened and, though it was still overcast, beyond the trees behind them Thaya detected the merest blush of pink, the whisper of a sun. So they were heading west, not that that changed anything.

Maggy stopped and held a hand up for quiet. Thaya strained but couldn't hear anything. How well *could* the old woman hear? Then the faint sound of voices made her catch her breath. A soft growl came from Tess, and then she was silent, ears forward, nose twitching.

Thaya leant on a thick oak and the bark beneath her hands moved. Stifling a scream, she stepped back as the tree trunk came to life. Why weren't the wolves growling? An arm appeared, then a hand, then a head. The Dryad emerged from the tree, a man, all tall and wiry, leaves and twigs circling his head like a crown. His skin changed from rough bark becoming pale green and smooth, and he narrowed his eyes at her, angry for being disturbed. The distant voice came again, and he looked to where it came from. His eyes narrowed even more, and his lips curled back to reveal rows of perfect tiny white teeth.

Maggy stared from the Dryad then back to where the voices were coming from. In the growing light, Thaya could just make out the pale road in the distance through the trees. They weren't nearly as far away from it as she would have liked.

The Dryad made a strange growling sound that came from somewhere deep within his throat. His hand dropped to his thigh and pulled a long thin dagger from its sheath that was tied with twine around his leg.

"No." Maggy shook her head at him and lifted her

splayed fingers. "The Spirit Wolves say there are five."

The Dryad paused his unsheathing, eyes glowering. "We are five, Wolf Speaker." He spread his hand wide, indicating the wolves and Thaya. Maggy chewed her lip.

The Dryad growled and barked at the wolves, uncannily matching their sounds, and then he was running with the canines, bounding towards the road.

"Wait!" Maggy yelped and ran after him.

Thaya trailed them warily, her brow clammy and Arto's dagger mysteriously finding its way into her palm. What could she do even with a blade? She had no idea how to fight at all. *A fight, praise the gods, why can't we just run? Bloody Dryads!*

Shouts and howling tore through the forest

"By the Creator, this is the last thing I wanted to happen. Curse the Dryads and their uncontrollable tempers!" Maggy hissed.

Thaya slowed near the road and peered through the trees. Fighting the wolves with shining metal batons or staves the length of her forearm were some very strange looking people. They were like humans in every way except that they were at least a foot taller than most men, and they were broader, and heavy with muscle. Their heads were elongated, long skulls encasing what must be huge brains to go with their impressive physiques. Their faces were handsome in a hard angular way, with strong chiselled jaws and noses, and dark brown hair and eyes. The lone female amongst them had dark hair that was long and curly, and she was as handsome and imposing as the men. Two wore strange golden conical hats, three wore golden breastplates, and all wore golden vambraces and grieves. A lot of their tanned flesh was exposed, as if they had come from somewhere warmer. Or perhaps they didn't feel the cold.

Thaya didn't know what she had expected the Nuakki to look like but it wasn't this. She'd assumed them to be ugly in some way, like the Vormae. After all, wasn't evil ugly? But they weren't. They were, in many ways, attractive, and this left her confused. Could they really be as evil as Maggy had led her to believe?

One landed his staff with a crack and fizzle of energy upon Teo's rump, causing him to howl in pain. This made Maggy leap out of the trees, walking stick and hand raised. Another staff landed on Tess, again with the flicker of magical power. This caused Thaya's anger to boil over too. She leapt out brandishing her knife, hoping to scare them more than anything.

The closest Nuakki spun to face the new threat, and the Dryad leapt to the moment scowling in hatred as he sunk his knife sickeningly deep into a Nuakki's back. The Nuakki's eyes widened, and with a groan, he toppled to one knee, then fell face-first into the dust. Thaya stared at the blood pulsing out of his back, unable to breathe. The Dryad spat on his slain opponent and lunged towards the female Nuakki. Beyond them, Teo and Tess mauled another, trying to take him down to the ground like prey.

Thaya couldn't move, not even to avoid the golden staff that swung towards her face. The world jerked and wobbled in an explosion of pain, and she hit the ground. Teo was already beside her, jaws snapping on the evil baton. She could barely see anything through the pain radiating from her cheek and through her skull, and the world lurched in fits and starts. *Magic, powerful, painful, magic!*

Breathing hard, she flopped onto her side, glimpsing the Dryad retreating whilst desperately dodging the blows from the enraged female Nuakki. She moved with a speed Thaya had never seen before, her staff of pain a deadly blur. Green blood trickled over the Dryad's naked torso, but the fire in his eyes told her he would fight to the death.

A closer staff loomed into view, crackling with pain magic. She strained to see the wielder, but he was a blur beyond the tiny streaks of lightning flashing around the stick as it descended upon her.

A meaty Nuakki hand grabbed the wielder's wrist, halting the staff's decent. Thaya blinked up at the bleary images of two Nuakki men as they argued in a harsh throaty language. The Nuakki wielding the staff scowled at the other restraining him and jerked his wrist away. Teo leapt over Thaya and clamped his jaws on the Nuakki's arm. He roared and cracked the golden stick down on his muzzle.

Thaya howled as Teo yelped, and she scrambled for her dropped knife. Thick fingers entwined her hair and dragged her along the dirt. She thrashed to be free.

"Thaya, no!" screamed Maggy. "Run!"

But how could she run? Her head still pounded with pain and now her hair was being ripped out of her head. She struggled and kicked, rolling over and trying to get on to her knees. A fist twice the size of her own slammed into her gut, knocking her back to the ground and the wind out of her lungs. Sucking in air, she curled into a ball.

The soft white underside of a wolf's belly leapt over her, moving too fast to tell whether it was Teo or Tess. The hand gripping her hair vanished, and she followed what her aching gut instincts and Maggy were screaming at her to do; she staggered to her feet and ran.

Gasping and stumbling she pelted up the road without looking back. She came to a T-junction, and ran left, keeping the forest on her left and a huge sloping wall of yellow rock on her right. The road rose gently upwards and she ran hard until her legs burned. She reached the crest and followed it round to the right, thankful for the downhill slope.

Ahead, the road was relatively exposed as it led towards a low rolling mountain just tall enough to reach into the clouds. Apart from clambering through the forest, and all the noise that would make, there was nowhere to hide except for the black yawning holes of caves high above in the rock face. Seeing a gap in the trees, she lunged for it, leaping over ferns and ducking under boughs.

A thorny bush caught her trousers sending her flying through the foliage. She landed hard. Dazed and panting, she lay stock still, half expecting a Nuakki to leap on top of her. She stuffed her sleeve into her mouth to muffle her gasping and strained her ears to listen. There was no sound, only a heavy, unnerving silence. Where were the others? Should she go back?

Rolling onto her stomach, she realised she still gripped Arto's dagger and it was red with blood. Had she managed to slice the Nuakki? She touched her cheek where the staff had hit and winced. There were cuts and bruises all over the exposed parts of her flesh, and the unexposed parts as well, as far as she could feel. Blood seeped through a rip in her trousers.

Tess bounded through the bushes making yelping noises. The wolf landed on all fours, sniffed her all over, and began licking her wounds as if she were her pup. Drops of blood matted her fur, too, mainly red but some green, flecking her grey and white coat. *Dryad blood. Did he survive?* Some of the wounds were her own but, like Thaya, the she-wolf appeared to be mostly whole.

"What about the others, where are they?" Thaya whispered, looking around, fearful that someone had overheard her.

The she-wolf sniffed the air then nudged her with her nose. Thaya got the message and stood. In a dazed stumble, she moved in the direction Tess urged her towards.

"But we have to help the others." She spun around, but the wolf planted her paws in the earth to block her path and growled softly.

"All right, all right. I'll bet Maggy made you do this." Unable to argue, she did as Tess 'told' her and clambered through the hazels and hawthorns. They moved through the forest with the road sometimes visible far to their right.

Satisfied she wasn't going to run off, Tess bounded in front and led the way. She stopped often to look back, whining a little to show her annoyance at Thaya's speed. Despite pushing through the exhaustion, Thaya couldn't move any faster through the thick foliage and was grateful when the tireless wolf paused at a stream to drink.

Thaya cupped the cold water and gulped it down, the muscles of her jaw aching painfully. She pushed her face beneath the surface, the frigid cold cooling her broken and bruised flesh. But Tess didn't let her rest for long and nudged her to her feet once more.

Where were the damn Agaroths when they needed them?

Though it was dark in the forest, above the trees she could glimpse blue sky and shards of sunlight fell through their boughs. They were gradually ascending and Thaya stopped to remove her cloak. The trees slowly changed from predominately broadleaves to predominately evergreens.

They stopped well back from the treeline when the road cut across them. Standing silently, Thaya watched the she-wolf lift her nose and smell the air for a good few minutes. Deciding it safe, Tess stepped slowly forwards. She paused, sniffed the air, then took a few more steps and paused again.

Then she bounded forwards across the open road and darted behind thick brambles on the other side.

Thaya bolted after her and collapsed. Peering through the bush, she scanned the dusty road. There was still nothing to be seen and, oddly, she realised she hadn't seen or heard any birds for some time now. Tess licked her cheek then bounded out again and ran along the road. She wasn't going to run in the open in broad daylight, was she?

Not about to be left alone, Thaya ignored her aching body and pounding heart and ran after the wolf.

The road was flat, and they made quick progress. They approached a corner and after they had rounded it the vista opened up into a vast landscape. Forests sloped down and stretched out for miles to her left, and ahead, rising into hills and beyond them, a range of low mountains all hazy and blue with distance. An enormous lake lay upon the horizon, and to her right the same low mountain they had been running at the base of. From this perspective, the mountain was much wider than she had previously thought, like some giant sleeping beast.

Tess turned and pelted up a rough track leading off the main road. At first exposed, the track soon descended into a shallow dip with great fallen boulders at its sides, shielding them from the sight of the road. Here, Tess sank onto her paws, her sides quivering with exhaustion.

Thaya pressed her sweaty back against the rock wall which had been nicely warmed by the sun, and slid down onto her haunches. Leaning her head back she closed her eyes and tried to calm her racing heart. What was happening back there? Why had that Nuakki stopped her from being beaten by the other? *They wanted me alive. The wanted to kidnap me, I'm sure of it*. She trusted her feelings.

The sun sunk lower, becoming a deep golden yellow,

and its rich rays spread over the forest, lake and mountains, making everything glow. *So, this is Lonohassa,* thought Thaya, and for the first time, she saw its beauty. Though once an enormous continent, it was said barely a third of it remained since the cataclysms. Was this really home? She wanted to feel a sense of belonging to the land, a place where she fit in. Apart from Maggy, she hadn't met any other Lonohassans, how did she know if she would even like them?

Dear gods, Maggy, are you still alive? Her first brief but brutal encounter with the invaders made her despise them as much as Maggy, the wolves and the Dryad did.

She reached into her backpack and pulled out a loaf of bread and an apple. She'd carried these whilst Maggy'd carried the cheese and apricots, the cooking pot and various other bits and pieces. A meagre dinner but better than nothing, and at least Maggy had something to eat as well. However, chewing on the bread caused shooting pains through her jaw and she was forced to eat at a glacial pace.

She examined the wall of stone in front of her. It was a soft yellow, just like the stone megaliths comprising the Old Temple of Brightwater. She laid a hand upon it, feeling the sandy texture. It even *felt* the same. So, the temple belonged to the people who had fled Lonohassa thousands of years ago, and using advanced technology and skill had taken part of their beloved land with them. She, too, had been forced to leave this fabled land, and now she had returned. She couldn't help but feel a part of them.

Curling up in her cloak, she nestled against the warm rock and watched the sky darken over Lonohassa. Thoughts of the people of this land and their fate filled her mind and her ears listened for any sound of Teo and Maggy.

14

WIND OVER WATER

THAYA AWOKE TO A BRIGHT MOON AND TESS WAGGING HER tail against her leg.

Heaving her body up, she slung on her backpack and set off after the eager canine, ignoring her leaden legs. She couldn't run, no matter how much Tess pressed her, and eventually the wolf gave up and settled into padding just a little way ahead.

The night had a cool breeze and the silver moon shone upon rolling dark clouds. The fresh smell of the pine forest far below reached her although there were no trees up here, just endless rock walls and fallen boulders.

The further she walked, the more she didn't want to meet this Gryphon, she just wanted to go home. *But there isn't anything back there for me anymore, there is only forwards.*

She focused her thoughts on the Saphira-elaysa and found a stronger purpose pulling her on. *Find him, that's all that matters.* But what if he was dead? Worse, what if he didn't *know* her? He might not feel the same connection, and if he did, he might resent it. Why did she feel such a pull towards this magnificent creature? All would be answered when she reached him, and yet he was so far away. Would she have to go to the enemy Vormae and literally reach a faraway planet? She pushed a hand through her tangled hair.

The thought was so crazy it was ludicrous, and yet that's exactly what Maggy had suggested. Just thinking about it made her head hurt. If only she'd been a Magi, she would understand these things.

The clouds began to thicken as the sky brightened with dawn and it grew colder, not warmer. Thaya shivered and wrapped her cloak tighter. Hopefully, the sun would break through at some point and warm her bones. The path remained sparse and barren with only boulders here and there to hide them, and she prayed the Nuakki were far away. No one was up here, maybe not even a Gryphon.

After another hour, Thaya stopped and collapsed against a rock, exhausted.

Tess whined and came trotting back.

"No, I'm not going a step further until I've eaten something," growled Thaya.

Reaching into her pack for another meal of dry bread and apples, she tucked in and stared up at the never-ending mountain they were climbing. It wasn't steep, but it went on forever. The peak was always just over the next crest or around the next corner, but it never appeared in front of them.

It began to drizzle. She put away her rations and got up, eating her apple as they walked. The food eased her growling belly but did nothing to soothe her aching legs. With a sigh, she pulled up her hood and trudged on.

When the drizzle stopped, she had lunch—dry bread and an apple—and enjoyed the brightening weather. Hauling herself over a boulder blocking the track, she caught her foot on a loose rock the other side and only just stopped herself from face planting into the earth. She stared at the rock as it clattered against the wall and saw that it wasn't a rock at all, but the skull of a goat or sheep, bleached white by the sun. Further on, there was a complete skeleton, bones picked dry.

"What are sheep doing up here?" she asked quietly.

They passed another skull; a wolf or dog's, and Tess paused to smell it. The wolf raised her nose, nostrils twitching and walked ahead slowly with her ears pricked forward and eyes keen.

Thaya followed.

They passed many animal skeletons, most appeared to be old, but some were fresher than she would have liked. She looked the other way as they passed a rotting sheep, part of the skin still clinging to the bones. The place began to stink, forcing her to wrap a kerchief around her nose and mouth.

The mountain levelled out and, finally, she could see the craggy peak; a rubble heap of boulders smoothed and shaped by the winds of centuries. Giant, cave-like crevices opened up on the leeward side, and Tess had her eyes locked on to them. The wolf paused some distance from a black crevice, sat down on her haunches, and looked back at Thaya.

Thaya squatted down beside the wolf, the hairs on her arms and neck rising, and her pulse beating faster. They looked at each other, then back at the gaping darkness.

A sound came from inside the crevice, a loud snorting or sniffing, then the dragging noise of something large moving. Wind gusted out of the entrance, picking up dust and debris, which it blew over them. She coughed and the wolf sneezed. What if it had heard them? Thaya covered her mouth and Tess shoved her snout into her paws.

"We should hide," whispered Thaya.

Looking over her shoulder, she saw there were some crags they could duck behind, but that defeated the purpose of their visit. They watched the dust settle and when no more noises came, Tess nudged her with her nose.

"You want me to go over there? Alone? No way!" She shook her head but Tess nudged her again.

Thaya stared back at the gaping hole to where part of a sheep's flesh had caught on a rock. It lifted and fell in the wind making it seem as if a giant monster breathed in and out inside the cave.

Inch by inch, Thaya stood and began to edge forwards, sweat dampening her brow as she moved towards the entrance. A noise came from within, thick claws scraping on hard rock. Thaya swallowed and glanced back at Tess. The she-wolf was standing now, her head lowered, eyes unblinking. Thaya turned back to the looming darkness, took a deep breath and tried to speak louder than a whisper.

"Uh, h-hullo? Excuse me, I-I mean no harm, but I-I'm looking for something called a Star Portal."

Silence. Nothing came roaring out of the cave or even moved inside.

She glanced back at Tess and shrugged. The wolf cocked her head.

Thaya stood straighter, arching her neck to try and see further in without going any closer. "Hello?" she called, louder. "Um, Maggy sent me. You know the old woman with the Spirit Wolves? She, well, she said you'd be able to help me reach a Star Portal."

Something moved in the darkness, followed by a great

long sniff. Tess growled and stood up, but she wasn't looking at the cave anymore but behind her.

Thaya stared back into the black entrance. "I just— Argh!"

Thaya dropped to the ground as a huge ball of brown feathers inset with furious golden eyes and an enormous beak exploded towards her. She clasped her head and clenched her eyes shut as wind and dirt gusted around her. Choking on grit, she realised she was screaming into the earth.

When no pain came, she opened one eye to see only sky. A roaring screech shook the ground, followed by Tess howling and the yells of...*people?*

Thaya jumped up and paused at the sight of the beast. The Gryphon was huge, half again as large as a horse and twice as wide. It had the head, torso, front legs, and wings of a great golden eagle, and the body, back legs, and tail of a lion. Its thick neck of shining feathers became deep red the further down its body they reached, and a line of dark red fur ran down its back along its tail to a furry red tip at the end. Its wings gleamed golden as it dived past her, the feathers interspersed attractively with lines of smaller magenta plumage.

With barely a twitch of its wings, it lifted and swooped far too swiftly for its size. Thaya fell back, but the bird-beast was not interested in her, what it attacked was a group of four Nuakki—the same warriors she had fought the day before. They had tracked her all the way here, and that alone sent chills down her spine. There was no Dryad or

Maggy or Teo running to help them, and now this patrol held vicious-looking spears.

Tess snapped at the heels of a Nuakki as it thrust a spear at the swooping Gryphon. He beat the wolf back with the blunt end of the spear and she shied away, blood on her white chest. Thaya had her knife in her hand and paced forwards, but the Nuakki were too busy with the Gryphon to notice her.

Tess limped over. She laid a hand on the wolf's head and stared helplessly at the battle. The Gryphon turned deftly, swiped a talon, and caught a Nuakki. Screeching, it plunged its beak into flesh until the man's screams turned to gurgles. The Gryphon hurled the limp carcass over the cliff. Unfazed, another man fearlessly leapt forwards, his tanned, muscled body sweating and bleeding. *Brave warriors.* Thaya couldn't help but be impressed by their skill. The enormous bird was not winning easily.

A large hand clasped around her mouth and nose, dragging her backwards and slamming her against a chest that was hard as wood. Thaya struggled pointlessly and peered up at her captor. Dark stubble shaded the broad chin of a Nuakki warrior. Behind him, she glimpsed at least a further five who were jostling forwards, weapons raised. More had joined the first. There wasn't much hope.

"Keep the girl, kill the wolf," her captor commanded in a deep voice.

Did he speak Lonohassan so she'd understand? He shoved her forward. Thaya growled and kicked as two Nuakki grabbed her; a female and a male, both dressed in shiny golden breastplates. Perhaps the armour marked them out as higher ranked? The female had slicked-back dark hair braided finely. She held a golden staff, the head of which formed a circle inlaid with lapis lazuli and white quartz that caught the light.

The Gryphon screeched so loudly her ears rang, and the Nuakki tying her hands momentarily turned back to their battling companions. The female began to speak in a language Thaya didn't understand; low and barking. The words made her feel sick and dizzy, and the gems within the staff began to glow.

The Gryphon must have sensed the magic or the spell or whatever was happening for it stopped screeching and dived towards her. The Nuakki female shouted and a deep vibration rippled out from the staff, like heat rising from a scorched road.

The Gryphon hovered just out of reach and held its front paws together. Between them, a ball of light appeared. The light exploded forwards, rapidly expanding and engulfing everything.

Rough hands released Thaya and she fell to the ground. All noise vanished and then a strange endless ringing echoed like a bell had been struck but the noise never fading away. Light and ringing vibrated through every cell in her body. People screamed and barely visible bodies writhed on the ground before her, yet she felt fine. Tess licked her palm. Thaya could barely see the she-wolf through the glare of light as she pulled off the half-tied cords around her wrists.

Enormous golden eyes loomed before her, and that terrifying beak. Giant claws reached through the light, encircling her and Tess. She couldn't move, not even to flinch as she was jerked from the ground. The light vanished and she screamed as the ground plummeted away.

"Stop that! And quit struggling or I'll drop you," barked a sharp voice. The talons around her tightened uncomfortably, preventing her from struggling or screaming. To her left, in the Gryphon's other talons, wriggled Tess. The wolf stopped struggling and hung limply, ears laid flat as she surveyed the land that she was never meant to leave far below.

Thaya peered up at the thick chest of the bird, watching the wind ripple his feathers, his black beak shining in the sun as they lifted above the clouds, head turning this way and that, spying the land for enemies.

"You can speak?" It was an obvious yet shocking revelation. An animal that could speak *and* fly, how peculiar! The Gryphon angled its massive head to eyeball her. Without deigning to reply it looked ahead.

"What happened back there?" shouted Thaya over the wind. If she kept him in conversation, perhaps he wouldn't think about eating her.

"Well," began the Gryphon, eyes narrowing, "you arrived with a horde of those bastards and forced me out of my nest for good! Now I'm carrying a stupid girl and a useless wolf. Nope, there'll be no going back there now, they'll be swarming that place for weeks, no thanks to you!"

"Oh," said Thaya, grimacing. "But I didn't mean to, I didn't even know they were there. Maggy sent me to find you and we were attacked by *them*. I don't even know if she's still alive. She said you could help."

The Gryphon muttered something inaudible.

Remembering the wonderful magic, she forgot about her plight in the talons of an angry Gryphon she had just forced out of its home. "How did you do that, back there? The light and sound...thing?"

The Gryphon took a long time to reply, clearly not wanting to speak to her—and yet he had saved her from the Nuakki when he could have just flown off. "It's not possible to explain such things to the ignorant and...*uninitiated*. Even your esteemed Magi know little of the ancient art Gryphons like myself are born steeped in. It's we who gave humans their knowledge. It's the Magi who call it magic! To us, the simple manipulation of energetic forces by using our mind and our in-built aptitude is as natural as breathing air."

"Magic explains it better," muttered Thaya.

The Gryphon snapped his beak and its grimace was almost human.

So it was magic, and it was incredible, and she wanted to be a Magi immediately. The Nuakki had literally fallen where they stood. The Gryphon's arrogant manner did not put her off asking more questions, there were just too many things to ask to stay silent.

"So, where are we going?" she asked jovially, angling her head to stop her hair flapping in her face.

"Where you bloody well want to go!" snapped the Gryphon. "I know Maggy, I met her many winters ago, but after this, that debt is most definitely paid. You wanted to reach the Agaroths, right? Hence all this bloody mess. Those unicorns—the *Saphira-elaysa*—" the Gryphon sniggered haughtily, "—had better be worth it, that's all I can say. Hah, look at your face. I know far more about everything than you think I do."

So, he knew Maggy? It didn't seem like a good time to pry. Clearly, he didn't care too much about other magical creatures. Maybe Gryphons only cared for themselves. Thaya looked at the sun, then peered down at the earth trying not to feel queasy and hazarded a guess. "So, we're going north then?"

"The place to reach them is in the highest place of Lonohassa, far to the north. As soon as I've dumped you there, I'm off. You can fend for yourself against the Nuakki. After all, it was your kind that welcomed them in the first place."

"And what mess?" Thaya pressed, feeling like she was getting somewhere.

The Gryphon didn't answer. Instead, he tilted his wings and lowered through the clouds. Far below, the most amazing sight unfolded. A beautiful green land lay to the right, tall deciduous trees blanketed gentle hills around which clear blue rivers flowed then poured into shimmering lakes.

But it wasn't the fertile land that wowed—it was the incredible human-made structure in the centre of the land utterly different to anything she had ever witnessed before, she had difficulty in comprehending how it had been constructed. It was a city; absolutely enormous, it had to be larger than the whole of Havendell. Apart from looking at maps, she had never seen a city or town from the air, so she had nothing with which to compare it. This city was completely round, constructed of concentric rings interspersed with rivers or canals. Each section of land and section of water were so perfectly circular, the stonemasons must have been able to measure it from the air.

It was hard to see clearly from this height, but there appeared to be roads made of yellow stone within the land areas, and there were buildings all along the roads, some tall and massive like the Illumined Acolytes' temple in Havendell Harbour, only much larger still, and all made of yellow stone just like the ancient temple north of Brightwater. Most of the other buildings were small, and she assumed these must be dwellings.

Over the water sections stretched bridges made of graceful arches, and between the houses and temples were green gardens and orchards. In the very large central rings lay fields and hedgerows.

A fertile land, rich architecture, perfect weather...She imagined beautiful people walking the streets, living lives of freedom and abundance, where work was a joy and music filled the air. Poverty and pestilence were unknown even as concepts.

"It's...amazing," Thaya whispered.

"It was, now look again." Whatever magic the Gryphon had cast to enable her to see, vanished, and a scene of ugly devastation was revealed. Two-thirds of the city lay in a jumbled ruin, the pretty, concentric circles utterly destroyed save for the eastern third—all that remained to suggest it had ever been there. Every house and building was gone, and only sections of circular walls remained. Thick, dark mud and sand covered everything, smothering the lush fields, dirtying the once crystal waters, and smudging the existence of a once beautiful city.

Thaya looked beyond the city and saw it didn't stop there. The entire land to the west was destroyed as if a giant tidal wave had swept everything away. *A tidal wave is what happened,* she told herself, *a great flood, earthquakes...perhaps the Age of Cataclysms never ended.* There were no fertile fields or green forests, villages or towns, everything had been flattened, even the hills were gone, and smothered in dark brown sludge. Far away, the sea was just visible on the horizon, ruddy and turbulent as if the violence still lingered in the waves themselves.

Thaya fell into a depressed silence.

"Those who survived, left," said the Gryphon in a low voice. "But not many survived. Up and down the land, east, north, south and west, but most especially from the west, the water, the giver of life, came and ravaged."

Thaya shook her head, trying to comprehend it; the destruction, the death, the devastation. *Imagine a wall of water rushing towards you, higher than the highest building, sweeping up and over everything, killing everyone.* The planet had betrayed her people. How could beloved Urtha have let this happen?

The Gryphon replied as if he had read her thoughts. If he had telepathy like Maggy, it wouldn't surprise her, everyone on Lonohassa appeared to have it apart from her. "No, Urtha allayed the damage as best she could, otherwise nothing would have remained and there would have been no one to tell the tale. And no, this was no natural phenomena. What the bastard Invaders tell the Survivors and those beyond Lonohassa is a lie. They spread the lies of 'natural catastrophe' to cover up that it was they who caused this destruction and seed distrust amongst the people against their beloved planet herself."

Thaya struggled to believe anything could create such devastation. Were they gods? "But how is that possible? What being could create such destruction?"

"I remember," the Gryphon's voice became deeper and quieter, and his words shocking. "They caused the earth to shake with their powers, and they lifted the sea from its bed. Both the quaking and the deluge they inflamed with their might, then crashed it down upon this place to wipe away the High Ones and the people, the knowledge and the artefacts and the libraries. All of these they wanted to destroy for this was the last place to be 'reduced.'"

Thaya remembered reading once that magical beings were immortal. Was this Gryphon immortal to recount so clearly these events? Had he witnessed them? "Why? Why did they hate them so much?" Thaya watched the destroyed city fall behind them, blinking back tears.

"Ultimately for control, for power. They had always planned to do this, even when they came with smiles and promises, fooling the stupid humans. They came in, invited by the High Ones, themselves greedy and yearning for more knowledge and technologies. So they came with their evil sciences, twisting the minds of those who let them in. Once they had gained trust, they turned, as was their plan. Your High Ones were too arrogant—arrogant like the Nuakki themselves—and ceased to listen to my kind. So we feel little pity for their demise.

"The ones you saw today, they are just the low caste, the foot soldiers. Expendable to their own High Ones. No, the Nuakki Elites are powerful, evil, they are as gods to your kind, and they should never have been let in."

"Are they still here, the Elites?" Thaya looked for some dominating structure, but the land was lost through the clouds as they lifted higher.

"No, they cannot stay. Their biology does not cope well with Urtha's density and her atmosphere. Long ago, before even I left my shell, they raped your kind and made many hybrids, some of them more human-looking, so don't be fooled by appearances."

The Gryphon's wisdom was awe-inspiring. The animal was so much more intelligent than even Maggy or any human she had ever met; she could no longer think of him as an animal. "Where are they from?"

"Rubini, the planet furthest from Urtha in our solar system. Nothing but a star in the night sky, even to my eyes."

The Magi were also astronomers, and Thaya stretched her mind to imagine it. Beings so advanced they could not only fly, but fly between the stars and cause the entire planet to shake and water to rise. What hope did they have? She slumped. "We cannot fight them."

"No," agreed the Gryphon.

Thaya's enthusiasm died in her throat and she fell silent, shivering against the chill wind blasting her face. Below, snow-dusted hills reached above forests and part-frozen lakes.

It was the Gryphon who spoke first. "Once this land was as warm south as it was north, but the Sky Ores were destroyed too, some were stolen and taken to Rubini. Now winter lasts much longer, and summer is a distant dream."

"How can you know these things?" Could she trust this bird-lion?

The Gryphon snorted. "You know nothing of Gryphons, nor the world. You are the most ignorant Lonohassan I've ever met. Thankfully, you also lack any of the arrogance now infecting your race—which perhaps makes you innocent but still ignorant. I'm afraid to say it, but the world is far larger than your little Havendell."

Thaya smarted. The Gryphon hadn't spoken angrily, and she couldn't deny his facts, but she hated the way he knew so much about her.

"I'm smarter and question more than most of my people," she growled softly.

The Gryphon continued. "The people beyond Lonohassa are simple, for the most part, undeveloped. Because of that, the gods of the evil ones have not been bothered too much with them yet. And therein, perhaps, there can be peace in ignorance. But the evil will not be able to leave them alone for long. Its greed knows no bounds. Dissatisfaction with your...*simple* life is apparent within you, which is why you come to me now. I had a dream someone would come seeking the old Star Portals—"

Thaya's eyes widened, "You knew I'd come to you?"

The Gryphon ruffled his feathers. "I didn't say you, I said

someone! When the Saphira-elaysa came, I lamented, for I saw those who followed them, and the struggle between the Nuakki and Vormae that would be played out upon Lono-hassa's shores once more. But beneath that, I felt a change occur, like the scent of pure air in a dank cave. *Change,* it whispered. And I learned that wherever the Pure Ones tread, they bring change from the Divine Creator of us all."

And the Gryphon would say no more, leaving Thaya to pick through his heavy, cryptic words.

15

THE VAST DARKNESS OF SPACE

THAYA AND THE GRYPHON DESCENDED TOWARDS A SNOWY lone mountain that was surrounded by low foothills and lakes.

To both east and west, far in the distance, lay the ocean, and to the north, more lowlands.

The lion-eagle descended in tighter and tighter circles towards the crater at the mountain's peak. Thaya closed her eyes against the dizziness that overcame her and let go of her breath when they skidded on the ground. The Gryphon released her and Tess, and she breathed in deeply, exercising her constricted lungs. Without the warmth of the lion-eagle's talons around her, the cold bit viciously.

A moody dark sky threatened a blizzard, and Thaya longed for warmer attire. The snow underfoot was so pure and fluffy she dipped her hand into it with a smile. Snow rarely fell in Havendell, maybe briefly once or twice a year in deepest winter and just enough to have some fun with snowballs but never enough to stay. If she and her brothers wanted to build snowmen, they had to trek up the mountain passes to do so.

Tess shivered too and she hugged the wolf for warmth and comfort as the Gryphon towered before them. His sheer size and fierce appearance continued to intimidate as he turned and walked to the centre of the crater, lion's tale swishing.

Seeing Tess chewing on snow for moisture, Thaya realised she was thirsty too. She scooped snow into her hands and allowed it to melt before trickling it into her mouth. The only effect it had was to make her insides as frozen as her hands now were, so she took out her flask and filled that up instead. The hairs on her arms suddenly rose and static charged the air. *Magic?*

The Gryphon had stopped in the centre of the crater and was looking at her with his ears raised. She hadn't noticed he had ears before, perhaps because they'd been lying flat against his head, but now they were visible she could see they were thin, pointy and feathered.

The energy didn't come from him, she could feel that much. She walked towards him and the energy built and grew until she could actually see the air wavering in front of her.

"What is this?" She raised her hand and felt an invisible force pushing back. "It feels strange."

The Gryphon nodded. "Ahh, like the ancient Lonohassans, you carry the necessary coding within you. What you feel is in your blood, and it's responding to the energy of this place; for before us is a portal—and not just any gateway to another place, this is a Star Portal, a portal that goes far beyond Urtha. And an Arothian one at that."

Thaya explained it slowly to herself. "Like the one Maggy's Spirit Wolves led me through, only it leads away from Urtha. But I could see that one, it looked different. I can barely see this one and I haven't gone anywhere although I'm virtually standing in it."

"The key to *that* portal was in your blood. You do not have this key, the correct coding, for this one, and so for you, it is locked."

Thaya thought about that. "I see. I guess, then, that's why the Agaroths don't need to guard it. That and being up here in this *freezing* place. Where does it lead—and yes, before you say it, I get that it goes to the Agaroths, but where are they actually?"

The Gryphon flicked his ears back and forth, perhaps wondering how he could explain it simply.

"Arothia," said the Gryphon.

"Is that near Rubini?" asked Thaya, pushing for more.

"No, it is beyond even the faintest star and in another system entirely."

Thaya imagined the vast darkness of space and how far away the furthest star might be. Did that mean all the stars were inhabited? Were there galaxies beyond even what was visible? She shook her head. "They came all that way to help us?"

"It seems that they did," replied the Gryphon, his tone implying he was as in awe of the thought as was she.

"But why us? What's so special about us?"

"That, I do not know. Perhaps they are as driven by revenge as they are by a desire to help those still of the light. The evil ones, despite their twisted powers, flee in fear of the Agaroths, such is their might. I myself would not willingly face one, but perhaps you can ask them yourself."

She followed the direction of his nod and held her breath.

Beyond the energy field, the snow lifted from the ground and swirled, and darkness gathered. Two humanoid forms solidified within the snow, and Thaya looked upon the marble-esque faces of a man and woman. Agaroths, both dressed in black from their shoes to their cloaks, their neck-chains and rings of silver gleaming brightly. Long, straight black hair was worn tied back, accentuating their sharp, sombre faces. Her eyes lingered on the man and then she smiled, it was he, the one she'd met in Brightwater.

The Agaroths walked forwards, black cloaks whipping in the wind, and the man spoke in his deep, almost whispering, voice, "We did not expect you to come to us, so this is indeed a serendipitous surprise." The corners of his lips curled up fractionally and his face softened almost into a smile.

"It's a surprise to me too," replied Thaya, "though it doesn't feel serendipitous, given how frozen I am." She hugged her shoulders with hands she could no longer feel.

"Then we should dally no longer," said the man. "You seek the Book of Maps, and for that, you must commune with our Council." He looked at the Gryphon and something unspoken passed between them. The Gryphon lowered his head and the man placed a silver-ringed hand gently upon his feathers. He then lifted his palm and placed it in the energy field, opening the portal in a flare of light, and causing the ring he had given her to glow faintly. The light spun into a vortex and a force-field pulled on her just like the one she had entered with the Spirit Wolves only much stronger.

He motioned her towards the Star Portal, and she hesitated, swallowed and stepped closer hoping it would be warmer in there. The Agaroths followed, but Tess and the Gryphon hung back.

"Are you coming?" she asked them.

"Our journey ends here," said the Gryphon, the wind ruffling his feathers.

She nodded, feeling sad. "I thought that... never mind." Her eyes lingered on Tess, wishing the she-wolf at least would come. She didn't know these Agaroths nearly well enough to trust them.

She hugged the wolf and Tess licked her face. "Please look for Maggy and Teo, they might be injured." A lump formed in her throat; she wouldn't let herself believe they were dead. The Shades and the cursed Vormae had started all of this; her prime grievance was with them. In the back of her mind, she saw the chained Saphira-elaysa thrashing in pain, his screams ringing through her head and trembling her soul.

She stood. "Am I to know you only as Gryphon?"

He angled his great head. "You cannot read even a name? I should have thought as much. Gryphons have a name for every year of our lives, and Vassa is mine for this time. It means 'Wind over Water'." He proudly spread his wings and gave a self-congratulatory nod.

"Thank you, Vassa, for saving us from them and bringing us here," said Thaya.

"Indeed." The Gryphon dipped his beak in acknowledgement. "My debt to Maggy is now repaid. May you find what you seek, Farseeker."

"And you, noble Vassa."

He smiled appreciatively at the term, or at least it looked like a smile, it was hard to tell with his beak.

'Farseeker.' Why had Maggy chosen that last name for her? Right now, as she stood before a Star Portal beside beings from another world, it certainly felt fitting. *Perhaps she knew all along I'd have to find my twin soul after that fateful day, and it would take me to places far away.*

She stroked Tess's head. "Rest and heal, and thank you, too, for protecting me." The wolf whined as Thaya turned to face the Star Portal. It looked so odd; a swirling mass of light upon the peak of a snowy mountain beneath a vast sky of dark clouds and flurries of snow. The Agaroths stood behind her. Each laid a hand on her shoulders, and with a deep breath, she let them guide her forwards.

Thaya expected this portal experience to be different to the first; gentler and more pleasant maybe, especially since the Agaroths were with her and this was a Star Portal, therefore much larger and surely more sophisticated than a smaller portal or Vortex. She'd also had more experience and knew what to expect. But it wasn't any different, and it lasted much longer.

The energy sucked her in, throwing her into an invisible torrent. Screaming, she tumbled, over and over, through flashing lights and howling winds of pure energy. She glimpsed the Agaroths close behind her; they weren't tumbling at all, but running upright, determined expressions on their faces, eyes glowing peculiarly. They moved gracefully, like angels. If it weren't for the utter terror, Thaya would have been ashamed of her graceless, screaming somersaults.

She closed her eyes and focused on controlling her bladder, but tumbling in the darkness only made it worse. Dear gods, when would this hellhole end?

Abruptly, the flashing light and howling tornado vanished into pitch black and half a heartbeat later she thumped face down into earth and grass, the air exploding from her lungs. Had it really stopped? She felt her body for breakages and blinked at the blades dancing in front of her face. They were similar to grasses in Havendell, only these were purple and quite fascinating and—

She surged onto her knees and vomited, choking violently. Her stomach gave her a second to gasp in air before clenching itself and purging its contents. Fingers clawed into the earth as she was sick noisily, again and again, interspersed between gasping and her whole body shaking. It was worse than before; it was definitely worse! Hands touched her shoulders, instantly calming the demon in her gut. She sucked in air and pushed limp strands of hair back from her sweaty face. She sat back on her heels as the retching receded. The grass didn't look so nice anymore.

Her gaze travelled up to the faces of the Agaroths. Their lips were pursed, eyebrows raised. She couldn't tell if they were concerned or disgusted.

"Sorry," Thaya mumbled, grabbing the flask from her pack to wash away the awful taste. Cool snowmelt soothed her throat and she breathed deeply. "Does it get any easier?"

"We're trying to work it out, but we're still not sure what the problem is," replied the female Agaroth with a frown.

"Fine," said Thaya. "It's obviously 'portal Sickness.' I'm clearly not made for portal travel." She swallowed more frigid snowmelt and the churning fires in her stomach calmed.

"I suppose, like the Gryphon, Vassa, you *do* have names? Since you know mine and have brought me here, perhaps you can tell me yours?"

The woman spoke, her long black hair lifting in the breeze. "We have only one name, and we do not change it for the seasons like Gryphons. We have tried twice to tell you them via telepathy, but it is apparent you are not yet able to receive our thoughts. I am Renatocca, and this is my cousin, Arendor."

Hmm, strange names, definitely not Havendellian or even Lonohassan. She also hadn't felt anything if they *had* tried to tell her their names. "Sorry, I suppose I'm...inadequate. I've never been able to read thoughts like some can, but thank you." She didn't know anybody who could properly read thoughts, even Toothless Betty couldn't, though she could interpret dreams.

"Feeling inadequate is not necessary if it does not serve you, there is only learning and applying," said Arendor. "In time, all things can be learned. Your race was meant to achieve much, like many others."

Well, that was encouraging. They helped her up and she forced herself to stand unaided, her eyes soaking up the surroundings.

The whole land was bathed in soft twilight, casting everything in beautiful shades of lavender and indigo as if the sun or the moon was purple. She glanced up, but couldn't see either in the sky, only thousands of stars more numerous than in the skies above Havendell, but fainter, as if they were far away. The breeze carried the subtle scent of flowers she did not recognise. It billowed over the grass causing it to move in waves like an ocean.

Beyond the meadow were trees similar to the great chestnuts back home, but their leaves were purplish rather than green. Butterfly-like fireflies floated above the swaying grasses, their bodies glowing amber between huge wings in shades of yellow and blue.

A deep peace emanated over the land, and something else she couldn't put her finger on; sadness or contemplation. She felt that to speak in other than a hushed voice would be wrong, so she whispered. "Is it sunrise or sunset?"

"It is neither," said Arendor, casting his gaze down. "There is only this now, never brighter, never darker."

"Oh," said Thaya. That would explain why they were so pale, but she didn't say it out loud. It turned out she didn't need to.

"Indeed, many aeons ago we were darker, burnished copper in the light of our beloved sun, now gone from us," said the woman, looking wistfully to the skies.

"But this now would be a time when we sleep, and sleep we do much of since the sun faded," added Arendor. He loosened the buttons of his tunic and untied his cloak, slinging it over his arm and revealing the strange gun-like weapon he had fired at the Shades. Hopefully, Shades were far from here; everything felt far from here.

She had forgotten again that they could read her mind and made an effort to control her thoughts as they walked along a path through the grass.

"What happened to the sun?" she asked.

But Arendor continued the previous conversation. "The day-beings of this planet remember there was a time to sleep and that is when the night creatures come out. When our faded sun rises, they in turn rest and allow the day creatures to rise, though the light remains the same. In six hours, the sun will rise and then we'll seek an audience with the Council of Fifteen.

"And no, worry not, there are no Shades here. Nothing will eat you, bite you, sting you or attack you whilst you're upon Great Arothia, for nothing violent has been allowed to remain. Every single bird, fish, reptile, insect or mammal that is predatory or violent in any way has been removed from our lands."

Thaya started at the thought. "All of them? How? Is that not itself violent?"

Arendor looked at her. "Your shock is understandable, but it was not done violently, they simply went to sleep and vanished when we removed their racial template from Arothia's core."

"You have the power to remove entire species just like that?" They were jesting, it couldn't be possible, but the Agaroths' faces remained serious.

"The appointed guardian species of any planet has the power to do this, as once your race also had. It is normal in the way of managing our homes. It's the corruption of your Councils that effected a loss of your Divine-given gifts. We agreed unanimously that in our dwindling years we would not suffer or allow the suffering of any being any longer. All who would not, or could not, agree to that were, lovingly, removed."

Thaya continued to struggle with the concept as they arrived at the top of a gently sloping hill. The path led down under the trees to a track of white pebbles that ground softly underfoot. Again, the trees' leaves were mauve in hue, and their trunks were more a muted orange than brown. As they reached the bottom of the hill, a beautiful lake came into view. Low cliffs bordered the far side and the land all around was forests and rivers with spans of grassland in between.

A creature the size of a rabbit lifted its head above the grass. Its fur was pale yellow, and its large eyes watched them as it chewed upon the grass. Rounded ears flicked back and forth, and its long bushy tail—much like a squirrel's—twitched constantly. To Thaya's surprise, it didn't run away as they neared but instead sat proudly on its haunches.

Renatocca reached down and stroked its head, a slight smile on her lips. "You may touch her if you like, she won't bite."

Thaya lifted her hand and the creature sniffed her fingers, its whiskers tickling her palm. Her fur was soft as silk and she cooed at her touch, not acting like a wild animal at all. But for all the peacefulness here, something wasn't quite right. Where did this sad feeling that emanated through everything come from?

"We are dying," said Arendor, answering her unspoken question. He started walking and she followed. "Everything you see that lives; the trees, the insects, even the little Poha, we're all dying."

"But everything dies eventually," said Thaya.

Arendor shook his head. "No, it does not. And that is not quite what I meant. Our race is dying, never to return here, and few of our children now survive into adulthood. Arothia himself is dying, and so, too, all the planets in our system, especially now the sun breathes its last. So now, we cherish the light." He lifted his hands and elements of light appeared above his fingertips, sparkling and twirling around each other like fireflies.

"Now we protect the light vigilantly, and we protect all those beings of the light attacked by the fallen. Through deceit, we lost ourselves to those of the dark. No, Thaya, do not be sad and downcast; we were lucky for we did not become like them for long. But though the light seed within each of us is closing, we adore the light like no other and live the remainder of our days more beautifully than even those of the light do, for we know truly what it means."

She didn't know what to say. A race that was dying, forever to be forgotten from the world? Nothing could be sadder to Thaya. The path turned into the trees and along it, glowing purple lanterns illuminated the way.

"This is an education to you as well. Our peace here is absolute, and should you bring violence, even in your words, you will be asked to leave and never allowed to return. We simply will not compromise the peace of our final years, and we have necessarily become ferocious against those of the dark—how else could we stand against them? So our ways are those of the warrior and we hone our skills out there upon the vast multitude of planets in this glorious cosmos. We hunt and kill the Fallen Ones whenever we can, wherever we find them in the Worlds of Light. Look, our dwelling lies ahead." He motioned.

The white-stone path led into a wide meadow surrounded by trees. Teardrop-shaped structures rose up between dozens of smaller elliptical pod shapes lying about the grass like giant eggs. Each pod was roughly ten feet in length and half as wide, and made of some pale hard material, like unpolished ceramic. They lay lengthways, and as Thaya neared, her eyes widened. The pods didn't touch the ground at all but hovered motionless above the grass. She touched one. Its smooth surface was warm, but it didn't shift even slightly under her touch.

"Someone sleeps inside," said Arendor.

Thaya snatched her hand away and his eyes sparkled in amusement.

"Is this a camp or something?" she asked.

"Yes, but it is permanent. I can see you are confused, let me explain. We cherish the outdoors and so a thousand years ago we moved away from our claustrophobic, sterile cities and towns to live amongst the trees and the animals and the stars as we were meant to do. In the past, in our ignorance, we let the Fallen Ones push us into cramped metropolises, thus diverting us from our true existence millennia ago. For a hundred thousand years we lived as those on other planets, within enormous buildings scraping the skies, far from the touch of the earth, and the sound of the rivers or the waves. All that has gone now, and finally, we find peace."

They reached the furthest edge of the meadow and the last of the pods. Arendor laid his hand upon one and the perfect oval silently split into two. The top half lifted up and over to one side, and inside, laid neatly, was a cushion, blanket and mattress of the softest rose material.

Arendor beckoned her into the pod. "Rest here. You are tired, as are we, and we shall await the waking of the Council of Fifteen."

"Where will you go? And how can I work this thing?" It operated by touch, but how could she do that?

"We'll be close, you need not fear. No Shade can reach you here, not even bad dreams will come. Simply touch on the inside here when you want it to open."

It had better open, she thought, climbing into the pod and feeling very odd. Her tired body was more than willing though and as soon as she sunk into the soft bedding, she felt sleepy.

Her stomach lurched as the top slid shut and she tried not to feel as if she were seeing the inside of her own coffin. It was dark at first, but her eyes quickly adjusted to the very pale purple light. It wasn't claustrophobic or stuffy at all, there was even a gentle breeze as if somehow the wind was able to move right through the pod. Perhaps it wasn't really solid at all... and as she wondered about it, she fell asleep.

16

WE ARE DYING

THAYA OPENED HER EYES AND WAS STARTLED BY THE PURPLE darkness.

Where was she? She had to get out! She slapped the sides of the pod and the lid lifted gently and smoothly, ambivalent to her panic. Hand on chest, she thanked the gods she wasn't inside a coffin and sat up to witness a peculiar sight.

Between the pods stood many Agaroths with their backs to her and faces lifted to the sky. She followed their gaze to a dark orb beyond the lavender clouds. It looked like a moon, but it didn't 'shine,' and its edges flared faintly. The Agaroths breathed slowly in and out in unison, opening and closing their eyes to the orb.

She slipped out of the pod and tiptoed to where Arendor stood. He didn't speak, leaving her to wonder at their strange ritual. There was a peculiar buzz in the air, more felt than heard, and she got the feeling that they were somehow communicating with each other using their minds.

Moving together, the Agaroths turned their gaze upon Thaya. She stepped back, the weight of their dark eyes alarming. Every Agaroth was at least a foot taller than she. *Don't think of anything, keep your mind empty,* she told herself. It was hard, especially on this planet so very different from her own, and beyond the fear, her stomach kept popping thoughts of breakfast in there.

"Every morning we greet the sun in his twilight years," Arendor explained. "Though his light is weak, we still feel his warmth, and for that we give thanks. It is good you are awake, for the Council of Fifteen await you." He indicated to the right with a nod of his head.

Thaya looked but could see only grass beyond the last pod, not even a path. She frowned and followed him. He paused at the edge of the pods and before him, the ground shimmered and a step made of smooth, dark purple stone appeared out of thin air. She looked back at the Agaroths who continued to watch her, their pale, expressionless faces disconcerting. He took a step up and, not wanting to seem foolish or ignorant, she lifted her foot experimentally. The step was solid! Immediately another step appeared above it and as she stepped onto that, more appeared.

In total, there were fifteen steps and when she stood on the last an entire plateau shimmered into being.

"A hidden temple? How is this possible?" She looked down at Arendor, but he said nothing and only gave his signature, barely detectable smile.

Thaya walked along the plateau and the air several yards high began to shimmer and solidify, revealing the most exquisite building she had ever seen. Dark purple stone had been carved in a manner to look like flowing liquid so that there was not a single straight line or sharp edge. The stone flowed up to form teardrop domes with several small ones surrounding a larger one, and within the walls and turrets were windows, each with a yellow light that twinkled merrily.

Thaya appreciated the temple's beauty with her mouth open. Slowly, she stepped towards the arched doorway through which welcoming warm light spilled. Not even with all the gold coins pouring into the Illumined Acolytes clutches could they create such a thing of beauty. Their temples, though dripping in gold, were dark mausoleums compared to the loveliness of this building.

She stepped inside to find long flowing walls reaching up to the domes high above. There were no objects or furniture inside, just a wide, sweeping open space that was immaculately clean and polished.

Her eyes settled on the people before her. Fifteen Agaroths, eight women and seven men, each dressed in violet robes, knelt on cushions before her. Their eyes were closed, their hands were folded in their laps and each wore a thick silver necklace with a brightly glowing white gem hanging at their midriffs.

"Welcome, Thayannon Farseeker, we are the Council of Fifteen." Many voices spoke, but not one of the Agaroths moved their lips. How they did that she would never know. "It gives us immense joy to have One of the Light visit us, but alas we do not have what you seek."

Thaya remembered why she had come. "The Book of Maps, but why not? I've come all this way and Maggy said you'd help. She said you had the book and from it, you'd be able to decipher how I can reach...*him*."

Had she come all this way for nothing? If they couldn't or wouldn't help, where did that leave her? She chewed her lip. Fancy palace, intimidating race and different planet or not, her emotions bubbled over. "I was nearly killed! I've lost

Maggy and Teo, the gods know where they are. Has it all been for nothing?"

The Agaroths shifted and wrung their hands in their laps. Were her emotions unsettling them?

When they spoke there was nothing but humility in their tone, though again their lips did not move. "You are in pain. We can see that your soul is torn in two, and with each passing day the hole within you grows, especially now your soul remembers and feels keenly that to which it was joined and then torn from so painfully. You must find this soul to which you are joined or your own soul will separate itself from your current form and you will die."

"Yes, that's why I'm here!" Thaya wrung her own hands.

"The Book of Maps was stolen from us most recently, but through the grace of the Eternal Spirit, the Leonites recovered it and now it is safe within their keeping. But even if they let you look at the book—for they will not let you take it—and you find where it is you must go, you will not be able to enter the realm of the Vormae and set foot upon Geshol. Even if you had the codes that would allow you to access and navigate the Star Portals there, how could you possibly face them?"

Thaya's heart sunk into her boots. "I don't know. I suppose I thought someone here would know. I only know what I have to do, not how to do it."

The Agaroths opened their eyes and looked at her, their penetrating gazes gleaming then turning dark again. The woman in the centre stood and the rest followed. She was older than the others, older than any of the Agaroths Thaya had met. Now she thought about it, all the Agaroths looked roughly the same age; around thirty. This woman looked to be in her forties or fifties, her shining hair still all black and tied elaborately into braids that wrapped and hung around her head.

"Greetings, Thaya, I am Arothia-Ra, First of the Fifteen." She spoke in a rich, deep voice and walked regally, as a queen might, to pause beside a man holding something covered in black satin.

Thaya nodded respectfully. Everyone always knew her name, but she knew no one else's. It was getting tiresome. "I'm honoured to be here but confused. Why didn't Arendor tell me? He could have. Why make me come all this way?"

The Agaroth paused, hands suspended over the object as she looked into the middle distance. Her eyebrows knitted together, and she whispered, "Because he does not yet know." She swallowed visibly. "Only two suns ago, the Vormae attacked, somehow breaking through our dimensional forcefield and entering through the tear. They must have discovered a new power to be able to do this and we are still analysing how it was done. Our Guards of the Book fought valiantly, many Vormae were destroyed, but a handful escaped with it, much to their detriment for we alerted the Leonites who closed upon them fast and spared none. It gladdens me to say the book was recaptured, but the lives of our Agaroths can never be brought back, and for us who birth so few, this is devastating. We have yet to tell Arendor that his partner is among those fallen, and others close to him remain severely injured."

Arothia-Ra motioned to her right and the entire back wall with its beautiful purple stone staircase melted away to reveal the outside. Row upon row of black shrouded figures lay neatly, side by side, upon the grass.

Thaya shivered, there had to be at least a hundred shrouded bodies. *They're dead? Dear gods, how awful, I wish I had never come.*

The Agaroths hung their heads. The pain emanating from them in the long silent moments became so potent Thaya struggled to breathe.

"I'm sorry, deeply," Thaya whispered. "I thought nothing harmful could come here, I thought we were safe?" Her words caused the other Agaroths to speak in hushed voices amongst themselves.

"So did we," replied Arothia-Ra. She moved her hand down, and the beautiful stonework reappeared. "But either we grow weak or the Vormae have grown strong. With their enslavement of the Saphira-elaysa, untold powers are becoming theirs to command. They have never dared to attack us before, although we have fought them many times on behalf of others. They fear us for what we have done and can do."

Thaya frowned, and the woman motioned to the ceiling above and swirled her hand. Again the stone melted away to reveal a sky full of stars, fainter now in the dark light of the sun. A long line of jagged rocks sprayed across the sky; some were enormous, almost the size of moons, others were mere pebbles in contrast. The asteroids revolved slowly around each other, lazily drifting across the sky. In the Book of Mystics, Thaya had read about the stories of destroyed planets becoming asteroids and strange creatures coming from them.

"We needn't fear the remains of Emmon, it is caught harmlessly in our orbit and serves to keep unwanted others from landing, even if they could pass through our barriers," explained Arothia-Ra. "But it seems our defences have been compromised and we must make urgent adjustments."

"Is that the remains of an entire planet?" Thaya asked. Had the Agaroths done that? Did they really have the power to destroy entire planets?

"Yes. Aeons ago, the Ordac Reptilians attacked our Emmonite brothers and sisters, sometimes with violent and bloody warfare but mostly with stealth and trickery. They planted seeds of evil in Emmon's core, weakening her and withering her and her people from within.

"The Emmonites and Ordacs became entangled with each other. Unable to watch them fall we tried to help and entangled ourselves with them. We were a refuge for fleeing Emmonites—we called them Emmords for they had become hybrids with the Ordacs—but the refugees themselves were compromised, carrying within them the Ordac evil seed. It is our fault, for we trusted them, and in our naivety, we let them come with open arms. For all our efforts, Emmon fell, and then so did we."

Thaya remembered the scroll she'd left lying on the ground within the Old Temple. "'We let the Gods in, and they destroyed us.' That's what's written on an ancient scroll I found, though I think they were talking about Nuakki gods."

Arothia-Ra nodded. "It is how many of the Higher Fallen operate. It is only those of, shall we say, lesser intelligence and aptitude who fight with physical brutality. The Higher Fallen are remarkably sophisticated, infinitely intelligent, and devastatingly proficient at destroying others. They infiltrate and corrupt from within. We lost control of our beloved Arothia and fought a bitter war, a thousand years of bloodshed.

"But we were losing, and so we did the last thing they would ever expect, we destroyed Emmon—our dying sister planet—and our own Arothia, and thus ourselves so that they could never take us. It was the noblest sacrifice we could make to ensure that they would be stopped for good, for if we took them down and fell with them, they would not be able to destroy another race. With their planet gone, nothing could sustain them no matter where they lived.

"Within one revolution around our sun, the Emmords were all dead, and we had fallen. Even to this day we still agree that it was the right thing to do; to destroy them, and thus ourselves, to save all others. We dedicate our dwindling years to destroying other Fallen Ones wherever we find them and protecting those of the light. But as you see, many such races are fallen, and so our work is endless."

Thaya listened in fascination to their story and considered the magnitude of it. It was clear to her who should be trying to free the Saphira-elaysa. "I'm not a warrior like you, not by a long shot, so surely *you* should pursue the Vormae and free the captured Saphira-elaysa?"

Arothia-Ra lifted the satin-covered object. "Indeed, and had you come two days ago, a legion of Agaroths would be with you. But now, with our defences compromised, I cannot afford to let any leave, at least not until we have safeguarded ourselves. We will not let the Agaroths end their days at the hands of the fallen."

"Then it's hopeless," whispered Thaya, her heart sinking. She would never find the Saphia-elaysa; she would never learn the secrets of her soul and heal that gaping hole.

"No, it is not. As have the Agaroths, the Leonites have secured a Star Portal upon Urtha from time immemorial to assist when they can. As you have reached us here, so too can you reach the Leonites. Return to Urtha and seek them out."

Thaya closed her eyes at the enormity of what Arothia-Ra suggested. "I would have to return home and hunt the entire planet for something I cannot see. I came here via the top of a mountain and I don't think my Gryphon ride is exactly waiting for me. Surely there must be some way to reach the Leonites from here? But even if I did, if I can't face the Vormae, what's the point in finding this stupid book anyway?"

"No Star Portals of Arothia lead to the Leonites, for Arothia has fallen, and the worlds of light are cut off from us. All Races of Light may come here, however, though few do so for the lowering vibrations negatively affect their spirits."

Thaya worried for her own spirit, though it was probably already harmed from everything that had happened these past few days.

The First of Fifteen continued. "We can offer no more advice than what we have said already. You may go to the Leonites or not, the choice is yours and yours alone. But if we find you in trouble, we will always come to your aid."

"Thank you," Thaya said quietly. She wanted more, but what could she do, what could anybody do? Was it worth even trying to reach the Leonites? It wasn't like she had any other options. If she went, there was a chance of reaching him, the Saphira-elaysa, or getting closer. If she didn't go, there was none. Besides, there was nothing else to do with her life now, Fi and Yenna didn't need her on the farm, for them, she no longer existed. The thought made her inhale sharply.

Arothia-Ra walked towards her, violet robes shimmering, and in her palms, she held aloft a gun. It was just like Arendor's with a singular short, thick barrel that shone like polished silver, and a grip made of smooth dark wood. Beautiful whirls and scrolls were etched into the metal, and amongst the scrolls were symbols, like those upon Arendor's rings.

She had shot Fi's gun only once after being goaded into it by her brothers. It had thrown her back against the wall so hard she had sworn the bullet had stayed still whilst she was catapulted backwards. The apple remained unharmed on the tree stump whilst the noise had deafened her for the rest of the morning. She'd never touched the thing again. So it was with reluctance that she took the gun passed to her.

"For me?"

The weapon was cool to the touch, lighter than it looked, and suggested nothing of its deadly purpose. She held it awkwardly and hoped it wouldn't fire by accident.

"A gift to you from us—from Arendor's accounts we feel you are deserving and in much need of it," Arothia-Ra inclined her head. "No being of light is safe from the Shades. Take the Fireshot and use it wisely—it is a formidable weapon. When it runs dry, soak it in pure water and then fire to refuel it."

It was a gift and yet it scared her, made her realise how vulnerable she was, and how alone. "I—I don't know what to say, uh, thank you, but I've never used a gun before, although I guess I could learn. The symbols, they feel strange, do they have power?"

"They do, but words cannot explain them. In time, you will learn them yourself simply by using the weapon, and they will become unique to you."

Thaya's eyes lit up. "I can learn them? That would be a bit like learning magic."

"Come closer, let me show you where you need to go." Arothia-Ra placed a cool palm upon Thaya's forehead, just like Arendor had done before, and her eyes and mind filled with light.

She closed her eyelids, and in the light an image formed. She gasped as a map of Urtha with lands and continents she had never imagined appeared. She recognised the turtle-like shape of Lonohassa, and to the right, far across the ocean, she thought she could make out Havendell. The map enlarged and focused on land far south of Lonohassa. She saw the giant trees of a jungle, and amongst the dense foliage lay the ruins of an ancient temple, dark stone entwined with thick vines and the roots of trees. Amongst the crumbling statues of long-forgotten gods, she saw the familiar swirling light of a portal.

Arothia-Ra removed her hand, but the map remained in her mind. "That is where you will find them."

Thaya let go of the breath she had been holding and shook her head. "But it's so far away."

Arothia-Ra pursed her lips and looked away. After a long time, she said, "It is not easy for you now so much of your technology has been lost and, yes, it is dangerous. Hmm, perhaps it would be wise for one of ours—I can spare no more—to accompany you, for I doubt the Shades will leave you alone for long."

Thaya nodded vigorously. If she had to travel to the ends of the earth and for the rest of her days trying to reach that which her soul yearned for, having a companion for some of it would be most welcome. That they would send one of their own just for her was a grand gesture. "I'm humbled for I would like that very much."

Arothia-Ra smiled, or as close to a smile as she could. She motioned with her hand and moments later Arendor entered. He touched the hands of Arothia-Ra, and then walked to each of the Council of Fifteen and touched their hands. Finally, he stood before the First.

The air buzzed faintly, alerting Thaya that they communed telepathically. Arothia-Ra took a deep breath, her eyes wide but unblinking as she stared at Arendor. If she was telling him about what had happened to the book and their people, including his mate, not a flicker of emotion passed across Arendor's face.

Arothia-Ra and Arendor ceased their communing and the man looked at Thaya. "I am sorry that you did not find what you were looking for. Hope is not lost and, though I would prefer to remain here and recuperate after my time away, I will honour the Council of Fifteen and return with you to Urtha to safeguard you in whatever way I can on this journey."

Relief washed over her. She'd have a companion. Thaya tried to match her manner and her words to their polite and stoic tones. "Thank you, Arendor. I'd prefer not to return either, and your company will be most appreciated. I guess there's no point waiting, although I could do with something to eat before we return."

"We are preparing everything an honoured guest from Urtha might require," said Arendor. Eyes gleaming, he held out his arm for her to take in an old-fashioned Urtharian gesture.

Thaya glanced back to the Council of Fifteen. Arothia-Ra nodded to her. Thaya smiled and nodded back, then let Arendor lead her into the perpetually twilit world.

17

WELCOME TO EARTH, BABY

THAYA AND ARENDOR WALKED DOWN THE STEPS AND BEHIND them the temple and staircase melted away to leave no evidence of its existence.

"Can you see the temple anymore?" Thaya asked curiously.

Arendor's eyes twinkled. "Of course."

"I guess it's hidden to strangers," she said, when he didn't elaborate.

They were greeted by Agaroths clustering around a food-laden table. Exotic-looking fruits, some small like grapes, and others as large as watermelons rested on ornate plates. Many had been cut open to reveal their juicy pink, purple and orange insides. The feasting Agaroths stepped aside to allow them access. Some spoke aloud as they ate, but most communed silently. Thaya selected a small pink fruit and several dark purple grapes and devoured them. As she ate, she wondered if all planets had human-looking beings or were some populated just with animals? Maybe some planets were all rock whilst others were all ocean with no land at all.

"The Cosmos is as vast as your imagination, and I don't mean to be rude, but your imagination is somewhat limited," said Arendor. Thaya's cheeks grew hot. "But it is good that you try to expand it. Everything you just imagined is true, if you can think it, then it exists. How else do you think you could imagine such things?"

"All things I imagine exist?" asked Thaya, biting into a sweet and tart pink fruit. Arendor nodded and she began to think of more outlandish concepts, creating crazy-looking animals and plants in her mind.

"That is good, expand your mind," said Arendor.

She didn't believe him, however, though it was fun to imagine anything existing.

After eating, she refilled her flask with water from one of the many amphorae beside the tables and put the extra fruit Renatocca insisted she take into her pack. "You are going to need it," she said.

Thaya smoothed back her hair, straightened her clothes and looked back the way they had come. This place was peaceful, beautiful and she wanted to stay, but on the gentle wind that blew through her hair, she heard a distant voice calling to her. A voice that was so far away she wondered if she would ever be able to reach it.

"I would offer you more rest if I thought you would take it," said Arendor. "But we must return, you are right."

"Thank you for all you've done, and your people," said Thaya. "You didn't have to protect me, but you chose to, and I hope you won't need to again. Despite what Arothia-Ra said, you don't have to come with me. This task is mine alone, impossible though it is."

"I'll accompany you to the safety of the Leonites, as is my word." Arendor's chin was set. There'd be no talking him out if it even if she wanted to.

With a silent nod, she started walking back the way they had come, the weight of the long journey ahead pressing down upon her. Neither spoke until they neared the swirling portal of light. Perhaps it was always there, or perhaps it appeared at Arendor's presence, but there was no Portal Stone to mark it. Maybe placing stone markers was a specifically Urtharian or human custom.

"I'm sorry for what the Fallen Ones have done to your people," Thaya said with feeling. They were doing the same to her own race.

Arendor's expression was blank. "Revenge will cool the heart," was all he said. He removed his Fireshot from its holster and lifted his other silver-ringed hand to feel the flows of the Star Portal. The swirling energies responded to his touch and flickers of light danced around his fingers.

"Now you may enter," he said.

"I go first?" she asked.

Arendor nodded.

Thaya swallowed, dreading the chaos about to ensue. She felt as if she were about to jump off a cliff, and the fear of throwing her guts up on the other side only added to her apprehension. Trying not to lose face, she forced herself forwards and held up her hands. The vortex pulled on her gently. As she walked closer, the pulling increased and suddenly grabbed hold of her and sucked her in.

Screaming, she tumbled through a flashing spinning tube of energy. She caught glimpses of Arendor. The man wasn't flailing uncontrollably, but upright and running, his feet pounding in sparks of energy as he checked his Fireshot. His face was calm and as unreadable as ever, and Thaya felt ashamed as another helpless scream tore itself from her throat.

Something changed, she couldn't say exactly what it was, but it was as if the energy tunnel she was trapped within suddenly dropped in frequency. A magical humming noise crackled, and streaks of dark light flashed.

The noise and light disappeared as fast as they had arrived, and everything became normal again, whatever 'normal' was in this crazy place.

Thaya thrust her hands and legs out desperately trying to halt her tumbling, or at least not spin so fast. She slowed a little, her feet not flashing over her head quite so often, but she couldn't control it any more than that.

The strange change came again, crackling frequency followed by streaks of dark light. Cold blasted through her very bones and she shivered. What was happening? Surely the tunnel should have ended by now? Urtha wasn't exactly near to Arothia, but it hadn't taken this long to get there in the first place. She glanced back at Arendor. He was running faster, the Fireshot swinging wildly in his hand.

She spun forward and cried out as a face flashed before her, a hideous face she had hoped never to see again, all bald and sickly white with slits for nostrils and no mouth. Heat blasted from behind her and the face vanished. Arendor caught up and grabbed her arm in a vice-like grip. She slammed against his chest and he held her there, his Fireshot aimed in front of them.

"Vormae," he said. "Get your weapon ready."

So, the face was real. Dear gods, she was still reeling from the spinning and now she had to fight? Breathing hard, Thaya fumbled for her Fireshot, almost dropped it, and aimed it ahead with shaking hands. As if she'd ever be able to hit something! Wind whipped all around them and the vortex extended endlessly ahead.

Another Vormae appeared, full head and body this time, swathed in dark red robes, and still impossible to tell whether male or female. Its three-fingered hands were raised and moving oddly as if it was weaving a spell.

Thaya screamed and fired. A fiery ball shot forwards from her weapon and whizzed harmlessly up into the air. Arendor, who had calmly taken time to aim, landed his shot moments after hers.

The Vormae exploded into flames. It screamed, hands flailing, and vanished. The entire vortex turned dark. A heartbeat later, flares of white lightning scoured it, illuminating everything eerily.

Three Vormae appeared only yards ahead, facing them as they floated backwards, seemingly impervious to the forces raging around them.

Thaya yelped as Arendor flung her behind him and then ran forwards, dragging her along. She heard him fire the gun again. A Vormae screamed. Pressure built rapidly, heavy and intense. Silence fell.

BOOM!

The entire vortex shook, turned black, and ceased spinning. The air vanished, she tried to inhale but couldn't. She flailed for Arendor, but his iron grip was gone. Air returned in the rush of a terrifying tornado, swirling around her and tossing her left then right like a rag doll. The vortex was gone, there was only light and wind, and she was falling.

The nothing ended when Thaya slammed against something flat, cold and hard. All air was forced out of her lungs, and every bone in her body creaked until they felt broken and her surrounding muscles turned to jelly.

There was noise, a ringing in her ears, a pounding in her head, flashing lights in her eyes, but beyond the mayhem that familiar, terrifying, queasiness swirled in her stomach. For the first time, she was grateful for it; it meant she was out of the portal and it was the one familiar thing she could cling to.

The flashing lights faded and her vision returned just as her stomach rolled. She saw grey paving stones, the edge of a curb and a metal grill in a road down which grey sludge trickled. She lunged towards it and heaved. Thaya was dimly aware of people passing her by, but nothing could stop her stomach doing its thing.

"Disgusting!" a woman growled.

"Ugh, get back home, tramp," said a man.

"I'm s-sorry," Thaya gasped between heaves, her eyes red-visioning with the strain. She glanced up to see a large metal box on thick black wheels careen towards her. She fell back as it zoomed over the grill. It was followed by another and then another. She grabbed her Fireshot and aimed it, but the metal carts whizzed past completely ignoring her. Several yards away, they came to a stop before a pole atop which a red light beamed. She could see the man in the driver's seat. He was busy watching the lights, not caring about her at all. She lowered her weapon. *They're not Vormae and they weren't trying to kill me.*

A man in a strange plain suit and white shirt pushed past her through the press of people. He glanced momentarily at her Fireshot, his eyes widening before his face creased into a grin. "Gonna do some damage with that blunderbuster piece of junk, are ya? Ha-ha." He shook his head and carried on, tucking his leather bag under his arm.

"It's real, you know!" Thaya shouted after him. "Hmm, strange accent," she murmured, unable to place it. But he was already lost in a sea of people—people scowling at her as they tried to get past on the pavement without falling into the road where metal carriages careened past.

Thaya wiped her mouth and pressed herself back against the wall, breathing hard. Where the hell was she? Where was Arendor? The Vormae could arrive any minute, although thankfully in these crowds, they'd never find her.

She looked around. The long straight street she was on reminded her of the main street in Havendell Harbour, only this was much longer and wider, and the buildings lining it were truly enormous, stacked one against the other with few passageways between them.

There were people everywhere, filling the walkways, hurrying and struggling to get through the throng. The clothing they wore was peculiar to Thaya's eyes, especially when compared to the people of Havendell. Here, women wore skirts or trousers and men wore similar trousers or smart, starkly-cut jackets like that worn by the man who had just pushed past her.

It wasn't just their attire that was different. These people had hair and skin of all shades, some were tall, some short, some fat, some thin, and they even spoke in different languages between themselves—it was as if an entire world of people existed in the microcosm of this place, and every single one of them was rushing to do some task or job that she could only guess at. At least they looked similar to herself or anyone in Havendell; they were not Vormae or Nuakki or even Agaroths. But one thing was very clear, she was a long, long way from Havendell.

The wide road had painted markings down the centre, and along it flowed two endless streams of horseless metal carts honking horns she couldn't see and moving faster than galloping horses. She was surrounded by an endless cacophony of laughing, shouting, hooting, wheels screeching, and everything in between—she could barely hear herself think. Panicked, she hunted the faceless crowds, but Arendor was nowhere to be seen. She'd recognise him anywhere for he'd be taller and paler than most of the people pushing past her.

The ground suddenly shook and an enormous metal beast of a cart reaching two floors high wobbled wildly into view. She stared in disbelief at the people inside filling both floors. When it stopped in front of her, people streamed out of it as other people streamed in. The tall cart gave a mighty blast of its horn making her jump then swung violently back into the traffic.

"Dear gods, tell me where I am!" she gasped. *I have to get away from here, somewhere quiet!*

She looked to her right. On the wall above the peoples' heads was a street sign. "Oxford Street." She read it aloud. Below the sign was a shop front with its wares displayed on stands in the street. Her eyes settled on a slight man with brown hair who was dressed in an oversized coat. His eyes darted this way and that, and he scowled at her as he shifted beside the stands of cards and strange packets of what might be food. His hand darted forward, grabbed some bright orange and yellow packets and stuffed them into his pocket.

Thief, thought Thaya. Havendell Harbour had plenty of them.

Screeching captured her attention. A vivid red vehicle without a roof skidded to a stop right in front of her leaving a trail of smoking black marks behind its thick wheels and an acrid smell in the air.

Thaya glanced at the driver and her mouth dropped open. "Arendor?" she gasped. He looked so different; his long black hair was cut short and brushed up into spikes. He glared at her, his eyes still dark and his skin still pale. The lights ahead had changed to green and the carts behind him honked loudly. He lifted his Fireshot, not at her, but to a small black box that hung on the street corner just above the sign. Rather than shoot a ball of fire, a small white ball of light blasted from it, shattering the box in a spray of dust and smoke.

The shifty man in the oversized coat looked wide-eyed from the disintegrated black box to Arendor. "Cheers, mate!" he yelled and ran off into the crowd.

Everyone had come to a standstill and a hundred eyes now cast their way. In a single motion, Arendor leapt out of the cart and hurtled towards her. The crowd fell back from him as if he carried the plague. Even Thaya tried to melt into the wall, his deadly, determined look was terrifying. He grabbed her arm like he had only minutes ago, and half dragged, half carried her to the red cart. The jerking, the chaos, the stench of fumes and street trash immediately made her unsettled stomach clench.

She doubled over, somehow managing to spray vomit straight into the same grate in the gutter as Arendor lifted her into the car. He dropped her into a seat and jumped into the next one behind the wheel. Her head hanging over the side, she covered her mouth in case her stomach took control again. He grabbed hold of the wheel and pushed a lever between their seats as the cart rumbled and trembled.

With an almighty screeching, the cart jerked forwards faster than a horse, and her screams joined the cart's. Arendor reached over, grabbed a black strap and pulled it over her, securing her into the seat. Gripping her seat, she closed her eyes as they narrowly dodged people and carts, sped through heavy traffic, and flew through lights of red, orange and green.

They made it onto a smaller, quieter road, and Thaya's vision caught up with her.

"Where in hell are we?" she gasped.

"Where are we?" he echoed, eyes wild as he looked at her incredulously then back at the road. Was he angry? Excited? She couldn't tell. He laughed crazily. "Where in hell have you been?"

"What? I just fell out of the Star Portal right behind you. You had hold of me and then you were gone!"

"Oh no," he shook his head vigorously, his actions unsettling her further. He held up a splayed hand. "That was five looong years ago. Five years! And where we are? This is Earth, baby! Your Planet Urtha—only some fifty-thousand years into the future, and I may have lost the light, but the people here are goin' down fast."

"Why, uh, why are you acting like this? Why are you talking funny? It's...unnerving." Thaya was scared now.

Arendor laughed loudly. "Acting? Talking? Ha-ha! I've been stuck here in this hell-hole for five fucking years! Five years, man... Look at me, do I fit in here? No! People called me a vampire, so much so I began pissing off the *real* vampires running this godforsaken place. And yes, this *is* hell, and this *is* how they speak down here, darlin', you'd better get with the program!" He laughed again and slapped the steering wheel, but not long after that, his laughs changed into sobs and tears appeared in the corners of his eyes. She felt like crying too.

White carts suddenly appeared ahead of them, blue lights flashing on their roofs and an awful wailing sound coming from them. Arendor yanked the wheel around and the cart screeched to the right, nearly throwing Thaya out of it. The white carts weren't interested in them, however, and sped away up a different road.

What was happening? She covered her face with her hands, wishing the nightmare would just end. Was this really the man she had known? The cart jerked and she gripped the edge of her seat, closed her eyes again, and did all she could to control her still somersaulting stomach.

"Gedoudda the goddamn way!" Arendor screamed and blasted his horn by pressing the centre of the wheel. People howled, but she refused to open her eyes as he continued to fume and curse.

Gone was his stoic, silent and wise character, instead she sat next to a madman.

After a long time, the cart ceased swinging wildly left and right, and the screams of people could no longer be heard. Instead, there came the growing roar of something huge. It was coming from above and grew and grew until it was deafening. Forcing her eyes open, they nearly popped out of her head as a white monster the size of a dragon zoomed above them. Its long straight wings didn't flap and, though high in the air, it was so large it looked close, far too close.

She broke into a sweat and started to shake.

"I can't do this, I can't—" she began, and then she passed out.

Arms wrapped around her and lifted. Blearily, she glimpsed black clothing, a white face, and a stunning amber sunset beyond a chaotic mass of building tops. A blazing red ribbon of light tore through the clouds gathered low upon the horizon, blinding in its brilliance. One of the closest buildings, a huge domed structure that was probably white in the daylight, was suddenly cast in vibrant red. A cool wind freshened her face. The people, the carts, the noise, and Arendor's craziness were all gone.

The Agaroth was calm and silent as he set her down in a crude chair made of fabric stretched over wood.

He looked at her through dark eyes. "I blacked out soon after I arrived, too. Woke up in a filthy gutter a day later. If a portal passage goes bad, it can happen." He passed her a canister of water made out of a clear, thin, bendy glass. She inspected the bottle thoroughly and unscrewed the lid.

"Plastic," he said as if that was enough to explain how glass could be bendy. With a sigh, he seated himself opposite her in a similar chair. Gone was his crazy behaviour. Instead, he was more like his old quiet self, though withdrawn and dejected, his shoulders slumped and face long.

She was too exhausted to ask questions, and just enjoyed the water soothing her sore throat.

He threw up his hands. "Sorry about that back there. It's been a...long five years. I realise that it's only been moments for you since the Vormae attacked and we got separated. Thusly, I've had plenty of time to work it all out; they were already there, hanging around Arothia. Maybe they were looking for you, or to attack our planet, I don't know. We can talk about that later, but anyway, they attacked us in the portal—and were probably only able to because they'd extracted the knowledge that was in the Book of Maps.

"Well, they managed to rupture and thus destabilise the entire portal. I extinguished two of them, but I couldn't close the rupture, and without the Vormae sustaining it, it rapidly spun out of control. I took a blast, it would have destroyed you if I hadn't, but it cost me my grip on you."

He shook his head. "Bah, it was so weird. I fell forwards into darkness and fell for ages before slamming into the concrete—exactly as you did—and arrived in this... *awful* place. I knew the Vormae couldn't follow once they had lost control of their rip, and you being so close, I knew you would be right behind me."

He scowled. "The people, they laughed at me rather than helped me. Much humanity has been lost here; it saddens me. They thought I was a tramp or a drunk. I could barely stand, and my clothes were smoking and ripped, every bone in my body felt like it had been smashed."

Thaya nodded, she still felt a bit like that now.

Arendor rubbed his eyes. "I clawed myself out of the gutter and staggered to a park where I collapsed on a bench, but even then, I found no rest. The police—the authorities in this place—forcibly removed me. Finding me of ill health, they took me to a hospital—a frightening place where the souls of the dead and dying get trapped! Make sure you never go to one.

"But anyway, none of this is of any consequence other than I've had to fight to stay alive every inch of the way. You have to have this thing called money to eat, to buy things, and to put a roof over your head. For a year I became the tramp the people thought I was. People feared me, my pale skin and black eyes, and the vampires of this cursed city began stalking me, thinking me one of them and invading their territory. I learned to stay in the sunlight, not that there's much of it here, pah."

Arendor took a deep sigh and ran a hand through his hair. "Well, I survived in the end, as most people do. But now you're here, I'm never going back to that office and that job, not back to that bastard who—never mind. None of that matters now.

"It's been so long I've...lost myself down here in the madness. I've learned to shut my mind to people's idiotic mundane thoughts, so much so I now know how it is for those like you who cannot telepath. A quiet, desperate, silent world fraught with misunderstandings...Ah sorry, this is of no consequence to you, you are tired.

"Long story short; I calculated your chance of arrival to be seconds or minutes after me, but only roughly at the same time every new moon." He picked up a pad of paper from beside him on the floor and flicked through it to a page listing times, dates and years. All had the same time of 11:53, though how he could be that exact, Thaya could only guess at. He tapped on an entry:

11:53 June 1st Oxford Street, London.

"This is today's date, and I actually felt the portal open, although it wasn't a real portal since that one has been destroyed in this time and day. It was a rip in space-time. Agaroths call them 'Atorents,' but they call them 'worm-holes' here, and this is what the Vormae are proficient at creating. I felt it open and knew you were coming. You arrived exactly where I arrived, at exactly the same time, five and a quarter years ago."

"You've really been waiting for me for over five years?" Thaya still couldn't believe it.

Arendor nodded. "I returned to the same spot at the same time every new moon. It's to do with energy and align-ments and the pull of the sun and the moon. It took me six full months to work it all out, and I've done nothing but study and research the whole time. Do you realise I had to get this thing called a 'job' just to survive here? It's been hell, but that's another story. Before I had worked it out, I went to the same spot *every day*, for six months."

Could he really have been here for five years? All that time alone in a foreign world? She couldn't imagine how hard it must have been. "But why? Why wait for me, you could just go on or go back to Arothia."

Arendor shook his head, eyes glistening. "I'm trapped here, Thaya. I'm an Agaroth, I don't have the codes to enter your planet's Star Portals—even if they weren't all twisted and broken. You are my ticket out of here, and now, thank the Infinite One, I'll be able to get free."

"So that was a...a *time rip?* And this really is Urtha but far in the future?" Thaya stood up. They were on a high building overlooking the rest of an enormous sprawling city. Now the sun had set, thousands of lights filled the streets making it impossible for the dark to take hold. The wind blew, colder than she was used to for June. She wondered where on Urtha they were.

"Surely that's impossible, I don't recognise anything! I... If that was a time rip wormhole thing, where's the Star Portal? Well, on thinking about it, we don't necessarily need one, any portal will do, though it won't take us back to Urtha, *my* Urtha. Am I trapped here too?" She shivered as tears welled up. She'd already lost her home and family, and now she was in a different time entirely and all of the people she had ever known and loved were long dead. What's more, the Saphira-elaysa was infinitely further away than he had ever been before. She stopped a sob and turned away to lean on the wall.

Arendor got up and rested a gentle hand on her shoulder. "I know. I know how you feel. I feel it too, this hideous *trapped* feeling—but we have hope. After five years working from my all too brief memory of the Book of Maps and studying the Ley Lines of this country, I've plotted on a map where they cross, and thus the most likely places where Vortices form and Portals open up. We'll start with the nearest and work from there. If it takes me aeons to get out of here, it will be worth it."

His words sparked a sort of hope. "Aeons? I don't know about you, but I don't have that long," said Thaya.

He looked at her and then away. "I forget what they did to you, the Invaders, so long ago now. You were like us, like our Infinite One's Children were intended to be, never suffering the unnatural disease of death. But now we all die, only some sooner than others. Funny to think that Agaroths have fallen and you have not, and yet you live vastly shorter lives than we. It's hard for me to accept that I will not share that fate." He looked away over the huge white dome that dominated the landscape.

Thaya stared at him, how long did Agaroths live? "What do you mean, you won't die?"

"Exactly that, but it doesn't affect our current situation at all." He took a deep breath. "I was chosen to be special, alongside a handful of others who are chosen over millennia. It's not really *special*, just difficult to explain. It's more of an enormous, and impossible, responsibility given to a select few Agaroths to preserve the future of our race. Only the strong can deal with it, for we were made immortals."

Thaya inhaled sharply. "Immortal? How is that even possible?" With some difficulty, she held her tongue to let him speak.

"The process takes years, decades in Urtha years, and it's not always successful for it can have unintended consequences because of the corruption in our blood. Often, those chosen die or become maimed, and for some, the process is ever ongoing or doesn't work at all. Still, the Council of Fifteen agree that it is worth the pain in order to protect ourselves and those of the light. You see, long after our race has died out, those made immortal will live on alone, holding the memory of our race in the Cosmos. It is a dark and lonely future as we slowly watch our family and mates pass away. And it means we will never be able to leave and reach the light. So you see, it is not a gift but an enormous responsibility."

Thaya imagined being forever trapped in time on Urtha or any other world, and never reaching the blissful heaven the preachers of Havendell always spoke about. The thought of it brought tears to her eyes, and in a quiet voice she asked, "So you survived and now you're immortal?"

Arendor nodded. "I was lucky, I survived the process undamaged, though my soul is somewhat scarred. My friend did not fare so well; he did not survive."

Thaya took a deep breath. "I'm sorry."

"Do not be, otherwise there will be sorrow built upon sorrow," he said. "But the weight of aeons presses upon me, especially here in this magicless, godless place. I can barely live another moment, and that frightens me—an emotion I had thought I'd long since conquered. The thought of returning home to Arothia and those I love keeps me going, and the fear I will lose her before I even get home keeps me fighting."

Thaya wondered who the 'she' was, then understanding dawned and a chill ran down her spine. "They didn't tell you."

Arendor looked at her, dark eyes searching. "Tell me what?"

"The Council of Fifteen...Arothia-Ra" Thaya suddenly wished she hadn't said anything and looked away, swallowing hard against the sudden lump in her throat. "Oh, it's...it's nothing. Maybe I misunderstood."

"No, it isn't nothing, tell me." He stood up straight, his poise demanding answers.

"I thought you were talking about someone else. It's none of my business." She shook her head and backed away, but in the next instant, Arendor's cold palm was pressed against her forehead.

"Forgive me," he said.

She felt not so much pain as intense pressure and her recent memories of the Council of Fifteen replayed clearly in her mind. She saw the rows of dark shrouded bodies once more and shivered again.

Arendor gasped, let go of his grip and dropped to his knees. Thaya swayed for balance as the pressure receded. "I-I'm sorry, I thought you knew when you mentioned revenge. I didn't know they didn't tell you about your..."

Arendor didn't say anything but sat on his haunches, frozen like a statue, his eyes staring blankly, which was worse than if he'd been sobbing.

Thaya started towards him, then paused, hand raised. Should she touch him? Hug him? What was acceptable Arothian behaviour? Instead, something extraneous came out of her mouth.

"You've changed your hair."

He didn't say anything.

"It's nice, but I liked it when it was long," she whispered. "Tell me how to help you."

Time passed and the Agaroth did not move. Thaya looked at the ground, feeling the most useless she had ever done in her life. Affection had never come easily to her—something which might have caused the end of most of her relationships. She realised now that it came back to the huge, unfillable, gaping hole in her life. The one she dared to believe finding the Saphira-elaysa would fill.

Thaya laid a featherlight hand on his shoulder. Still, he didn't move, perhaps he couldn't even feel it. Why hadn't they told him? She needed more information to understand. "I'd make you a tea or cocoa or pour you some wine if I knew where such things were. I wish I could ease your pain."

Arendor blinked and shook his head as if he had just come out of a trance. "Let's get something to eat and drink, I'm far too sober." He stood and strode towards a rusty metal blue door which creaked dramatically as he opened it.

She hurried after him. Was he all right? Was she safe with him? *He might be mad and in unimaginable pain, but I'd still trust him with my life.* "We're going out there? Again?" The noise, the speeding carts, the people...Thaya wasn't sure if she could cope with it and began to feel what Arendor felt, a desperate need to get away from here.

18

PIZZA, PASTA, AND TASERS

WITH THOUGHTS OF DINNER, THAYA'S STOMACH STARTED growling as she followed Arendor down the grey stone steps.

Many floors later he shoved open another metal door at the bottom and they stepped out into the night.

The streets were only marginally quieter than they had been earlier, and now the steel carts shone with bright red and white lights that blinded her.

"What happened to the horses? How can they even move without them?" she asked.

"Engines," said Arendor. "Cars are faster and, I guess, better for horses? Technological advancements; though the way energy is harnessed here is destructive and poorly done, deliberately so by the Fallen Ones in control. Another story for later. We have a lot to talk about.

"As for the horses, on Arothia you will never see that. No living creature should be confined and forced to work for others."

Thaya watched a car screeching fast around a corner

and the people hurrying out of the way. "I'm not sure if they're better for people," she muttered.

She stayed close to the Agaroth and tried not to look too hard at anything. There was so much she didn't understand and she was, frankly, too hungry to even think straight. The people back home in tiny Brightwater knew so very little of the world. So little, she felt frightened.

They crossed a street then took the next right. Arendor pushed upon the glass doors of a building that looked completely made out of the stuff and held one open for her to enter. A blast of warm air and the smell of something delicious made her stomach growl.

As she entered, she caught her reflection in the glass and her blood ran cold. "Wait!"

Arendor paused as she stared at herself in dismay. She didn't look great, to be honest. Dirt stained most of her clothing and her hair cried out for a brush. There were bruises on her face and neck—if only she had some cream and powder to cover them up! Some eyeliner would be great for her eyes right now, too. She smoothed her hair and clothing, pinched her cheeks, and rubbed her teeth.

"Relax, it's not posh. You look grungy. Anyone can fit in in this city, no one will pay you any attention, trust me."

"Great for you to say, I have to live in this unkempt body," she grumbled. "I need a wash; my clothes need a wash. If I'm going out for dinner, I'd at least like a bit of face paint and perfume."

Arendor shrugged. "I suppose I should have thought of that. You could have washed back at mine, I guess."

Thaya shrugged. "Well, there's no point worrying now we're here. I'm hungry."

Arendor nodded and pushed the door open again.

A man dressed in one of those strange black suits and a pristine white shirt greeted them politely. "Table for two?"

"Yes, please," said Arendor.

"Right this way," said the man. He whirled around and grabbed two thin books from a shelf.

Arendor was right, the man barely looked at her.

The Agaroth took her hand and led her into the plushest tavern she'd ever seen. A great chandelier twinkled above, though not with candles but with strange glowing glass bulbs that cast soft lighting over the many white-clothed tables set with shining cutlery, glasses, and even flowers in the centre. Around these, people sat talking quietly amongst themselves as music played from somewhere, though she couldn't see any musicians. Diners ate from shining white plates—not the mismatched, chipped variety she was used to eating from in the local tavern—and they drank wine from fine, clear glass goblets like rich people did. The food looked strange, wide flatbread dishes covered in red sauce and melted cheese. Others ate from bowls filled with long strands of something pale yellow.

The smart-dressed man seated them at an empty table and handed out their menus. Arendor ordered wine and water while Thaya lost herself in the two pages. Her eyes kept lifting from the page to stare at everything. Most people were dressed smartly and were clean. Feeling terribly self-conscious, Thaya smoothed her hair back once more and checked herself again, especially for signs of vomit. Thankfully there was none, but her attire had certainly seen better days. The tussle with the Nuakki had given Maggy's clothes more than a few tears. If only she'd packed some rouge and kohl before the Shades had invaded Brightwater, or at least just a hairbrush.

"I told you to relax. This isn't a fancy place, and the waiter hasn't chucked us out," said Arendor.

"Could have fooled me! This is the most expensive place I've ever been in," Thaya began, then hushed when the couple next to them glanced their way. She buried her face behind her menu.

"We'll clean your clothes tomorrow, maybe get some new ones. Then we're leaving."

Thaya nodded. Apart from the names of meat and vegetables, she had no idea what any of the food was. She suddenly stopped short with a sharp inhale. The words on the pages were not Havendellian, they weren't Lonohassan, so how in hell or heaven could she understand them? What's more, unless the Agaroths upon Arothia were all speaking her language, which she highly doubted, how could she possibly understand what they had said to her?

She looked up to find Arendor watching her. She said, "Havendellian is a different language to Lonohassan. I learned Lonohassan a long time ago and assumed my ability to speak it now was because of that, but now I wonder. How is it I can speak it so easily? How can I also converse with you and all Agaroths? Surely Agaroths speak an entirely different tongue that I've never learned? How can I understand these people here perfectly and read this menu, yet now I'm looking at it, these words are not Havendellian?" As she asked the questions, she felt afraid, for it was one more thing about the world, about herself and the cosmos, that she did not know or understand.

Arendor's almost coal-black eyes held hers for a long moment, then the faintest pained expression passed across his features and he sighed and set his menu down. "There is so much you have to learn, how can a being learn what I know in such a short lifespan?" He spoke to himself and pinched the bridge of his nose between finger and thumb.

"I can learn, and I might live longer than most," Thaya matched his quiet tone, controlling her anger. "The more I know, the more chance I'll have at finding him. I have to try."

Arendor's expression softened. "You're eager and willing, I'll give you that, though few of your people are. Curse the Fallen Ones for what they have done to your race, but never mind, most things can be learned—or remembered.

"So, this is how it works. Every passage through a portal and an exit through the gate affects the coding of your blood, of the tiny particles that make up your physical body. When you arrive at a destination, you take on the energy of that place, so every gate exited gives you a certain knowledge of that place, which includes the language of the people living by the portal. In your case, this is indeed lucky, since telepathy cannot be learned."

The waiter returned with the water and a bottle of wine and filled up their glasses. "Are you ready to order?" he asked.

"Yes," said Arendor. "I'll have the Pasta Special."

The waiter turned to her and Thaya began to panic. She looked at the man to her left busy sawing through a wide round flatbread and pointed at it. It looked good and smelt delicious. "I'll have that."

The waiter surveyed the dish. "Pizza Margarita, very good." He wrote it down on his pad and turned away. Thaya hoped it was good—anything to stop her growling stomach would do.

As soon as the waiter had gone, Arendor grabbed his glass, downed the wine, and filled it up again. Thaya decided to sip hers, feeling it instantly hit an empty stomach and bring warmth to her cheeks. The Agaroth fell into a sombre reverie, staring deep into his glass as he twirled the stem between his fingers.

She watched the strange man who had come so violently into her life. *He's in mourning, maybe I can help by taking his mind off things, for what good it will do.* "What were you shooting at back there?"

Arendor blinked, rising up from his thoughts, and spoke flatly. "A CCTV camera. It's a non-magical device that can see and record events; people, traffic, crime—that kind of thing. Before you ask, I shot it because there are a handful of extremely powerful others who know how the world, the cosmos and reality *really* work, not this kind of fake illusion everyone is lost in." He waved his arm around, indicating everything in the tavern.

"And it's not a tavern, it's a restaurant," he said, reading her thoughts.

"Oh," said Thaya. She smiled, glad that he had read her thoughts, and not shut her out. These 'powerful others' were clearly not the good guys. She had no idea how a device could 'see' and "record" people; perhaps it was like a crystal ball the fairy tales of her childhood mentioned. She didn't have the energy to understand the thing further and considered his last words instead.

He was right, the people here were just as lost and unaware as they were in Havendell. Did they still have knowledge of the cataclysms that destroyed great civilisations thousands of years ago? Did anyone know anything anymore? Had the Shades not come and forced her to flee, she would never have known anything about anything either—although that gaping emptiness would have always been there, urging her to look deeper.

Why were they not taught about the invaders—*it's our*

history, for heaven's sake! And who were the Acolytes of Light really? Everyone just blindly believed what they were told and didn't dare to find out anything for themselves. *They're scared, scared of what they might find, and having found it, what it might mean. But they weren't even interested, they didn't even want to know about the giant temple staring right at them, they preferred to remain ignorant than to question.* Why weren't they interested in the past, or even in the future?

"Painful as it can be, it is good to question," Arendor agreed. "We did not question. We believed our fallen leaders blindly because of our good nature, and put other's needs before our own, and so we fell. Your race of humans is also falling through ignorance. I am truly surprised they are still here after all this time but then there is a lot I, too, do not know about this planet. While I'm stuck here, I'm like everybody else, in the dark and not in a position to easily find the truth. But all that matters now is that we leave here and get back to Urtha. And now we both have a very personal vengeance against the Vormae." His jaw clenched and he took a long draft of wine, draining half the glass.

Thaya remembered the Shades swarming Brightwater and Solia floating face down in the water. She let go of her breath slowly, feeling depressed. "I'll let my vengeance go if I can just free the Saphira-elaysa. Everything else is just a sideshow. But don't you want to return home first? What about her, your partner? You can talk to me—"

He cut her off. "There is nothing to say because she is gone forever and I'm stuck here in the mortal world forever, and that's pretty much it. It is beyond sorrow."

Thaya opened her mouth, then closed it again. What else could she say? She did not know the ways of the Agaroths. She touched his hand. "Well, I'm here, and you have a friend in me."

He looked up and a faint smile turned the corners of his lips. The waiter arrived with their meals, hot and steaming and smelling delicious, and gave her a strange utensil; a small blade made into a wheel with a handle.

Thaya checked the room for etiquette and rolled the knife awkwardly over the bubbling cheese and tomato sauce covered bread. She lifted a piece to her mouth and had never tasted anything so delicious. "Mmm, hunger makes everything taste divine. It's almost as good as Yenna's cooking."

Arendor approached his pasta with far less gusto, pushing the tubes around his plate and seemingly preferring his wine. He poured the last into their glasses and signalled to the waiter for another bottle. Catching her expression, he hesitated then said to the waiter, "Just one more glass, please."

"Yes, Sir." The waiter nodded.

If the man needed to drown his sorrows, Thaya understood, but she didn't want him to become too intoxicated in this strange world. "Don't mind me, I just didn't think that Agaroths were...drinkers."

"It's the only way to survive this...magicless place," he said, and with a deep sigh he slumped back in his chair.

He didn't say any more, and she lost herself in devouring her pizza. She paused to sip her wine, her gaze drifting around the room until it settled with a start on a familiar-looking man facing her. He was seated in front of an attractive slender woman, her dark brown hair tied up into a perfect twist and her full lips painted rich rouge. Thaya stared harder at the man, he was so familiar with his light brown hair and green eyes—only now his hair was cut short like every man wore it here, and his beard was just stubble.

Arto? No, it couldn't be, could it?

Arto's lookalike caught her gaze and his eyes widened. Thaya spluttered on her wine and set down her glass, coughing. *It's impossible!* But he looked so much like Arto, he could have been his twin. She forced her gaze down to the remains of her pizza, but her gaze kept drifting back to him, and what's more, his eyes kept coming back to her. Thaya was under no delusions; the woman he was seated before was surely more attractive than she, dressed elegantly, and at least clean, so it wasn't *that*. His brows knitted together as if he were trying hard to place her too.

The woman turned around and scowled at her. Thaya's cheeks burned and she stared down at her empty plate. When she dared to look up again, the woman had thankfully turned away. Arto's double also had colour in his cheeks and he stared hard at his food.

Arendor sighed. "What is it? I don't think we have time for...flirting, or causing trouble, which is what will happen if you two keep staring at each other."

"I wasn't flirting!" Thaya shrilled, coughed, then lowered her voice. "I wasn't flirting. I know that man and he clearly recognises me, but it's...it's impossible! That man is Arto, the captain who saved me when the Vormae attacked us trying to leave Havendell Harbour. And, yes, it is absolutely impossible, unless he followed us through that worm-rip *thing*."

Arendor's eyes flashed peculiarly as if a light had passed within them before they turned dark again. An air of deep concentration and silence gathered around him. "Anything's possible. You might live short lives, but many of you choose to come back, and many are *forced* to come back by the Fallen Ones. That probably *is* the man you think it is, only in a new time and place."

Thaya stared at Arendor. Either he was mad or her world was crumbling. She had often entertained the idea of reincarnation the mystics from the west had described. The idea of an eternal soul in the Higher Realms choosing to incarnate in a singular physical body for the purposes of exploring external creation, and the lessons provided therein, was a concept she felt drawn to. But she never actually considered it a *reality*. For a moment, she just looked at him as her mind went into overdrive.

"All right," she said evenly. "How come he looks the same?"

"Easy. Often, though we have different parents in many lifetimes, the soul remembers the imprints of previous bodies and these are out-pictured in the final physical form. This is well known amongst many advanced races. There are differences, however, though mostly because the soul has chosen those differences. Look again—no don't stare like that! Discreetly...are you sure he's the same?"

Thaya waited until the man had turned to discuss something with the waiter. "Hmm, his hair is paler, and his nose bigger, but otherwise he's the same, I know it." *And still attractive,* she thought, but didn't say aloud. She blushed and looked away as the man turned back to cast her a glance.

"A more interesting question would be; why is he here, with us at this time and place?" asked Arendor.

"You think it means something?" she asked.

"Yes, everything means something, but what? If he is here with us now, there is a strong draw between your two souls, a connection in the past. Something that links you or draws you together."

Thaya didn't quite know what to say, she'd only spent a short time with Arto, not even enough to learn anything about the man. She shrugged. "I don't know. There's nothing obvious."

Cold air blasted into the room as new people entered the restaurant. Arendor looked beyond her to the door and froze, any remaining colour draining out of his already pallid face.

"We're leaving!" He downed his wine, plunged a hand into his pocket and threw coloured paper and coins onto the table. He grabbed his coat from the back of his chair and slung it on.

What's got into him? Thaya thought, looking at the newcomers; two men dressed in sharp black suits and their skin almost as pale as Arendor's. They, too, had dark hair and might have been Agaroths had they been taller and had more attractive features. Their eyes were black beneath low brows, and wide foreheads and heavy jaws made them look strong and bullish. The men were expressionless. She doubted they had any muscles in their faces to even smile, and they looked completely out of place, a strange air or energy hanging around them. *They're not human!* She didn't know how she knew, she just *knew*. Her stares were cut short as Arendor dragged her off her chair.

The strange men spotted them and one pointed. They reached into their jackets and pulled out black guns—like hers and Arendor's, only much smaller and stumpier. Everybody screamed and scrambled for the floor, knocking glasses and plates of food off the tables in their haste.

The first man fired.

Arendor moved with super-human speed, a blur in her eyes as he ducked the strange double bullets exploding from the gun. A shimmering thread connected the darts to the gun, missing the Agaroth and embedding themselves into a chair. The second man's gun fired.

Thaya tried to dodge and failed.

Two darts struck her. Immense pain exploded through her body as she convulsed. She fell to the sound of scream-ing, shouting and flaring light, the pain overwhelming her terror. Everything went blurry and muffled.

Slowly the pain receded, but her body was useless jelly that someone else was hefting around.

Cold city air engulfed her, helping to bring her round. It was not exactly fresh, but at least she was outside and it was Arendor who carried her like a rag-doll, and he was moving fast. He jerked and the ground suddenly sped away beneath them making her gasp. He landed on the edge of a three-story building and pirouetted along the wall like a ballerina, carrying her as if she weighed nothing.

He jumped again and she screamed as the familiar large domed building loomed below them. He landed with a thud and they slid down the dome, jarring to a stop upon a large, circular balcony.

Thaya moaned and lay there, struggling to get her bear-ings. "What the hell happened?" Her vocal cords trembled as he lifted her to half sitting and steadied her against the railings.

"Shhh," he said, and peered through the bars. He had his Fireshot at the ready.

Relaxed footsteps and the sound of people chatting in the streets below could be heard. The minutes passed slowly until Arendor dared to relax.

"You were tasered," he said. "It's an electric shock meant to neutralise you, rarely, it kills."

"Why? Who were they? Do they know me?" It didn't make any sense; she'd never met those men before.

"No, but obviously I was too slow taking out the CCTV," said Arendor. "I arrived late, thanks to the bloody traffic.

That was just one camera too, scores more will have seen you fall out of thin air, and some people watching would have seen and felt the portal opening. Anything unusual or paranormal, and the Fallen Ones' hybrids come, the Nedromas; soulless beings with dead eyes, and always dressed in black suits. And no, they are *not* human, they are alien hybrids employed by the evil running this place and much of the world. They work for the vampires, who themselves are also alien hybrids. We have to get out of here as soon as we can, they won't stop now."

Thaya remembered the vampires of legend; pale, human-like creatures with sharp fangs for drinking people's blood, and an allergy to sunlight. The worrying thing about *those* stories was that they were told as if they were actual historical events, and the vampires were described as real, unlike in most Urtharian fables.

"No, not *those* types of vampires." Arendor shook his head. "They died out centuries ago and were merely an experiment gone wrong. The real vampires in control *choose* to drink the blood of their victims, although they don't need to, to survive, and they choose to perform sacrifices—animals, humans, anything—to call upon demons and dark powers from fallen places. As I said, they are aliens, and to stay on this planet for longer they consume the blood and body parts of humans in order to look more human."

Thaya felt sick at the thought and wondered how much time Arendor had spent studying his enemies here. "And what about the Vormae? Are they here?"

Arendor looked at her and laughed. "Oh, they are good and well and in league with the human hybrids. The Vormae, the Nuakki, the Ordacs—they are *all* here, and many more 'baddies' to boot. Each and every person you've seen today? Well, they all carry, in varying amounts, the DNA—the blood—of the Fallen Ones. The human race is going down, baby, and this is how it's done. And what's more, no one out there believes it or knows about it. The Fallen Ones are hidden. They work in the shadows and they corrupt from within. Urtha's story is a long, sorry history, like every planet which has been infected by the evil ones. It began thousands of years before your time, on several occasions. Your people let them into Lonohassa, just like mine did on Arothia, and then they wreaked havoc as any virus does."

Thaya felt sick, the cheesy pizza not sitting right after being tasered then trundled at a gallop along the tops of buildings. Knowing the downfall of the entire human race was because of the actions of her Lonohassan ancestors made it even worse.

"But why? What do they want with us?"

"To do tests on us, to drink our blood and thus consume our living codes that will enable them temporary access to the planet's Star Portals. Then they can spread to other systems and infect them too. They wish to reach the Divine Creator and take it down too. They hunger for power and food, for they've cut themselves off from the light of the Infinite One and it can no longer sustain them. So they must feed off others, hence they are vampires. Perhaps even the Vormae are here right now, looking for you. Maybe *they* sent the Nedromas. Perhaps Shades don't work too well inside restaurants, who knows?

"Anyway, let's go. Time is against us now. We have to get inside this building and closer to the portal, it's the only thing that can get us out of here." He grabbed her hand and dragged her along again, half crouching to remain behind the railing.

"Wait, inside here there's a portal? What is this place?" She gasped for breath, struggling to keep up with him on jellied legs.

"St Paul's Cathedral," he explained. "Those Acolytes of Light you have in Havendell and elsewhere? Well, they're here too, doing what they do best—controlling religion. Only they're called something else to hide their history and identity. There's a portal here, and Portals are sacred places of reverence for all beings of any planet. So the evil ones take control of them and use their power for their own ends. The portal is still here, only its ancient purpose has been deliberately hidden from the people."

"Why would they bother?"

"To control them, silly," said Arendor, and smiled sympathetically at her. "A people who don't know their own history or the power at their fingertips are easy to control."

Thaya thought about the Old Temple again. "Yes, but even back in Havendell people have already forgotten their history, so not much has changed. They don't even want to know what went before."

They came to a thick wooden door, locked, handle-less, and impossible to budge. Arendor smoothed his hands over it and paused where there should have been a handle. She felt energy charge the air followed by the sound of two loud clicks. The door swung open towards them silently.

"How did you do that? Magic?" Thaya stared.

He dragged her into the darkness and pulled the door shut. "What, unlock the door? Some would call it that, yes, but it's easy, more of a trick."

"I can't do it," she said.

"You will, with training. I can show you. Since there isn't any magic left on this planet, or too little to mention, what I used was will, intention, and the energy of my soul, rather than using the planet's natural energy. Although it may be considered 'magic' my ability with it is incredibly weak here."

"I want you to teach me." Thaya imagined seeing no locked door as an obstacle, and the ability to go anywhere at will.

"Yes, in time, but not now," he whispered. "Let's get this over with."

They were going to find this portal and get out of here. Thaya couldn't wait. "So, you want me to lead us into the portal because I hold the keys to it in my blood?"

"You're finally getting it." His eyes flashed in the dark and the ease with which he moved suggested he could see perfectly well. "This place is dark," he added quietly.

"It's all right for you, I can't see anything." She stumbled against something hard, possibly a table.

"No, it's *dark,* evil, hard to breathe, and yet I sense the faintest glimmer of light. Focus on the feel of this place. Allow your spirit to read the energy. Can you feel it? You must hone the subtle skills given to you by our Creator; we all have them. You are so helpless, but you must become strong to survive, especially in this world."

Thaya nodded even though he couldn't see it. She was useless and a coward, and felt quite sorry for herself, really, for the world in which she had lived her whole life had been a complete lie, well, perhaps not a lie, but certainly not the truth. The world and cosmos were infinitely more incredible than she had ever bothered to imagine, and it was equally as dangerous and unfathomable, especially right at this moment.

Now that she focused upon it, the place did feel strange. She sensed darkness, but an unnatural darkness. It sat alongside a sense of hope, human hope, but down there in the depths beneath the building, a cold darkness lurked. The hope she sensed was a candle in that darkness. It was cold too; she could see her breath now, but outside it had been warm.

Arendor moved and she followed, bumping into tables and chairs and cursing each time. She was glad when they paused at another door. He opened it a crack and candle-light spilled in. He peered through and a moment later opened it further and stuck his head out to look left and right.

"Anything?" asked Thaya.

"Not really. Focus on the portal, try to feel it."

Thaya closed her eyes but could only see darkness, a thick swirling mass of black liquid tar that was mesmerising and pulling her into it. She opened her eyes and took a sharp breath.

"Did you see it? The blackness?" he asked. She nodded. "But nothing else?" She shook her head.

He held his breath wondering what to do. "Let's get to the ground floor and try again."

Crouching low, they exited the dark room onto a walkway and bannisters. The domed roof rose high above them and candlelight flickered against the ornate cornices of the upper building. They ran along a floor paved with stark black and white tiles, trying to keep as quiet as possible.

Sticking to the scant shadows, he led her down a winding staircase. Footsteps sounded, hard soles on marble flooring getting closer and closer. Arendor pressed himself back against the wall and held his finger to his lips.

The footsteps paused and a man cleared his throat. "Come out, there's no need to hide from us," his polished voice crooned.

Arendor leaned his head back and let go of his breath. Then he lifted his hand and moved his fingers in quick darting motions. His rings flashed brightly, and a shadowy mist quickly gathered around them. Swiftly he ran, pulling her behind him, the shadowy mist following. They burst into the main hall, skittered across the black and white tiled floor, and fell behind a large altar dominating one side of the room.

Thaya glimpsed a figure standing on the edges of the candlelight on the other side of the room. He stood with hands on hips, a gold ring of a square design on his little finger catching the light, and his head cocked expectantly. He, like Arendor, was dressed in black save for a blood red lining to his very long black jacket.

"Stay here or get to safety when I create a distraction," whispered Arendor, his eyes gleaming dangerously. He reminded her of a cat about to leap on a mouse.

"Who is it?" asked Thaya.

"One of them; a blood-drinker. Human for the most part yet works for the dark ones. I can smell and see it all over him. One alone is not dangerous, for me at least, and they have poor magic, but we don't want to bring more. We need to keep a low profile. Can you feel the portal?"

Thaya closed her eyes and felt for that familiar dark energy, and a kind of pulling towards an opening. She let go of her breath and shook her head. "Nothing." However, she still 'saw' in her mind's eye that faint glow of light far away.

Arendor sighed. "Okay, never mind. Let's assume it's not functioning and get the hell out. I'll get rid of this guy, you make it to the door, okay?"

Thaya nodded though her palms became instantly sweaty.

She must have looked terrified for he paused, and his

face softened. "Feel for the portal, Thaya, you can do it. It's somewhere here or not too far away. Don't tremble like that, find your courage, for it is also there, somewhere within you."

Before she could respond, Arendor jumped up and ran out into the open.

19

HUNTING STAR PORTALS

GRABBING HER FIRESHOT, THAYA PEERED AROUND THE ALTAR.

Arendor retained his cloak of shadows as he moved across the floor, nothing more than a faint spectre. The other man's eyes were drawn to the shadow and a smile twisted his lips. So, he could see magic then, and he had some skills. Hopefully, Arendor had not underestimated his opponent. *He's been alive for the gods know how many years and he knows what he's doing, there's nothing to fear.*

Too transfixed to move, she watched as the shadows thickened and Arendor emerged from the sooty black. With his back to her, he strode towards the man, Fireshot clenched at his side, and flickers of light dancing around his free hand. He moved like a cat, shoulders bunched, head lowered.

"Ahh, there you are. My, you really *aren't* human, are you?" the other man said, a look of wonder on his face and a strange hunger in his eyes. The man was handsome, there was no denying it, with a straight nose, flawless skin, perfectly arched eyebrows, and yet he repulsed her. He was enrapturing, and yet she wanted to run as far away from him as possible.

Arendor raised his Fireshot and fired.

The other man moved with uncanny speed, a blur in which his human form changed and became more...*reptilian*. His skin mottled to a faded green and his face extended into a blunt snout, but it was his eyes that really gave it away—large golden orbs split down the middle with a black pupil. Those snake eyes narrowed with hatred and the man-reptile dodged the flaming ball. It smashed against the wooden wall panels behind him, extinguishing in a spray of sparks and leaving a smoking blast mark. The man stopped moving and his human form returned.

Thaya blinked, not believing what she had just seen, had Arendor seen that? He must have.

"Where's the other one, the girl? She arrived like you did five years ago. We have the footage and we know you've been returning to that place often." The man grinned and pointed up at a small black box nestled in the corner of the ceiling. It was similar to the one Arendor had destroyed. "And now we have this footage."

Without making a sound Arendor raised his left hand, silver rings gleaming, curled his fingers as if gripping something and pulled down clenching his fingers together. The camera was torn from the ceiling and crumpled in the air. Not just one camera was wrenched from the wall but all five dotted around the room were torn from their nails and clattered in pieces upon the floor.

The man's smile faded as Arendor's smile grew. The deadly look on the Agaroths' face scared Thaya more than the strange man. *A warrior race bent on revenge and always willing to fight to the death...*

"You only need to worry about me, Inigo Price," said Arendor quietly.

The other man grinned. "A psychic, very good, we're in for a fun night. And we can see clearly that you're not of this world, so where are you from? Where is she from?"

Arendor threw his free hand forward. Shadows shot from his fingers straight at the reptilian man, wrapping around him and lifting him bodily from the floor. He squirmed and struggled but could not break free. Arendor clenched his fist and the shadows tightened, choking the man until he spluttered and his face turned red.

Cold hands grabbed Thaya, hauling her off of her feet into a powerful grip before she could yell. Another figure clad in black loomed in front of her. Instinctively she raised and fired her Fireshot. Beyond the flaring ball, she glimpsed the dark face of a woman with predatory eyes and red lips twisted into a smirk. Those lips opened to scream as the shot hit her square in the chest. She made no sound as fire and shadows engulfed her. The shadows quickly became black ash that scattered on the floor. Nothing remained of the woman but a heap of soot.

Thaya couldn't breathe. Too shocked to fight the arms that tightened around her, she hung limply. She'd just killed a woman, with the tap of her finger, she was gone. The Fireshot was wrenched from her flaccid hand and she became aware of a man growling behind her. Two more black-robed people stalked forwards, a man and a woman whose eyes blazed in fury.

Thaya lost them from view as the man choking her swung her into the main room. "Let him go!" he growled.

Arendor paused, turning slightly to regard her helpless state. A flicker of annoyance passed over his face and he paused throttling the man called Inigo. Taking his time, he lowered the man to the floor and released his grip until the shadows let him go.

Inigo crawled on his hands and knees, choking and gasping.

"Restrain him," growled the man who held Thaya.

The man and woman padded towards Arendor, strange thin plastic strips in their hands. Other men and women emerged out of the far doors, their black robes with the blood-red lining swishing on the floor as they strode.

Thaya's eyes were drawn to Arendor. The Agaroth had slipped a ring from his finger and surveyed the humans striding towards him from all directions. The ring flashed in his palm, making Thaya wonder if it was reflected light or the ring itself, then he tossed it into the air and hurled himself at the nearest man and woman, bowling them to the floor.

Time slowed.

The ring flipped over, spinning and glinting as it reached its highest point before pausing then tumbling to the floor.

Arendor was already up and moving so fast he was virtually flying towards her. He flicked his fingers forward. The man restraining her grunted, convulsed, and released her. In the chaotic blur, the faces of the people were locked into screams and curses, their eyes wild with fury.

The ring hit the floor with a tiny 'clink' and sent ripples out through the black and white tiles like a pebble dropped into a pond.

"The floor." Thaya stared. "It isn't solid!"

Arendor grabbed her as the ring bounced and hit the floor again. Everything turned hazy and insubstantial apart from the Agaroth pulling her off her feet. The people faded into grey mist and the whole world vanished. Shouting could be heard, but it was muffled and distant.

"Can you run?" asked Arendor, his voice was loud but distorted.

"I think so," Thaya said, though very much doubted it. Even her voice sounded weird.

She found solid ground beneath her feet and Arendor took her hand, dragging her onwards. They pelted through a grey mist that became thicker and thicker until it was like wading through soup.

After several yards, the density began to lighten, and she breathed cool night air. The mist started to fade and ahead a grey road and cars became visible. She glanced back to see the ominous cathedral towering into the sky. Somehow his magic had enabled them to run through the walls!

Arendor urged her along faster.

People appeared out of the dissipating grey mist, strange men in uniform with black caps and bright yellow vests with 'Police' written on the back. She stared at the black and white chequered ribbons around their hats just like the chequered flooring of the cathedral.

Reality sharpened and she noticed the entire front of the cathedral and beyond had been cordoned off with tape upon which was also written 'Police'. The uniformed people surrounded the entire building and were clearly hunting for something, but they didn't even look in their direction, the fast disappearing grey mist had hidden their exit. Any passersby who got too close to the cathedral were quickly ushered back by the police. *They're not trying to help; they're trying to keep people out! Are they working with the black-robed people inside?*

"*They are.*"

She heard Arendor's unmistakable voice in her mind,

not her ears. She stared at him, but there was no time to question, for the grey mist faded further and the Agaroth ran faster. Their feet beat on the pavement as they hurtled down the street, and people moved out of their way, proving they were now visible.

When they finally lost sight of the cathedral, Arendor slowed. He stopped inside the mouth of a dark side street, Thaya bent over gasping for breath. The Agaroth wasn't even breathing hard.

What had happened? Were they safe? Heart pounding, Thaya closed her eyes and behind closed lids saw something strange. A pale light that wasn't there when she opened them. She calmed herself and focused on it. There it was again! A definite strange energetic pulling sensation.

"Let's keep moving," said Arendor.

"No, wait, I feel something. And it's coming from over there." She pointed across the street.

"A portal?" Arendor's eyes lit up.

Thaya chewed her lip. "How could I know? But I feel something pulling, and a faint light when I close my eyes."

"I think it is. Hurry, lead the way." He shooed her onward.

She trotted along the street, the pull growing stronger until it brought her to the front of a shop. An ornate metal grate covered the wall of the lower section below the window, and she bent down to stare through the bars to see a pane of thick glass. Beyond, all she glimpsed was the rough stone of an unimpressive boulder.

"'The London Stone,'" Arendor said, reading the small plaque on the grate which she had ignored.

Thaya closed her eyes. "The energy, the light, it appears to be coming from this stone. But how can this be a portal? It isn't possible."

"Yes, it is," Arendor whispered and knelt beside her. He peered through the grate and his eyes filled with longing. "And it's our way out of here. Ancient structures hold a lot of power, given to them by the powerful Magi of the past. This would have once been part of a greater structure. Incredible that power remains, even in this tiny fragment."

Thaya had trouble imagining the rock may have once looked like the Old Temple in Brightwater. "That's an ancient structure? Even so, it's locked behind a grate and sealed by thick glass, we can't even get close."

"Indeed." Arendor rubbed his smooth chin. "Alternatively, why was any of it preserved at all? Someone must have known. Let's find a way in, we need to be able to touch it."

He felt around the wall and pulled on the grate which didn't budge. "No luck. We'll have to get to it from the other side."

"I don't know about this," Thaya murmured. She looked down the street and licked her lips. Streetlights illuminated everything and though there was no one there the Black Robes could arrive at any moment.

Being the middle of the night, the door was, of course, firmly locked, and Thaya didn't fancy breaking in—yet their lives depended on it. The Black Robes and police were hunting for them.

"Use your magic trick, you know, the 'unlock door' one," she urged.

Arendor was already holding his hands over the complicated-looking lock. She heard many clicks, and then he simply pushed it open. She shook her head in amazement. With a quick look around them, he dragged her inside and closed the door.

Another door barred their way, this time made of thick

glass. Again, Arendor held up his hands and the door unlocked with a few clicks. They entered cautiously and crouched down by the wall next to the stone. Another grate and pane of glass blocked their access.

Thaya sighed. "Well, we have to get it off. At least in here we'll have privacy."

At her words, Arendor lifted his hand, clenched his fingers and pulled. Behind them, a camera was wrenched from the wall and crushed into pieces. "I almost forgot; we may have been too late for that one."

"They're everywhere," said Thaya. 'To prevent crime or to look for people like us?'

Arendor laughed briefly, a rare sound. "I'd like to think we were that important. They serve many purposes, for the master likes to look after his slaves. Right then, we have to try harder. Let's hope no one can hear or feel this."

He took hold of the grate and closed his eyes. There was a faint rumbling and then a loud squeaking. The thick screws locking it against the wall began unscrewing and one by one fell to the floor. He wrenched the grate free and set it down.

The next barrier, a thick pane of glass, was completely sealed into the wall with no way of unlocking or opening it.

Arendor sighed this time. "Okay, we'll do it the old-fashioned way." Arranging his rings, he punched the glass so fast his hand was a blur. The glass shattered but did not fall to the ground as she expected. He pushed his Fireshot into it and wrenched pieces away to make a hole large enough to fit a hand through. He looked at her expectantly.

"I just need to touch it?" asked Thaya. It was too simple, surely she had to cast a spell or invoke some god?

"Will it. Call to mind your Lonohassa, where you wish to

go. Ask it clearly to take you home or to a place more powerful than this so we can get out of here."

Thaya nodded and took a deep breath. The Agaroth knelt behind her and placed two strong hands on her shoulders. She closed her eyes. The pull was definitely coming from the stone, it was somehow calling to her and was that joy she sensed, too? Joy coming from the stone that someone had finally recognised what it was.

With an encouraging nod from Arendor, she held a clear vision of Lonohassa and placed her hand upon the cold hard stone.

Shock waves coursed through her; cool, sharp, shaking her entire body. It came through her hand and flooded out of her into the stone, an exchange of essence, information, will and desire. A torrent of energy filling her body and mind with images and feelings; fury, devotion, ecstasy and emptiness.

She found herself standing alone upon a grassy hill, forest and hills rolling away all around her, and a cold wind whipping up her hair. *The stone!* To her right, her palm still touched the stone, it looked as it had a moment ago only it was wild and free, no longer caged like an animal. It was telling her something, showing her what it remembered.

Everything vanished.

She looked down at the ground as a bird might and glided gracefully through the wind currents over a treeless plain. In the distance appeared a ring of enormous ancient stones standing like Magi frozen in the mist. Their grey surfaces smoothed by the aeons were identical to the caged stone she had just touched. Suddenly she was hurtling towards them.

As she neared, light flared, saturating everything until there was only light. A soft rumbling pushed back the silence and wind rushed past her. The world jolted and she fell hard onto grass, arms sprawling to keep her face out of the mud. Arendor thudded beside her feet first and jumped nimbly to a stop as if he had done this a thousand times before.

"Urgh!" Her whole body felt as if it were spinning. Blades of grass danced in front of her face, and above, a night sky filled with hundreds of stars lit up a wide-open plane. Strange mounds dotted the land all the way to the horizon, and apart from the odd copse, it was mostly flat grassland.

She enjoyed a brief moment of calm to take in the view before her stomach clenched. Barely making it onto her knees, a horrific noise rose up from her gut to her throat and she hurled the contents of her stomach onto the grass.

"Dear gods, why?" she gasped between wretches.

She could do nothing but endure. Thankfully it was short-lived, and her stomach slowed its churning. With shaking arms, she pushed herself onto her haunches, smoothed the hair back from her sweaty face, and drank from her flask. Why the hell did that always happen?

"Are you all right?" Arendor approached her cautiously now she had stopped spewing everywhere. He squeezed her shoulder.

She nodded and wiped her forehead.

"Hmm, I thought we'd come here," said the Agaroth looking thoughtfully around him. "But...but this isn't it. I've been here so many times I can't even count them, but it doesn't lead where we need to go."

"Where's here?" Fighting the dizziness, Thaya got onto her feet.

"Stonehenge," said the Agaroth.

"Stone what?" Thaya frowned and looked at the enormous stones.

Arendor nodded at them. "Far more ancient than they tell the tourists visiting, and designed for a purpose no one in this present reality could ever fathom. It's not to map the stars or the rising sun specifically, and it certainly isn't for sacrifice or burial, although dark deeds have certainly been committed here." He became withdrawn and spoke as if to himself as he surveyed the land. "I can feel that darkness keenly; there's a whole ocean of it occurring right now far beneath our feet, but I will *not* get side-tracked. I must keep my attention only on the current problem, and those people cannot be helped. There is so much darkness in this world, it would take aeons to fix it all, and then, maybe the solution is more simple..."

"Funny looking henge." Thaya shivered and broke him out of his dark reverie. "What is it exactly? Why would the stone bring us here? And what was it created for anyway?"

She walked towards the stones and clambered over the ropes enclosing them. A trilithon towered above her, and she laid a hand upon it. The world darkened, the sound of her sharply inhaled breath echoed, and she was sucked rapidly forwards and backwards, and yet the stone remained before her unmoving. Beneath her hand, the stone's surface became smooth and unweathered, its edges sharper. *How can that be?*

Every single stone in the circle was now topped with a lintel forming a perfect ring and a hazy mist drifted around their bases. Tall, slender figures moved in the mist, white-robed people gracefully stepping between the stones, wide hoods loosely covering their heads. They were singing, their gentle voices creating an odd vibration she could detect in the stone beneath her palm. The words were more like sound tones and incantations, moving through her as they did the stones, each tone spoken precisely and deliberately.

Thaya stared entranced at the spectacle. There were equal numbers of men and women, and they walked and turned in perfect unison as they intoned. It was a strange mesmerising slow dance where they raised their hands to the heavens every now and then. It had a strange effect; the energy of the place became charged, powerful, awaiting, it made her both sleepy yet fully aware, as if in a waking dream.

Their singing and dancing were deliberately performed, but why? As if in answer to her question, thoughts came from the stone itself, but she didn't have the concepts to describe them. It was like a tide of darkness sweeping towards her from far beyond the planet. It hit the stones and collected there as if drawn to them, then it rose up the uprights, flowed along the top lintels then down the other upright into the ground where it was sent back to wherever it had come from. *The stones, they're channelling the darkness away!* Whatever the people were doing, it was somehow helping this to happen.

But what is this darkness, exactly? No, don't look at it! But the flowing blackness was seductive, drawing upon her, willing her to follow it. The scene darkened until she could barely see the white figures. Their singing faded and distorted noises replaced them. Down below her feet, evil pooled in caverns; man-made caverns filled with giant crystals.

"Crystals aren't evil," she whispered.

"No, but they are powerful and can be used to do evil,"

Arendor's voice echoed in her mind. Where was he? She couldn't see him.

Wailing came from somewhere, mournful and pain-filled.

"Return now!" the Agaroth commanded.

A loud clack sounded from somewhere, and she blinked. The blackness and the stones and the people vanished, and she stood swaying on the grassy plain beside the weathered old stone.

Arendor's pale face was luminous. "We cannot help them."

"Help who?" Thaya frowned.

"Never mind, just don't look at the darkness. We must get on with the task at hand, we're being followed."

Why wouldn't he answer the question? The thought of the reptilian vampires arriving stopped her pursuing it and she followed him.

"What you saw," he continued, "was what this place does and where it's connected. It's a giant plug—" he struggled for words when she frowned, "—a device that forms a connection to another device. In this case, the stones are the plug, the connecting point, and sadly it is not connected to Lonohassa, where we need to go."

"So where does it connect then? I held the intention of Lonohassa." Thaya's frown deepened.

"That stone in London is connected to these stones and to *all* stones, all stones that have been charged, that is— look, we don't have time for this," the Agaroth shook his head, wondering where to begin. "That stone brought us here because it's connected to these stones, but also because this place must be closer to our objective. What you witnessed, I witnessed, too. It was the creation of this place —incidentally it was created long before even your time."

Arendor sighed and his shoulders sagged. "Your Lono-hassan Magi understand these things better, and if they had been doing their duty of teaching and sharing knowledge properly, all of the peoples of Urtha would understand too, and the planet would not be falling! So just believe me when I say that the darkness you see is coming from a black hole, a place of dead light, a place—a universe in fact—that is utterly fallen."

Thaya inhaled sharply at the thought. An entire universe feeding upon others. It was hard to imagine.

The Agaroth lifted his hands. "This place, this Stone-henge, seeks to re-route the black energy and send it back to where it came from. But the darkness gathers here as a result. Let me tell you there are people enslaved just beneath our feet, humans like you. They suffer unimagin-ably at the hands of the Fallen Ones here, right now. They are born into darkness and they die in darkness with no one above ground even knowing of their existence. They are fed to the evil flowing here to keep it flowing in abundance. I hear their voices and I see their faces, but we have to leave, now.

"You would drown in moments if you knew all the dark-ness in all the worlds in all the eras. Focus, Thaya, focus on getting us out before we become trapped here. Focus on the Saphira-elaysa whose calling burns within you every moment of every day. Yes, I can see your thoughts, you know this, barely a moment goes by when you do not think of your twin soul. If you do not find him, you both will wither and die."

Thaya stared into his penetrating black eyes, seeing intelligence and a world reflected back she could barely imagine. The things he must know...she was barely a child to him. He pushed into her mind images of the Pure Ones;

beings of light with spiralling golden horns, and from them all, *he* stepped forwards, burnished silver and indigo glory banishing the world of horrors from her mind. She found herself nodding back at Arendor.

He smiled faintly. "Good, now I need you to focus. Where is the Star Portal? It's somewhere close, the London Stone wouldn't have portalled us here if it wasn't. Now I know what you're thinking, but don't assume it must be another stone, otherwise it would have taken us to that stone instead. Ancient stones like these are markers, they are not necessarily the Portals themselves. Besides, the crust of planets shift—especially beleaguered ones—and markers come out of the alignment. Focus."

Thaya struggled to clear her racing mind of thoughts. She had an overwhelming and desperate need to run home and shut herself away in her bedroom. *Those days are gone, they can never be brought back, and now my life is a whirlwind where there is only be and do and survive.*

20

WHERE ANGELS FEAR TO TREAD

THAYA LOOKED FROM ARENDOR AND OUT OVER THE ENDLESS plain stretching under the stars, the cool wind gently lifting the hair from her shoulders.

Reality is not what I thought it was, not even close. The world is far too large for me and I'm cast out alone within it. An icy breeze touched her soul and she shivered. *Out there is a gateway, a Star Portal that will take us home, I must find it. I must.*

She closed her eyes and a clear vision awaited her as if it had been there all along. She saw herself from above, hovering like a bird as she had been earlier. She floated forwards and described what she saw. "I see us and green lands, rolling hills, only I'm in the air looking down. There are fields below the hills, filled with crops, but no portal is discernible.

"Hmm, wait, I see..."

Her vision gently rolled over a field and a large, geometric shape with perfect intricate lines was revealed in the crops below. "Someone, some-*thing*, has *drawn* an enormous shape in the crops, circles flowing into each other and then outwards. It's beautiful, and it's...*powerful.*" Energy hummed around the shape and it sparkled when she looked harder.

Arendor's voice came from far away. "Yes, crop circles, they mark places of power as well—the giving or leaching of power. Most are grown rather than drawn. One mustn't forget that control is power. Some of the geometric designs are negative and created by the Fallen Ones from adjacent dimensions. Other shapes are created by those of the light to undo them, a kind of counteractive positive energy. Think of how spells and enchantments work, these crop circles are similar in a world devoid of magic. Sadly, the people here do not know what they are. Regardless, they are not what we are looking for. Keep looking..."

Arendor's voice faded and her vision moved forwards again. A high bank of hills and a white shape carved into it came into view. She stared at the enigmatic figure. "I see a horse, a white horse, and yet, and yet, surely it was a unicorn once?" Her voice was a whisper, and she knew it was foolish and not the truth to think it had been a unicorn and not a horse, but in that instance, she felt for all the world that this was a message only for her, that here lay what she sought.

Arendor spoke, his voice urgent, but she only half-heard parts of it as she stared at the horse. "White horses abound in the landscape, there...we cannot possibly...try looking for more..."

It's a message for me, surely? "Find me," the horse figure said. "Search for me with all your heart, and I'll be there."

Thaya opened her eyes. "It's there," she said quietly, so quietly the effect was as if she had shouted.

Arendor paused mid-sentence and stared at her. With the briefest nod, he said, "Take us there."

"North." She nodded in that direction and set off at a jog.

As they moved over the land, she tried to match what she saw from the ground with her vision from above. It quickly became obvious that what didn't seem far whilst floating above it, was miles away on foot.

Their journey lit only by starlight, Thaya and Arendor forged their way through fields and copses, passing several strange mounds, and a few lone standing stones that had never quite made it to the henge and given up where they stood. Every time she wanted to rest, every time her legs complained, she imagined the vampires behind them or the police in their strange dark uniforms and chequered hats, and she pushed onwards without pause. She imagined being caged deep beneath the ground in endless dark caverns, no one ever knowing of her pain or her existence, and those thoughts made her forget about her fatigue and pushed her onwards.

"That's what will happen if they catch us," said Arendor. She had become so used to him replying to her thoughts—and still so incapable of controlling them—that she didn't even blink anymore. "They'll test on us, do painful things, try to extract our power. They'll drink our blood, and take my seed and your eggs and create beings from them, our Great Creator only knows what—"

"Stop it!" Thaya shouted, halting.

He stopped short. "Sorry, it's just, I know what they do. It vexes me that I cannot stand and fight them. I would do something if I could."

"I just don't need to hear anything like that right now." Thaya scowled.

"Right, of course, sorry."

She carried on and tried not to think about what he had said, thankful she couldn't read his thoughts.

They came to a fence bordering a wheat field and clambered over it onto tractor tracks. A farmhouse stood two fields away, a square ominous shadow in a dark landscape. Better not get too close, farmers always had dogs, and that's the last thing they needed chasing them.

It was difficult keeping a direct route to the white horse she saw in her mind. Pushing through the undergrowth, wading through mud, and anything else in their path was slow going.

When they came to a road headed in the right direction, she started along it with a relieved sigh.

"No." Arendor took her arm and steered her across it to another fence.

"Hey, why can't we use the damned road? We'll get there much faster," she hissed as he trundled her over the fence and into the trees.

"Because." He spun her around. "Look."

Through the trees and away along the road, a lone car slunk, its headlights blindingly bright. It approached slowly, too slowly. The lights flashed in their direction as it rounded the bend.

"Get down."

He forced them down into the gorse. She stifled a squeak as thorns scraped her arms. The car prowled past, its backlights gleaming red. Another slow-moving car followed several yards behind it. She let out a breath, pulse-quickening.

"And they're just the ones we can see." Staying low, Arendor led her away from the road and into the bushes. "Keep moving. Dawn is not as far away as I would like."

Knowing they were being tracked made her even more

weary and frightened. She longed to sleep, to sink into the grass or even the mud and close her eyes. But whenever she closed her eyes, even just to blink, those bright headlights were there, hunting.

They approached another fence and clambered over it silently, too tired to speak, once more pushing through endless ferns and brambles the other side.

Two more fences and three fields later, the sky began to brighten into a pretty pink as they staggered through a field of barley. *Better stick closer to the hedges in the growing light,* she thought, and copied Arendor ducking down lower in the exposed gaps between the fields.

A hill rose ahead of them. She prayed it was her hill. They passed the last tree and her heart leapt. "The white horse!"

It was another mile away, maybe more, but there it was. A beacon of whiteness in the darkness of the hill tinged pink with the onset of dawn.

"Yes, but do not slow, I think we've been spotted." Arendor grabbed her arm stopping her from looking behind. She could barely place one weary foot in front of another. "Can you feel it? It will be a specific spot or at least a concentration of energies. You have to find the strongest point."

Thaya was so tired she doubted she would feel anything, but when she closed her eyes, she felt the energy as strong as ever and it was tireless, unlike her body. "Forwards, I feel it pulling stronger now." It was the right place. She imagined returning home to Lonohassa and grinned. *Returning to another nightmare!* She forced the grin to remain.

She paused at the base of the hill and stared. It was much steeper than it had looked in the distance or from above. Well, there was no point delaying. She started the climb towards the white patch that was the horse.

Her boot scraped a pale rock and she picked it up. "Chalk," she muttered, noting the smudges of white it left on her fingers.

A little further and the energy was positively humming. Thank the gods her feelings were right.

"Do not think of 'gods' for there is only One True Creator of All," said Arendor beside her. "The rest are, at best, pretenders. At worst, they are deceivers, evil, and nothing but the creators of the Fallen Ones who are bent on destroying the light and all those from it. The 'gods' of Lonohassa of which you speak *are* imposters, invaders posing as gods who wow and woo your leaders."

Thaya smarted. What Arendor said was blasphemous and most people would be put to death for it, but he could be forgiven for he was not from Urtha. She thought of the 'gods' most people worshipped and called down curses from or gave thanks to in their daily speeches; Cirulef the light bearer, god of the Acolytes of Light; of Zinith the Dark, and of Eed the Nameless One. Imposters and deceivers...she never liked their holy books full of fire and brimstone.

"Aliens, invaders, all of them." The Agaroth pressed, side-glancing her to be sure she heard as they staggered upwards. "Eed is not one being, but a collective of Ordac High Priest half-breeds from a fallen matrix. Nameless because there are so many of them!

"Zinith is long absent. A Fallen One of great power who came to Urtha a million years ago and influenced the people incredibly negatively. She is not a god, not even in her own system—a fallen system with a black star which has moved so far away from Urtha's and fallen so deep into the dark, you will never see that 'god' again. Your people are praying to an absent god, no wonder their prayers don't get answered.

"And if you ever see Cirulef and his minions, run, run, run."

Thaya listened speechless as Arendor railed out blasphemy, half expecting the gods to strike him down where he stood. An Illumined Acolyte would have frothed at the mouth and passed out had he heard the Agaroths' words. She was never one for religion, the austere temples that dominated the landscape scared her, and the sombre clerics made her shiver, but what Arendor spewed out was hard to hear, and if a cleric were near, he would be flayed and hung outside the temples.

"*Flayed and hung...that's not the action of a loving god, is it?*" Arendor's voice echoed in her mind.

"No, I suppose not," she said aloud.

"Indeed," agreed Arendor. "Forgive me, but I cannot watch you do this to yourself. You should know these things. At least tell others on your planet—some already know—though it will make your life undoubtedly hard back in Brightwater."

Thaya nodded dumbly. The Agaroth spoke the truth, and yet her *religion* had just been stripped easily from her, his words tearing her beliefs away as easily as unwrapping a parcel. Was there any good god or any reason to anything? In a matter of moments, she had been spiritually flayed.

Arendor spoke in a softer tone, though how he could speak walking up this steep hill at all was beyond her. "Do not cling to that which no longer serves, fill it with something better. Fill it with the truth. Think only upon the True Creator." Arendor smiled faintly and placed in her mind images of white golden light. It grew within her, surrounding her, filling her with warmth and peace. Forgetting the Old Gods, her mind and spirit became filled with a desire to know this True Creator.

The light he put in her mind faded, much to her disappointment. She looked at Arendor who now stood in the centre of the white horse, his arms raised expectantly and his eyes burning with thoughts of home. His gaze travelled back the way he had come, and he lowered his arms. "And speaking of Lonohassa...let's get to it. We'd better move quickly."

Thaya followed his gaze and her blood turned cold. Running through the fields of barley they had just passed were scores of men, all dressed in black suits, all exactly the same as if they were exact replicas of each other. *They ARE copies of each other, I can feel it as the truth. But how?*

"Clones." The thought in her mind came from Arendor. *"Biological entities created from the blood-codes—DNA as they call it here—from one individual. Highly expendable soldiers. And no, they have no souls."*

Clones? The thought alone made her shiver.

Swallowing, she closed her eyes. The portal energy was there, waiting, pulsing. She needed to touch something, to earth herself like the protective lightning catchers did back home. She dropped to her knees and dug her fingers into the chalk, opening herself to the energy of the place. It filled her in powerful waves of darkness and light. Wind roared in her ears and rolled through her body, tugging at her hair and clothes.

Arendor was shouting, but she couldn't make out his words in the rushing din. Loud bangs and flashes boomed beyond the crescendoing energy, but there was nothing she could do to help him, the power of this place held her completely. She couldn't breathe, and either the ground was falling away or she was rising above it for there was nothing solid beneath her anymore. *It's working, it's really working!*

A hand grabbed her shoulder, silver rings gleaming brightly in the strange light, reassuring her. Arendor commanded an element of directional control and he pushed her forwards, adeptly traversing the Star Portal. The loud bangs and shouting faded away in a roar of energy.

The Agaroth's firm grip prevented her from spinning out of control, but he couldn't stop her stomach somersaulting and already she felt sick.

"We're going home!" Arendor said in her mind. His voice was filled with a joy she had never seen him express physically.

She didn't dare relax, not until she saw the lands of Lonohassa firmly beneath her feet.

The energy built until she thought she would explode, and light flashed so brightly she couldn't see. An immense rushing sensation filled her as the energy moved. It was too much to process and she began to detach, drifting somewhere between the Star Portal and semi-consciousness.

The light dimmed. She floated slowly for several blissful moments, then slammed into the earth and rolled helplessly.

"Guh." She came to a stop upon cold, hard rock, her body quivering and every muscle in her body turned to jelly. Her stomach lurched, and she catapulted onto her hands and knees and heaved.

It lasted a long time.

When it finally subsided, the weakness and dizziness remained. Trying to focus she stared up into Arendor's joyful face. The biggest smile curved his lips—this was the happiest she had ever seen him. They were on top of a mountain, the same mountain housing the Star Portal to Arothia, and a frozen landscape slumbered in the dusk-light. The wind whipped snow as hard as ice around them making her shiver and long for the gentle green slopes and warm summer winds they had just left.

"That was unfortunately fast," a deep, non-human voice said. "Did it not work?"

Thaya stared at the Gryphon who stood just beyond Arendor. The eagle-lion was poised at the edge of the crater as if he was just about to take off.

Arendor made a shrill noise, almost like a laugh, and sunk into the snow. He scooped up handfuls of the stuff and rubbed it into his face. Thaya pushed herself away from her own vomit and shoved snow into her mouth, the frozen water bringing cool clarity despite her shoulders shaking from the cold, the journey, and disbelief.

Arendor stood and came over. He wrapped an arm around her and helped her to her feet. "It looks like we have returned at the very moment we exited. We made it, after so, so long. That was *awful!*"

Thaya raised her eyebrows, trying to compose herself. If she was having trouble taking it all in, she could barely imagine what Arendor was going through.

"Honourable Vassa." He inclined his head respectfully to the Gryphon, and the eagle-lion nodded appreciatively as the Agaroth spoke. "Please assist us further, for we have been to hell and back. Five years have passed for me, and a day or so for Thaya fleeing the Fallen Ones. Please take her to the Leonites far to the south. You will be richly rewarded by us, the Agaroths, with anything you require, I promise you."

"Anything?" the Gryphon's ears twitched.

"Anything," said Arendor and walked towards the

Gryphon, beseeching. "Please take her immediately before more evil befalls us. I would go with you, but for the first time in my long life, I feel utterly weak. I must return home, to Arothia, to regain my strength. I will need only a few days to regenerate my power, my resolve, my health, then I will return to you."

He held a hand up to brush Thaya's face. She took it and squeezed. "I can only imagine how you must feel." After five long years in hell, he would be returning to an empty home without his partner. It would not be a happy time for him, and pain stabbed her heart.

The Gryphon eyed the Agaroth as the man approached. "And why must she go there?" Vassa asked, but after a moment's thought added, "Is this place warm?"

Arendor paused before him and nodded. "Yes, and tropical and filled with warm-blooded animals and high peaks upon which to land." Arendor's eyes sparkled. Without waiting for confirmation, he spun around and strode back to Thaya, his black cloak flapping, the fire still alight in his eyes. "Please understand, brave little Thaya, I cannot help you whilst I am weak. I will bring others with me when I return. I see you still have the ring; this is good, I will use it to find you."

He touched the ring, making it grow warm and glow a faint orange. She wanted to say something but was too tired to make any decisions or even to think clearly. She longed for rest, for warmth and sleep, and a huge dinner or breakfast, whatever time it was. But she didn't want him to go at all. The thought of being alone, in this world or any other filled her with dread.

It was so cold, she stammered. "You must g-go, return home. You've been g-gone years, whilst for me, it has been d-days."

He took her face in his cold hands, looked into her eyes, and spoke directly into her mind, *"I see within you untapped power, bravery, a soul that can become strong if you but let it. Conquer your fears, find your courage, and you will go where even angels fear to tread. The light of the Creator burns within you, let it shine."*

She placed her hands over his and blinked away tears. "I'll try," she rasped.

"You've come so far in just the short time we have been together. The fastest Star Portal learner I have ever known," he smiled.

"Necessity," Thaya said bashfully. "I can find them but not control them."

"In time," Arendor said and kissed her forehead. He whirled away.

Thaya chewed her lip as the Agaroth lifted his palms to the sky. His silver rings, bracelets and chains pulsed with white light, and she felt energy gather fast around him. The light grew into a throbbing oblong of pure white-blue that surrounded him. He lifted a hand in farewell, and in a flash, he was gone.

The Gryphon stood beside Thaya; the heat of his body very welcome. More than anything she craved companionship, and this Gryphon, for all his intimidating size, great claws and sharp beak—not to mention his terrifying magic — would have to do. She laid a hand on his feathers, a bold move to touch a dangerous being, but she was too tired to care. The Gryphon blinked as if touched by the gesture and ruffled his feathers.

A demented screeching shattered the peace.

Her hand flew to her Fireshot and the Gryphon reared on his hind legs. The screeching grew and she covered her ears. It sounded mechanical, like the broken brakes on a carriage, only infinitely louder. The entire mountain shuddered and something struck Vassa, lifting and hurling the Gryphon right off the mountainside as if he were a mere toy.

The vessel appeared above her, whatever had cloaked its presence vanishing. Thaya looked up at the enormous cigar-shaped ship, unlike those of the Vormae, and a white beam burst down from the centre. She couldn't scream, she couldn't move, she could only stare, mouth open in horror, as the light ensnared her and put out her consciousness.

21

GONE

DISTORTED, DREAM-LIKE IMAGES OF STRANGE FACES AND voices faded into and out of the light.

The curl of a nose, the slant of an eye, the movement of lips—nothing close or clear enough to focus on properly. Time passed piecemeal with sparse chunks of wakefulness interspersed with nothingness.

It could have been hours, it could have been days—how do you measure time when you are beyond it?

Thaya landed on her feet as if dropped from a height and crumpled onto the ground, her legs too weak and sore to hold her up. She couldn't see because there was a sack or something over her head. Her knees ground into something grainy and damp. *Sand,* she thought. She couldn't move her arms because they were tied tight behind her back. Large, powerful hands grabbed her shoulders and pulled her upright.

There came a winded grunt as someone else landed beside her to her right. From the gasping, it sounded like a man. Someone else shifted and groaned softly to her left. Other thuds were followed by more groaning. Her heart pounded in her chest and she was frozen in fear. Where the hell was she, and what was going on?

Movement, then a gasp to her left was followed by a flare of energy. She saw it as orange light even behind closed lids and felt intense radiating heat. The person screamed, and the magic hurt Thaya too; she felt burning, but from within the cells of her body. She flinched and shied away.

The sack was torn from her head, leaving her hair, which was thick with static and sweat, sticking uncomfortably to her face. She blinked into a warm, sunlit world where a wide, yellow sandy shore stretched out for miles. In the distance, dark cliffs ambled lazily into rich green pastures and then forests. The sky yawned azure blue, and white gulls screamed as they wheeled and dived above.

A figure stepped in front of her, and she blinked up at the towering form, but her focus faded in and out, revealing her present reality in only blurs and smudges. Through the haze, she saw bronzed skin and a powerful form. *Nuakki!*

Her vision sharpened and her mouth dried as her eyes travelled over gilded sandals and perfectly manicured, tanned toes. Polished golden shin guards reflected the sunlight painfully, and she couldn't help but note huge, well-muscled thighs. His creaseless white tunic and pristine golden breastplate gleamed magnificently in the sunlight. In one hand, he held a short golden staff with a rounded pommel. Power emanated from it. It had not been he who had taken off her sack, the Nuakki standing behind her had done that, and beyond the one in front stood many more Nuakki, male and female, all dressed in their strange, almost ceremonial armour.

She sighed, her ribs hurting with the effort. There was no way she was escaping, not this time.

Blue eyes gleaming, the Nuakki smiled—not a smile of

warmth, but a smile of dominance, like a murderer might smile. His large, strong hand curled gently under her chin, then he gripped her painfully and dragged her onto her feet, his hand the only thing that supported her. He turned her face left and right, inspecting her, then raised his stick. It hummed and pulsed, then all her clothes burst into flames. She screamed from the burning heat, but then it was gone in the next second and all her clothes had disintegrated. All her fine hairs were singed and her skin was pink.

He took his time inspecting her, then he shifted his grip to her neck and held her out to the crowd of Nuakki behind him as if she were an animal for sale at a market. The realisation struck her. *That's exactly what I am!* Shame filled her, overcoming her weariness and burning hot skin, and she made a futile effort to hide her nakedness.

To her left lay a man, also naked but lifeless, a trickle of blood coming from his nostrils. To her right, an endless line of people stretched; men, women, children—all head-bagged and bound as she had been. Her body was dirty, bruised, and she smelled. Her shame deepened at her grimy and unwashed state. Ashamed! As if she should care? She hated herself for it.

The Nuakki all inspected her. One by one, the males stepped forwards, shook their heads and stepped back. The last eyed her for longer than the rest, and she surprised herself by giving him an angry snarl. It forced its way up her throat and past the Nuakki's grasp. It made him chuckle.

When the last one finally shook his head, the Nuakki who held her shrugged and dropped her to the ground where she folded back onto her knees, hunching down in the dirt to hide her breasts and everything possible.

But he was not done with her yet. Blinking through her hair strands, she watched him hold up his short staff and raise a palm towards her. Upon his hand was a mark, a golden symbol of lines connected by swirls embedded in his palm. The staff glowed, the mark swirled, and he barked intonations. She felt woozy and suddenly he slammed his hand against her forehead.

Like a magnet to metal, she was bolted to his hand and instantly paralysed. Terrible excruciating pain exploded through her brain and tore through her body. She couldn't breathe, she couldn't fight. There was blood in her mouth and it bubbled out of her nose. She fought her bindings, feeling the rope tearing into her wrists. She screamed, louder and louder, and began to convulse yet still his palm remained connected to her forehead. She had always feared being struck by lightning, it must feel something like this— only this didn't stop, it rolled through her again, over and over.

He removed his hand and the pain simply went, along with everything else that had comprised herself and her existence. All that Thayannon Farseeker had ever been or known or understood—was gone.

Thaya knew only one thing, she just *was*.

There was wetness around her eyes, caused by the terrible pain that had suddenly ceased. She no longer had words to describe the things she now experienced, not even to herself, she just endured them. She had no language, it was gone. Recognition of objects, their names and labels and functions...it was all gone. Screaming came from others around her, but she couldn't move, all she could do was lay barely breathing, face pressed against the coarse wet sand, like the man to her left and the older woman beyond him. It went on a long time.

Finally, the last screams were replaced with silence.

The Nuakki spoke amongst themselves and then walked away, their shiny gold armour and bright white tunics disappearing into the distance. She closed her eyes and drifted.

———

Something touched her arm, making her jump. She focused on a red-tanned face, and the boy-man smiled. He was small and slender with a thick mop of black hair cut just above his eyes. Thaya looked at this strange being who appeared to mean her no harm, not like the larger others had. Even though she didn't know what this creature was, something told her he wouldn't harm her. Her basic instincts remained intact although nothing else had.

The non-threatening boy-man helped her to sit up, and she saw other beings similar to him helping the other people who were naked and prone on the ground as she had been. The naked people had blood on their faces, and their eyes were vacant and wide, like newborn babies. She saw herself reflected in those faces.

The boy-man pulled some fabric over her head. It was the same as he wore, and she immediately felt less vulnerable and a little warmer.

"Clothes," he said, and pointed to the material now covering her. She fingered it and frowned. "Clothing," he said gently.

He struggled to inch her onto her feet, but she pirouetted and fell on her face. Again he tried, but she couldn't remember how to stand and fell time and again. The effort left her spent, and despite the strange but encouraging noises coming from the boy-man as he tried to lift her, she couldn't stand or even get on to her knees. She just lay.

A large hand shoved the boy aside and a huge figure loomed over her. Thaya whimpered, terrified of this new being and his threatening expression. He grabbed hold of her shoulders and she cried out in pain as he wrenched her up and half-carried, half-dragged her along the sand. Again, the world turned dark.

22

AMWA

THAYA AWOKE IN DARKNESS.

She was in an enclosed space and the soft snores and slow rhythmic breathing told her several others slept nearby. A light came towards her. As it neared, she saw it was carried by the boy-man. It illuminated his gentle face in orange. The light he held flickered and when he was close enough to touch, she felt warmth coming from it. She lifted her hands and enjoyed the heat. She touched the light and jumped from the searing pain.

"Don't touch." He copied her motion and shook his head.

She didn't know what his noises meant, but she didn't try to touch the flame again.

The boy-man made more noises with his lips and pointed at the flickering heat. "Fire." He repeated it and motioned to her.

She placed her bottom lip against her teeth like he had. "F-f-uh," she managed.

"Fuh-eye-er," he repeated more slowly. "Fire."

"Fuh-fuh-er," she tried again then sighed heavily and rubbed her eyes. Immense fatigue rolled over her.

He made some more noises with his lips and smiled.

In the light she glimpsed several other people sleeping under rough blankets a few yards away. They were in a large cavern, and on the far side more flickering fires appeared, held by the helpers like her boy-man, and they were tending those awake.

He lifted something hard, hollowed and round to her lips, and made noises. Liquid sloshed within and she drew away, but he smiled encouraging and lifted it to his lips, swallowing some of the contents. He was infinitely patient, and infinitely kind, unlike the Nuakki.

"War-ter," he said then pointed at her. "You."

Thaya allowed him to tilt the device to her lips and she swallowed. The liquid was cool and delicious, and she grabbed it from his hands, thirstily drinking it all. He gave her some more, pouring it from a tall device beside him, brown like the earth beneath them.

A certain amount of clarity returned, and her blurred vision sharpened. She could see the dark cavern more clearly now, though she didn't know the words for it, she only knew it wasn't outside on the beach where they had been before.

"Water," she repeated.

The boy-man laughed and clapped his hands, making her laugh too. She began to cry with the joy of getting a word right, but also because something was terribly, terribly wrong with her. Where was she? Who was she? *What* was she?

"No, no," said the boy, raising his finger and waggling it, but the sobs came from deep within, shuddering her whole body.

He pulled her into skinny arms that had surprising strength and rocked her back and forth. She clung to him and tried not to wail as she sobbed against his chest.

When her shoulders stopped shaking, he pushed her back and continued her lessons unabated. Raising his hands, he pointed back at his chest, "Amwa," he said. "Amwa."

"Amwa," Thaya repeated and he smiled. He did not ask her name; he knew she would not know it, just as he no longer knew his original name.

Amwa, she said over and over in her mind. It meant a lot; she wouldn't forget it.

"Bowl," he said, pointing to the device on the ground laying where she had dropped it.

"Bowl, water," Thaya said.

He became excited and pointed to the dark objects the fire licked. "Wood."

She repeated the word back perfectly and he moved on to other objects. These words came more easily than the first few as if he were unlocking the language she knew already within her.

In the first long hours of her new life, she relearnt a hundred nouns; the verbs, being more abstract, were harder. "Ja-ump," she repeated after Amwa when he jumped in the air again. "Amwa jump."

"Yes," he nodded.

She couldn't decipher the connecting words, or the connective conjunctions, or the adverbs or adjectives, and counting took even longer than the words.

"Sleep," said Amwa, and he put his palms together and tilted his head upon them, then pointed at her.

He lay down and pulled a rough frayed blanket over him, his large brown eyes watching her. Thaya was exhausted, but a desperate need to learn burned within her. Beyond the emptiness of her mind, her soul remembered who she was, if only she could reach it deep within her.

She lay down and pulled up her blanket. It was rough and scratched her skin, but at least it was warm. Her fingers resting lightly on the earth, she watched the fire dancing and the long shadows it cast on the walls and she cried silently, the whole cavern trembling as her eyes filled with tears that emptied continuously until a dreamless sleep put out the light.

———

Three Nuakki dragged her to her feet, jerking her awake. She knew the name of her slavers now as Amwa had taught her them. Her hands were clasped into thick iron cuffs and she was attached by a heavy chain to a man-slave in front. The man-slave was much older than her, and his hair was all white and dishevelled. He listed to one side.

The Nuakki in charge, a tall, powerful male ranked higher than most of the others with his golden breastplate, short stave and headpiece, ordered about a human man who was dressed in a simple tunic, much like the clothing Amwa wore. He wrapped a chain around her waist and chained someone else behind her, and another behind them. The Nuakki savagely struck his short golden stave on the back of the man in front. Energy sparkled, making her eyes widen first in wonder and then in horror as the man screamed and stumbled into a walk, jerking her along with him. The man had other bruises from previous beatings. His whole body was covered in them.

She glanced back and saw Amwa standing alongside scores of other slave-servers, all with their hands clasped in front of them, heads bowed and their eyes fixed firmly on the ground. She lost sight of him as she walked in the long chain through the fire-lit cavern, passing other grim-faced Nuakki who watched them, their meaty arms folded, and their strange hats made of stiffened material making their elongated heads look even longer. She kept her eyes low, afraid that she'd be beaten like the man in front.

They passed many dark caverns leading off into the darkness, but where they led, she couldn't see. Maybe they went on forever. "Mine," Amwa had called it, but she didn't know what that was, only that it was where she lived. Regardless, this place was endless.

A faint light grew ahead of them, different to that cast by fire. Through the swaying figure of the old man in front, she blinked into the bright light wishing she could shield her eyes with her bound hands. The old man stumbled and the Nuakki struck him with the stick. He stumbled repeatedly until just the threat of the lifting staff made him shuffle faster.

They emerged into a wider, brighter cavern and the old man, blinded, tripped over a rock, falling to his knees. Thaya rushed to help him, but the Nuakki's stick was already descending. The man howled as the stick struck and sparked upon his shoulder. That staff of pain flashed towards her, smacking into her cheek. Immense pain and sparks exploded in her vision and she gasped in agony. She fell back against the person behind her, desperately trying to get away from that agony stick.

Satisfied, the Nuakki turned away from her and again, began to beat the old man even while he was struggling to get onto his feet. Thaya tried shutting her eyes, but she could not shut out the man's cries of pain or the jerking of the chains that bound them together. When she opened them again, blood trickled from his shoulder, nose and mouth, but he was on his feet and slumped against the wall. As soon as he pushed away from the wall, the beating stopped. Thaya had no idea how the man did it, but he continued walking on wooden legs, blood streaming from his face and gashed shoulder, splattering crimson over his tan tunic.

They stepped fully out of the endless caverns and it was so bright Thaya was temporarily blinded. How long had she been in darkness? How long had Amwa been teaching her there, deep beneath the world? She blinked upwards where the light was so bright it hurt her eyes and enjoyed its caressing warmth. *Sun,* she said in her mind, recalling the image Amwa had drawn in the dirt of a circle with short lines radiating out from it. *Sun,* she repeated in her mind, the word reassuring her. If only Amwa were here—alone, she was terrified.

They walked past baskets filled with the same tan coloured clothing every non-Nuakki appeared to be wearing. Behind the baskets stood Nuakki women, faces scowling or simply bored as they looked down upon the ragtag group of chained slaves. The first woman eyed her up and down, sorted through the basket of clothing, and shoved a bundle into her arms before wafting her away to deal with the next.

With her hands cuffed and chained to the man in front, Thaya struggled to hold the stuff. As she paused and grappled, the Nuakki with the Pain Stick strode towards her.

Thwack!

Stars danced in her eyes and her arm felt broken. How she managed to not drop her bundle was beyond her. The Pain Stick rose again. She hastened forwards flinching, but thankfully the pain never came again as the Nuakki's attention was taken up by another slave further down the line. He bellowed and she hurried on hugging her bundle to her chest.

The next baskets contained strange long objects with hard bottoms and a fabric top. The woman stared at her feet then selected two and put them on top of her pile. They were quite worn with holes in the toes and ominous dark red spots splattered over them. Thaya didn't pause too long to inspect them and was shunted along to the next section.

More Nuakki women stood in a line, all holding shiny, sharp-looking metal objects. Fear trickled down Thaya's back, there was something dangerous about the metal objects they held. A guard paused the man in front and the Nuakki women stepped forwards to inspect them all. The women were huge; as tall and muscly as human men. One of them grabbed hold of Thaya's hair, bundling up the strands and scrunching them up with distaste as if she were a filthy animal.

Thaya squinted and hunched as the sharp metal object rose above her head and made snipping noises. Her golden-brown locks were suddenly tumbling all around her. That feeling came again, shame, and far beneath it, the faint stir-rings of anger. Perhaps it flickered across her face for the woman grabbed the tufty remains of her hair and yanked her head painfully backwards. Seeing her fear, the Nuakki woman smiled cruelly and threw her forwards.

She stumbled against the man in front. He braced himself and prevented her from falling to the ground. Had he done that to help her? He glanced over his shoulder and she made a quiet noise, she hoped it was a "thank you" like Amwa had taught her.

The next row of women reached into huge deep baskets and pulled out hard heavy objects. A wooden thing with a long piece of metal in one end was shoved atop her pile. Nuakki guards hurried them on brandishing their pain-sticks menacingly.

The last row of women gave them each a soft, round, brown item that smelt so delicious that Thaya's mouth began to water and her stomach rumbled. She didn't know what the round objects were but her stomach appeared to.

The Nuakki guard who had led them here now marched them around the corner and towards a dark gaping mouth in the side of an enormous cliff face. The other two guards followed at the rear. They were being taken to another cavern, different to the one she had come from. Was Amwa there? She wanted to see him, but the diminishing light and warmth from the sun made her shiver. She did not want to go back into darkness.

However, darkness swallowed her up and plunged her into the cold. They walked deeper into the abyss, and her eyes adjusted slowly to the dim glow of small fires held on the wall within metal cases. She didn't recognise anything here and the unfamiliarity was frightening. Her eyes kept going to that small brown ball on her bundle and each time, her stomach rumbled.

The Nuakki paused beside a wall covered in toolmarks. He slammed his hand down on the man in front's bundle forcing him to drop it, and his round ball rolled into a corner. Thaya quickly dropped her bundle beside the man's, and the Nuakki gave a rare nod of approval, a smirk on his handsome face. Everyone behind copied her actions.

The Nuakki spoke, his deep voice harsh as it reverber-ated around the chamber. Thaya didn't understand all of his words, but some were familiar as Amwa had spoken them last night. Had he known she would be taken today and what was in store for her?

"...take...dig..." was all she could pick out.

The man in front didn't understand either and he bore the full brunt of the Nuakki's impatience meted out with the Pain Stick. The man finally, with trembling hands, took hold of the wooden object with its curious piece of metal. He turned to the wall the Nuakki pointed at, dragging Thaya along with him.

"Dig!" roared the Nuakki, slamming his hand down on the man and forcing him to his knees.

Thaya was also forced to her knees and flinched as the Nuakki lifted his arm and struck the wall with his pain-stick. Sparks flared and a boom shook the chamber making everyone whimper.

Thaya grabbed her wooden and metal object, and knelt beside the man, copying his actions as the other slaves fell to their knees and did the same. She struck the metal part against the wall where a thousand other chip marks lay. A chunk of reddish-brown stone flew off. When no chastisement came, she assumed this was what the Nuakki wanted them to do, and the others followed her actions. She struck and hit the wall to the sound of a hundred other strikes, and all she could think about was that soft brown ball laying somewhere behind her. She couldn't stop to put it in her mouth, the guard would probably kill her.

Chink, chink, clang. Her tool struck the wall along with the tools of scores of other people beside her, and the quiet slap of the guards' bored footsteps echoed behind them as they paced.

The hours passed, and her arms ached.

Someone paused and in the corner of her eye, she saw slender female hands resting the tool on her lap. The guard pounced on her.

Smack!

It was followed by a scream of pain. The resting tool jerked into the air and hammered against the wall.

Thaya renewed her flagging efforts, feeling the plaintive growls of her stomach fade away, despondent. The hunger came and went in waves, each stronger than the last.

The Nuakki barked and a couple of slaves paused their hammering, alerting Thaya that she should do the same. He dragged the man beside her to his feet. Dutifully, if weakly, she and the rest of the line stood. Her legs were stiff from kneeling on the hard floor for so long and she closed her eyes, praying they'd hold her up.

The Nuakki motioned them to pick up their piles of belongings, then marched them back along the tunnel. They trudged past the dim sombre walls that enclosed them and eventually the pale light of day grew ahead.

Sunlight and warmth, how she longed to feel it. She trembled all over with a fatigue she had never known, and a hunger that gnawed even within her bones. She grinned foolishly when the Nuakki made them sit down on the damp sand to eat their rolls. The sun vanished behind a cloud and a cold wind blew beneath the greying skies, but she didn't care as her fingers tore into the brown spongy food. It was dry, flaky, and hard to swallow, and it was delicious. She wanted more, ten more, but there was only one.

Nuakki women approached and bowls like the one Amwa had given her were shoved into their hands. A Nuakki man poured water from a large amphora into them. He walked down the line sloshing and pouring the water continuously causing the people to desperately lift their cups, eager to fill them as much as possible. Thaya managed to fill hers, but the woman beside her knocked Thaya's bowl in her panic and half spilled out.

Thaya glared at the woman, but the Nuakki only

chuckled and did not return to fill it up again. Thaya noticed all the Nuakki were grinning, amused at the peoples' ragged, desperate state. Stronger stirrings of anger clenched her belly, but she cast her eyes at the ground and down-turned her face in case they noticed. She drank the water. It wasn't clean, and grains of sand marred her last mouthful.

The Nuakki made them get up, then another guard with a silver and gold staff and an air of authority came to stand by the first in line. The other guards and Nuakki women clustered behind him.

The Nuakki with the gold and silver staff eyed the man briefly then said a word Thaya did not know. '*Dis-card*' she repeated in her mind, trying to find something it matched and failing. The word, or the meaning behind it, made her shiver. Two guards unshackled the old man and unlinked him from her chain then dragged him away. He hung limp in their grasp, skinny and spent with his head lolling.

The Nuakki stepped in front of her, his dark torso rippling with muscles, his gold armlets almost blinding in the light.

Thaya stared up at him, forcing herself to not even blink. Her brain a sponge for information, she memorised his face in a moment, the faint lines around his lips, the deep brown of his eyes, the curve of his nostrils that left him and all Nuakki forever sneering. She fought with all her might to still the anger growing in her belly, along with another burning emotion for which she had no name.

If he noticed it in her eyes he didn't respond, if anything he looked at her with a bored expression. He grabbed her left hand, lifted it and examined the palm briefly before dropping it. He spoke a different word loudly, and again she didn't know what he said. '*Keep*' she repeated in her mind but had no reference as to what it meant. She expected the guards to unshackle her and drag her away, but nothing happened, and he moved on to the next.

He examined the woman beside her in the same fashion and barked the same word he had for Thaya. Nothing happened and the woman remained shackled to her. The next was a man, tall and younger than the one they had taken away.

"Keep." Again the same word was barked, and the man remained shackled.

The Nuakki came to another woman. Thaya could just see that her hands were covered in dried blood and her nails were split. Those slender hands which had previously dropped the tool now trembled uncontrollably, and Thaya wished she could offer her some comfort.

"Discard," he commanded.

Nuakki guards unshackled the woman and led her limping away.

Thaya couldn't see any more from her position, but down the line came the barks of 'keep' or 'discard,' and if the latter, the person was always dragged away. Thaya could only count to ten people, but there were many more after that. At least ten were taken away after being labelled 'discard.' Where they went, she would never know, but she did not see them again.

The Nuakki finished their assessment and ordered them to pick up their belongings. Now in front, Thaya was forced to lead the others back into the cold dark mines. Their shortened line was placed against another wall, and there they struck at it once more with their crude tools.

Clang, clang, chink, over and over and over. Why? Thaya did not know. She tried to ignore her aching arms, her rumbling belly, and focus only upon the wall in front of her and the strike of her tool against it. She looked forward to the little things, like when a tiny spark flew off her tool on certain parts of the rock, and the faintest brush of fresh air that reached them from outside. Her world was the red-brown rock in front of her, and in a way, she found some contentment. So long as she didn't pause, so long as she ignored her screaming arms, no harm would come to her, no pain-stick descending, no calls for 'discard.' She found herself thanking her jailers.

She worked in a daze, so much so that when the Nuakki barked for them to stop she nearly didn't hear him. Dutifully she got to her feet when he motioned, and clasped her hands together, trying to hide their trembling from him lest he shout 'discard!'

The Nuakki marched them down the right fork and deeper into the warren. They moved through endless tunnels until she was sure she would never see the light of day again. They walked on and on until she recognised elements of her tiny world. Her eyes brightened. There was that funny curve of the rock, and there the tilting, wonky wall light. The entrance to their cavern was just over there... and look! That was where Amwa and she slept. They had come through the rock to their home, it was all connected in one giant maze of tunnels.

She watched in dumb silence as her shackles and chains were removed by the human slave helpers, their gentle hands moving fast, and smarted at the raw skin puckered around her wrists and ankles. She had ignored it for so long her skin was numb. The chains were taken away, the guards departed, and they were left to their own devices.

In the distance, to the far side of the cavernous room, a huge barred door grated and ground shut, the Nuakki guards locking it firmly from the other side.

Almost laughing at her release, Thaya slumped back

against the wall, closed her eyes and slid down onto her haunches.

Hours might have passed before something cool and moist was laid over her wrists. She winced at the sting and stared at Amwa who was crouched down before her. The sting became numbingly soothing and a faint smell came from the white bandages he wrapped around her wrists and palms. She liked his flawlessly smooth, red-brown face and his thick shock of black hair that reflected the firelight. It was a relief to be in his company and hopefully he would begin his lessons again soon, she had to know the words for everything.

Sensing her need he said, "Bandages," and pointed to the strips of white cloth. She repeated the word then he made her sit back so he could tend her raw ankles. As he worked, she wondered why his hair was not messily shaven like her own and those she had worked alongside but was allowed to be longer with a precise cut. Other people helped the workers and they too had short, cropped hair. She couldn't ask him why; she could only wonder.

"Shoe," said Amwa, lifting the two red spotted objects she had been given earlier.

"Shhhooo," she repeated.

"Put on," he said and pointed to his own feet encased in similar-looking objects. Understanding dawned on her and, keen to look like him, she stood and pushed her foot into the material.

"Tie," he said, pointing at the string holding the two flaps. He showed her his neat tie, but she had no idea how to do what he asked.

"Tie," he repeated and set about doing it for her. She watched him work the strings in awe. He then undid them and motioned for her to do it.

She tried but couldn't even remember the first step. He undid his shoe and worked slowly. She wrapped the string one over the other, then looped it around and under copying his deft fingers. She learnt it quickly, her fingers remembering what her mind had completely forgotten.

She put on the other one and laughed; the ground was no longer cold and rough beneath her feet. Her eyes kept returning to the red spots on the shoes and she traced a finger over them.

The world trembled and an image flashed in her mind —sunlight, blue sky, Nuakki with sharp metal objects, a terrified scream followed by bright blood spraying. Thaya gasped.

"No," said Amwa sharply, firmly grabbing her hands and pulling them away from her shoes.

She chewed her lip; she had upset him. Would he hit her? "N-no," she stammered.

His frown melted into a smile and he drew her close. "No Vision," he said. "No Sight. Don't think." He rocked her back and forth like he had the first time and she found the tears pouring out of her again.

He pushed her back and continued her naming lessons. She learned more words, mostly to do with their bodies; 'toes' and 'fingers,' 'nails' and 'ears,' and she counted further this time but still did not understand anything more than simple sentences. She couldn't speak like the Nuakki spoke to each other, each word rolling into the next.

Amwa tapped his chest then he drew in the dirt the outline of Lonohassa like he had drawn many times before. He then drew many dots to the south of it. "Amwa from here," he said, tapping his chest then pointing to the dots. "Islands," he said. She nodded but didn't quite understand what he described.

"Me, child," he said, and drew a small human next to a large, nothing more than stick figures, but she understood what he meant.

"They—" and he indicated the Nuakki with a special hand gesture, then he wiped his hand across his brow. "You, they—" and he wiped his hand across her brow.

Her stomach clenched and she tried to breathe through a constricted throat. "Gone," she gasped and began to shake.

He grasped her hands and squeezed. He had only been young when it had happened, there couldn't have been much memory he had lost, but then, the wiping did other things to you.

"Blanking," said Amwa and wiped his hand over his forehead again. "But the Nuakki call it 'Cleansing'; making us pure for them. All of us have been Cleansed, purified for our masters." He indicated the room and raised his hands to the air as if to indicate further. "But now, so long has passed, I remember pieces and I pray to the gods every night to give me back to myself."

He pointed at the islands again. "Others have told me, taught me, like I am teaching you. Big trees." He drew tall trees with huge long leaves in the dirt. "Sun, hot, and the sea blue like the sky." He described his beautiful homeland and she saw it clearly in her mind. She imagined living there, she imagined being free as Amwa spoke.

Amwa paused with a yawn and pointed at himself again then at her. "Amwa," he said.

"Amwa, I know." She repeated him, frowning. She knew this word, had he forgotten? He pointed at her again and waited, nodding encouragingly. She realised what he wanted her to do and her frown deepened. What was she called? She had a name, didn't she? She searched in the darkness of her mind, through the blank places that should have been her memory, and found nothing, not a whisper.

She shook her head, slumping her shoulders as the world wobbled in her eyes. He did not press her and instead stroked her shoulder, but she understood the disappointment on his face.

They laid down to sleep that night, and many nights thereafter, and she let the tears fall. At night before falling asleep, she always cried. She didn't know why she cried, it wasn't the bruises on her body from the Pain Stick, it wasn't her aching arms and stinging ankles and wrists. It was because something within her was broken, an important part of herself was missing that she couldn't remember, and perhaps never would. Whatever dreams she may have dreamt in the past, her sleep was always dreamless and empty now.

23

NOW, YOU BELONG TO ME

THE WEEKS PASSED.

Every day was the same for Thaya; spent in darkness and mining the endless rock. Then one day, the metal door screeched open earlier than usual, jerking her awake. She pushed herself onto her feet as others stirred. Amwa was already gone and his bed pallet cold. He must have left some time ago to do his own tasks, whatever they were.

Two new Nuakki males and her usual overseers hustled into the cavern speaking amongst themselves. The higher ranking slaver with the Pain Stick pointed at her, and the other overseer pointed at two others she couldn't see. Her heart pounded as they strode over and put a single iron cuff around her wrist. She had no ability or desire within her to resist, the thought simply did not cross her mind. Her mouth went dry, what had she done? But they didn't look angry or shout at her. Two other men were also cuffed, one slightly older than her, and one younger. They were chained together, with her in the centre, and then they were marched out of the room.

She tried not to think and instead wondered about the

other human men with their roughly shorn sandy hair and tanned skin. They were fit, so had they tried to fight their Nuakki captors and were to be punished? Would they fight now? From their slumped shoulders and hanging heads, she didn't think so. Something had been done to them to make them weak, she was sure of it. The anger she felt inside, she couldn't seem to bring up within her to resist.

She stared at the older man's broad back as he lumbered forward. Were they from this place? Lonohassa, Amwa had called it, or were they from lands beyond? Lands she could barely wonder at. Amwa had said she might be from northern Lonohassa where the people were paler, but her face was not typical Lonohassan. Even though the language came readily to her and she learned faster than most, he wasn't convinced she was Lonohassan, so where was she from?

Thinking about Amwa took her mind off wherever the Nuakki were marching her through the dark tunnels. Amwa said he *was* Lonohassan, but from islands off Lonohassa's coast far to the south. Southern Lonohassan's looked like him, black-haired, brown eyes that were slightly slanted, and skin that was deeply tanned and almost red. Northern Lonohassans were fairer and paler, so either she was from a mix of the two or she wasn't from here at all.

The entrance loomed and Thaya stepped outside into the bright sunlight squinting, a pang of fear knotting her stomach. *Discard.* No, they weren't going to kill her, she'd worked hard and been good, and they wouldn't kill these fit young men who could lift twice as much as she in the mines...would they?

The Nuakki marched them over the sandy plain. The sudden vastness of the sky and the wide-open space was overwhelming as it pressed down upon her, and she glued her eyes upon the ground only daring to glance a little left and right now and then.

They passed near to a fence made of wood and wire, the other side of which stood round domed dwellings made out of the same sandy stone that dominated this place. Between the round dwellings, people walked, people like her! She stared and stared at them, they weren't chained but free! How did they get free? Few looked in her direction and those who did quickly looked away. Thaya could only wonder.

Further on, a group of children clustered at the fence, their freckly faces staring at them unabashedly. One little boy with a mess of brown hair pulled a face and stuck his tongue out. Thaya wanted to laugh or scowl back, but a guard shoved her onwards, forcing her to look at the ground to avoid tripping.

Someone started shouting. Thaya side-glanced the fence trying to locate the voice. An old woman's weak voice, it came from somewhere beyond the clustering children. But their path was taking them away from the fence and where the shouting came from. Thaya dared to look back over her shoulder and saw an old thin woman with long straggly white hair that had not been cut off like hers. She was pushing through the clustering children and shouting a word over and over.

"Thaaayaahh," she screamed again, but Thaya didn't understand. What did Thaaayaahh mean? She'd have to ask Amwa. The woman was staring right at her too. An uncomfortable itch nestled between her shoulder blades, but there was no way she could scratch it with handcuffs on.

The Nuakki ignored the whole situation and marched them around a huge lumbering chunk of rock, and she lost sight of the old woman, the children and the dwellings.

Thaya looked ahead and stared at the enormous place unfolding before her. Opposite a long and wide stretch of golden sand, a darker cliff face rose from the sea far to her left, high into the azure sky and along into a deep valley to her right. The towering rocks were covered with wooden scaffolds and holes burrowing deep inside. Along all the levels of the scaffolds were hundreds of people dressed as she, being ordered around by Nuakki guards. They milled everywhere, building more scaffolding, emerging from and disappearing into the hundreds of holes bored into the rock face, carrying baskets laden with rocks on their shoulders, or empty baskets waiting to be filled.

The whole place must be one enormous mine, thought Thaya, how far and deep it stretched, she could only guess at. How many slaves worked them? Finally, the question she should have asked Amwa months ago dawned on her; what were they looking for?

The Nuakki led them to a large, circular, black iron furnace, about six feet wide with fire burning out of the hole near its base. Black smoke billowed from the top, twenty feet above them. Male and female Nuakki guards tended it, prodding at the flaming coals with long metal poles.

Words were exchanged between their guards and the Nuakki tending the furnace. When communing between each other they spoke Nuakki, and Thaya did not fully understand them, but when they ordered the slaves around, they spoke Lonohassan, as Amwa had taught her. But Thaya's empty mind was thirsty for information and, slowly, purely by listening to them, she was beginning to learn the Nuakki language.

They unchained the man in front of her and made him kneel with his left arm extended over a flat-topped boulder. Fear tickled the base of Thaya's spine. An iron pole sticking out of the furnace was removed, its end glowing red with such heat, she could feel it five feet away.

Two guards clasped the man in position while a third lifted the pole to his splayed open palm. The man jerked back and tried to pull away, but for all his strength, the Nuakki were larger and stronger and held him firmly. Thaya tried to pull away too, but the chains prevented her and her Nuakki guard scowled and brandished his Pain Stick. *Must be good to not be 'Discarded'.* She swallowed.

The brand descended onto the man's open palm and he screamed. The brand hissed, smoke and the smell of burning skin filled the air as his howls echoed through the valley. People walking the scaffolds paused only briefly before continuing with their eyes cast firmly on the ground as if this happened every day. Thaya could barely breathe as she stared in horror, too shocked to move as they dragged the man away, his whole body crumpled around his injured palm.

Thaya found the will to resist as strong hands dumped her onto her knees. In a daze, she clasped her left hand to her chest, but the Nuakki yanked it away and held it down on the stone. The fight came to her and she did the only thing she could do; she whipped her head down and bit the restraining hand. She tasted blood, heard him grunt. The hand swiped her back and his other hand blasted across her face. She glimpsed a gold ring inset with a ruby before it tore into her cheek. The world danced with stars and pain and droplets of blood.

Her higher-ranked overseer growled and lunged at the one who'd struck her. They grabbed at each other's breast-plates and shouted as she swooned between them. Other Nuakki struggled to pull them apart.

In the commotion, Thaya glimpsed the dark blue sea in

the distance and the white-tipped waves of a vigorous shore. If she ran, she could go there, to the sea. She was unchained this moment; she could be free. She glanced over her shoulder, wondering if the human man behind her would come, would he fight? But his head was lowered, his shoulders slumped, and he was chained.

Thaya ran.

Time moved fast and so did her legs. Her feet slapped the beats of freedom into the cold damp sand, the wind lifted her hair, the smell of sea salt flared her nostrils as the waves in the distance galloped towards her. She was as free as the gulls above and she'd never have to live in a dark cave again or be struck with the stick of pain. *I'm free!* The wall against which she struck her tool hour after hour would be a distant memory, and never again would chains chaff her wrists and ankles until they bled. *I'm free!*

She did not get far.

Something slammed into her back and bolted through her whole body with flickering pain. She was hurled into the air where she first spun and then crashed to the ground. The pain didn't stop but intensified, violent electrical energy that made her teeth chatter and blood burst from her nose. Pain Sticks could attack from afar? How was that fair?

Heavy, armoured feet thudded on the ground, hands grabbed and dragged her dazed body. The pain lessened and moments later she was thrown back down beside the flat-topped stone. Her left hand was wrenched forward and this time tied down. Her sudden bolt for freedom must have caused an end to their tussle for both Nuakki stood silently beside her, faces grim and jaws clenched with pent up anger. Too stunned to resist, her whole body quivered, and she watched in silent horror as an iron brand was lifted from the furnace.

"Not that one," her slaver said gruffly in Nuakki.

The brand was exchanged for another; a silver, slender length of metal but still with a terrifying orange glowing end. Thaya closed her eyes as her whole body began to shake.

The pain was immense. It spread from her palm, seared up her arm and flared through her whole body. She didn't scream, she gurgled. When the smell of her own burning flesh hit her, all the blood seemed to rush from her body and she went along with it.

When she came to, she was being carried in a pair of strong arms. She could feel the sway of each step lolling her from side to side. Azure sky framed the face of the Nuakki carrying her; the higher-ranked overseer. Dark eyes narrowed as he stared ahead, smooth tanned skin drinking up the sunlight, pale red lips pursed into a thin line daring anyone to get in his path. But no Nuakki did. She saw them step back as he passed, gazes lowered.

His tall hat was a canvas of red, white and blue whirls, and she could see clearly the Nuakki lettering marking his high rank although she couldn't read it. His golden breast-plate rubbed painfully against her shoulder, but he clasped her so firmly against him, she almost struggled to breathe. Her hand throbbed maddeningly. Someone had bandaged it and it flopped weakly over her belly. Her body still shuddered from the electrical bolt that had slammed her to the ground.

Where was he taking her? Was she to be 'Discarded' for her disobedience? But her angle was such that she could see only him and the sky, not where they were headed. She wondered what his name was. *No, I don't care, I'll not see him as human!* This was her slaver, the one who'd beaten her with a golden stick of pain, the one who'd caused her to be branded, the one who'd chained her, and probably the one who'd just bolted her with shock. She despised him, but he was the only one who could make her life easier—or infinitely more painful.

They walked through a doorway, its smooth stone arches rising twice as high as her captor. Another Nuakki brushed into view, a male wearing a tall white hat that arched to a point and was decorated with beautiful gold thread. Thaya could only glimpse the shoulders of his attire, and the golden staff with a crook at the top which he held lightly in long, veiny hands.

He was older than her captor with deeper lines and creases upon his hard face. His eyes were so pale and watery they could have been any shade in his youth, and they were so cold, Thaya shivered. He held a dark air of power and spoke in sharp words. Her overseer lowered his eyes dutifully, marking the other as superior, and he replied with composure, but the only word Thaya could pick out was 'She,' and assumed he meant her.

A long silence passed between the two, the older man's eyes boring first into the Nuakki and then into her, whilst the slaver kept his eyes lowered, his shoulders straight. Icy, unseen fingers stole over Thaya. They slithered over her ankles and thighs to places she did not want them to go, over her arms and shoulders and chest. They reached even into her heart and lungs making her gasp with the cold, before lingering on her lips. Pain stabbed into her mind and she cried out. The stabbing pain receded, and a twisted smile touched the older man's lips whilst her overseer's jaw clenched dangerously.

Other Nuakki rushed over, speaking urgently to the older man and blessedly tearing his attention from her. The repugnant icy fingers retreated, leaving her mind to throb along with her hand.

No longer of interest to the white-hatted Nuakki, her slaver walked away, carrying her along impeccable white hallways of high arched ceilings interspersed with golden support beams. She couldn't see much, but she got a good look at everything above them. He carried her up a winding staircase, along more wide, pristine hallways and up another flight of stairs.

They entered through a door of pale wood that had been carved with intricate leaves around the edges. He shut the door behind them, and she sensed they were alone. Long white chiffon curtains cascaded from tall windows that reached from floor to ceiling and billowed gracefully in the warm breeze.

He released his powerful grip and set her down upon a deep, red velvet chair that had thick golden arms. Then he poured red liquid from a gilded amphora into a crystal glass and passed it to her. Thirst gnawed at her, but could she trust him? To disobey would not go well. She lifted the liquid to her lips and tasted it. Cool and sweet, it reminded her of the honey they were sometimes given with bread. She couldn't resist her thirst or the delicious liquid and drank it quickly.

He took the glass away and stood erect, staring down at her, his body filling her vision. She held her injured hand against her chest and wished for him to stop staring. Averting her gaze to the open balcony door, she tried to see beyond the chiffon curtains concealing her view. She was unbound. She could try and run again, but she was two floors up at least and would never survive the fall.

As if reading her mind, the Nuakki firmly shut the door then walked away into the next room. He returned swiftly with a golden egg the size of her hand and sat in an identical chair opposite her. He reached over and took hold of her injured arm.

"No!" Thaya gasped and pulled away. Nothing could make her go through that again, at least not while she was conscious. She readied herself for a fight, a fight which she would not win.

Unperturbed, he roughly grabbed it again and yanked her forwards so her hand was upon his knee. When she resisted, he twisted her arm in a way that shot pain up her body forcing her to whimper and be still. Pulling the bandages off, he forced open her clenched fingers making the wound sting and the smell of burnt flesh fill her nostrils.

"Please!" she cried, but he pushed the golden egg firmly into her palm.

The pain was ice cold and she gasped, sweat instantly rolling down her face and back as she froze in pain. It throbbed through her hand in excruciating waves until she could feel it no more. Then he simply pulled the egg away and let go of her hand.

The pain had completely gone, not even the burning throbbing remained. Panting, she retreated slowly back into her chair and stared at her hand in disbelief. The burnt flesh was gone, the horrific bloody black scab had healed, and in its place was a shimmering golden symbol of a single line swirling into the centre.

She touched the symbol; the skin was tender and sensitive, but it didn't hurt.

"You will not work in the mines anymore. My gift to you." He gestured to her with an enormous hand.

Thaya didn't know if the gift was the branding or not working the mines anymore, and whether either could be considered a gift. Her heart sank, what about Amwa?

"But," she began.

The Nuakki raised a warning finger, and she knew not to speak. Instead, she sucked in her lower lip and bit back the tears.

"Come," he said.

Fear stabbed at her heart. "Discard?" She stared up at the Nuakki even though she knew she should have kept her eyes lowered.

This amused him for he smiled, lifted her branded palm and pointed at the golden symbol. "No. Now you belong to me." His eyes gleamed and the way he said it suggested this was a great honour, so why did she feel devastated? No more Amwa, no more lessons, no more friends. She felt more a slave now than she ever had in the mines. He didn't notice and stood.

"Wash," was all he said and, taking her arm, led her across the white marble floor, past an enormous four-poster golden bed laid with red sheets and into a washroom.

A huge white bath nestled to one side, and above it hung great golden taps. These he turned causing water to magically gush into the bowl. Steam began to rise from the water, and when it was half full, he turned off the taps.

"Undress," he commanded.

Undress? Thaya looked down at her muddy and frayed attire. Shame, reluctance—she simply stood, head lowered, clinging to the neck of her tunic. The Nuakki turned and she flinched, waiting for the Pain Stick to knock her to the floor. It did not come and instead, large hands grabbed hold of her tunic and pulled it over her head. There was no fighting this powerful man, but she refused to assist him. It was warm and steamy in the room, but she stood there shivering in her poorly woven undergarments.

Less roughly, he slipped the last garment from her shoulders, and she visibly shook. Gently, he wrapped an arm around her waist, and lifted her into the bowl, pushing her down when she was unable to move.

Warm water wrapped its silken arms around her, trying to hug and shield her against her own surging emotions. The thin layer of bubbles on the surface provided a welcome cover over her naked skin.

He cupped the water and poured it over her hair and shoulders, displaying a tenderness she didn't think the Nuakki possessed. They were hardened warriors, and she was a weakling human—like Amwa, like all those she worked with. What this Nuakki was doing was surely not allowed, surely sacrilege. She was nothing more than the horses and mules they used to cart around the rocks, and yet here he was, bathing her, healing her wounds, allowing her to be near him. She had been chosen and given a status of honour, so why did her heart pound?

Before she had been branded, he'd struck the Nuakki who had struck her. Why? Had she unwittingly gained this man's favour? She was compliant and hard-working, and rarely did she suffer the Pain Stick beatings frequented upon many others.

He lifted a bar of soap—this wasn't like the grainy grey soap they used in the caverns to wash their faces in the muddy puddles, this was scented with flowers and made of silk that glided over her skin as he washed her shoulders. The mud, the blood and the sand fell away revealing a smooth tan and lithe body she was not accustomed to seeing. She was thinner than when she had first started in the mines, however long ago that was.

Amwa had told her about days and weeks and months, and she had started marking the days down, although a fair few weeks had already passed before that. There were fifty-three scratches on the floor beneath the foot of her sleep-mat. Fifty-three, the number burned into her mind for today. But what was she counting for? What was she waiting for? In that time, her body had become thinner but stronger, and wiry cords now braced her shoulders, taut ripples layered her belly, and her thighs belied her thinness with jostling muscle.

She had learned to work and sleep on an empty stomach most days, as had they all. Though her dreams were blank, while she drifted to sleep, she thought only of food, of mountains of brown rolls and endless bowls of golden honey.

Firm hands pushed down on her shoulders, motioning for her to go under the water. Fear shivered through her as she took her last lungful of air and submerged. She could never relax with the Nuakki, their sudden, unpredictable rage was all too frightening.

Moments later, those large hands lifted her by the armpits and she wiped the water from her face and pushed back her short hair. Those hands lingered there, danger-ously close to her breasts, making her fight with every ounce of her being to not shake between them. He could crush the life from her without breaking into a sweat.

Slowly those hands withdrew and stroked the back of her neck, touching her hair. She heard him sigh. Was he sad about her shorn locks? His hands drifted away and then the softest white blanket was dangled in front of her. Standing up, she grasped the towel and quickly wrapped it around her. This was her armour, her defence against the world and its prying eyes, and she instantly felt less vulnerable.

The bath was so big, she couldn't easily get out of it, but he lifted her and led her back into the first room with the chairs and the bed. Again, he stood looking at her for a long moment. As if reaching an internal decision, he pulled the hat off his head which was so long she wondered at his enormous brain within, the intellect, the command of the very elements all Nuakki appeared to possess. She didn't know if she should look at him or lower her eyes anymore, but he didn't say anything when she stared.

He unclasped his golden braces and dropped them on to the chair, then undid the straps of his gleaming breastplate to reveal a tanned torso heavy with muscle, setting her own to shame. *No, I can never fight him, not with power, nor intellect, nor magic.*

With complete indifference and lack of the shame that she felt, he undid his heavy belt and let his lower clothing fall to the floor. Thaya's pulse raced, gut-wrenching fear tightened her stomach painfully. She didn't know why she was afraid, there'd been plenty of naked males in the caverns and there was nothing fearful about them. This Nuakki was not going to kill her. He had not hurt her, at least not today, and now he had chosen her and spared her from the mines—there was nothing to fear. But her mind raced around her sparse memories and circled the black hole that lay at the centre of her existence. In that black hole lived everything that was missing from her mind, everything that should be hers but was taken.

Silently and slowly he stepped closer, thigh muscles bulging, his manliness swaying. She stepped backwards, clinging to her towel until her back came up against a bed pole. He took hold of the towel and when she tried to resist, he tightened his grip and firmly pulled it away. She stared hard at the marble floor, noting every chip and speck and the faintest flaws that were there.

A huge hand cupped her breast, tiny in his hand, and massaged. She couldn't move, she couldn't even breathe. He was so close, so much larger than she, and what was happening filled her with terror. The events unfolding tried to make contact with similar events that had occurred in that impenetrable black hole in her mind. Those familiar events within the black-hole were a reference point and they were not terror-filled but contained warmth and told her she shouldn't be afraid. It left her terribly confused, but one thing she was sure of—she could do nothing to stop what was occurring right now.

24

OSUMAN

THE NUAKKI TOOK HOLD OF THAYA'S CHIN AND LIFTED HER face until her eyes met his.

Why did he want her to look at him, wasn't it sacrilege for slaves to look at them? He wasn't smiling and there was a faraway look in his eyes. If he had been human, she would be able to read him more accurately, even with her limited vocabulary and experiences. And that was it, wasn't it? This was what was wrong, he was not human. A Nuakki female would know what to do, and a Nuakki female would be comparable in size and physicality. Between two distinct species this should not be, but she was utterly owned and he could do whatever he wanted.

His hand drifted down from her breast to her stomach and then around to her buttocks. She felt him hardening further. His free hand went behind her neck as he curled the other under her bottom and lifted her onto the bed. She stared into his eyes, willing him to stop, but his gaze was filling with something else, and they were reaching a point where he would not be able to control himself.

He lay down beside her and now both his hands

engulfed her chest. Far too soon, a hand snaked down to push her trembling legs apart. Thaya closed her eyes, hunting in the black hole that was her memory for a hundredth time, searching for the familiar reference point she knew was there. *Where are the missing parts of my life? I'm an adult and yet only fifty-three days do I remember clearly.* Perhaps it was a good thing she couldn't remember any similar event, this would only sully any good memories.

It was the multifaceted shame she struggled with, shame for her nudity, for her trembling body, for her powerlessness, but mostly she was ashamed for her complete and utter mental and physical weakness. In these moments, she utterly loathed herself and her existence.

When he lifted his massive body upon her, she closed her eyes. He held her hands and brushed her cheeks, showing a tenderness and caring she never dreamed the Nuakki possessed, but he did not stop, and a different pain thrust within her. *A different species... it's all wrong!*

She gasped, tears smarting her eyes, and she tried to pull away, but this made him less gentle and he held her down more firmly. She suspected he was trying to restrain himself, maybe he was afraid of her smaller size, but nothing he did could possibly make her enjoy this. She longed to be back in the caverns, longed to be back with gentle Amwa and his smiling round cheeks. Now she wondered if she would ever see him again. *As soon as I'm alone, I'll kill myself,* she decided. That day in the mine when they'd awoken to find an older woman hanging from a lamp hook, strangled by her own clothing, she'd learned the words 'death' and 'suicide'...and freedom.

As the Nuakki's painful thrusting became more urgent she tried to lay as still as possible, it hurt less if her muscles did not clench, but this lack of doing something to stop him also made her hate herself more, as if she were somehow assisting this crime, somehow condoning and accepting it. She pushed herself into the darkness of the black hole until she could no longer feel her body nor the pain of physical existence.

The darkness became her saviour, and she smothered herself in it for as long as she could.

But the darkness did not remain complete, and far away appeared a pinpoint of light. It grew, moving towards her—was this where her missing memories lay, were they returning to her? The harder she focused upon it, the faster it grew and took shape. A blue-white light showed something loping on wide paws beneath a body of pale fur. The body had eyes and a snout—it looked like the dog Amwa had drawn for her in the dirt, and the one she had glimpsed in the distance sitting obediently beside its Nuakki master as it watched the slaving humans. But this dog was larger, its ears were pointed, and its eyes were alight with untamed fire. Behind it, another light appeared, another dog like the first. In her previous dark dreams and empty mind nothing had ever appeared to her from the black-hole, so what were these hounds of light?

The first paused, lifted its head and howled—a long mournful sound.

"Wolves," a word whispered in her mind. Had the hounds put it there?

"Wolves," she whispered back. "Spirit Wolves."

The words caused painful sparks in her memory, making her cry out. Something was trying to break through to her from the darkness, if only she could grasp it. Images of lost memories flashed, too fleeting for her to hold on to, but they were there.

"Help me," she sobbed, and the wolves pressed

forwards. She reached to touch them, but suddenly every-thing was rushing away, and she was falling fast back into her body.

She gasped and opened her eyes, losing the wolves, losing the memories, and stared up into the flushed face of the Nuakki. He was frowning. Was that concern slanting his eyes? Thaya didn't care, she almost felt fearless of him as she clung to the Spirit Wolves in her mind.

The Nuakki stroked her hair and in his deep voice said, "Osuman." She frowned, and he tapped his torso. "I am Osuman."

She nodded slightly, respectfully, for the manner in which he spoke showed her that him telling her his name was a great thing. She had no name to give him in return. She was nameless, and he didn't ask.

He lay down beside her and she curled up away from him, almost jumping when he placed an arm over her and pulled her against his chest. He kissed the back of her neck and pressed his face there. After a few moments, she felt wetness on her neck and realised it came from him. She froze in shock; Nuakki could cry? Even the men? The world flipped and her mind scurried to help her know what she should do. He had taken her and yet he was the one crying. Was it remorse for what he had done or for the mess of everything here? What was going on in this mad nonsen-sical world where despair and sorrow built upon despair and sorrow?

Half an hour or more passed and they remained like that until he silently got up and pulled on his clothes. She heard him leave the room only to return seconds later bearing a tray of fruits in shades of yellow, orange and red, but the only fruit she recognised were the oranges. He set the tray down on the table beside the bed, and from a drawer beneath it, lifted a thin cord that shimmered silver. This he looped around her wrist and she heard it snap shut through some mechanism she couldn't identify. The other end he tied around the bedpost. In silence, he left the room.

Thaya did not move. For all the hunger she felt, she knew nothing could pass down her throat at this moment. She closed her eyes, hoping to see the Spirit Wolves but they were gone. She surprised herself by falling asleep.

The wolves were in her dream, sitting with their bushy tails wrapped around their haunches, one female and one male. Both had grey and white fur in identical patches on their bodies. They were too similar to each other for them to be mates, so she suspected they were brother and sister. They stood and opened their jaws to let their tongues loll out. Unafraid, she reached forward, and the female nuzzled her hand.

"Where have you come from?" she whispered. "Are you here to save me?"

The male wolf sat back and howled. A white and golden light grew before them as if the wolf had called it. Thaya held her hand towards it and the faint light touched her fingers, exploring. The light grew and indigo eyes flickered open from a sea of white, and a golden beam became a horn, long and straight and twirling. Thaya gasped as her entire body was filled with a longing that felt strangely familiar.

The image ended as the bed shaking startled her out of the dream.

Osuman looked down at her from his seated position at her side. In his hands, a silver bowl contained something slightly steaming and deliciously fragrant. Outside it was dark, and the lamps on the tables gave off an amber light. How long had she slept? Most of the day appeared to have passed. The sleep they got in the mines was never long enough, but without daylight, she was always unaware of how much time was really passing.

Thaya pushed herself up and took the spoon he held for her, then the bowl. Her hunger roared so keenly she plunged her spoon into the milky green liquid. She was too hungry to tell what it was, but she hadn't tasted anything this exquisite in all her fifty-three days.

A few splashes had Osuman grabbing her discarded towel and shoving it under her bowl. He took hold of her hand holding the spoon, and with calm deliberate movements, showed her how to eat it without making a mess.

"Manners," he said firmly.

Manners, she wondered curiously. Was it an action or a name? She was hungry and wanted to drink out of the bowl, but Osuman demanded obedience, and so she let him teach her.

When the bowl was empty, he took it away then returned and again undressed, unashamed of his nudity in her presence. She froze, her body still aching from earlier, but her shoulders relaxed when he pulled on a long silken gown. He passed her a neatly folded bundle of the same material and she gasped when she touched it. It was so soft it was like bubbles passing under her adoring fingers. He motioned for her to put it on.

Keeping the covers tucked under her chin, she tried, but the cord around her wrist prevented her. He reached across her and simply touched the chord and it unlocked itself from her wrist. You only had to touch it to unlock it? Had she not been asleep, she might have tried to escape. What a stupid lost opportunity that had been! Then again, only he could probably unlock it. Her glimmer of hope vanished.

She pulled on the garment and got out of bed. It fell around her body, a sleeveless simple dress that cascaded from her shoulders to the floor. Silvery and clinging, she didn't know if she loved or hated this Nuakki thing.

Osuman nodded approvingly and passed to her a small, palm-sized object with bristles. She stared at the strange thing, turning it over and over until he took it from her and started brushing it against her short hair. It snagged immediately and fell to the floor. Laughing, she grabbed it and tried herself, taking time to work through the weeks and months of tangles. He turned away and seated himself on the chair, picking up a pile of tan papers.

She watched him as he leafed through them, engrossing himself. Did all Nuakki take human partners? If so, then what had happened could no longer be considered unnatural. Had he stopped overseeing the mines? She did not know enough words to ask, and perhaps she was not allowed to ask anything of him anyway.

Her hair tangle-free, she set the brush down on the table and glided towards the window. Was she allowed to look out? She decided to try. She felt Osuman's eyes upon her, but he did not get up when she pushed the chiffon curtain aside.

Outside was a small balcony, but otherwise the view was

disappointing. It was dark beyond a sparse courtyard of pink
flagstones lit only by flaming braziers at each corner. A
depressing number of Nuakki soldiers paced the square,
their golden breastplates gleaming in the torchlight. She
was a dismally long way from the ground, too.

She peered into the darkness. Out there was her freedom. Her eyes picked out lights in the distance, perhaps the
lights of the village where the 'freer' people lived. Faint
figures moved across the light now and then, people going
about their business. Her eyes were drawn to a distant still
figure standing behind the fence at the edges of the light.

Thaya stepped closer to the window and rested a hand
upon the cold glass, her breath steaming it up. Could it be
the old woman who had shouted at her? She saw little more
than the silhouette of a small slender human, hair a wild
mess upon their head. She squinted, trying to be sure,
certain it was female but unable to see further.

Osuman's hand on her shoulder made her jump and she
dropped her gaze, her heart racing as if she had done something wrong.

"Come," said the Nuakki, leading her away.

Fear churned in her stomach, but all he said was,
"Sleep." He slipped off his robes and turned out the light,
beckoning for her to join him. It took all of her strength to
step towards him, and a little more to slip out of her
garment as he lifted the covers. He enfolded her in his arms
and did nothing more. He fell asleep, his great chest rising
and falling slowly, and she extricated herself from his arms,
more because they were heavy and hot than through any
particular revulsion. She wanted to hate him but dismally
found that she did not.

Thaya stared into the dark for hours before sleep found her, and there the Spirit Wolves awaited.

"Why do you come to me, what do you want?" she asked as they wagged their tails.

She went to the nearest, but he moved away and looked back as if asking her to follow. The she-wolf trotted behind her and pushed her with her snout. Where would they lead her if she followed? She couldn't escape the Nuakki in the dream-state, could she?

The wolf pushed on her again, harder, and the he-wolf lifted his snout to the air. Light floated down upon them, and Thaya and the wolves looked up. It sparkled with effervescence and she wondered if it were magic, especially when the wolves were as entranced by it as she was. The light condensed, becoming so bright she had to squint, and indigo eyes blazed open, the horn of the ghostly being sparkling into life.

"Thaaayaahh," a voice whispered from beyond the light. It wasn't coming from the being but sounded like a human's voice; a woman's.

A piercing noise broke through the beauty of the moment, and both wolves pushed on her. Beyond the being of light, something else moved.

"Thaaayaahh, run!" said the voice.

Fear iced her spine and she gave in to the pestering wolves, leaping along with them away from the light. *But I want to be with the light!* She dared to look back, but now the light was cut through with waves of ominous black and red.

Another flare torched the air above them and the whole ground upon which she ran shuddered.

The bed shook violently, dragging her out of the dream. Osuman jumped up, a long bronze blade already braced in his hands—ready to fight even in his sleep! His eyes wildly hunted the room as she clutched the sheets. It wasn't just her dream; he'd felt it too.

A boom sounded from outside and the whole night sky flared red—the same red as in her dream a moment ago. Pounding footsteps and then shouting sounded in the hallway. Osuman flung a sheet around himself and unlocked the door. Nuakki barked at each other. Thaya understood only, "attack again," and perhaps a name, "vormay," repeated over and over.

Osuman growled and slammed the door. Growling Nuakki curses, he threw on his clothing and armour.

"Dress!" he shouted at her.

She jumped out of bed and pulled on her new dress. *If they are under attack, this flimsy material will make great protection*, she thought sourly.

Booms sounded outside followed by more flares. She'd heard thunderstorms in the caverns but, though terrifying, they were always distant. This was right above them, shaking the whole room.

Osuman grabbed the silver chord and snaked it over her wrist. Just as he was tying her to the bed, an explosion rocked the building, making her scream as plaster fell on her head.

Cursing, he secured the cord around his belt instead, tying her to him. He thrust her under his arm like a doll and ran outside into the hallway. With a shiver, she noticed the golden Pain Stick in his belt alongside a knife and a long golden stave which curled into a symbol at one end. In a jolting, lurching, sickening journey, they galloped down two flights of stairs and out into the night.

They emerged into a courtyard surrounded by peach and cream stone buildings where the air was charged with chaotic energy. Thaya stared at the astonishing pandemonium. Nuakki guards were shouting and running across the flagstones in a tidal wave from right to left. Like immovable rocks in a river, elite, white-robed Nuakki with their funny conical hats stood amongst them, shouting orders and gesticulating wildly.

Fleeing in disorder were people such as she, dressed similarly in simple silken clothing. *So, I'm not the only one. The Nuakki do take human partners,* if that's what they were. 'Special slaves' may have been closer to the truth, though she had yet to learn what tasks she would be performing apart from in the bedroom.

But the mayhem on the ground became nothing compared to what was occurring in the sky. From great metal ships, silent light flared in huge white, red and blue beams, so bright it made it seem as if it were day. There were two types of vehicles; some were much smaller, round in shape, yet more numerous, and then there were the far fewer, but larger, cigar-shaped vehicles. The smaller were attacking, darting between the larger ships faster than birds. Orange beams burst from their undersides, striking the buildings below with ear-shattering booms and turning them and anyone inside into ash and rubble. Even the larger, two-storey buildings shuddered and partially collapsed, the screams of the occupants cut off abruptly. Bloody footprints and splatters patterned the flagstones, here a blood-soaked handprint, there a dripping pool. Blood wherever she looked.

Osuman set her down and ran, dragging her along until her lungs were ready to burst. An enormous explosion blasted them sideways, shattering a corner of the palace they had just come from. He tumbled through a manicured bush and onto the grass, with her sprawling on top of him. She glanced back. A third of the building's front wall had vanished, exposing rooms, hallways and stairwells. Was that Osuman's room that now lay gaping open to the elements?

He jumped up completely unscathed, and then she was gasping and staggering behind him again, the cord around her wrist rubbing painfully. Pretty, rose-lined pathways wound between the buildings, but the orange beams struck the ground exploding dirt and petals over them as they ran. The hair on her arms stood on end and her heart raced with her legs, but fear couldn't dampen the excitement of being outside and the hope of freedom even in death.

They stumbled out on to a huge open plateau flattened and decked with peach flagstones upon which a cigar-shaped ship languished on thick metal legs. Nuakki soldiers streamed towards it, taking the steps that led into a gaping doorway on its side two at a time. There were no humans here at all, but Nuakki swarmed everywhere. Osuman must look odd to them with her chained to his belt.

Through the din of explosions, shouting, and crumbling buildings, a lone shrill voice called out.

"Thaaayaahh!"

Thaya spun around, her eyes surveying the flashes in the sky and the rubble illuminated beneath, lingering upon the unmoving bodies of Nuakki and humans strewn beneath peach and cream bricks. Her gaze travelled along the fence to the lonely, skinny figure of an old woman. She clung to the wire of her cage, shaking it with her bony fingers, trying to capture her attention. Pain stabbed in Thaya's mind, making her double over. An old woman with scraggly white hair and the clearest blue eyes she had ever seen.

Osuman jerked her cord angrily and she staggered and

lost sight of the woman. The Nuakki aboard the ship shouted furiously at him, made cutting movements with their hands and pointed at her. He shouted back and shook his head, carrying on towards the steps, dragging her along.

They never made it to the ship.

The whole world lit up as a bright white light blinded Thaya. There was no sound, only the feel of cool energy coursing through her, then something slamming into her back so hard she would have thought it a physical object if she could have seen it. Then, both she and Osuman were hurled forwards as an enormous *boom* splintered the world.

Time swayed. Thaya lay on her back, eyes blinking up in the flickering light to the round ship barely twenty yards above her. She couldn't see Osuman and the chain about her wrist was gone. She closed her eyes, and in the darkness faces appeared, ugly, and neither Nuakki nor human but something completely different. They had no mouths and their huge bulbous pale heads were covered in thick veins. Large watery eyes blinked back at her.

"Run, Thaya," a voice said.

Just as she was getting onto her knees, another explosion rocked the world, sending her flying. She rolled to a stop on the hard ground and blinked open her eyes. The ship had vanished as fast as it had appeared, leaving her with ringing ears and partially blinded sight. She turned onto her front and pushed herself once more onto trembling legs. She had been blown against a wall, now partially collapsed, and the Nuakki ship that should have been behind her was gone. The entire area where it had been was a blackened, scorched pile of ash with unidentifiable bits of metal here and there, smouldering.

On the other side of the blackened area, a group of Nuakki were staggering to their feet. Beyond the billowing smoke was the old woman still clinging to the fence.

From the darkness enveloping the other side of the part-destroyed wall leapt two Spirit Wolves, pale blue and even more ghost-like in the strange light. Thaya's eyes widened and she stepped back. It could not be! But here they were, bounding towards her like they had in the darkness of her mind.

She braced herself as they neared, but the wolves ran right through her—they weren't solid like in her dreams—and circled back the way they had come. She must follow them; they were asking her to. Freedom lay in the darkness beyond that broken wall.

She lumbered forwards only to pause at the wall when a Nuakki shouted at her. After months of obedience beaten into her, her legs stopped by their command and she clung to the wall and looked back.

Osuman stood several yards away, held up by another Nuakki, blood covering his breastplate and half of his face. Their eyes met and he held her there as strongly as if he'd gripped her shoulders. Pain flickered across his features—was it the same pain that made him kiss her neck and cry into her hair? Other Nuakki started towards her, but he grabbed the wrist of one and barked an order.

Far to their right, light flared from the sky again, striking another docked Nuakki ship and incinerating half of it. The ground rocked under the assault and another blast blinded her again. The attacks by the smaller alien ships were ferocious and unrelenting. Ears ringing, eyes smarting, she turned and fled after the wolves.

THE KNOWING

S<small>KITTERING</small> <small>BEYOND THE WALLS OF HER PRISON, THE SHADOWS</small> embraced Thaya.

The smell of pine trees, as Amwa called them, became the sweet scent of freedom. For all the explosions, the flashing lights, and the screams of the dying, her fear vanished, and she abandoned herself to the night.

The Spirit Wolves glowed from ahead, leading her on, and she ran on tireless legs, her heart pounding, her breath fast and shallow, her mind a whir with wild thoughts. Her soft shoes tripped over roots and rocks, bruising her feet, and branches smacked into her face and tangled her hair. She ignored it all. The Nuakki could be right behind her, she daren't look back.

'Run Thaaayaahh,' the old woman had screamed, and so she did.

Over hillocks and through glades she hurtled until the sky brightened and she fell more times than she took steps. Only then did the wolves slow. Her trembling marathon paused, she looked up at the pink touching the sky. The explosions were a dim drum-beat in the far distance. Her legs wobbled and she collapsed down into a dip between two trees and lay there panting like an animal. The wolves stood before her and, thankfully, did not make her get up.

She closed her eyes, and bit by bit her pounding heart slowed along with her breath. When she opened them, the wolves were gone. Had they ever been there? She hoped they had for she was too spent to hunt for them. In the growing light of dawn, in the forest of pine, Thaya fell into an exhausted sleep.

When she awoke, two wolves of flesh and blood stood before her, the gentle breeze brushing their mottled slate and snow fur, pink tongues lolling between fangs.

She yelped and rolled out of her bolt-hole onto her feet, but the wolves silently watched her from large brown eyes. The slight wag of their bushy tails had the effect of calming her.

The she-wolf yapped, turned, walked a few paces, and yapped some more.

"I follow?" Thaya pointed at herself.

The she-wolf yapped and both wolves trotted away.

I can't do anymore! Her legs still burned, and her feet were blistered and bloody with splinters. Her shoes were barely shoes anymore, but strips of fabric partially held together by thread. The clothing Osuman had dressed her in was torn, muddy and blood-stained from the hundreds of cuts and scrapes covering her body. Still, she limped along —at least the wolves appeared to be in no rush.

What if the Nuakki were looking for her? She strained her ears, but there was only silence. Osuman had let her go, but why? Had he pitied her? Had she unlocked some emotion within him, long buried beneath the harsh rules and codes the Nuakki bore? Did he realise deep down that what they were doing was wrong? She could not know, but she found, through his peculiar actions, the ability to forgive him, and in forgiving him, she found herself being set free.

She swallowed against a desperate thirst. Osuman would feed her, Osuman would protect her. *No, I will not think it!*

There was no path this far from civilisation, but the ground was mostly bare, sandy earth, and the large gaps between the trees allowed easy passage. The he-wolf ran off into the forest, leaving the she-wolf to lead her.

He returned sometime later carrying a limp and bloodied creature. Thaya had no word for it, Amwa had not drawn this, and when the wolf dumped it at her feet, she noted its long bushy tail and dark brown fur. It looked sweet and gentle and she felt sorry for it. The wolf nosed the carcass towards her.

Thaya gagged despite the deep pain in her empty stomach. When she did nothing, the wolf picked it back up and they ran through the forest again.

An hour later, both wolves paused in an unremarkable patch of forest and scented the air. They dropped their snouts to the ground and circled between the trees. The she-wolf paused at a clump of earth and began digging it up spraying dirt, moss and roots behind her.

What on earth was the wolf doing? Thaya went to inspect and bent down to the rapidly deepening hole. The wolf uncovered rough brown fabric and stopped digging, wagging her tail as she looked at Thaya who reached into the hole and hauled out the coarse sack. The wolves clustered close, sniffing the bag excitedly as she began pulling out the contents.

She held up a jerkin made of a pale green fabric and

turned it over and over curiously before setting it aside and inspecting the rest. A pair of thick woven leggings, a simple shirt, and beneath them, toughened boots.

"Where did you find these?" She frowned. Had the wolves buried this stuff? Why? And why were they helping her? She laid a hand on the jerkin and chewed her lip. "It... seems familiar..." but nothing came to her from the black-hole.

She threw off Osuman's clothing and pulled on the shirt, tunic and leggings. They hung loose around her skinny frame. She wanted to put the boots on too, but her splinters hurt too much; she'd have to get them out first and although the clothing offered her warmth and protection, it couldn't feed her.

The he-wolf whined and nosed the bag, clearly wanting her to empty it fully.

"Let's have a look." She felt inside and pulled out the remaining item. It was a peculiar, solid object, heavy for its size, tubular, and made of silvery metal decorated with intricate writing and symbols all over it. One end curved into a wooden handle that fit snuggly into her grip.

A weapon. She shivered and looked around. Weapons were forbidden. At the end of every day in the mines, their pickaxes were taken from them and their bodies searched. Although there were no Nuakki here, she still hastily put the weapon down and hugged her arms.

The he-wolf sniffed the air then trotted off into the forest again. The she-wolf settled nearby and tore into the animal captured earlier. Seeing the wolf eat filled Thaya with desperation. Could she eat the raw animal? She was sick and faint with hunger, yet the thought made her feel sicker.

She turned her gaze onto the boots and focused on the painful task of prying the needles and splinters from her feet. The carcass devoured, the she-wolf came over and licked her wounds on one foot whilst Thaya worked on the other.

She tore strips of material from her Nuakki garment and wrapped these around her feet before sliding her feet into the boots. Standing up, a wide smile spread across her face; the boots fit perfectly, the ground no longer hurt, and her feet were warm. She picked up the sack, she could use it to carry things and she didn't want to leave any evidence of her passing. Something small and shiny tumbled out and rolled on the ground.

"A silver ring," she murmured, looking at it lying within the needles and twigs. It was like the gold ones the Nuakki wore only thinner and without any gems.

The ring shimmered at her touch. A strange sound rang in her ears, and the pain of forced memory made her dizzy. She closed her eyes and a man's pale face looked back at her, human in more ways than the Nuakki, but obviously *not* human. His skin was white as marble, and everything, from his hair, to his eyes, to his attire, was black.

Each moment of her past remained trapped in the black hole within, and the rare rebirthing of them into her conscious mind was a painful endeavour. She couldn't link that face to other memories or events, it just floated there, detached—she only knew that she had known him once. Maybe he had hurt her or maybe he was a friend, how could she know?

I would not have kept his ring, had he hurt me.

But knowing he was a friend and not an enemy hurt more, and she clasped the ring in her hand, longing for Amwa's gentle presence. Had her only friend survived the attack by the Vormae, as the Nuakki had called them? She recalled the ugly face of the aliens she had seen in her mind.

Was that truly how they looked? The sharp sting of another memory rising made her wince. Several Vormae stood before her and a human man with brown hair lay slumped and groaning at her feet. She stood against a cold wall in a small metal room and strangely glowing objects flashed all over the walls and ceilings.

Three Vormae loomed before her, watery eyes wide, expressionless faces terrifying. *"Run Thaaayaahh."* Echoed the old woman's voice, forcing Thaya to open her eyes. She stared blankly into the middle distance. *Thaaayaahh, is that my name? Who is the old woman? Did she send the Spirit Wolves to me?*

She pushed her index finger into the soft brown earth and wrote letters in it like Amwa did when teaching her.

T-H-A-A-A-Y-A-A- H-H

She stared at it, whispering the word again and again, imagining Amwa were here with here now. *"No, look,"* he would say, *"always simple, simple is better."*

"Not quite right," she murmured. She scrubbed her hand over the letters and wrote them again speaking aloud each one.

T-H-A-Y-A.

Warmth trembled through her body and the world wobbled with her sudden tears. There were no images or memories, just feelings. *Thaya. It's a name, I feel it. It is my name. If I see Osuman again, I will tell him my name is Thaya! Oh Amwa, I have a name!* "Thaya. Thaya. Thaya." She said it again and again, loving how it sounded, loving how it belonged truly to her.

Grinning, she tried the silver ring on each of her fingers, but it only fit her thumb, so she slipped it on that. The Nuakki wore rings, especially the women, and she felt a certain kind of dignity and prestige come over her. The ring brought her close to a forgotten friend, and she tried to remember his face more clearly, tried to bring back the memories from the darkness.

The he-wolf returned with another furry creature, dropped it on the ground between Thaya and the she-wolf, and trotted off again. He returned quickly and gently dropped a mouthful of purple berries—berries she had seen on the Nuakki fruit platters. Thaya all but ran to them and stuffed them in her mouth one after the other, grimacing at their sour taste as she devoured them.

They weren't enough to slake her hunger that burned like fire in her belly, and when the wolves ripped into the carcass, chomped on organs, sinew and bone, she joined them and they let her, she was one of them. The blood was more sour than the berries, and her stomach churned in revulsion, yet she forced herself to eat as one of them, on haunches using fingers and hands to deliberately decry the 'manners' taught to her by Osuman.

She was glad when the wolves finished it off and lay down to fight the rising nausea. But they did not let her rest for long, and soon began nudging her with their wet noses until she groaned and got onto her feet.

"But where are we going?" she sighed, her weary legs complaining as she followed them through the forest. *But I'll still follow them to the ends of the earth rather than return to the Nuakki.*

Had Amwa's gods sent the wolves to her? Amwa prayed to gods some nights. He'd draw them in the dirt, two male and one female, though only stick figures. He called them Ciru, Zin, and Iyd, and said they'd created humans and put them here, but though they sounded familiar, she couldn't feel them when she closed her eyes like he seemed to be able to do. Maybe they weren't speaking to her. Had these gods created humans to be slaves for the Nuakki? She wanted to feel the devotion bright in Amwa's eyes but couldn't. For her, the gods were as absent as everything that had happened to her before the...*blanking*. The 'Cleansing' she shivered at the word the Nuakki used for wiping away their memories and everything that they were.

Why would the gods create us only to take away our memories, memories of them, too? She pushed the thoughts away and scrambled over a fallen tree. If she thought too much, her head began to throb—was that part of the Cleansing too? She frowned in confusion. Nothing made sense about her or the world. *Don't think, don't think, otherwise the tears will come and then the Pain Stick!*

The wolves had slowed to trot, ears pricked forwards, noses twitching. Thaya felt a change in the air, a charge that made the hairs on her arms rise. She lifted her hands and stared at her fingers, there was the faintest shimmer coming from them.

"Wow, my hands!"

Her gaze lifted from her fingers and she stopped abruptly and stared at what the wolves were looking at. A huge, single stone thrust out of the sand and dirt, clothed in cosy moss and adorned by ivy. Dark grey and cracked in exposed areas, it was peculiar in a land of only pale yellow or pink stone. It stood alone between the trees at an unnatural angle—clearly, someone had put it here.

The wolves turned to look at her.

"What is it?" she asked them, wishing they could reply with words. They watched her as she stepped closer and lifted her hands to feel the energy. The shimmer intensified and tiny sparks bounced off her fingertips.

"The energy, it's coming from the stone," she whispered. Amwa had never said anything about stones having magical properties, but this one she could *feel*. Why had the wolves brought her to it? Slowly, she reached out a hand, aiming for the bare patch of grey between the moss and ivy.

Energy exploded between her and the stone, sweeping over her like a wave as the world vanished. She looked into a vast open space that stretched out above, below and all around her. One by one, as if someone had turned them on, lights appeared in the darkness and were connected by a silken thread of shimmering light. She gasped at it, an enormous latticework of lines and orbs made of pure golden light. It was as if she were hanging in the night sky alongside the stars, only all the stars were connected by delicate lines of vibrating, humming threads.

The stone appeared again before her, but it was a massive thrumming, glowing obelisk. A thin beam of energy led out in a straight line from the stone and linked it to an orb of light in the distance. That orb had three lines of energy connecting it to several orbs even further away, and they again were connected to many more. There were *thousands* of orbs of light. Thaya stared open-mouthed.

She had the strong feeling that what she looked upon was a map, like Amwa had drawn of where they slept and where they worked, and the tunnels they walked between that connected the two. Only this was a *living* map, she couldn't describe it as anything other than that, but the light was alive, the orbs were alive, even the dark spaces between the light thrummed with life and energy.

Something was drawing upon her, pulling her forward but she was resisting. She dropped her hand from the stone's surface and the living map vanished along with the energetic pull. Mouth still hanging open, she stared at the grey monolith for a long time. Her world was so pitifully small and nonsensical, but she wouldn't let herself cry, not now. And what would happen if she didn't resist?

It took an age for her to lift her hands again, both of them this time, and touch the bare patch of grey. The wolves had brought her here, what else was she to do? *I won't resist this time,* she said, spreading her fingers wide and pressing them against the stone.

Her entire being was sucked forwards into what should have been solid rock. Lightning flared all around her and then surged forwards into a tunnel of flickering energy. She screamed and tumbled through it, cartwheeling head over heels. She clenched her eyes shut but that made it worse. Something about the energy, the way it flickered and sparked, caused memory to flicker and spark in her mind. She'd done this before but why? She screamed and trembled, clutching for something to hold onto but there was nothing.

Darkness spewed around her like black liquid poured into a whirlpool, and it swirled around the light. The entire tunnel shuddered, and in its actions, memory of another occurrence came clearly into her mind. The pale-faced man with black hair running, a device in his hand identical to her own—the faces of the Vormae looming before her.

The tunnel of light didn't make a sound, it simply vanished.

An instance of darkness engulfed her and then a blinding light. A high-pitched wailing sound scoured her ears, and her body was paralysed, becoming as rigid as a plank of wood where only her eyes could move.

She was not aware of losing consciousness, but in the next moment, she was somewhere completely different, blinking up into the faces of several, exceedingly ugly, Vormae. She sensed rather than knew that time itself had shifted—and there was a huge chunk of it missing. *Another black hole to add to the others*...She was beyond terror.

A withered, three-fingered, spindly hand touched her forehead, its repulsive fingers wrapping around her crown like cold wet rope. She screamed as bolts of energy crashed through her brain, like the Pain Stick, only worse. She bucked and strained against invisible restraints, causing the pain to intensify but unable to stop herself convulsing.

Impossibly, she felt them inside her head. They were looking inside her mind, ravaging through it, careless of the pain they caused. But there was nothing for them to find— her mind was empty.

And then, something happened.

The black hole that was the centre of her being, that was always there when she closed her eyes or tried to remember her past, wobbled and then shattered. Pain bolted through her. She screamed from the depths of her soul as a tsunami of memories, emotions, feelings and forgotten abilities, ploughed in and drowned her.

In one incredible rush, Thaya lived her whole life once more, but this time with complete recall. Images attached with emotions pulsed through her faster than light. From her inception in the womb to the moment she touched the light of the Saphira-elaysa, from when she fled Brightwater and the Shades, to the endless plains stretching out around Stonehenge with Arendor at her side.

Again, she lived through the Nuakki pressing his hand against her forehead, breaking her apart and 'Cleansing' her mind of everything that she was. Billions of moments that made up her life could not be mentally processed, nor the emotions endured, and she drowned within them.

The clerics of all three gods taught that when you died you reviewed your life. This was her review, and she was dead, the Vormae had killed her. That was why, beyond the deluge of memories and feelings, a pale light grew. Well, she would meet it with strength and dignity. *I shall run no more! I'm no longer a slave, and I never was. I am no longer afraid for nothing more can be done to me. I am Thaya, Thaya Farseeker, and this, I am!*

The feel of the light that kissed her face took her breath away. It was warmth, comfort and joy, it was complete understanding and utter forgiveness—she had felt it once before when she had first touched him, the Saphira-elaysa, but this was so much more, this was so absolute, this was...*huge!*

The light itself was conscious, wrapping her up in loving arms as she stood in an infinite open space. The light cleansed away all her pain, wounds and grievances, turning her body, her mind, and her soul into pure harmonious light too. *I have become the light; I am the light!*

A knowing came upon her. She didn't know how else to describe it, but this light was the source of everything that there was in all of creation; it was the First Cause, it was Eternal, and from it, she had come.

This Eternal First Cause was consciousness itself, and it was intelligence itself, and it was love itself. And it spoke to her with full sentience.

"Remember."

She remembered then why she had come to exist, why she had chosen to *be* at all. A task so simple, and yet so divine. She repeated what she felt, although words were feeble and lacking compared to the Knowing. "I shall return to free that which is the light. That is, and has always been, my heart's desire."

Here, there was no time. Here the light didn't fade or move away, it was her focus of attention that changed, and she turned to look back into the cold, lonely darkness.

Electricity pulsed through her in agonising waves, jolting every muscle, cracking her teeth against each other as her jaw snapped shut, pulsing her heart with arrhythmia, and crushing her brain in a vice.

The pain faded and a groan crawled up her throat. Cold fat fingers pulled open her eyes, causing them to water in the blaze of harsh white that shone into her face. Beyond the cold light, bulbous heads clustered, thin-cheeked, watery-eyed, mouthless, slack-shouldered and skinny.

Gone was the warm loving light and the feeling that nothing could hurt her again. Gone was the joy, the infinite understanding, the Knowing. Her body shook with pain. Saliva seeped from the corners of her mouth, and her eyes watered from the cold bright air. She couldn't move, she could barely breathe, and the stench of those *things* flared her nostrils.

One of them lifted a thin metal rod and pushed it against her stomach. The whole of her insides felt as if they were being jumbled, twisting and contorting.

Thaya filled her lungs and screamed.

26

IN THE BEGINNING

ANOTHER SCREAM ECHOED BEYOND THAYA'S; HIGH-PITCHED, inhuman.

Saphira-elaysa!

She knew that sound—it haunted her memories. The Saphira-elaysa appeared in her mind's eye, a shimmering being of light that changed from white to purple to black. He thrashed and reared, fighting against chains that bound him, his golden horn slashing at unseen foes.

The rod twisted, the agony increased, and she and the Saphira-elaysa screamed again. *He's feeling my pain!* she realised. Where was he? He felt so close! She felt as if he were right here with her.

"Stop," she pleaded.

To her surprise, the rod was removed, and the pain ebbed away. Opening her eyes, her vision returned slowly. The Vormae had turned away, their grey-white skin stretched taut over balloon-like heads as they clustered together and convened. She strained to hear them, but they spoke silently with their minds—after all, how else could they speak without mouths?

She didn't think they stopped the pain because she asked them to, she got the distinct feeling they were analysing the effects of what they were doing to her. *I remember them now! Dear gods—no, dear Eternal Spirit! Everything has returned to me, and these creatures act without remorse or empathy.*

She looked down. Pale metal clamps bound her hands and feet to the hard thing she was laying upon, although she wasn't exactly 'laying,' rather tied upright and suspended from the floor. Again she was without her Fireshot, her only weapon, and again her ring was gone. *At least they let me keep my clothes! Dear Arendor, I remember you, how could I forget? My only friend in this awful world.*

She began to cry at the hopelessness of the situation. How did she think she could ever help the Saphira-elaysa when all that had happened had proven her impotence and weakness? Did she really think she could find her twin soul and free him from the Vormae? *I didn't think, I just had to do, and now we're both here, doomed to the mercy of the Vormae, and they don't appear to have any.* But one thing they retained in abundance was extreme intelligence and a supremely advanced technology, even to that which she had witnessed on Earth.

The Vormae ceased their communing and turned to face her, their pale, sickly eyes opening wide. One pressed closer and a strange voice spoke in her mind, strained to a low pitch, cracked and gasping and hard to understand.

"You will display to us your...*connection* to the Saphira-elaysa. You will lead us to...*understanding* them."

"I won't help you unless you free him," Thaya said aloud, her voice shaking and feeble.

"You will display your connection." The closest Vormae inclined his head, and she realised he was not asking her, but telling her. She swallowed audibly as they reached impossibly long fingers towards her, but they did not touch her and instead fiddled with something on the side of the pallet to which she was strapped.

They turned away and started walking, and her pallet followed them without them even holding it! It floated above the ground, not even wavering an inch. The Vormae remained close, surrounding her floating pallet, their black and red robes swishing. *Black and red, they remind me of Inigo Price and the vampires we fled from on Earth. That was so long ago, and how I hated it...but I'd do anything to go back there just so I wasn't alone.*

The Vormae moved with a long loping gait, rising slowly up and down with each step as if they were bobbing on rolling ocean waves. She tried to look around but found a band clamped over her forehead prevented her from moving her head. They walked along a corridor devoid of colour, everything pale grey and white from the floor to the wall panels, to the ceiling.

Along the ceiling, bright lights illuminated everything and banished all shadows. If she ever escaped there was nowhere to hide, not even a nook in the walls! Plastic, that's what the walls reminded her of, that strange flexible material that made up the bottle of water Arendor had given to her. Perhaps the walls were more solid than that; the grey bits were some kind of metal, not shiny but brushed and dull.

They walked for a long time, unhurried. A wall panel made a hissing sound, sank back into the wall, and then slid soundlessly to the side tucking seamlessly into the wall itself. Through it stepped two more Vormae, identical to the three who surrounded her, even to their clothing. They were all clones of one another, like ants.

Beyond the newcomers, Thaya glimpsed an identical corridor to the one they were in stretching far into the distance, white and grey and devoid of any character. This place was enormous, but for all their intelligence, the Vormae lacked any creativity; everything was a carbon copy of everything else, even their own bodies. There was no character, no beauty—everything in their environment was purely functional.

A Fallen Race, Arendor had described them as. Did 'fallen' mean losing your creativity? It certainly meant losing your empathy and feelings as far as she could tell.

They walked for hundreds of yards, passed another 'hidden' door with its strange sliding panel, and two more Vormae stepped out silently to join them. *Are they speaking to each other telepathically?* Thaya couldn't tell.

Her entourage was now significant; a large group of foul-smelling, ugly Vormae surrounded her, and all thoughts of escape were driven from her mind. She gave in to the depression. Whatever lay ahead? Well, hopefully, it wouldn't last too long. It would be painful, yes, but then she could just die. *They haven't killed me yet, they want me alive for some reason.* What if she remained strapped like this for days? Maybe even years while they performed their tests on her until she could take it no more?

She closed her eyes and focused on her breathing. They wouldn't know how to keep her alive. Having no mouths meant they surely wouldn't have food on board, would they? But that just brought up the question of how they *did* sustain themselves? Perhaps they lived for thousands of years like the Agaroths. And how long did Nuakki live? At least she was free of them and would never have to find out.

They halted and she opened her eyes as they turned right down another long, characterless corridor. They paused again before another insignificant wall panel. The panel slid aside and Thaya's mouth dropped open. Within was an entirely different world.

The 'area' into which they stepped was so vast she couldn't even see the ceiling. It was dark. Dim orange lights nestled in corners barely illuminating their surroundings. What they did illuminate was intriguing; plants, ferns, trees, bushes and grasses swaying in a faint breeze as if they stood outside in a jungle. They weren't real, were they? But, looking down, she realised there was too much detail for it to be fake; brown and decaying fallen leaves littered the ground, here a tear in a leaf, there a mottled blemish—all genuinely life-like.

The walls, though dark and hard to decipher, were concave and covered in swaying ivy and clematis, their extravagant indigo beauties nodding dolefully amongst other climbing plants she couldn't name. A stream trickled beneath them and its rushing sound echoed through the cavern. As her eyes adjusted from the bright lights in the corridor to the darkness, she identified old oaks, giant sycamores and silver-trunked birches standing beside other trees she had never seen before. Between their trunks, extensive ferns and grasses made their homes. The Vormae had created a whole forest oasis inside this...*place,* wherever and whatever it was.

Thaya peered up through the branches and into the canopies, half expecting a bird to fly out tweeting loudly, but she saw no animals; no bees or butterflies danced among the flowers. There were, at least from her position, no

animals or insects, only vegetation and the stream. But...
why had they created any of this?

The door slid shut behind them, plunging them into the
gloom. A Vormae stepped forwards, his wide feet crunching
upon leaves and twigs. He made a noise, it sounded as if it
came out of his nostrils, low and whiny at first then crescendoing into screeching that made her wince. He stopped, but
the noise echoed loudly, the breeze vanished, and everything became still.

Blinding white light burst above them forcing her to
squint, but the Vormae just stood unblinking and moved
forwards with her still floating between them. *The Vormae
are unaffected by the light?*

Thaya blinked as the light dulled slightly and she stared
into the lush forest as they moved along a rough path.
Ahead, the trees opened up, and in the centre was...some-
thing. She strained to see, but her vision was blocked by the
Vormae swaying in front of her.

They stopped and the Vormae parted to stand beside
her. Strange sounds came from their nostrils and their
watery eyes opened wider as they stared entranced at the
horror before them.

Thaya couldn't breathe.

Entrapped, surrounding a pool of liquid silver, were ten
shimmering white Saphira-elaysa. Around their bodies
twisted silver chains like the one Osuman had put on her,
and these chains bound them to the ground so tightly they
were forced into kneeling on their front legs whilst their
hindquarters remained thrust and resisting into the air.
More chains snaked over their elegant heads thrusting their
noses against the earth, forcing their golden horns to dip
into the pool. They were statues of gleaming white crystal

ready to shatter; flanks quivering, eyes barely open, and each pitifully gasping from pain.

"How can you?" Thaya rasped, but no words could do justice to the horror she felt. Did the Vormae not see their pain and suffering? These creatures of light should be frolicking and free, bringing their blessings to all beings of the cosmos, but instead they were captured and chained—sacrilege on the deepest level which defied comprehension.

They moved closer, step by loping step, and she saw that not all the unicorns were shimmering white. On the far side was one which was grey. From his hooves to the horn that should have been golden, and the hair that should have been white—he was all one block of slate hewn from a single stone. A real statue. *But why a statue when the rest are living?*

"They are dying, and you must stop them," the broken, nasally voice forced its way into her mind answering her unspoken question.

"Then let them go," Thaya growled. She wouldn't speak to them in her mind, they shouldn't be in there! "They are better dead than caged by you. Filth."

The voice continued emotionlessly, ignoring her words. *"These are all that remain here. The others we captured have perished; they all perish after fifty revolutions of the sun."*

Thaya caught her breath, fifty revolutions of the sun? What did that mean?

"Fifty Urtharian years," the voice replied.

Thaya sagged. Chained like this for fifty years? How many had perished here? She would have staggered had she not been strapped to a board. She took deep breaths, her insides still aching from the rod they had used on her.

"One thousand." The voice answered her thoughts again, frankly and without emotion.

Thaya struggled against the bindings and screamed, a terrible sound that echoed throughout the chamber.

The Vormae all turned their eyes upon her, faces expressionless.

"We must have them all, or we shall perish."

The nearest Vormae walked closer, the slits of his ugly nostrils widening as he lifted his grossly long hand.

"No!" Thaya flinched from the cold hand of pain as it wrapped around her head.

She screamed as bolts of pain exploded through her brain. In the pain came images from the Vormae, the Vormae's memory forcing inside her mind and imprinting there.

Scores of Saphira-elaysa struggled within a red light. They pawed the ground and swung their horns but could not break free of it.

Chains snaked around them with a life of their own and tightened, forcing them to their knees and their noses to the ground. When their horns dipped into the strange pool of liquid silver, they screamed and bucked. Their pain bolted through Thaya's head and she screamed as they did. Light pulsed out of their horns into the liquid and it began to glow golden. Their light began to fade, and their screams died as their struggles ceased.

"After the initial bleed, they become passive, but the life-essence extracted reduces to minute amounts, it is not enough."

Thaya shook her sagging head and tried to manage the pain as the hateful voice continued.

"They're connected to a greater life-source, and we must open the flow. In you lies the answer."

"No," Thaya said aloud, but it came out mumbled. Her whole head throbbed.

"We will not perish."

"Die!" Thaya hissed and closed her eyes against the pain.

Was there any way to set them free? She focused her mind on the liquid pool, what was that? It was thick and viscous—

"Element Vodon, unknown to your race. It's the only substance capable of harnessing the life-force from these containers."

Element Vodon? They called the Saphira-elaysa 'containers'? Thaya moaned as a new wave of pain hit her and with it more images flooded into her mind. She looked upon vast floor-lit rooms filled with endless rows of glass pods—like the pods the Agaroths slept in, only long and thin and functional. Inside each pod lay a supine Vormae and every pod was connected by a tube through which flowed this Element Vodon liquid metal. There were hundreds, possibly thousands, of resting Vormae.

"You would destroy one species just so another can live?" Thaya panted, cold sweat rolling down her face and everything dancing deliriously before her.

The hand removed itself, and she slumped against her restraints, her whole body drenched in cold sweat.

The question confused them for the voice in her head took a while to reply. *"What species would not?"*

Thaya barely heard it. All she could focus on was the absence of pain. She had no answer. Would she willingly die so another might live? Yes, perhaps for Arendor or Maggy, maybe even for Arto and Solia, definitely for her family. But would she condemn her whole race to save another? She hadn't the strength to reason through such a question. She could only feel, and she felt that what they were doing was wrong.

"If you hadn't destroyed yourselves, you wouldn't need

to," Thaya's mouth spoke the words, but they were not her own, even her voice was of a lower timber. Who had spoken through her? She lifted her head and so did the Vormae.

"Lower the One," the voice commanded but not to her and she wondered why she'd heard it. Had they unwittingly opened up telepathy between her and them, or simply forgotten to close it? Only a Magi would know. What had spoken through her to them?

Two Vormae lifted their arms, long fingers reaching up and bulbous fingertips flaring. Shards of lightning arced from them into the air above the Saphira-elaysa. A giant ball of diffuse light glowed above the Pure Ones and slowly began to lower towards them through the tree canopy.

A very odd sensation flowed over her skin and bloomed within. The light began to pulse brighter and deeper, more golden in colour with each beat. It pulsed in rhythm with her heartbeat, and when her breath and pulse quickened, so did it.

Within the light, something moved. A golden horn tossed, a hoof lifted, an elegant neck arced. Nostrils flared and brilliant indigo eyes opened. *Is it him, my lode star?* Thaya felt a rushing sensation. Her breath came in short gasps and she struggled to control the rising panic. Her whole body tingled with energy, and she felt increasingly detached and faint.

Those indigo eyes locked onto hers and the light surrounding it burst forwards, engulfing her and throwing the Vormae to the ground. Thoughts, feelings, words...all tumbled through her in a torrent. And Thaya knew.

He and I are one. He was as much a part of her as her own hand. The knowing filled her. Soon, after so long-held captive, she would be free, and all loneliness, emptiness and pain would end.

The Saphira-elaysa's memories came to her and she witnessed his capture.

Terrifying light beaming down from round metal ships, trapping him. The young adult stood no chance against them. His shame and fear were her own as he was lifted from the ground and chained, just as she had been enslaved by the Nuakki. But his imprisonment lasted years, not months, and he watched others of his race die in chains around him, only to be replaced by more of his kind. Yet he lived on, unable to break free, unable to even find salvation in death—for no matter what the Vormae did, they could not bleed him dry. The life-force just would not flow from his horn. But his presence calmed the other Saphira-elaysa, and something about him extended their life-force. So they kept him, and for that, he hated himself even more. He was Saphira-elaysa, but he was forever changed, forever different, in more ways than just the colour of his hair. She reached for the light—his light—and he reached for her.

"I know you," whispered Thaya.

"I feel you," replied the being in her mind that was so much more than just a Saphira-elaysa; a part of her soul itself.

Tears spilled down her cheeks as she felt herself rising towards him. The straps restraining her cracked and broke, and she was free. With that same direct knowing she knew that nothing in the cosmos could stop what was occurring in this moment, and that beyond her and him, something much more was with them. It was divine, it was a Witnessing, it was the Light itself.

It was the same all-encompassing, divine feeling she had experienced only moments before when the Vormae had unwittingly unlocked her memories and all that the Nuakki had taken from her was returned.

The Eternal Spirit flared within the centre of her being, the creation point, the endpoint, and all that had been done and undone would be made whole now.

The Saphira-elaysa thrust his horn forward and she grasped it like she had in the beginning.

Anything that was not light, vanished. Her body became shades of gold as his became silver. Her mind joined with his and their souls melded; two souls twinned in perfection, harmony, and joy. Thaya wanted to remain in this state forever, but it was he who initiated the change.

There was a task to complete, the reason why they were here at all. She felt his will direct down, and she followed him. Her physical body returned to her, and she wrapped her arms around his powerful neck as the harmony and joy receded. The darkness of the forested chamber returned as the light vanished.

And the bloodshed began.

No longer chained, the Saphira-elaysa swung her onto his back where she clung desperately, leapt ten feet and lunged. His horn speared through the chest of the nearest Vormae as if it were made of butter. He plunged so deep his forehead rammed against its chest. Thaya stared into its white watery eyes, for the first time displaying any emotion, the emotion of shock. He jerked violently, hurling the Vormae away, brown blood gushing out of its nose, earholes and chest as it slumped to the floor.

The Saphira-elaysa's motion was a blur. Magic flared from his horn causing all the Vormae to fall to their knees. He reared, hooves slashed, and the head of a Vormae split and crumpled. Power surged between her and him, and for all his helplessness over the years, he had in their joining become invincible. She could feel his need for magic and she willingly gave her energy to him, filling him with all that she had. She had never really felt magic within her before, but now it flowed within her, unlocked by the Saphira-elaysa.

Thaya wanted to help him fight, but he moved too fast for her, she could only cling to his neck and wrap her legs around his back. She sensed he wanted her to do nothing anyway. This was his vengeance.

A Vormae ran at them and rammed a silver rod into his stomach. He shrieked and staggered, and the pain hit her too, her intestines twisting and tightening.

She kicked out savagely, knocking the Vormae back but nothing more damaging. Her soul twin whirled around and slashed his horn. Thaya gulped as the Vormae staggered, half its head sliding off of its neck. Never had she thought the Saphira-elaysa capable of rage and violence. But they had to get free, and her companion knew no other way.

Revenge, that's what I feel. It coursed through her as it coursed through him, making his body quiver with it. She didn't want the Vormae to live, she hated them as much as he, but she didn't want to watch them die. And so she buried her head against his neck, just where his soft silvery-white mane ended, and prayed for it to end.

He reared and struck. The Vormae made strange noises, nasally screams, as they died. It felt like an hour had passed, but it could only have been minutes, maybe only seconds, before the Saphira-elaysa stopped moving, his sides heaving and his breath coming in powerful snorts.

His head hung down, the blood and gore of the massacred Vormae lying around him. He was exhausted and repulsed and struggling with something deep within him.

They had so little time to spare, and so she urged him on. "Free the others before more come."

He said nothing as he walked to the closed door and

plunged his horn into it. The whole panel sprayed sparks, and blackened cracks snaked all over it. She prayed it was sealed shut. Calmly he turned, stepped over the disfigured bodies of the Vormae, and walked towards the chained unicorns. All of them had fallen to the floor, their haunches no longer thrust into the air. He lowered his gore-covered horn and pressed it against the chain of the first Saphira-elaysa. A spark burst where he touched, and the chain split and fell away.

The freed Saphira-elaysa did not move, did not even open her eyes. Thaya slid off his back and touched her nose while he moved on to the next. She ran her hands over the female's head. "Wake up," she whispered.

The female slowly opened her golden eyes, appearing confused as she turned her head from left to right. Thaya wasn't strong enough to help her stand, but she tried to steady her as she got onto trembling front legs, legs she might not have used for years.

Thaya moved onto the next one freed; a male struggling to his feet, and then onto the next. All of them were confused and weak. One male fell twice before straddling his legs wide and panting with his head down.

She winced as sudden pain crackled in her head. Cold waves of fear washed over her. Danger—the Vormae. Somehow, she could feel them, as if what they had done to her had left her the ability to sense them.

"More are coming!" she cried.

27

UNGROUNDED CONSTRUCTS

"GET UP!" HER SOUL TWIN COMMANDED SHOVING HIS NOSE into the male he was trying to rouse.

Thaya stared at him. It was the first proof that unicorns could actually speak with their mouths. His voice was almost human, deeper perhaps, and with more tones. She didn't know why she was surprised; the Gryphon could speak, and apparently, all magical creatures could. She'd only ever encountered Dryads before, and being humanoid it was no surprise they could speak.

All but two of the ten Saphira-elaysa stood, all of them keeping their heads hanging low, eyes half-open, noses to the floor and breathing heavily. They were closer to death than alive. How were they ever going to get out of here even if they *could* fight?

Thaya looked to her Saphira-elaysa twin and her soul shivered. He stood beside an older female, the broken chains of silver fallen around her, but she was not rising. She was set back on her haunches and her nose pressed against the ground. Grey tinged her horn, and she didn't shine like the others. Her soul twin held his head against hers, their horns crossing, both their eyes closed. Danger gnawed at Thaya, crawling over her skin, but he needed this moment, the fallen Saphira-elaysa needed this moment.

Slowly, he lifted his head, and turned away from the dying unicorn to the grey one Thaya had thought was a statue. Her mouth went dry. A devastating scene, sorrow adding to sorrow. The male looked to be in his prime, strong, powerful, perfect in every way, but the Vormae had brought him down, had bled him dry, and all that remained was his statue of stone. For that's what he looked like, an object, a granite figure like the leaping dolphin fountain on the quay in Havendell Harbour. Is that what happened when unicorns died, they turned into statues? Or was it just what the Vormae did to them? It should be impossible that such beings could die.

Her soul twin pressed his head and his horn against the dead unicorn, and when tears fell down his nose, the room shivered for Thaya.

A blast made them jump. The Vormae were trying to open the door. *So close!* The unicorns lifted their heads, their shared fear palpable. They clustered together then one female led them, stepping through the trees towards the stream. Thaya followed, wishing they would run, but where to? The female dipped her horn into the water and it sparkled and fizzed. The others did the same and the whole stream became aglow with shimmering light.

More explosions rattled the door, scorch marks began to cover it turning it into an ugly patchwork of black and white.

The unicorns lifted their horns and lowered their noses to drink. Thaya dropped down beside them and scooped the water into her mouth. It tasted pure and clean, as delicious as cool spring water, and energy filled her with each mouthful. This was more than just water; they'd done something to it. If all the myths and legends were to be believed, then Saphira-elaysa could purify all liquids and this was proof enough for Thaya.

A huge explosion rocked the ground and a giant crack appeared across the door, large enough to see movement the other side.

"The door!" Thaya cried.

"Hold on to me," he said.

Thaya grabbed hold of his neck and paused wondering if she had done something improper. Was it all right to touch Saphira-elaysa in this manner? Fire sprayed through the crack in the door, and the gap doubled in size. Forgetting any perceived protocol, she swung herself onto his back, hoping that whatever he had in mind he'd do quickly.

One by one, the unicorns stepped into the water and began walking downstream, with her and her twin bringing up the rear. Couldn't they go any faster?

"Hurry!" Thaya cried. She could almost hear the Vormae breathing. But the unicorns ignored her, and she realised they were doing something. A soft mist began to flow from the first unicorn and joined with the energy of the next. The mist-energy grew exponentially as each Saphira-elaysa added to it.

"Magic?" she asked.

He didn't answer, he had his eyes closed and the energy sparkled blue in the air around him. He was collecting and directing it.

Thaya inhaled sharply as the Saphira-elaysa at the front melted into white light. The next unicorn did the same, and then the next. One by one, they became waves of pure white light surrounded by the blue. Thaya's pulse raced.

"Do not resist," his deep voice comforted her. "Flow, like the water."

Magic surrounded her, she saw his horn dissipate into silver light, followed by his head and neck. She held her breath and closed her eyes, doing everything she could to not resist *something*. A cool wind blew, passing right through her skin and even into her bones! Every cell in her body began to thrum with energy.

It's okay, it's all right. I'm safe and this is all normal! After all, what were Portals and Star Portals? And she'd gone through plenty of those.

She opened her eyes and looked out into a world of silver, azure, and gold energy. Gone was the forest, the stream, and even the Saphira-elaysa, all was just insubstantial, mesmerising light. The energy drew together and lengthened like a rainbow road leading ahead, then it burst into spiralling white light.

Moments passed within the light, then the Saphira-elaysa appeared ahead and she was seated atop her soul twin once more. Now, they moved fast. Rather than running, they flowed and moved with the energy itself! *Definitely not like horses!* Faster than a gallop, the Saphira-elaysas' gait was completely different to a horse's. They ran so smoothly, with greater elegance and speed, and so fast Thaya had to cling tightly. Daring to look down, she stared at the pure energy flowing like a river beneath them.

Black lightning cracked above, and she ducked with a yelp. *Vormae!* They weren't going to let them get away that easily, their very existence depended on their vampiring off the Saphira-elaysa.

"You have the power within you if you dare to use it." Her twin soul's voice came distorted around her.

What did he mean? She didn't even have her Fireshot.

She chewed her lip remembering what Arendor had said, '*I see within you untapped power, bravery, a soul that can become strong if you but let it. Conquer your fears, find your courage, and you will go where even angels fear to tread. The light of the Creator burns within you, let it shine.*'

What power did they both mean? Had she found her courage yet? Could she dare to hold power like Solia had? She wanted to say, 'yes,' that she felt the power within her, a glow within her heart, within her solar plexus, that had always been here, but now she was with him, her lode star, she *felt* it come alive. Perhaps all humans had this feeling somewhere inside. But she didn't know what it was, and no one had ever shown it to her, much less told her how to use it. Maybe Maggy knew more, maybe it was part of the forgotten and lost powers that had been stripped from humans over millennia.

"But I've no idea what it is or how to use it!" she said.

"Raise your hand, let it flow," he said. "Now, here of all places, nothing can stop it. I'll help you." His voice was ever calm despite the tornado of magic around them.

Bruised sludge seeped into the energy above them alongside the shimmering forcefield of the tunnel they ran through. It pushed forwards ahead of them, bulging and churning, trying to break the Saphira-elaysas' magic.

She felt him nudge that power within her. It was the only way she could describe it to herself and she raised her hand as it built within her. It was like feeling fully alive, an essence, a power, a will—it grew with its own energy, chaotic and uncontrollable, but there.

Like a cork exploding from a bottle, golden energy burst from her extended left palm straight into the sludge above them.

The sludge screamed and recoiled and fell behind them.

"Haha!" Thaya laughed in triumph and awe, but he remained silent, almost grim. She couldn't hold the power for long. The Nuakki brand on her palm ignited in agony. The magic dissipated and she sagged with sudden exhaustion. She breathed deeply and clung on to his neck, his gait so smooth she doubted she could ever fall off him.

A wailing scream came from behind them and the walls of their spinning tunnel of light bulged. Shadows emerged from the walls, long spindly hands made of smoke reached towards them.

"Shades!" Thaya's blood ran cold. They filled her with the same choking terror she had felt in Brightwater.

She ducked down, dodging a ghostly claw. The shadows became more substantial and crawled out of the walls. Her twin soul lowered his head and ran faster, leaping over one, dancing to the left to avoid another. They weren't winning this fight, they were barely fleeing it. The Shades, unfettered by solid form, moved faster than the Saphira-elaysa and flowed around them. Her mount flailed a hoof out, and a Shade screamed and vanished into puffs of smoke. He stumbled trying to strike another, causing him to drop a few paces behind the others. Shades shot past them, reaching out to attack those in front.

One appeared right beside her. She screamed and fell back from its grasping hands, but razor sharp claws raked across her cheek, solid and slicing. She smarted, blood trickling from the wound. Another reached around his neck, dragging its fingers and drawing blood where it passed. He snorted and Thaya punched at its hands. It lost its grip and fell away, mouth opening up in a howl that engulfed its whole face.

Ahead, Shades swarmed the others, clawing their sides and leaving bloody rakes wherever they touched.

Thaya swallowed. They couldn't fail now, they just couldn't!

She lifted her hand again, trying to cultivate within her the same energy she had used before. It was still there but weak and unwilling, churning her already bruised insides. She tried to force it forth. It travelled from her solar plexus to her palm and her brand burned in agony. She cried out and looked at her hand. The Nuakki mark was no longer gold but red and bloody. She held it against her chest.

"You cannot use it again so soon," shouted her twin soul. "What is that on your hand?"

"A Nuakki bran—"

She started to answer, but the tunnel trembled violently, and they plunged into darkness.

The air became so thin she felt faint, all she could do was pant and sip it. She'd experienced this all before—the Vormae had won. "They've taken control of our portal," she said. This was similar in every way to a portal, and if it was that, it meant Saphira-elaysa had the power to create their own.

"It was never strong to begin with," her mount replied, his quiet tone worrying her. "We're too weak, even with nine of us. They hope to confuse us in darkness so we'll lose our way."

Waves of magical light radiated from his horn, flowed along his back and flared out from his sides. The energy grew until it radiated out from him looking like shimmering purple wings. Ahead, all the Saphira-elaysa were doing this, the light of their magic the only thing illuminating the darkness.

"Hold on," he said, and he bent his head down and ran faster. He reached the next Saphira-elaysa and passed alongside her. Magic flared between their horns and burst forwards to the next, and then the next. Magic radiated around all of them until every single one had powerful wings made of light.

The dark tunnel first trembled then split above them. A vast night sky filled with stars was revealed as the tear widened—and then the entire tunnel burst open, collapsed, and flattened beneath them. Thaya held her breath and stared down at the incredible sight. They ran upon a black pathway through the very stars themselves! All around them shone stars, large and small, near and far, millions more than she had ever seen in her life. The sky was aglow with them, vivid and alive with starlight as they hurtled along on a road between them.

The black road shivered and shattered.

She and the Saphira-elaysa did not fall. Instead, they spread their wings and tucked their legs beneath them. Heads high, they flew—or rather, glided—through the stars. There was no wind with which to fill their wings, therefore normal wings could not work here. Only wings of energy could navigate the space between the stars. But how could she breathe if there was no air? *Magic, something to do with that shimmer around us. We are not supposed to be here, floating around in space...* and she suddenly felt faint.

Fighting against the sensation, she asked, "Where in all the worlds are we?"

"In a lot of trouble," her soul twin replied.

"Can you create another portal?" A stupid question, she

thought, the Saphira-elaysa would have done that already if they could.

"There's no water out here," he explained.

Thaya looked behind them, her heart leaping for joy as she saw only stars and no Vormae. "I can't see them, we got away!"

His lips downturned, surprising her that he could grimace.

Suddenly, an enormous black cloud ballooned from below and swallowed them, blanketing out the stars.

The air became thick and hard to breathe, and it turned deathly cold. The Saphira-elaysas' wings vanished into darkness, the magic stripped from them. Out here, the Vormae were masters of Space.

Thaya's screams were cut off when they slammed onto hard ground. Her mount staggered under the strain, his shoulders quivering. Their wings were gone and there was nowhere to run. Thaya started to dismount, her weight was surely a burden to him.

"Don't," he said. He didn't run but turned around as the other Saphira-elaysa clustered beside him.

Thaya tried to see into the darkness then it suddenly deepened and swarmed towards them. The formless faces of a hundred Shades appeared, eyes flashing between white and dark, a bulging mass of shadows that wailed and groaned like phantoms.

Her soul twin stamped a cloven hoof and lightning flared from it, snaking towards the Shades. It flickered when it touched them, and they screamed. Other Saphira-elaysa stamped their hooves, sending flickers of magic at the Shades, but they learned fast and began to dodge them. Halted for only a moment, the Shades slunk closer. Her companion tossed his horn menacingly, trying to buy time.

Time for what? A few more seconds of freedom? wondered Thaya. They'd be imprisoned again, only it would be worse than when the Nuakki had her. She'd be strung up like the Saphira-elaysa, or even worse, strapped down and tested on by the Vormae until her body was spent and her life force drained. She rolled her shoulders; she couldn't let that happen.

"Better to die here," she murmured, but what could she do? She had no weapon, no fangs or claws, no horns or hooves...How she hated being human!

The Shades leached closer, but he didn't back off, and she keenly sensed he felt it was his duty to protect them all. The other unicorns bunched close behind him, their fear tangible in the air—an unnatural emotion for these creatures of purity, and a terrible crime to be done unto them.

"More come!" said a female from the far side.

Behind them, another wall of Shades heaved forwards. Everywhere Thaya looked she saw Shades. They were utterly surrounded, and the blackness deepened, the air turning thick like soup.

Her soul twin lunged forwards, his horn sparking with fire, and the Shades fell back, screaming. Thaya enjoyed seeing them afraid.

Something crashed beyond the Shades, followed by a boom. Was it magic? Was it Vormae technology? Two more thunderous cracks shook the air and then utter mayhem descended.

The Shades behind them screamed and surged forwards towards them, fleeing from something unseen. The Shades in front scattered and fled in all directions. Her mount spun around to face the rear assault, his horn flashing as he drove the Shades away from him. The darkness lifted to an ominous grey smoke that wafted all around.

Crack!

Another ear-splitting detonation blasted. The Shades in front of her exploded into strips of shadow that rained like confetti around them. The remaining Shades wailed in terror, a horrible sound that had her clasping her ears. Beyond the fragmented and wailing Shades, tall, pale-faced people walked.

Thaya's eyes settled on one man, his black hair long again, his Fireshot raised and flaring.

"Arendor!" she screamed.

A Shade grabbed her from behind, yanking on her hair, flipping her off her mount's back and pinning her to the ground. The unicorn roared and reared and smashed his hooves upon the Shade, shattering it into shadow fragments. She stared at his planted golden hooves, one barely an inch from her head, the other just brushing the side of her ribs.

She couldn't breathe as their eyes met. Such accuracy... she wondered if he could harm her even by mistake as he reared away to fight the next Shade.

Cold hands grabbed her arm, and she looked at Arendor as he pulled her to her feet. Shades wailed a deafening cacophony all around them.

"This construct is failing," he shouted.

Beyond the wailing came a throbbing that vibrated her eardrums and drummed through her whole body.

"What?" she shouted. What the hell was a construct?

A Shade lunged close, claws scraping at them. Arendor dragged her behind him and triggered his Fireshot. The Shade was quicker and vanished before the flare struck.

"It was a trap!" he shouted over his shoulder. "But the Vormae have lost control of it. The Leonites are trying to ground us."

This whole construct *thing* was some kind of Vormae trap? Thaya jumped away from a Shade that loomed beside her out of the ethers. Too close to her for Arendor to shoot safely, he whipped out a silver blade. Her soul twin was quicker. His horn tore apart the Shade. It screamed, its hands clasping its howling, severed head as it dissipated.

"Where's your weapon? You've lost it again!" Arendor sighed.

"I didn't mean to, it was the Vormae!" she cried.

He threw her his blade. She only just caught it without hurting herself. She looked at the silver dagger; long and thin, even the hilt was all silver, and it shone brighter than any metal she had ever seen. She *could* fight if she had to, but she'd prefer to use her Fireshot or the power that had come from within her. Had her twin soul put it there? Had it actually been his power she had channelled? No, it was her own. The Vormae had unlocked it somehow, or maybe he had, but it was her own, just never tapped into before. Maybe it had been inaccessible until she found her Saphiraelaysa. She looked from the dagger to her blistered palm, even the thought of calling forth magic made it sting painfully.

But what about her right palm? Now she was no longer clinging to her mount, she had both hands free. She stared at her other palm forgetting the battle raging around her. *Goodness, I need a Magi's Anatomy class...all the things I could have been taught had I not lounged around in Brightwater lamenting over Eddo.*

She realised Arendor was shouting at her.

"You never grounded it from the start, that's why you're here!" he shouted as if it were a revelation.

She shook her head, what on earth was he talking about?

He rolled his eyes and grabbed hold of her with one hand, the other slamming against her forehead. Images pushed forcefully into her mind.

She saw his memories, an image of herself touching the London Stone trapped behind glass in a world devoid of magic. Then she was touching the Portal Stone with the Spirit Wolves beside her after she had escaped the Nuakki.

"Focus!" shouted Arendor, pirouetting them away from a swelling sea of Shades. Her soul twin was there between them, and another Saphira-elaysa male beside him. Energy flared erratically and that vibrating throbbing had become unbearable, shaking her insides and making it hard to stand.

"But how?" Thaya pleaded.

Her soul twin was right beside her, panting and bleeding from a thousand scratches. She clenched her eyes shut, and in her mind saw the incredible latticework of stars and energy lines.

"It's you they want. You have the power," her twin soul's voice said in her mind.

"But I don't know how!" she screamed. She tried to think. *Grounded, I never grounded the...portal!* They had done it before, the Vormae had hijacked their portal and she and Arendor had ended up on Earth thousands of years into the future. *Dear gods, please don't go there again!*

Thaya had no idea what she was doing, nor any idea how to execute it, but she clung to the image of the Portal Stone she had touched last in Lonohassa. *But I can't return there, it's too close to the Nuakki!*

"Of course," said her twin soul. She squinted at him to see his lips curling into a smile that made him look odd. As lightly as a feather, he brushed his horn against her forehead.

She saw herself as a child again, bathed in golden sunlight, surrounded by Saphira-elaysa as she sat giggling in the pond. An unmarked portal lay there, of course! She only had to reach for it.

It was enough.

The construct collapsed and a massive force sucked her downwards. Lightning flared and the palms of her hands burned with fire.

28

LEONITES

BEAMS OF LIGHT SHOT DOWNWARDS PAST HER AND FORMED into a field of soft white.

She hit that field and her fall slowed. Moments later, she splashed into liquid and hit the bottom, sprawling face-first into frigid water. She sat up gasping and stared at a comical sight.

All around her, Saphira-elaysa and Agaroths fell into a shallow river. She watched as they plunged into the water, their faces a picture of shock as they rolled and tumbled. Surrounding them all were peculiar beams of dense white light that throbbed with energy. Where were the Shades? Her stomach clenched but none appeared, not even a shadow could be seen in the light. She laughed and flopped onto her back. The water was freezing, but she didn't care, they were free. Free!

Her soul twin steadied himself on legs that wobbled like a newborn colt's, and Arendor rolled onto his knees, gasping and wide-eyed.

Thaya laughed harder.

"Hmmm," said her Saphira-elaysa, shaking the water from his mane unamused.

"Laughing," nodded the Agaroth, glaring at her through his dripping strands of dark hair, and making her laugh even more. Every portal exit had ended in disaster for her and this was no different, but she was glad—no, smug—to finally not be alone. But there was no sickness, thank the gods, the Eternal Spirit, and whoever. And there was no body-racking vomit!

"Well done for grounding, we couldn't complete it without a clear directive."

Thaya lifted her head at the perfectly smooth, cultured voice and stared at the being walking gracefully towards them. He—at least she thought it was a he—had a face more akin to a lion than a human, and his skin, or fur, was tawny. He didn't have a huge mane, but rather a short mass of thick, darker tawny hair that covered his head. His face was more blunt than a cat's, and his eyes more human and deeper set. His mouth was somewhere between the two, with thin, human-like lips, and definite cat whiskers. He walked perfectly upright on two legs and had two arms with hands and fingers just like a human. Very short fur-covered all of his skin that she could see, even his fingers, and he had claws and not nails. He was dressed in a long tunic girded loosely with a belt.

Behind him, other cat-people walked, similarly dressed. She'd been right in her judgement that the first was a male, as some of the others were distinctly female with soft curves indicative of hips and breasts. Thaya found herself staring at their long tails swaying beneath their robes. *The Leonites Arendor has spoken of many times, they have to be.*

"The Vormae had recaptured you, and they were not letting go." The lion-man raised his eyebrows at her, his pale blue eyes sparkling with intelligence. "They were about to destroy us all in the process, even themselves. They're getting desperate. I would not stay here, they can trace the energy signature for hours, and they never give up."

The Leonite extended his hand down and she found herself staring at the tips of his retracted claws. His whiskers twitched and she realised she was being rude and took hold of his proffered hand.

"Well done, Thayannon Farseeker," he purred, pulling her to her feet, his eyes narrowing with pleasure just like little black and white Moggie did back home. "You've freed some of the Saphira-elaysa, which we have never success-fully done."

"It isn't enough and two died..." her voice trailed off as she wondered how many more might be trapped by the Vormae, their life-force bleeding away for decades.

Arendor and her soul twin came to stand beside her, the Saphira-elaysa's long white mane tickled her cheek as it lifted in the breeze. Arendor laid a companionable arm on her shoulders and lifted his other palm. The Leonite pressed his palm against it and both smiled like they were good friends.

"Well-met, Harvenfeer," said Arendor. Something passed between them, but Thaya was not privy to it.

The Leonite spoke, answering aloud an unheard ques-tion, "Perhaps, my friend, but this one is so inexperienced, there is much she must learn—if she is willing to learn at all."

"Learn what?" asked Thaya, becoming suspicious under the scrutinising gazes of the Leonite and Agaroth.

"One has come who will free the Saphira-elaysa," shrugged Arendor, as if what he spoke of was of little conse-quence. "And I propose we offer you an...*education*. With knowledge comes power, and many gifts, should you so choose to accept. No peoples from Urtha have been taken off planet for education and training in a thousand years. We have found that those who are not enslaved by the Fallen Ones are in league with them. Our hope for this planet and your kind dwindles."

Thaya looked from one to the other, then at the Saphira-elaysa by her side. "I, er, of course, would be honoured, but not if it takes us apart. There are so many questions..."

"Indeed," said the Leonite. "When the time is right you'll come to us seeking answers of your own accord. Then you will be ready. Until then, and to begin with, Urtha and her Wise Ones have much to teach you. Find the Magi of Urtha, learn from them, then come to us."

Thaya found herself nodding. He made it sound so simple, but she had no idea where the Magi were.

The Leonite bowed. "Now, we must leave. The Vormae only stay defeated for a short while. They will return, they always do, and we cannot keep our shield up indefinitely, it weakens us. Through the power they take from the Saphira-elaysa, the Vormae have become strong and thus bold. Their attack on the Nuakki was unprecedented, as was the invasion of Arothia. We'll protect you from afar for a short while. I wish you luck, Thayannon Farseeker, in these difficult times."

The Leonite turned to her soul twin and she watched, intrigued, as the lion-man bowed his head in reverence to him. The Saphira-elaysa lifted his own as they silently communed, and an air of sadness hung about them.

The Leonite nodded once to them all, then turned away, his entourage following. The beams of light that had remained since they'd grounded, deepened and thickened around the Leonites, and then they vanished into them.

Moments later, the beams lifted into the sky and disappeared. Thaya stared from the ground to the sky, but there was nothing to see; the Leonites were gone. She realised her jaw was hanging open and shut it with a smack. The way they had left had been sort of like vanishing through a portal, and now she thought about it, there was an unmistakable pull here. There *was* a portal here but no Portal Stone marking it. It felt stronger than a Vortex, and so far, appeared to remain in one place rather than rove. Perhaps it was better remaining unmarked. At least she knew it was here and it was a place she would never forget.

"Harvenfeer is right," said Arendor, interrupting her line of thought. "The Vormae do not stay defeated and they are relentless. We, too, shall leave and return to the heavens to fight them this day." His eyes were alight with excitement at the thought of fighting again.

Thaya looked at her warrior friend, recalling everything that she had been forced to forget about him. So much had happened, so much had been changed. He looked curiously at her as she first smiled and then threw her arms around him. The surprise of her actions made him pull away and he awkwardly patted her on the back. When she released her hold, her cheeks were wet.

Silently, he gently laid a cool palm on her forehead and she let him read everything that had happened, holding nothing back. His expression blank, he let his hand drop and looked at her for long moments. There was more said in his silence than there ever could have been with words.

Finally, he spoke. "The Nuakki have always been cruel since the day their fallen gods made them. But this experience has changed you; you are older, wiser, braver, and I see within you a growing power. You must know that we tried to reach you but we could not. Now I know why. Without the ring and with your mind blanked we would never have been able to reach you."

"I was alone, in a dark place." she said softly. "Many still remain there. But you came, in the end, and perhaps that's how it always is; never alone forever, not really."

His eyes suddenly glistened with rare emotion. Did he feel alone? Did the darkness gnaw at him? His race was falling, but he still felt the light. "You remind me of why we fight. Yes, I feel the darkness, but we still see the light. Never alone, we fall with grace."

Thaya bit back the tears. The Agaroths could be saved, couldn't they?

But Arendor slowly shook his head. He cupped her cheek in his cold hand, "You have your twin soul now, and the whole is always greater than the parts. Do what Harvenfeer says and go to your Magi. For now, our paths part, but I will see you again."

Thaya laid her hand over his and then they parted. The other Agaroths, five in total, stood amongst the Saphiraelaysa, heads bowed in communion, their eyes alight in awe of the Pure Ones. The unicorns beheld them, not so much with aloofness, but with complete exhaustion. They had been scarred deeply, and changed in some fundamental way, just as she had. In their shared pain, she found comfort.

The Agaroths left the unicorns and followed Arendor. Whereas the Leonites had vanished into the light, shadows formed around the Agaroths, melding with their black hair and clothing. Arendor turned to look at her, a half-smile on his face as he threw her something. She caught it and laughed at the Fireshot.

"I think you dropped this, but don't lose it again, I'm not giving you another one. And you may as well keep this, a token of our friendship." She barely caught the little silver ring he tossed to her; it was the same one the Vormae had taken. He must have taken both back from the Vormae. She slipped it on her thumb and smiled. With a wink, he disappeared into the shadows and the wind blew them away.

Thaya tucked the Fireshot into her belt alongside the silver knife he'd given her. Her smile faded as she looked at her soul twin. He hadn't spoken since they'd arrived. The other unicorns lifted their heads and watched them both.

"I suppose you must go, too," she said, her voice suddenly cracking with emotion. She hadn't thought about this part.

He raised his nose and looked first skywards and then back at the Saphira-elaysa. The look lasted for a long time.

When he didn't answer, she said what she felt was the right thing to say, though her heart bled. "You should go to them. Recapture the time—the life—that was lost."

"I'm one of them, and yet I am not," he replied. "We are both...changed from that moment, and I can no more be apart from you than from my own horn."

"We need time," said Thaya, nodding. "Time to work out what happened to us all those years ago, and more recently. Now I no longer have a home to return to."

He lifted his head and looked far away beyond the clouds clustering above. "I thought I had a home once, now I'm not so sure. The Ellarian Fields will always be in my heart, but something else calls to me, I hear it whispered on the wind, but I know not what or where it is."

"You may join us for a little while in the Ellarian Fields," said a female Saphira-elaysa walking close, her golden eyes mesmerising. "A gift from us to you for helping free us." Her mane floated like silk and her coat shimmered so that she didn't quite seem real but had stepped for just a moment from the Lands of Fae.

Thaya had never heard of the 'Ellarian Fields' before, was it a place where unicorns lived? Wherever it was, excitement rippled within her. Anything to spend a moment longer with these creatures.

The female unicorn continued. "But you could not stay for long even if you wished to, for our home is beyond the Mortal Planes and your mortal body made of carbon could not thrive there. But if you want to visit, the offer will always be there." The female dipped her golden horn in a friendly gesture.

"Thank you, of course, I'll come—" Thaya began, but paused as she looked around her.

The pond was as it had been a quarter of a century ago, and just as beautiful and serene with the wide stream trickling through it. There were more trees than before, and the path to the side was gone, swallowed up by creeping bushes and moss, but it was otherwise frozen in time.

To the right, there was no longer a village green where the children had been playing, now it was an overgrown meadow of grasses taller than herself. On the far side, by the trees, she knew there'd be the remains of a destroyed village if she went and looked, but she wasn't going to.

Funny how the Nuakki wiping her mind and then the Vormae unlocking it again had made every single memory more vivid than before. She remembered more of her life than ever she had. Events long since forgotten, she now remembered with a clarity as if they'd happened yesterday, and, she supposed, they had. But why then could she not recall the people of the village—not even her parents—to which she had supposedly belonged?

She swallowed the sudden lump in her throat. "I can't come with you, though with all my heart I want to."

She swept her eyes over the swaying grasses. Saplings

hovered tentatively at the meadow's edge as the trees readied to move in. She let go of her breath, they were at the very beginning, where it had all begun. Where the Saphira-elaysa stood now, she had touched her twin soul, and her future had changed forever—or maybe it was destined to always be so. Were these the same Saphira-elaysa she had seen all those years ago? She'd have to ask her soul twin to be sure but she didn't think so. *How amazing it is to be here again but, hmm, there's something wrong with the picture.*

"Something's missing," she murmured, trying to see past the clustered Saphira-elaysa, "or *someone.*"

Maggy! Thaya imagined the old woman was there now, just as she had been decades ago, with one muddy sock drawn up, the other fallen down around her skinny ankles, and her hair a tied up mess of grey and white strands falling around her scrawny shoulders. Thaya covered her mouth as tears wobbled her vision of the past.

'Thaaayaahhh!' screamed the old woman, shaking the fence that imprisoned her, and the tears slid down Thaya's cheeks. Her soul twin nosed her gently but said nothing. She would come to know that he spoke little.

"Maggy," she gasped. "I have to free her!"

***

"You can't do this alone," he insisted, his gaze darkening with foreboding.

"But you must return with your...people." Herd? Family? Thaya didn't know how to refer to them.

"The Vormae destroyed my family long ago—I watched them die." He spoke quietly and Thaya exhaled sharply, remembering him as a baby, dancing between his beautiful parents' legs.

"I'm deeply sorry." She knew it was a weak and feeble thing to say, what words wouldn't be? "All the more reason that you must go to your people."

"And you should be with yours," he replied, his fathomless eyes unblinking.

"I don't have anyone…" she trailed off, he already knew what she was going to say, and his expression told her he felt the same—they were alone in the world. But his people were right here, so why did he feel alone?

He turned his head to glance at the waiting Saphira-elaysa. "They are my people whom I'll love forever, but I have gone beyond them, maybe beyond what is acceptable for them. For now, I'll leave and return to them another time."

If the other unicorns heard, they didn't say anything. Noting this, she wondered if they had already come to some kind of mutual agreement.

"Then come with me." Thaya stepped close to him and laid a hand on his neck, feeling his silken soft fur that shimmered pearlescent purple and silver. He felt so familiar to her and she understood then how identical twins felt about each other.

"That is my soul's desire," he replied, and her heart lifted with joy.

———

He stood with the other Saphira-elaysa in a silent circle, their horns lowered to the centre point between them, their eyes closed. He shimmered dark against their light, his darker hair making his tail and mane appear even whiter. Was he the first unicorn to be coloured so?

Thaya could feel the sadness that settled upon the group

as a tangible thing. She wondered if they were sad to be losing the brother they had been imprisoned with for so long. He had changed and they didn't understand it, had yet to determine whether it was for better or worse. But what was done was done, why else would the Eternal Spirit have wanted them together? Whenever she called to memory that awesome light, it overwhelmed her.

She watched the Saphira-elaysa commune for so long, she began to worry the Vormae would arrive.

"Ahem," she coughed when the sun began to weaken and cast orange ribbons over the treetops. "The sun is setting."

Her soul twin lifted his head and they all opened their eyes. Their horns shimmered and a golden light fell around them. Each unicorn dipped their horn to him as they turned into the light and disappeared within it. When the last vanished, Thaya wiped away her tears and ran to him, splashing through the water and burying her face against his neck.

"Let's find safety, I remember a place not far from here." His soft words wrapped around her. "But first, drink."

He lowered his mouth to the stream made pure by the Saphira-elaysa and drank deeply. Thaya did the same, scooping up the sparkling water and sucking it into her mouth. It was the purest, coolest, most divine water she had ever tasted, and she splashed it over her face and neck. She caught a glimpse of herself in the water and immediately missed her waves of golden-brown hair. It was growing back, however, and was already past her ears and just about long enough to tie back with a band. She saw a little of what Arendor had mentioned, too; her hazel eyes held the shadows of hard lessons learnt, but there was a glow within them, a glow that reminded her of Solia. Was it the blossoming power within her?

Cold water sprayed all over her, making her gasp. The Saphira-elaysa did it again, literally dousing her with the stuff. "You evil imp!" she squealed, and dodged another soaking as he bellowed with laughter. She splashed through the water, pirouetted and kicked it all over him making him rear up. His fore hooves smashed into the water sending a veritable tidal wave over her. Spluttering, choking with laughter and utterly soaked, there was no way she could win this fight or outrun him. Well, she would have the last laugh and she fell backwards into the pond fully submerging herself so he couldn't soak her anymore.

Still laughing, he made his way to the bank as she clawed her way back out. "Clean now?"

"Actually, yes, thank you." She nodded and walked past him with her nose in the air. She *did* feel clean and also completely renewed.

As a second thought, she looked at her blistered left palm and bent to immerse it in the water.

"You've been branded," he stated, inspecting the gold mark that was surrounded by red and swollen skin.

"A Nuakki slave mark. He made it golden when he...took me," she said. She couldn't speak of what happened, not yet, and shame heated her cheeks even now.

Her twin soul's eyes glowered. "Peace and acceptance might come with time, but the brand will make your magic...painful."

"Is there a remedy?" Thaya asked hopefully.

"Use the other hand."

"Great!" She scowled. "Well, anyway, let's get moving. I don't want to stay here until it's dark."

Birds readying to roost tweeted their final calls as they left the stream and walked along the bank.

"You know, you're like a twin to me in ways I don't understand, but I still don't know your name." Thaya smiled at the unicorn. "I am Thayannon Farseeker, but you already knew that, like everyone else."

The Saphira-elaysa blinked. "I am...I am. Your language has no words." He tossed his head and an image came into her mind, making her start. His telepathy was startlingly clear.

Darkness, a midnight sky, then a growing light on the horizon that turned the sky purple. The beautiful light illuminating everything was so bright and so radiant, she was forced to look away.

"Is that the dawn? Is it a star? In the darkness you would come to me as a guiding star bringing me hope, leading me on—my lodestar." She tried to think up names for the image she saw.

He cocked his head. "It's a...there are no good human words to describe it. It's the light of home—the Ellarian Fields—and it is also purity, and the light of the Creator."

Thaya felt this was a little extravagant, but then she didn't know Saphira-elaysa and how they spoke. Why wouldn't beings of purity speak in such magnificent terms? She suspected they, like Gryphons, and possibly all magical beings, were a little full of themselves. She was also jealous. Her name had comparatively little meaning.

He lost his grandeur and spoke quietly. "In our language, the sound-tone for what my parents called me is Ellumenaah-Ahrieon. I find it a sad name. Ellumenaah means to light up, to illuminate, or the light's action. Ahrieon in your words would translate into 'future perfect,' or 'hope made real'...it's harder to explain. After the change, and especially after I was captured, I was given a new name and became Khy-Ellumenaah-Ahrieon."

Thaya rubbed her chin. "Hmm, I can barely pronounce those names. I suppose I could call you Khy or Ahrieon or something? What does Khy mean?"

He looked at her sharply, was that fleeting pain in his eyes? He looked up at the faint emerging stars. "Khy means apart, different, changed—many things, and all of them negative. Applied to a being it also means; Outsider. One Who Has Left."

Thaya frowned. "That's not good. Who could name you as such?"

"But it *is* true," he said, rippling his shoulders, his eyes bright. "The words don't lie, Saphira-elaysa never lie. This name is correct, and I see now why I was thus named—it's surely a blessing, not a curse...The more I think on it, yes, that *is* my name and you *should* call me it. Khy I shall be known as, for now and forever."

"But I don't want to call you a bad nickname," replied Thaya. Couldn't these magical creatures just use names that meant nothing? It was just a name after all—or was there more to naming things than she understood?

He shook his mane. "Now I've said it aloud, I embrace my...*difference*. My second family with whom I was imprisoned gave it to me. They meant no malice. Saphira-elaysa speak only truths and hold only pure intentions. The word is the truth, and so I shall make it mean 'truth' for me. I *am* the truth, and I am change."

Thaya frowned at the way he spoke. It made sense, too much sense, and yet she struggled to understand his manner. "Khy," she repeated the name to herself, doubtfully. There was nothing wrong with it, but 'Lodestar' sounded much nicer, though perhaps he wouldn't go for that.

"Then I shall call you Khy unless you prefer something different. Look, the stars are coming out in the east. I guess we'd better get going."

The sky had turned a deep orange, and the dragonflies skittering across the pond now lowered themselves onto nodding reeds to rest for the night. Groups of twittering sparrows darted into their favourite roosting trees and chattered noisily.

Dinner wasn't looking likely and Thaya's belly rumbled. She scanned the bushes and trees as they walked, hoping for apples or blackberries—anything to satiate her hunger. The Saphira-elaysa had done something to the water, otherwise she would have passed out from hunger long ago. Still, she needed more sustenance.

"What is it?" asked her twin soul Khy, picking up on her restlessness.

"I'm starving, aren't you?"

He frowned. "You mean, you require sustenance again?"

"Again? I haven't had any!" Now Thaya was confused.

"But the water..."

"Water is not enough to sustain a human!" she huffed.

There was a lot they needed to learn about one another, Thaya decided. They might be twin souls but their bodies were vastly different.

"You live on only water?" Thaya tried to imagine this and failed.

"Water and sunlight, but we must purify and bless the water first. Most of it on this planet is impure."

Thaya looked at him, the muscles rippling over his body, his luxurious coat, and baby soft mane and tail. *All that is sustained by water and sunlight?* His belly and girth *were* far less rotund than a horse's, and he was lither than a deer, but still. Yet he was telling the truth, and she suddenly felt impure and lacking. What happened if you were in a desert and it was cloudy? A hundred unlikely scenarios tumbled through her mind. *Just water and sunlight?*

"Well I, and all humans, need food, food of any kind. And right now I'm missing about five meals." She noted how Maggy's clothing hung loosely around her. When she'd first put it on it had been much snugger, and her bust, lamentably, much fuller.

"So that explains the taverns everywhere, then," said Khy.

"Are you sure you want to stay here, on Urtha?" Thaya burst out. "I mean, it's going to be vastly different to any life you should have lived."

"And what about you, do you want to stay here?" Khy asked.

Thaya looked towards the setting sun where clouds of orange ribbons were fading to dark and the first western stars were coming out. She turned from the west and looked east to where Brightwater now settled down to sleep. Fi and Yenna were there, would they remember her now? She could return and find a house, maybe not in Brightwater, but somewhere in Havendell. The thought was...*horrifying.* So much had happened, she couldn't imagine returning to a mind-numbingly simple and mundane existence. She stood here with a Saphira-elaysa, bless the light, and had had experiences with four alien races—two of them extensively negative! She had heroically gained her freedom—twice— and her journey had only just begun.

She continued along the bank. "You're right, we *have* changed. We can't return to our normal lives and pretend nothing has happened. The world has changed, too, and I feel that it is waiting for us."

Khy stepped over a muddy patch and nosed a reed,

watching an irritated dragonfly buzz into the air. "I feel that, too, in a different way I suppose. There's more I haven't said. My kind don't approve of what happened between you and me, they don't think the way I've changed is good because they believe it portends their fall. They don't understand it, none of us do, and I don't know where our journey is taking us or where it ends, but I know that my heart is still pure and uncorrupted, and I feel the Great Spirit within me."

Thaya nodded. "Your words echo my feelings. What happened, happened for a reason, it's up to others to deal with it. For us, there's a whole world to explore, and beyond."

"Onwards then?" said Khy.

"Onwards." Thaya smiled. "But first, Maggy."

"No, first food," Khy corrected.

She laughed, it didn't matter where in the world she was, as long as she was with him. "Which way though, and how do we avoid danger? There are Nuakki..." She shivered.

"Most Slavers are far to the south and east, or at least they were decades ago," said Khy. "To the west, I smell the ocean, it is at most a hundred miles away."

Thaya's shoulders slumped. If only she knew this place better. "There could be ports along the coast, and thus food, but it would take days to get there."

"Half a day." Khy shrugged.

"What?"

"We Saphira-elaysa do have *some* abilities you know." He snorted. "I wish you'd stop thinking about us in terms of horses, I can read your mind better than you know."

"Sorry," said Thaya, staring at the ground. "The only thing is, food might be east, but Maggy is south and west. If we can find the main road, perhaps we'll find sustenance along it?"

Khy lifted his head and closed his eyes. "I can't smell roads, but I can feel the energy of many beings passing in one place. They leave an imprint, like a lingering smell but of energy."

Thaya closed her eyes and tried to feel the energy around her just like Arendor had urged her to do. She had abilities, everyone did, and she was determined to improve them. But she couldn't feel anything that Khy did.

"The signature is very old and faint—nothing has lived here since that time..." Khy turned towards the old village green. "There's an overgrown road leading out from here onto a wider track. Perhaps along it, we'll find something."

Thaya nodded, her growling stomach overcoming the disappointment in her abilities. They both hunted for the road and came to a long grassy section, the remnants of a long-overgrown track.

"I suppose if we follow it as best we can, we'll get to the main road eventually," said Thaya with a sigh.

The grass turned into thick vegetation, and they pushed through brambles, nettles and ferns. Sadly, it wasn't quite autumn here, and the blackberry bushes were covered in flowers, not berries, but their plan worked and before long they clambered over a ditch and onto a sweeping dusty track.

Many wagons' wheels crisscrossed over it, some still sharp and surely only a day old. She looked at the darkening orange sky and turned left on the road. Left was south according to the sky, and ahead the long sweeping track curved between tall poplars swaying lazily in the breeze.

29

WILD & FREE

THAYA FELT UNEASY OUT IN THE OPEN.

Her hand rested on her Fireshot, and her eyes scanned the dim road. Did the Nuakki patrol here? Were there any free people left at all? Lonohassa was a huge continent, or it had been once, and the slaving operations might only be in the south. Still, she constantly checked behind them, hoping Khy's senses were sharper than her human ones.

"You'll feel any danger, hopefully not too late," said Khy. "Learn to trust your feelings."

"Easy for you to say," she murmured. "What if the Vormae come? What if people see you? They'll fall all over you and we'll never get away. Worse, they'll try to snare you."

"To them, I'll look like an ordinary horse." Khy tossed his head.

Thaya looked at him, noting again his horn, cloven hooves and long tail whose hair did not start at the base but a third of the way down. Not to mention his other-worldly indigo eyes and shimmering coat. Her mouth dropped open as his horn suddenly vanished, his hooves became dull and round, his fur became grey with hints of mauve and his body became stocky. Only his eyes remained a little odd, still indigo but not as bright. He looked like an aged racehorse.

She stared in shock then burst out laughing. "So, I'm not to think of you as a horse?"

Khy bristled. "Got any better ideas? It's how they'll see me. The spell won't work on anyone who knows the truth or anyone who can use magic well."

"No, it's great, honestly," she said, marvelling at his change. "I wish I could turn myself into a big man with a huge sword." But it would probably only get her more hassle. Brawlers loved a large man, or at least they did in Havendell Harbour. If she was going to stay on the road, as she saw it, she sorely needed training in pretty much everything, with foraging being a good start. "As long as we keep a low profile, no one will bother us."

Thankfully the road was made of light-coloured sand and stone, and as the night enveloped them, it remained relatively bright. Perhaps her time spent in the dim Nuakki mines had honed her senses because she found walking in the dark easy. Still, when the moon finally came out from behind the clouds, she was grateful for the extra light.

A wolf howled in the distance and was answered by an owl. Rather than be afraid, she found the wolf's lonesome call comforting. Where were Maggy's wolves? She prayed they were looking after the old woman. Maggy and Amwa might have been killed in the Vormae attack, but Thaya wasn't giving up on them until she was sure.

"Walking is easy on the road. Let's go faster," suggested Khy.

"I'm not running," said Thaya, and eyed his nice

comfortable back eagerly. To ask if she could ride him felt insulting; he wasn't a horse but a magical being.

"I'll carry you," said Khy.

Thaya grinned and gleefully climbed onto his back when he scooped lower. It was obvious they'd travel ten times faster in this manner.

She squealed as he broke straight into his unique gallop, smoother and more arcing than a horse's, as if he ran on clouds rather than dirt, and had an invisible extra pair of legs. She squeezed with her legs and clung onto his mane, hoping she wasn't hurting him. A saddle or rein would make it easier, not that she'd ever dare try to control him or even wanted to. No, *he* very much was in control.

The wind whistled past and she hoped he could see better in the dark than she could at this pace. She tilted back her head. *Wild and free, that's what we are.* A strange sense of knowing his next move settled upon her. There, a boulder had fallen into the road and she moved lower against him to aid his leap over it. A sinkhole had swallowed the road to the right, and she leaned to the left with him as he navigated it. They were not steed and rider but one being, and she found herself tiring, just as he tired, as if their energy had been combined and spent equally.

He slowed. It wasn't a canter, just a slower form of his 'gallop,' and then settled into a fast walk. There was no trot, which she was particularly grateful for. With no saddle, she'd be chafed raw, even if his fur was remarkably soft.

Khy slowed even more and stopped when he reached a crossroad. The road going across was twice as wide as the one they were on. Two shallow banks bordered it and tall trees cast shadows beyond them. The wind rustled the leaves, creating a good blanketing white noise to dampen the sound of their passing and an owl hooted again but far away.

Thaya squinted to the left, her sharp eyes picking up the faint glow of a lantern barely visible through the trees. Another traveller? Fear and excitement shivered through her. She didn't need to tell Khy what to do, he was already heading towards the light, his furry ears, half again as long as a horse's, pricked up with intrigue. *At least he's fearless,* she thought.

Moving at the pace of a trot, the light neared. Soon, a glass lantern appeared, swaying drunkenly from side to side in opposite rhythm to the cart it was attached to. A plump old man with a weather-beaten hat pushed low over his head hunkered down over the reins.

"Good evening, good sir," hailed Thaya politely, but her hand brushed the handle of her Fireshot.

"And what's good about it?" replied the man gruffly.

Thaya didn't let her smile waver. His horse was friendlier, and the old grey stallion pricked his ears forward and nosed Khy companionably. Her soul twin remained stock still. Was he afraid to act like a horse, or just shocked to meet one?

"It's not raining, and the night is warm," Thaya said from between clenched teeth.

"A woman out alone on these roads? You must be mad." The man lifted his reins and made to move off.

Thaya burst out. "Is there a tavern nearby? A pub or shop, maybe a farmstead—anywhere I might be able to get a bite to eat?"

The man nodded. "Back yonder, five miles. Colt Run Tavern, although most nickname it Cut Throat Tavern. Your choice, your life. Yee-haaah." He snapped the reins making the poor old stallion jump, and the cart creaked away.

Thaya and Khy stared ahead at the dark empty road for long moments. "It doesn't look very inviting," she murmured. Her stomach growled loudly. "Right, let's go eat," she said breezily.

Khy set off at an easy lope that ate up the miles.

Just past a knot of alders appeared a tavern, golden lights spilling out from its windows like eyes lighting up the night. The building was a single-story mess. Wood panels had fallen off the walls and those still attached were rotten. Its sign was half hanging on with an indecipherable picture eaten away by time and weather. It might have been a colt, it might have been a throat—either way, she was going inside.

A lone woman entering a tavern in the middle of nowhere... what could go wrong?

Remaining in the shadows of the nearby log-shed, she swung off Khy and stared at the door. They both jumped as a man burst out of it swaying wildly, a tankard sloshing in his hands, and fell onto his knees. He giggled, lifted his pint to his lips and guzzled whilst falling straight forward onto his face. The tankard clanged on the ground and rolled away, but the man didn't move. His broad-brimmed hat hid all of his features, but his rotund belly suggested he wasn't a fighter. She looked at Khy and he looked at her.

"Are you sure about this?" he asked so clearly in her mind, she started.

Her stomach growled loudly in reply. She tried replying with her mind by saying the words silently.

"Yes, any trouble and I'll run out. We can get away faster than any drunk. Besides, I'm not worried about anything human." The thought of Nuakki sitting in there enjoying a pint of ale sent cold shivers down her spine and made her brand tingle.

She smiled when Khy nodded. He could hear her, this

was great!

"*And what do I do in the meantime?*" Khy asked. Was that annoyance in his voice? Did he feel he was missing out on something?

"*Umm, I don't know. Stand here and act like a horse?*" Thaya didn't mean it at all like it sounded, but Khy snorted, much like a horse.

Rolling back her shoulders, she walked towards the door, pausing to inspect the man lying, and now snoring, into the earth. Dirt blew in and out of his nostrils and he stank to high heaven of sweat and alcohol. Grimacing, she lifted away, but with a second thought, she reached down, carefully pulled off his hat and dumped it on her head. She winked at Khy and he shook his head frowning.

"I'm only borrowing it," she hissed. Maybe he was a bit of a worry-guts.

Hand resting on the Fireshot concealed in her tunic, she pulled the hat down low and stepped through the door.

Dense fug greeted her. The smell of smoke and food and booze made her reel for a moment, and she fought to maintain her composure. Keeping her face shaded under her hat, her gaze darted around the room. The tavern was well-lit by the many lamps lining the walls, which was a relief to the alternative: threatening shady characters sitting in dingy corners. A wide bar stood at the opposite end, and rows of drinkers' pews, tables, benches and chairs filled any space. The cold slate flagstones were sparsely covered in sawdust, and all conversation ceased as she made her way to the bar, her boots resounding harshly on the floor.

The hairs on her neck prickled as ten pairs of eyes

watched her. She refused to look at anyone other than the huge barman busy polishing wine glasses behind the bar, eyes regarding her under shaggy brows. Thaya pulled her hat down lower and affected a cocky swagger which ceased when she bashed into a chair leg. She cleared her throat and continued walking normally, trying not to limp.

A long low whistle came from a corner, bristling her shoulders with irritation. She could have been *any* woman —even a hag—and all eyes would have been upon her. There were no other women to be seen, and eyes and silence followed her all the way to the bar. *I can always run, Khy is waiting.*

She reached it sweating and dumped herself down on a barstool. Don't be elegant, don't be polite, she half intended to spit on the floor. The air was charged as everyone waited for her to speak. The only person not interested was the bored-looking barman.

She leaned forward over the bar. "Are you serving food?" she asked quietly, wanting no one else to hear her voice or detect any accent.

The barman sighed and set down the glass he'd been polishing. Planting his hammer-like fists on the bar he bent his head towards her.

"What?" he shouted, making her jump off the bar stool.

She rolled her eyes and sat back down. "Have you got any god-damn food?" She shouted back, matching his volume.

For some reason, this seemed to break the spell laid upon the whole tavern. People turned back to their drinks, paused conversations resumed, and half-finished jokes and insults completed themselves, ending in raucous laughter or shouting. The barman blew out his thick, bushy moustache, eyeing her suspiciously as he relayed their extensive menu of 'stew.' Apparently, it was the only unimaginative thing available that night.

The barman bellowed her order through a hatch behind him and poured her a glass of red wine which was probably not a good idea, but she drank it anyway and remained at the bar, feeling somewhat safer next to the huge but audibly challenged barman.

A dumpy, red-cheeked, red-haired waitress appeared moments later with a steaming crockpot, cutlery and wedge of bread clutched in her hands. Phew, another woman. All eyes descended upon her instead although conversations didn't cease. She set them down before Thaya and winked at her in a way that made her own cheeks redden. With a smile and a toss of fiery curls, she disappeared back through the swinging doors to the kitchen.

Thaya tucked into her food. She'd never heard of cheese-covered fish stew before and she barely chewed or even tasted it as she wolfed it down. If it had any bones she didn't notice, and in moments the food was gone, along with her wine. She wiped her mouth with the napkin and an unpleasant feeling crept over her skin. The barman was watching her like a hawk as he polished a pint glass, his moustache twitching like a feral mouse, his beady eyes squinting.

He knows, she thought. *He knows I've got nothing to pay for this!* Thaya had been so hungry she hadn't even thought about paying, and it had been many months since she last had paid for anything at all. Her brain went into overdrive. There was a window to her left. It was half open on a hinge and a cool breeze blew in. It was her nearest exit, but it was on the opposite side from where she'd left Khy.

She looked around the room. Men sat drinking, but there was caution about them. Their eyes flickered over everything, missing nothing, just as hers did. She knew that they knew she was an outsider, and outsiders everywhere brought trouble. Sweat now beaded on her brow as well as her back. How could she have been so stupid? *I was too hungry to think!*

She could offer washing-up services, but the tavern wasn't busy with eaters, and the serving maid looked more than capable. Her panic began to increase as she ran swiftly out of ideas.

"Any work around here?" she asked the barman. Amiable conversation might win him over, and perhaps find a way to pay.

The barman snorted. "You and everyone else... Not sure what a skinny lass can do around these parts. Runaway, are we?"

"What?" Thaya's hand tightened around her Fireshot at the man's accusing tone. She was a grown woman, not some teenage whelp.

The man's hammer-like fist darted forward faster than a cobra and grabbed hold of her left wrist. He half hauled her over the bar and two other men leapt to either side of her.

"Explain this," said the barman, stabbing a fat finger at the glistening Nuakki slave mark on her hand.

Nestled in her blistered skin, the golden mark shone out proudly.

"You belong to your masters, runaway." The barman's scowl deepened.

Stupid! She'd been worrying about paying and all along it was her mark that had betrayed her! But then what did humans care? She never thought she'd have to hide the mark from *them*. A hundred thoughts ran through Thaya's mind. They knew about the slavers, clearly, but did the Nuakki have human spies?

She realised the truth of the situation rapidly; her old skill was still there and possibly sharper honed by the Vormae unwittingly unlocking all her memories and potential. They didn't employ humans; humans were worthless in the Invaders' eyes. *No, they just don't want trouble, humans never want trouble!*

There were unsavoury traits within her own species; everyone wanted an easy life, just to be, even though the whole world was being enslaved. By their compliance, they assisted all that was unfolding. They were cowards, just like she was, just like she *had* been! *I'm not a coward anymore.*

These simple folks thought she was a runaway from the Nuakki, and she was, she supposed, but she never belonged to them to begin with, she wasn't theirs to take, no one was. The barman hadn't acted before because until she had started eating, he hadn't spotted her mark.

A couple of choices unfolded in her mind, spurred on by the realisation that she could feel Khy's increasing agitation outside, as if he had somehow felt her panic.

She could fight, or she could appeal to the barman's humanity—and it was clear from the glare in his eyes that either needed to occur before she could escape. From her twisted position on the bar, she couldn't see the man to her left, only his muddy boots. They were large boots, for a large man, heavy with metal toes and more for fighting than for farming. The man to her right was short and slender, but sinewy cords knotted his tattooed forearms and his small eyes were hard. A scar ran the length of his left cheek, too neat and straight to be made by anything other than a blade.

Still, these men had no reason to harm her, and the

barman didn't know she couldn't pay, he'd only seen her brand. Her human side won over and she decided to reason rather than fight, but she didn't loosen her grip on her Fireshot. "You're right, in that they captured me, but you good men are not in league with slavers, are you? For that would be enslaving your own kind."

The man's lips thinned to a dangerous line, and he tightened his fingers around her wrist. "They come here, every month, looking for runners like you. At first, I tried to help 'em escape, but the bastards found out, and they raped and murdered my wife before my very eyes. So don't appeal to my pitying side, I have none."

"Then take revenge," growled Thaya. Was he just going to accept it? Have his wife murdered and do nothing about it whilst they came and did what they willed? Humans were doomed. Disbelief made her bold. "For the gods' sakes, man, they've murdered your wife!" She looked into his pale brown eyes and saw grief battling with unreleasable rage. He was going to let her go and say no more about it, she was sure of it.

"That's a gold mark, Ebo. And they'll pay gold for gold, and you know it," said the sinewy man.

"Yeah, man, you know they'll come and find out," said the other, his voice slow, making him sound low of wit. "They'll use their powers again—you know, them devices that make you talk. Then they'll kill you, not pay you, and kill us too."

Thaya gasped, she couldn't believe it, her own kind bartering her as if she were still a slave, still owned and able to be bought and sold. Whoever the advanced ancient ancestors of this land were, they were long gone. What cowards these men were. How dare they!

Events unfolded rapidly. She didn't mean for it to

happen—she didn't actually know *how* it happened—but the same energy that Khy had somehow unleashed through her built up rapidly in her solar plexus, flooded along her left arm, and exploded out of her palm straight into the barman's face.

He screamed and fell back, releasing her arm. The other men jumped away, yelping. Her branded hand blistered agonisingly and Thaya screamed and fell to the ground. The front door exploded into the tavern, wood and splinters showering everyone. Through the pain she could barely focus on Khy, heaving in the doorway, veritable smoke coming out of his nostrils as his eyes blazed with rage.

The men looked from the screaming barman rolling on the floor, to the huge odd-looking horse that had burst into the tavern, then to Thaya who lay groaning and gripping her bleeding palm.

Thaya felt Khy's magic build as she had felt her own fill her insides, only his collected in his horn and with perfect control. The space between her eyebrows where the telepathic third eye sat, burned.

"No, Khy!" she gasped.

These men were, so far, innocent. Khy wasn't human, he didn't have the same feelings, connections, and understandings about people that she did, and whether she was right or wrong, these men had suffered enough and didn't deserve to die.

Hugging her throbbing palm to her chest, she got to her feet and ran to Khy. His horn blazing red light and his rage contained but still vivid, he backed out of the door.

In moments, she was on his back clinging with one hand, and they were flying along the dark road again.

Thaya dared to look back. The lights of the tavern were swiftly disappearing, and she could see nothing following them, *yet*. They should get off the road, but the foliage was so thick either side, they'd never be able to move fast through it. She prayed they wouldn't meet another soul.

The night deepened as clouds drew themselves over the moon and Khy slowed, his breath coming easier than hers despite him doing all the running. Slowly she released her grip on his mane and relaxed her knees. Her left hand still throbbed painfully, and she held it against her chest.

"I told you to use your other hand," said Khy. "I knew something like that would happen."

"I didn't do anything, it just kinda...*came out!"* she said, looking at her palm and grimacing at the puss weeping out.

"It's that mark, it distorts your magic, makes it erratic and uncontrollable," said Khy. "The gold conducts it and causes some of it to reverse into your own flesh."

"But what, exactly, is it coming from my hand? I know magic is energy, but is it a type of energy? Like sun energy, or fire energy, or electricity like lightning? I just want to understand."

"Soul energy," said Khy. "And yes, I suppose it would be like solar energy, or more like star energy. It's the fire that burns within the soul."

Soul energy? It felt right, but she didn't understand it any better. Another one for the Magi to explain. *My soul's energy is hampered by the Nuakki symbol.* She closed her fingers over the hateful mark. It might be pretty, but it made her feel as if she were still owned, and those men back there proved it did. Her body ached all over and she longed to lay down. "Let's get off the road, find somewhere to rest for the night."

Khy silently agreed and headed off the carriageway, pushing his way through the foliage. Thaya slid off his back and took pains to cover their passage by pulling the flora back into place. Who knows how good the Nuakki or their human minions were at tracking.

After half an hour of searching in near-complete darkness, Thaya gave up looking for a good spot and settled on the damp ground beneath a sycamore. She leaned back against the trunk and closed her eyes.

"At least I ate," she sighed and massaged her aching thighs whilst Khy stood motionlessly, looking back the way they had come.

After a moment he said, "They're looking for us, but they don't understand our tracks." Thaya noted his clouded eyes, was he seeing into the far distance? "It will take them all night to reach us here. For now, we are safe...from them at least."

Thaya nodded and yawned, wishing she had a soft blanket to curl up in. "At least it's warm enough to not need a fire."

She lay down on the damp ground and tried not to think about breakfast. Khy came over and nuzzled her neck, then lay down beside her. She rolled over and pressed her face into his warm back and drifted fast asleep.

Thaya awoke with the dawn, warm sunlight spilling through green grasses dancing before her face in the breeze. The sky was already a clear azure and it looked to be a beautiful day. She wiped her eyes. Khy was already up and standing statuesque in the sunshine, and she took a moment to admire him.

He stood in meditation as he received his sustenance from the sun's rays. His horn shimmered as if soaking up the golden rays, and his pristine body shimmered lavender silver in the sunlight. His tail lifted spritely, and his silky hair wafted in the wind. His eyes were closed, his long, elegant neck arched, and his deep, powerful chest rippled with muscle. The whole forest surrounding him beat with life, from the almost luminous green leaves above him to the butterflies circling his feet. Birds chirped in the branches, hopping closer as they peaked at this glorious creature. The forest worshipped his presence, and she wondered if, in return, he brought light and life into it.

He opened brilliant indigo eyes and looked at her. Stepping like a dancer he floated closer, lowered his horn into the grass, and rolled a perfect red and green apple towards her. She picked it up and he followed it with two more.

"There's a tree about half a mile away, and these are the best ones," he said.

"You got these for me? Thank you!" Thaya beamed and tucked into one, its tart, sweet juice filling her mouth. She finished it and threw the core into the bushes whilst Khy continued to stand in the sunshine. If only she could fill her stomach with sunlight!

Munching on apples, her thoughts quickly led to Maggy. Where was she now? Would the Spirit Wolves find her again? And what about dear, gentle Amwa? Was he still alive? How far away were they? It could take them months to traverse hundreds of miles, and she had no map to follow.

But I have a different kind of map! The realisation struck her. She looked at Khy, but he had his eyes closed. She didn't want to disturb him and so closed her eyes and called to mind the portal map she had seen when she'd touched the Portal Stone; the three-dimensional latticework of light connecting all points that were portal openings. There were far too many points to memorise, and they mostly looked the same. But all she had to do was find another Portal Stone and attempt to connect to the one near the Nuakki slave mines. Thaya opened her eyes and mouth, but Khy was already speaking.

"I see you've found an answer to our predicament," he stated.

Thaya paused and frowned, "Yes, how did you know? Just what happens when you're standing there lounging in the sun?"

"Beyond our obvious connection, the light reveals all that we need to know," explained Khy mysteriously. "In truth, everything we need to know is there all around us all the time, but we get lost in our own...adventures, thoughts, emotions. Emptying the mind allows the light to fill it and remind us what's important."

Thaya nodded slowly. "Okay, sounds great, must try it some time. So, there's a quick way to Maggy and—"

"Portals," Khy finished for her.

"Yes," said Thaya, glad to not have to explain something she didn't quite understand.

Khy continued. "Before you ask, the one back there in the river wouldn't have worked. It is not anchored, and it's probably swarming with Vormae."

Thaya shut her mouth. "I hadn't thought of that. But all I have to do is find one, a good one." She narrowed her eyes and peered into the undergrowth as if one might be nestled there. Arendor's face came into her mind, encouraging her to focus. She closed her lids, but the only thing she could see-feel was Khy's radiant presence; a pulsing rainbow of energy in her mind's eye.

"Maybe if we walked along the road, I could feel it out as we went," she suggested.

30

SOULFIRE

THEY WALKED ALONG THE ROAD.

Warm honeyed sunlight beamed down upon them, yellow wildflowers twirling around bold irises in the grasses between the road and the forest. Bumblebees and butterflies pirouetted amongst them and birds chittered in the branches.

Ah, today...today, the world is perfect. Thaya ran her hands through her hair and stretched them above her head. It was hard to imagine the misery the slave-miners would be suffering this day—or that any suffering at all could be occurring in this world. How could it be? How could the light of the Eternal Spirit have touched her today and not all others? There was something about the world she needed to understand, and she hoped the Magi would be able to tell her.

Lost in confused thoughts about the Infinite One and the nature of suffering, she felt the familiar brush of energy tickle her senses. *Hmm, I know that feeling.* Moments later, she stopped short in shock. Just at the crook of a bend in the road, naked in the clear light of day, stood an ancient grey

Portal Stone. She blinked, expecting it to vanish, but there it remained, mottled slate rounded with age, standing proud at about ten feet tall.

She hurried towards it, the energy increasing in waves she could feel but not see. Hands tingling, she held them towards the stone. *Don't will anything yet, hold back and just look.* That's what she told herself, but as she licked her lips, dread unfurled in her stomach. Every single Stone portal passage had ended with her throwing her guts up or being captured by the Vormae.

Khy sniffed the stone with interest, and she pressed her hands against it, bracing herself. Soothing energy cooled the heat of her blistered hand, and that familiar strong tug she resisted from letting it swallow her completely.

Another world opened up before her, one of the star-like orbs suspended in space and connected to each other by a thin cobweb of lines like the finest lace. Each point was connected, for the most part, to the nearest points, and they to the next. It was a beautiful golden lattice made of light. *Stunning, a living energy map of the stars!*

But which one led to the place the wolves had taken her to? The thought made her shiver. The Vormae had come, but that hadn't been the wolves' intention, and it didn't mean the Fallen Ones were there waiting. Still, she felt cold.

"If you can open an Interplanetary portal, I can protect us over a short distance," said Khy.

"Do you know where they go?" she asked, resisting the growing pull on her body.

"No."

She sighed. Pushing thoughts of Vormae aside as best she could, she focused on the nearest point and held the image of the wolves' portal in her mind. Focus and intention were all it took. She ceased resisting the pull. It was lucky then, that Khy's shoulder was brushing hers for she had forgotten to hang onto him.

A scream tore itself from her lips and her stomach somersaulted.

The ground vanished as she was sucked swiftly forwards. A great rushing filled her ears as the entire lattice careened towards her. Immediately she began to tumble over and over, scrabbling madly to hang on to something, but Khy was just out of reach. In the glimpses, she noticed he wasn't falling shamelessly but remained upright, veritably floating in the flickering maelstrom that was their portal passage.

The passage was very short, and the unexpected ground hit her hard. She rolled over on earth and grass before thudding into a boulder and hugging it for dear life. She gasped and lay on the ground trying to catch her breath. Lifting her head above the grass she stared up at an enormous cathedral-like structure that looked to be made out of pure crystal. Three clustering spires reached up to the azure heavens, each shining white and pure.

"Wow," whispered Thaya.

Her awe was quickly tarnished as she got to her feet. At the cathedral's base, scores of buildings—maybe even hundreds—that surrounded it, had been smashed to rubble. Remnants of stone window frames and doors stood out clearly amongst the fallen walls. An enormous pile of crystal-rocks suggested more crystal cathedrals had once stood here. What had caused such destruction? That any towers survived at all was a miracle.

She scanned the devastation for life, but the place was abandoned, the wind the only voice to whisper along the empty halls that remained. Was it old or new? The time-weathered rubble suggested old, but the spires were sharp-edged and shiny, suggesting new. *Perhaps crystal doesn't age like stone,* she thought. The green forest surrounding them had respectfully declined to reclaim this once beautiful place, leaving it open to the sky, the sun, and the stars.

Thaya longed to explore it, and Khy was already stepping forward, his ears pricked, but time was catching up with her and her still tumbling stomach began to shudder. If she didn't act fast, she wouldn't be able to make another journey again for an hour.

Snatching hold of Khy's fast disappearing tail with one hand, she slapped her other against the fallen Portal Stone beside her; shocked to note it was a beautiful fallen obelisk of shining white crystal.

The portal Map opened up again, and again she focused on the next nearest portal. If they had to leapfrog to Maggy in this manner, she'd do it. *Please be the one,* she prayed.

Khy reared as he was dragged backwards. She closed her eyes and swallowed a retch as they spun into the maelstrom again. At least she now somersaulted in time with her stomach, it had the odd effect of calming her queasiness.

In only a few heartbeats, she flopped weakly into stabbing pine needles. Thank the Creator this journey had been shorter. She didn't feel any better, however, and barely had the strength to roll over before retching at the base of the ivy-covered standing stone. There was nothing in her stomach to come up.

"Dear gods, curse hell," she gasped. "I'm sorry!" She

meant sorry to the stone, not the gods, whom she now knew were evil off-worlders. She'd never pray to them again!

The empty vomiting episode lasted longer than usual, perhaps because of the double journey, and she descended into a painful, noisy fit of retching and trying to breathe, which made her sound remarkably like a pig.

Finally, the heaving abated, and she pressed her cheek against the ground. Khy's nose stroked her back.

"Sorry," she gasped and sat up, pushing her lank hair back from her sweaty face. "I can't stop it."

Khy shrugged his shoulders in a remarkably human gesture, "Everybody is different, maybe this is your 'thing.'"

"I wish it wasn't." She sighed and looked around. The sandy, pine-needle covered ground, the cyprus trees, the moss and ivy covered stone—yes! This was the place. But without the wolves to guide her, she had no idea in which direction the Nuakki settlement was.

Khy stood still, his head raised and nostrils flaring. "Vormae have been here, I can smell them." His back shivered.

Thaya nodded. "They attacked the Nuakki. When the wall collapsed, I escaped in the mayhem. I don't think they're here now, but we can't be sure. Perhaps you should stay somewhere safe."

He lifted and dropped one hoof, shifting nervously from side to side. "We're here now," was all he replied.

She looked around the forest. "I don't know which way it is, but I'm sure the sun rose in that direction and set over there, meaning they must be to the north."

"North-east, the scent comes more strongly from there," said Khy.

"Then let's go." Thaya clenched her jaw and started walking, her body not quite sharing her mind's determination. There was a stream this way too, she could drink from it and refresh herself.

They made their way through the forest and down the banks of the stream where she crouched to drink, but Khy stopped her from drinking and insisted he must purify it first. "Water is an advanced being, it has memories, like you and I, and it reflects feelings and emotions. You wouldn't want to drink dirty and blood-stained water full of vengeance and rage, would you?"

Thaya's frown faded. "No, I guess not. I didn't know that about water." And she had a hard time seeing the substance as an actual being. Despite their twin souls, it was clear that Khy saw the world in a vastly different way to her. For him, it was all energy, frequency and matter, truth, light and darkness, and he had powers to command the elements she could only dream of.

Wide-eyed, she watched as he swirled his horn in the dark water and turned it crystal clear and virtually fizzing with effervescence. It was as if the water was happy. She scooped it into her mouth and swallowed. How could water taste delicious?

"It was worth the wait," she said, rising.

They set off again, following the stream for a little while before crossing it and continuing north-east. Why was she returning to a place she hated? What if Osuman was there waiting for her? She shivered. She knew the Nuakki, he would never give up hunting her. And what exactly was she going to do when the Nuakki settlement loomed above the tree-line? Was she going to waltz in there Fireshot blazing?

"I don't suppose you have a plan?" asked Khy.

Damn, he'd read her thoughts! "Um, I'm working on it."

"I've seen the Nuakki many times," said Khy. "They're formidable warriors, expert Magi, and adept inventors. And in none of those attributes do they care to use the Eternal Life frequencies."

"They are indeed inventive," growled Thaya, remembering the way they'd struck the slaves with their Pain Sticks, and the total removal of their minds upon enslaving. "I was hoping to come up with something. I was hoping Maggy's Spirit Wolves might come."

Perhaps they still might. She chewed her lip, she didn't want to speak aloud her half-baked ideas, but even if she didn't share them, he'd be able to read her mind anyway.

"If it comes to it, I was thinking about turning myself in." Had she actually thought that idea through at all?

"Never," said Khy, shaking his head.

Thaya rubbed her forehead. "I can't give up on Maggy, I won't. It may be the only way to find her—her and Amwa. It's not like I'll be able to see them from the gate. What if Amwa is chained in the mines? What if Maggy is dead? I need to know or I'll never be able to rest."

Khy didn't say anything, but she could feel him trying to think up something.

An hour later he said. "It's there, ahead through the trees."

Thaya inched forwards, peering through the foliage of brambles and knotweed. Sure enough, the peach and salmon stone of the Nuakki buildings peeked through. Heart beating hard, she squatted down in the bushes and scanned the area. Rubble still lay everywhere, and many buildings had vanished, black scorch marks marring the paving stones where once they had stood.

Voices came.

She pressed herself to the ground and spied two Nuakki guards walking, their golden breastplates shining, curved short swords in their belts beside golden Pain Sticks. She could barely breathe, the hold they had over her was still strong.

So, the Nuakki had not all perished in the attacks. What had the Vormae been looking for, exactly? Could it have been a war of territory? If so, they hadn't won.

She glimpsed a woman walking behind the guards and held her breath. The dark-skinned woman was clothed in a silk tunic identical to the one she had worn once. She wasn't chained to a Nuakki, though she walked behind them with her gaze lowered. Thaya ground her teeth. The empty-minded, fearful slaves would never assist her if she brazenly attacked.

There were more guards in the distance—the entire area was being patrolled by Nuakki, their eyes constantly flickering skyward. *Clearly on high alert after the attack.* She wasn't going to be able to slip by them easily. Maybe if she just waited and watched for a few days, she'd be able to spy Maggy. It was quite a big 'maybe' and she didn't fancy surviving on apples, if there were any, *or* dead squirrels. Time to explore a little more.

She pulled back into the trees and tiptoed to the left passing many windowless, block-shaped buildings. Keeping to the trees, she paused near the tall wire fence. Beyond it was a wide, open area with guards, slaves and servants working on various tasks. A dog barked in the distance, followed by a long howl. Far too many people and watchdogs, there was no hope of slipping in unseen!

The dog howled again and was joined by another. *Strange, dogs don't normally howl like that.* Thaya stared through the leaves, fence and milling people, to a pen filled with animals on the far side.

Amongst the medley of mewing cats and barking dogs, a

large, grey and white wolf stood on his hind legs, huge paws splayed on the cage, thick tail wagging. He lifted his head and howled. Another wolf came beside him, tail wagging and nose smelling the air.

Teo and Tess! Thaya nearly fell into the open. "They're alive," she whispered, "but captured." She frowned, wanting to be joyful yet feeling more afraid. Did that mean Maggy was alive and here somewhere? Maybe they had been captured trying to free her. She couldn't know. At least her trip here hadn't been for nothing, she could try and free the wolves, and they would lead her to Maggy.

Thaya gripped her Fireshot and planned her attack, her eyes never leaving the marching guards.

"Okay then, here it is," she said to Khy who was beside her. He pricked his ears forward with interest. "I see two Nuakki here close by the fence, and four more marching. Obviously, there are many more we can't see, but we just need to get in and get out as quick as we can. The slaves and servants won't hurt us, but they won't help us either. Hmm, is my Fireshot any match for their weapons? Hmm, maybe we could capture a servant and I dress up as them—Khy, wait! Curse it!"

Thaya's heart somersaulted into her throat as Khy leapt through the trees towards the settlement at a gallop. The wire fence tore apart like paper as his horn shredded it. Nuakki guards froze in shock at the charging beast.

Gulping and sweating, Thaya unholstered her Fireshot and leapt after the crazed unicorn. Trampling over the destroyed fence, she dodged past the screaming slaves and servants. A white-robed Nuakki priest appeared from around the corner and raised and pointed his golden staff at Khy. Thaya halted, aimed her Fireshot, and pressed the trigger. A ball of fire streaked towards the priest and exploded into flames on contact. He screamed and fell to the ground, the fire raging until he became a sickening pile of ash.

Thaya trembled.

A Nuakki leapt into Khy's path. He rammed his horn forwards, embedding it to its base right through the Nuakki's chest. The man screamed and gurgled as the unicorn wrenched his horn upwards, lifted the heavy man right off his feet and hurled him against the wall several yards away. Thaya stared as the Nuakki slid limply down the wall, leaving a thick bloody stain.

Another Nuakki leapt in front of her, Pain Stick staff descending. She flinched back, but it caught her cheek. Lightning cracked and jolted through her. It felt as if she'd run into a brick wall and then she was falling.

In a blur, the Nuakki vanished from her field of vision as Khy's hooves crushed upon him. She raised her right palm to her pounding forehead, and something peculiar happened. Energy in her hand—was it Soulfire like Khy had said?—flooded from her palm into her head and cleared the pain jolting through her body. Confused at her sudden clarity and strength, she got onto her knees and picked up her dropped Fireshot. Her cheek was bruised and bloody, but the painful energy had gone.

Khy was beside the animal cage and lowering his horn to the heavy lock. The lock sparked and fell apart like cheese. Nuakki guards ran towards them from all sides as slaves and servants ran away in all directions. The Nuakki had rage in abundance, and usually slaves and servants bore the brunt of it.

Thaya looked behind her and frowned in dismay; not one slave was trying to escape through the destroyed fence. They didn't even know what freedom was, they didn't even know they were slaves. That made her angry and she raised her Fireshot at the closest Nuakki, noting his scowling face, and his raised bronze sword.

He disappeared in a ball of flames.

Thaya gasped, confused and conflicting emotions running through her. She'd killed him in anger, it didn't feel good but it was necessary.

The mayhem swiftly turned to chaos.

Teo nosed open the door and all the animals streamed out, but instead of running away, they clustered around Khy.

"Fight for us," he said to them, but he must have said it in their minds because his lips did not move.

Thaya stared as the cats and dogs dispersed, leaping with glee onto their slavers and torturers. Cats clawed bare calves, dogs grabbed hold of ankles, and a cacophony of growling, mauling and mewling filled the air.

Danger tickled Thaya's back, and she whirled in time to dodge an electrifying blast cast from a priest's staff. She glimpsed its golden circular top throbbing, and the Nuakki grinning beyond it.

She raised her Fireshot and fired. The flaming ball burst towards him faster than an arrow, but the priest vanished, and the flames scattered harmlessly into the air. The priest reappeared several feet to the right. Thaya blinked. Now *that* was magic. The Nuakki's smile deepened and his eyes glowered so powerfully they began to turn red. They enjoyed this, the fight, she realised, and she swallowed.

Thaya aimed her weapon but was reluctant to lose another shot. Lightning snaked towards her from the Nuakki's staff and she dropped to the ground. It fizzled barely inches over her head and struck the wall behind. Masonry and rubble showered upon her. She rolled to her feet, but the Nuakki was before her, his staff charged and ready to release the latent energy flickering around its tip.

She raised her hand in a futile attempt to shield herself and felt energy gathering there. Flickering blue magic burst towards her. With her will, she released the power gathered in her right palm. Golden light spilled out and flared violently against the blue. The Nuakki growled and intensified his efforts. Blue energy flowed in greater waves as the staff vibrated and hummed. Her golden magic throbbed and the staff buckled then exploded.

The Nuakki blinked, his hand empty and burnt, and the blackened fragments of his staff falling around him. Thaya stared at her open palm, noting the absence of pain or blistering. The Nuakki shot her a look and roared. Several yards behind him, a legion of Nuakki guards charged.

Thaya backed up until her rear bumped against Khy's. Behind her surged another legion of guards and they were quickly surrounded. The wolves and other animals had vanished, gone to safety, she hoped.

"Now what," she hissed to Khy. "This was your great idea!" Now they were going to be captured and undoubtedly tortured until dead.

"Get on, what are you waiting for?" growled Khy.

She threw herself onto his back. He reared and turned in a tight circle. As he spun, her eyes swept the sea of Nuakki and she glimpsed a face she recognised. Osuman? Cold chilled her to the marrow. Was that a flicker of recognition in his eyes? He was lost from view and forgotten as they pelted towards the broken fence, forcing apart the approaching Nuakki.

Khy leapt into the woods, fast catching up with the rabble of fleeing dogs and cats. She wondered if he had some sort of link to their mind, advising them when to fight and when to run. The Nuakki couldn't keep up but they would pursue. Did they know they had a Saphira-elaysa in their midst? She could only assume they knew Khy for what he was and not some ageing racehorse. The Magi priests would surely know. He was still in danger. The Nuakki had nearly destroyed Vassa without a care. No creature—magical or otherwise—was safe from the Invaders.

Khy lurched down the hill, branches whipping their faces and bodies. The rush of the stream filled her ears and he jerked to a halt in knee-deep water. He thrust his horn down into the swirling eddies and flicked it back up again and again until the air shimmered and tingled around them.

A thick mist rose, engulfing them, and the noise of shouting quickly faded in the dense fog. Calmly, he walked downstream.

Thaya glanced behind them but couldn't see or hear anything beyond the fog. "Are we—"

"Shh," whispered Khy. "Don't break the spell."

Her heart pounded in her chest. Though she couldn't see or hear the enemy, she knew they were there beyond the thick white. The moments ticked by, and the clop and splash of Khy's hooves became soothing. She released her grip on the Fireshot and tucked it into her belt but didn't dare speak.

Half an hour might have passed when the roar of the river could be heard, alerting them to a waterfall ahead. Khy stood still, ears pricked forwards, then he turned and stepped onto a grassy bank. The fog evaporated and the sun shone down through the cyprus trees.

Teo and Tess stood beyond the fog, tails wagging as if they'd been waiting for them to arrive.

"Tess!" Thaya slipped off Khy's back and buried her face

in the she-wolf's thick mane; her life-saver and unforgettable companion.

"Well, that was exciting!"

The old woman's voice made her freeze.

Thaya stood and peered around Khy's wide rump. "Maggy?"

Getting onto her feet was the skinny, wizened frame of Maggy.

The old woman grinned, her blue eyes perpetually youthful and mischievous. "Ahh, you made it, I knew you would!"

"Maggy!" Thaya pulled her into an embrace and squeezed. "I remembered again; my memories returned to me. The Vormae took me once more. They did something and it returned my memory the Nuakki had erased. I had to come back; I couldn't leave you," she gushed breathlessly, then pulled away to look at the old woman. Both of Maggy's cheeks were bruised, and she was weak despite the strength of her gaze.

"Dear Thaya, you shouldn't have come for me," the old woman sighed. "My full life is done, and now you have many enemies who've seen your face."

"I would do it all again in an instant!" Thaya rasped, her eyes filled with fury as she looked across the river, daring any Nuakki to emerge.

Maggy took her face between her hands. "I know what they did to you, I saw it in my meditations. It's what they do to all who work the mines. But revenge will be your undoing, as it will be their undoing."

Thaya closed her eyes, sagging. "I want to hate them, but I don't. Instead, I feel...*sorry* for them."

Maggy peered at her, frowned, then took Thaya's palms and inspected them. She was less interested in the blistered and branded palm than in the good palm. "I saw what you did back there." Maggy nodded, her eyes glistening. "I know that Soulfire magic. You have the power of our ancestors; when this world was young, and we were as gods. Why... how, I don't know, but you have the old power."

Thaya watched the woman inspect her palms. "Maybe it was the Vormae. They didn't mean to but... they were looking for something within me, something that would help them capture Saphira-elaysa, and more efficiently drain their life-force."

"Possibly," Maggy said, although she looked dubious. "But I always felt the power within you, even way back when you were a child. I knew it was there even before you touched the Saphira-elaysa." She looked at Khy adoringly and laid a gentle hand on his shoulder. He snorted appreciatively.

"I will have to meditate long and hard on it, but what the Vormae have probably done is unlock the potential within you and revealed your connection to Khy. Your soul connection to this Saphira-elaysa, and he to you, is unbreakable. To what end and purpose it occurred, only you can discover. I doubt there's a Magi now in all of Urtha that can match your power, though you use it poorly. You'd better go to them and learn control before you destroy yourself. This world is changing faster than I ever thought possible. It remains to be seen whether for good or for ill." She murmured the last as if to herself.

Go to the Magi, that's what they all said, and she knew she had to. "I don't understand how any of this has happened, but what you say is the truth about the Vormae. I can feel again the truth of things."

As she rolled Maggy's words around in her mind, a more important issue pressed upon her. "Maggy, do you know of a young man, he looks more like a boy, called Amwa? He was with me in the mines. He has tanned skin, almost red, a mop of black hair and a smiling face. He said he was from southern Lonohassa—maybe one of the Island People? I have to find him; I won't let him die in there." She looked back towards the Nuakki settlement, but there were only trees. Her shoulders slumped as Maggy shook her head.

"You can't go back there, Thaya." Maggy gripped her arm. "You cannot risk being captured again."

Thaya chewed a fingernail and continued staring into the forest as a warm breeze lifted her hair. *I'm going back. Leaving Amwa is simply not an option.* She patted Maggy's hand and smiled at her but said nothing as she planned her return. Thaya knew Khy had read her thoughts, but he said nothing. Perhaps he agreed.

31

FREEDOM WORTH DYING FOR

THAYA HELD HER HANDS UP TO THE WARMTH OF THE SMALL campfire.

She was even more appreciative of the cloak of mist surrounding them that Khy had again created. It swirled around them protectively, but still they spoke in hushed voices, for Khy had warned not all sound could be muffled.

He stood silently at the edge of the mist, resting with his eyes half-closed. Teo and Tess lounged by the fire, whilst she and Maggy spoke quietly to each other about all that had happened. Bellies full of fish from the river and sponge nuts from the trees (Maggy was truly resourceful, no wonder she had survived so long alone), everyone was contented, although Thaya hid her restlessness.

"I remember lying there at night, listening to my Spirit Wolves howling for me," said Maggy. "It broke my heart to see they had been captured, but at least I knew they were alive. The Nuakki tried to wipe my mind, but somehow it never worked. I wanted them to kill me or to set me free, but they realised my suffering would be worse if they caged me, so that's what they did. But I knew I'd never die in there; I knew I'd die free. So I waited for freedom to come to me, and then you came."

Thaya listened to Maggy, smiling in sadness and grimacing in anger as she told her tale. "The whole world doesn't even know about the invasion and destruction of Lonohassa by the Fallen Ones. They know only of the cataclysms."

"They know a mighty civilisation fell," Maggy corrected, "but they don't know what it means, and they won't know until they see what was lost. But long before that happens, the Nuakki will come and enslave them too."

Thaya started at the thought. Would they attack Brightwater?

Maggy chuckled quietly at the look on her face. "You don't believe they'll stop here, do you, girl? Hah, no! They want Urtha, all of it, and they'll take it with them all the way to hell. We can fight 'em if we like, but it's one hell of a battle, and they are not the only fallen to fight over it."

"The Vormae," said Thaya.

"And the Ordacs," added Maggy.

Thaya had never seen the reptilians before, and she didn't want to. Unless of course that Inigo Price was one of them...She shook her head, Shades alone were more than enough. She told Maggy everything about them, the Vormae and her abductions.

"They took you to their ship, the Mother Ship from which all the little ones come." Maggy nodded knowingly. "The Vormae destroyed their own planet Geshol, and thus themselves, that's why they look the way they do, that's why they're dying. They can't reproduce. They can't use Portals; their decaying organic bodies have lost the ability to do so. Displaced from their own planet, they are forced to feed off others to survive."

"Like vampires," said Thaya thoughtfully.

"Exactly," agreed Maggy.

"No planet, just a 'Mother Ship'? The craft must be enormous," said Thaya. The term was peculiar, especially when she'd always thought of ships as being water vessels, and not made for the air. A far more advanced race with advanced technologies, what hope was there? Surely the Magi knew what was going on, why weren't they doing anything to help?

"It's the size of a country," said Maggy spreading her arms wide. "I saw it once, a long time ago. We have these Viewing Mirrors, or had, the Nuakki took them when they took control. These Viewing Mirrors could look into the sky millions of miles away—and as such, they could look into the past and future. Through them we saw the crafts of many different aliens, many hovering around Urtha, like scavengers around a kill." Maggy shivered and fell silent.

Thaya joined Maggy in a deep yawn and looked at the low burning embers. They settled down to sleep, but images of giant Vormae ships tearing into their skies filled her with dread—and to think she had been on one! *I survived, most don't. I must be grateful for that.*

She'd intended to stay awake and work on her plan to find Amwa, but sleep quickly sucked her under.

It didn't last long and a few hours later she found herself blinking into the now cold embers.

Quietly she stood. Maggy was turned away, her side rising and falling rhythmically. Khy was closest and slept standing up, his eyes moving back and forth under closed lids, making her wonder of what he dreamt. Teo and Tess were circled up together tail to nose. Teo opened his eyes and watched her as she quietly stepped into the protective mist surrounding them, but he did not rouse. What if the Nuakki were just beyond? *I have to try; I have to be brave!*

She stepped a few feet forwards and the mist and those within it vanished. There was just a bare patch of ground beside the river where they were camping and trees beyond. *Very clever,* she thought, *I must learn how Khy did that.*

Thankfully, there were no Nuakki and she looked into the bright, moonlit forest feeling rather small and alone. *I can't have anyone come with me, I've asked so much of them already, I daren't risk them being captured again.*

Besides, only she knew how the mines worked and where Amwa might be, the others couldn't help. They'd never let her go off alone, which left her only this choice. She'd sneak into the slave mines—the Nuakki were sloppy guarding slaves because they relied on their 'Cleansings' to keep them dumb and docile, and they only ever left one guard on duty outside the slave pens. The Nuakki were also lazy, which usually meant this particular guard would be dozing. They relied on a complicated, electrically locked door to discourage slaves from trying to exit, something which she knew she'd easily be able to disable now her mind had returned. One guard was enough for her Fireshot to take down.

She'd be returning to hell, but this time she had a full memory and a heart full of vengeful rage. She just needed to acquire a slave's clothing and hide her weapon under her sackcloth.

There were large gaps between the trees which made for easy journeying as she formulated her plans. It might be possible to get Amwa out without them noticing a thing. She paused. Amwa would never leave the others, just as she would have never left Amwa if she'd had the choice when

Osuman took her. Something to do with the Cleansing; their total innocence and complete vulnerability made them cling to one another all the more. Their ties ran deep, that's why she was returning to him now.

She ducked low under the trunk of a fallen tree. No, Amwa *would* bring the others for her, and help them all escape. She'd arm them with pickaxes and try to sneak out as many as possible before the alarm was raised. Yes, they'd get free, but there'd be mayhem, and people would die. She paused again and stared into the middle distance.

Freedom was worth dying for.

She pushed through a particularly thorny bush and almost fell down the rocky cliff the other side. It was a shallow cliff, but enough to break bones at the bottom. Beyond, she stared across the expanse of sand turned silver in the moonlight. *Where the hell is this?* Her shoulders slumped; she was completely lost. Surely she'd been heading north, but this had to be west? What now? Go back and try again? She spun around, but how would she ever find her way back to the others? She wasn't great at tracking, not even her own footsteps. The wolves were likely to find her first.

Damn it!

To her left a dark sea rolled, the sound of waves pounding against rocks echoed up the valley. Opposite, much taller cliffs of dark rock reached into the sky and extended to her right where it disappeared around a corner. Maybe the valley curled around to the mines. Maybe this was that long stretch of sand where she'd tried to run to freedom all that time ago? The thought gave her hope and she looked for a way down. The low cliff rose the further inland it went, and so she turned south towards the sea where it levelled out.

It was hard going. The rocky, uneven ground rose to trip her at every opportunity. The trees became sparser and gnarly the closer to the sea she got. Strong sea winds blew, stunting all that dared to grow. She had to wiggle back and forth through the foliage several times before coming across an animal track that wound down to the sand below.

The track offered little in the way of cover, and in some parts was completely exposed, but there was no other obvious path. The whole journey was taking far longer than she had anticipated, and the night, and her chance, was wearing on. The others might already be looking for her.

She was about to step onto the path when something in the distance caught her eye. A light or flash or something. She squinted out to sea, but a lot was moving out there, it was probably the white horses catching the moonlight.

There it was again; a glowing yellow light just above the waves, far too low to be a star. She lost it in the swell, then it appeared again. Thaya stared as the light illuminated the great wooden hull of a galleon cresting a wave. The light was gone in an instant, but the moon emerged from a cloud and illuminated scores of lumbering ships. *Ships. Ships made for water. Urtha ships!*

"They look like human ships," said Khy.

Thaya nodded. "Yes, they do—What the!" She started and turned. "What the hell are you doing here?"

She stared at the Saphira-elaysa blinking innocently in the moonlight.

Beyond him, Maggy silently emerged from the bushes, crouching low to avoid being seen, her eyes wide and trans-fixed on the ships. The wolves pushed through after her.

"We heard you leave, and when you didn't come back, we went to find you." Khy nodded behind them. "The Nuakki mines are back that way."

Thaya slumped. "Well, there's no sneaking away from you lot is there? I'm not lost, I was just taking a detour, and it looks like it was a good idea!

"What are human ships doing here, and why haven't they got many lights on?" she muttered. The rattle of enormous chains told her the anchors were being dropped. It was hard to tell from this distance, but it looked like smaller raft boats were being lowered over the sides.

Could they be slave ships? Were the humans in league with the Nuakki? The Nuakki didn't need humans to capture slaves, they took them themselves using far more advanced ships and technology. Besides, no human would willingly work with them, would they?

With virtually no lights on in that perpetually turbulent ocean, how do they not smash into each other? *Warships. Expert captains.* It dawned on her and her heart began to race.

"Praise the light, they're invading!" She laughed and jumped.

"Can it be?" Maggy's eyes lit up with hope.

The first rafts began touching the shore—was that a glint of a blade or armour in the moonlight? No larger than ants at this distance, Thaya watched the soldiers jump out, heave the rafts up the sand, and gather into formation. They were fast and orderly, and in moments the beach was filled with soldiers. When the moon shone down, it glinted clearly off armour and she saw a score of mounted knights, their steeds proudly stomping their feet. There were a handful of others not wearing armour but robes with hoods. *Magi?*

They flew no banners and wore no tabards. Beyond Havendell to the north, the King's emblem was a white flower on a midnight background—or was that the Emperor's? Curse it, why hadn't she paid more attention at school?

She chewed a fingernail, they were going to attack and looking at their numbers, they had a very good shot at it. Amwa and all the slaves would be freed! She wanted to jump for joy.

"Come on, let's go down to them." Before anyone could stop her, Thaya scrambled down the scree and jumped onto the sand. The wolves followed silently, but Khy made such a racket with his hooves it sounded as if half the cliff was collapsing. He skidded beside her, regained himself and shook his mane. Maggy made it down last, not fast but still fit and able, and then Thaya was racing across the sand, her hands raised to show she was unarmed.

"Hey!" called Thaya, hoping they wouldn't shoot her in the dim light. She could see the archers at the rear, but they hadn't raised their bows yet.

Most of the army turned to stare at the peculiar group coming towards them, led by a woman waving her arms. A knight turned his heavy, chestnut stallion towards her and urged it into an easy canter, quickly closing the distance between them. His plain steel breastplate reflected the moonlight dully and the visor of his helmet was half-lowered so that most of his face was concealed. His hands were encased in gauntlets of chainmail, his left hand holding the reins of his powerful steed, and his right warily gripping the pommel of his sheathed sword.

"Halt," he commanded.

Thaya dutifully stopped and lowered her hands.

"Escapees? Lonohassans? Declare yourself," he commanded.

"Yes, both," said Thaya breathlessly. There was something about his voice and the curve of his cheek that was familiar, and were those green eyes that beheld her behind his helmet? She peered at him and frowned. "Arto?"

The man flipped back his visor fully and stared at her. "Thaya?"

To her delight, a familiar, handsome face was revealed. A long straight nose, defined chin and a flattering shading of stubble—it was none other than Arto. Everything came back to her in a blow and she doubled over breathless. Standing beside him on the ship, Solia floating face down in a sea of blood, drinking in the tavern with him and his men, chatting together in the lantern light before she'd left and the Dryad had accosted her, then, most bizarrely, seeing him again, thousands of years into the future on Earth.

Most importantly, however, she was acutely aware of the mud and grass stains on her clothing, her unbrushed hair, and how much she would have liked a bit of eyeliner or rouge on her lips. She should have washed in the stream last night, no matter how cold it was.

"Are you all right? What in all that's pure are you doing here? We're about to attack!" he said, his eyes clouding with worry.

Thaya took a deep breath and steadied herself on his steed's shoulder. "I think so, just overwhelmed. And I was about to ask you the same thing! Why are *you* here? The Nuakki, they took me but...it's such a long story. I got free and I've returned to free the slaves."

He looked incredulous. "Just you, an old woman, and... and some *animals?*"

Thaya glanced back at Maggy, Khy, and the wolves.

Could he see what Khy was? Khy's power of concealment shimmered subtly and if she looked really hard, she could see the shabby racehorse he pretended to be. Arto didn't look amazed, and he wasn't a Magi, so he probably didn't see a Saphira-elaysa. "Well, I was going to go alone, but they followed. You see, I know the mines, and I'm looking for someone very dear to me."

Arto rubbed his eyes as if struggling to comprehend. "After my ship was destroyed, I found myself employed as a hired sword and entered the army of a powerful baron to the east...but, that's also a long story. Things progressed from there and now I'm captain of this unit.

"There's no time to explain this so let me just say, a deal with the Nuakki turned sour, and gold was stolen from my employer. After what happened to us and the people of Havendell Harbour, I was seething, I needed revenge. I couldn't reach the Vormae, but I learned we could attack the Nuakki and so the contract suited me perfectly. It's not like I had a ship to manage anymore, so I gladly picked up my sword.

"However, my current *employer* isn't honourable, the bastard deals with off-worlders, but I'd sooner see these Invader dogs put to the sword and get paid for it. Until then, get yourselves to the safety of the ships where there's food and shelter. With the Creator's blessing, I'll see you at dawn."

Before she could reply, he'd slammed his visor down, turned his steed and was galloping back to his unit of neatly assembled soldiers, leaving Thaya to stare.

"*You* lot should do what he says," said Thaya, "but I must find Amwa."

"We should *all* do what he says, but I would do the same as you regardless," Maggy replied and gave a grandmotherly smile. "You would be wise to wait until after the first attack. In the mayhem, you'll be able to free the slaves."

"But they'll be killed too!" Thaya ran a hand through her hair.

The soldiers were marching now, the sound of their boots pounding ominous beats on the valley floor. Were they enough to take on the powerful Nuakki? Behind the marching units, her eyes settled on the handful of blue-robed Magi riders. She could sense the energy humming around them even from this distance. They gave her some hope.

There was no way she was going to hide by the ships though, mind-erased slaves would panic and run every-where. They wouldn't know these soldiers were here to help. No, she had to get there first and sneak in as per her first plan.

She took a cord from her pocket and smoothed back her hair into a low ponytail. "Khy?" He pricked his ears forward. "Shall we run?"

"I see no other option," he replied.

Heart fluttering, chin set into a grim expression, she climbed onto his proffered back. "Maggy, I'm going to get there first. I need to get in before the alarm is raised, and if there's trouble, the army will be right behind me."

The old woman nodded. "You do what you must, my little brave one, though now not so little. There are a few things I can do from afar, you'd be surprised, the old magic is still within me too." She grinned knowingly. "And the wolves won't be far."

Thaya nodded and took a deep breath. "Let's go."

She may as well have shouted and cracked a whip for Khy leapt into a run, his head straining forward and the ground flying beneath them. Thaya clung to his neck, hanging on for dear life as the soldiers whizzed by. A knight on a chestnut horse turned towards her, she thought he shouted, "Thaya," but the wind roared in her ears.

They rounded the cliffs and slowed as silence descended. The cliffs protected them from the wind and the noise of the sea, and the mines stood straight ahead.

"Let's get into the shadows," Thaya whispered. Khy slunk like a wolf into the dark strip at the base of the cliffs.

His horn shimmered slightly, and he said, "I have concealed us."

"Good, you must teach me how to do that."

The place was deserted apart from two guards each stationed at the two main entrances. Even she was surprised at the lack of Nuakki here. Perhaps the Vormae attack had them all stationed in the Nuakki living quarters. The Vormae weren't interested in gold.

She dismounted and tiptoed ahead. Khy followed. Flattening herself against the dark rock only yards from the first entrance, she turned back to him. "Maybe you should stay here."

Indigo eyes looked from her to the dark entrance and the Nuakki guard dozing on his feet, then back the way they had come. He didn't quite know what to do, and neither did she, she was making it up as they went along led only by her need to free Amwa. If it bothered him, he didn't say.

Khy twirled his horn and a shimmering cloud formed above it then floated towards the Nuakki guard. The guard lifted his head and turned to look their way just as the mist engulfed his face. The Nuakki's eyes drooped and he leaned back against the wall, his head hanging. Hopefully, he would sleep until she was done. She laid a parting hand on Khy's cheek and scurried towards the entrance. She didn't look back as she plunged into the cold gloom of her old prison.

———

Darkness swallowed her. She waited as her eyes adjusted to it then stepped forwards. How would she ever find Amwa in this maze? It was a monumental task; these mines were cavernous, endless. Her fingers trailed the cold wall and with that came memory. *It's right then left, but not the first or second right—that's it!* So, it looked like she'd be able to find her way to her old area, but if Amwa had moved there was no chance.

As she walked deeper inside it became pitch black even for her heightened senses. *I'd find my way better if I could see.* There would be some light where they slept, but between her and there, they always put out the lanterns at night.

She rubbed her palm and a thought came to her. Could Soulfire create light? She held her right palm up, closed her eyes, and imagined energy flowing from her core to palm. Her hand tingled and grew warm, but she couldn't see any light. Closing her eyes again, she brought a little more until a glow appeared. She stared at her softly shimmering palm where a semi-circle of golden light rose a couple of inches. *Amazing!*

She held it up and walked forwards scattering the blackness in front of her. It wasn't enough to see far ahead, but it was enough to find her way. The tunnel split again, and she took the left fork, further amazed that she remembered. It was as if the way had been branded into her mind like they had branded the slave mark into her flesh.

The tunnel narrowed and straightened as she expected,

and the walls closed in tighter. She never remembered feeling panic or claustrophobic before, perhaps because this was the only world she had known, but now a cold sweat made her back clammy, and the air became thin and stale. She pushed forwards; she couldn't give up now

After some time, a comforting soft glow appeared in the distance. Many tunnels branched off this one, but her destination lay ahead. Her pulse quickened as she approached the familiar door to her prison. She anticipated her and Amwa's happy reunion then paused. The door was open, why? She couldn't hear any snoring or people talking softly, had they been moved? Turning cold, she stepped into the cavern lit by a single, low burning lantern.

She realised her mistake before she had even set her foot down, and a small squeak of surprise escaped from her lips. The entire cavern was empty. Where before fifty sleeping slaves should be laying before her, there were none. The heavy iron door was always shut and locked, always, why had she not been more cautious?

Her eyes drifted up from the floor to the broad-shouldered, heavily muscled Nuakki standing before her, bare arms knotted in front of him, brown eyes glimmering, and his impossibly tall head unusually helmet-less. He carried no weapons and wore no armour, and as she took in his powerful, deep chest, she knew he needed none, not for her.

Terrible powerlessness stole over her, and with quivering shoulders, her gaze slid down to the ground as she whispered, "Osuman."

32

THEY HAVE NO NAMES

"Lonohassan Viewing Mirrors are quite remarkable."

Osuman spoke in perfect Lonohassan as he paced slowly towards her. "They showed you returning to me, and I couldn't quite believe it. But now you're here..." Each step closer reduced her freedom by one, yet she found she couldn't run, she couldn't fight—why was this? He held a terrible power over her, and it wasn't magical, it was purely psychological.

She stepped back. He pressed a small device in his palm and the door began to slide, metal grinding on metal that echoed loudly around them, before shutting with a dreadful finality. Her bottom pressed against it and she could retreat no more. He raised his other hand. It was huge—*he* was huge, and she flinched as he gently stroked her face.

"You fear me so much." He smiled, but a frown knitted his eyebrows together.

"Is it any surprise?" she replied, her voice almost a whisper.

His face hardened and he leaned in close. "Your mind has been polluted again. It must be Cleansed for you to return to me." He grabbed hold of her chin and fumbled in his pocket. Did he have the power to erase her mind again? Her breath quickened.

"The Vormae captured me, they did something and it all came back!" She hated the way her voice had taken on a pleading tone. She'd survived so much, she had been through so much, and now she was reduced once more to a simpleton girl in this alien's presence. Had she not found her strength and courage? *It's outside waiting for me!* Thoughts of Khy brought a little determination.

Osuman paused, his turn to be surprised. "You survived the Vormae? It's not possible."

She pushed her face forward. "Where's Amwa? Where are the slaves? I did *not* come back for you, I came to free them—"

He moved so fast and then she was flying across the room. When she hit the floor, the agony in her left cheek started, followed by her hip and knee. She began to sob like she had before. It was happening again, and she was powerless before him. She could barely see through her rapidly swelling eye as he lifted her with a sudden tenderness that scared her all the more.

She noticed the light in her palm had gone out and her hand was cold. She tried to muster the strength to kindle the Soulfire, but it froze within her.

"I've been thinking all this time only about you," he said.

As he stroked her swelling cheek, she became aware of the struggle within him she had sensed so long ago. There was the light, and there was the dark, and his confused reactions were driven by whichever side entrapped him in the moment.

There is light in them, there is hope for the fallen Nuakki, she thought. But she was not in a position to help him, and right now, her very life and freedom depended on getting as far away from him as possible. She knew what she had to do, but could she bring herself to do it?

He danced his fingers along her chin. "I don't know this Amwa, they have no names."

Thaya was surprised he bothered to answer her question. It showed an element of respect.

He continued, "The slaves were moved to the north mine when a large gold vein was discovered. This one has proved far less fruitless. Your hair has grown long." He smiled and stroked it, and she supposed it was a compliment. "I like this...new you."

Fearful anger blossomed within her and she narrowed her eyes. "This is not the new me, it's the *old* me you bastards tried to erase! Well, it didn't work for long. And *I* have a name and it's Thaya if you ever bothered to ask. We all have names!"

She felt the Soulfire stir within her at last, only a spark but it was there.

Osuman drew back, his mouth curving down. "We're going to have to fix that attitude." He sighed and pressed something into his palm that looked like a piece of flat, swirling silver. "I didn't want to do this, but I can see there is no choice. To stay at my side, you must be obedient."

Osuman lifted his hand, his other tightening on her hair and pinning her back. The moment Thaya had been dreading was fast approaching, and tears began to blur her vision, making her task harder. She focused on her Soulfire, culturing it, fanning it like she would a fire but with her mind. She was learning to control her powers; she just wished her lessons didn't always have to take place *on* the battlefield.

His dreaded palm loomed in front of her face, and she

saw the silver device was a peculiar symbol. The first time her mind had been erased, the Nuakki had just used his palm. Perhaps it was different the second time around, or perhaps Osuman didn't have the power to do it unaided, maybe only priests could. Why did he have to do this? She'd let him go if he let her go but he never would. Couldn't they all be free? Couldn't they all be happy? That world felt very far away.

His palm touched her forehead and terrible pain sparked there, but unlike before she knew what it was, and she was ready for it. *I rise above it. I'm stronger in body and mind, so much stronger than before!*

Tenderly, she lifted her left hand and laid it against his face, so small against his cheek, and her thumb caressed his smooth tanned skin. His eyebrows twitched, surprised at her tenderness, and a soft, genuine smile turned up the corners of his mouth, but he did not release his palm and the pain grew. Fighting it, Thaya had little time before the pain and confusion overwhelmed her. She lifted her right palm and pressed it against his chest then moved it closer to the sternum where she knew from many nights lying beside him and listening to it, was where a Nuakki heart lay.

With a sigh, she released her Soulfire in a single torrent.

Light flared between them. Osuman jerked, his face twisting in pain and surprise. Tears blurred Thaya's vision, but her right hand did not drop away even when blood poured over it. Her left hand burned in agony and smoke rose from between it and his cheek as his skin blackened. His eyes locked onto hers and his palm dropped from her forehead.

The pain vanished. He sunk to his knees, bringing his face in line with hers.

Tears filled his eyes, and in Nuakki he whispered, "Why?"

She fell with him to the ground. His eyes fluttered, then closed and he was still.

Thaya swallowed and trembled all over. What had she done? "I didn't want to do this, but you left me no choice!" Her cry echoed around the chamber.

Her left palm still burned ferociously and suddenly it sparked. She stared as the golden spiral brand flared then faded. The blistered skin shrank and became smooth, and the burning ceased. Instead of a blackened brand or golden mark, just a smooth, pale white spiral remained. *Through his death I am free.*

She stroked Osuman's face. *How far have you come from your own world to enslave the people here? Do you miss home?* She felt sorry for this warrior race. Their dark deeds only served to enslave themselves and lock them into a world devoid of freedom and happiness. A world filled only with fighting and taking and lack. She might have been the slave, but compared to the Nuakki, she was forever free.

A deep shudder vibrated through the tunnel swiftly followed by another. *Explosions. The army has arrived! Amwa...*

She jumped up and grabbed the small black device Osuman had used to close the door. She couldn't quite determine what it was made out of, it felt like a mix of metal and ceramic, but when she squeezed it, she felt some mechanism inside click and the door began to slide open. Casting one last look back at Osuman's prone body, she turned and ran back into the dark.

Thaya paused at the exit and stared at the chaos. To her left, a legion of Nuakki smashed into the human regiments in a cacophony of screaming, clashing weapons, and explosions of magic. An arrow whizzed inches past her face and she fell back into the cavern. The army had just arrived, but how had the Nuakki got here so fast?

Everything slowed down as she unravelled what had happened and made a list of assumptions—assumptions that her 'ability' told her were correct. The awake guard had noticed his sleeping partner and awoken him, breaking Khy's spell. Either one had then run off to raise the alarm, reducing the army's element of surprise. Where was Khy? He must have moved away to avoid detection.

She peered back out. At least she was behind the front-line. The archers were level with her, which meant the humans were pushing back the Nuakki. *Pray that it stays that way!* The humans outnumbered the Nuakki, but their foe was much larger and more intelligent. The outcome was unknown.

Behind the archers stood a line of Magi, hands and staves lifted to the air as they commanded the magical forces. Lightning arced from their palms over the heads of the soldiers and straight into the Nuakki. It flared against a mauve shield and created an awesome yet deadly magical light display. Anyone caught in it burst into flames.

Khy had spotted her and pounded towards her, soldiers scattering in his wake. Sprays of blood mottled his sides, and gore slid down his horn. He pranced before her, saying nothing, but eyeing her all over for any damage, noting her swollen cheek and eye. Neither spoke, they didn't need to. She laid a hand on his neck and pressed her face into his hair, the familiar smell of him drowning out the chaos, making her feel like she was home.

She lifted her head and looked from the battle to the gaping maw of the other mine a little further along the cliff. "They're in that one. I won't be long this time."

"Use your Fireshot first, think later," said Khy, "otherwise your other eye will be swollen, and you'll never get out."

With a chuckle, she flattened herself against the wall and inched towards the entrance. Every explosion made her flinch. Blood sprayed the wall ahead and below it slumped a bloodied soldier, sword still in his hand. He wasn't moving and one of his arms was a mashed and bloody stump with white bone visible.

Thaya's hand went to her mouth, and she gagged. What price life? What was in it for him, other than pay? The man didn't deserve to die. The Nuakki probably hadn't done anything to him, and he probably didn't even hate his enemy. *Who sends these people, these humans, to die?* She imagined a rotund, over-fed, bejewelled prince swathed in velvet and gold, his greedy eyes gleaming brighter than the gems on his fingers as he did business with the Invaders for his own gains.

'We let them in...'

Evil, greedy leaders send people to their deaths and damn the world to hell. They must hate their own kind to do such things!

The screams of the dying raked her ears and her pulse pounded with anger. She didn't know who she despised more, greedy humans or the invading aliens. *But we weren't always like this. What made the prince greedy where others are not?*

'...the Hidden Darkness will move amongst us pretending to be as us, infiltrating in silence, dominating from the shadows,

twisting and destroying all things holy...' Thaya shivered as she remembered the ancient scroll.

A spear smacked into the wall barely a foot in front of her face, striking with such force it embedded itself into the cliff. She stared along its vibrating staff and saw a soldier being lifted by his neck by a Nuakki warrior. His furious kicking drummed harmlessly upon the Nuakki's breast-plate. The Nuakki twisted his hands, there came a sickening crack, and the soldier went limp. The warrior roared and hurled the soldier against the cliff, his lifeless body sliding down the rock face to Thaya's feet.

The Nuakki locked eyes onto her and lifted a Pain Stick. Electrical energy flared and surged towards her. She flat-tened herself against the wall with nowhere to run.

Khy leapt in front of her. The energy struck his horn where it crackled and collected, connecting the two by light-ning. Khy and the warrior battled for control. The Saphira-elaysa jerked his head and the energy flared. The Nuakki howled in pain and tried to throw his weapon down. Khy reared and the Nuakki flew into the air. With a toss of his head the energy snaked and snapped, hurling the warrior across the battlefield.

The rearing Saphira-elaysa caught the attention of the closest Nuakki and three turned to them. Swords and spears raised, they shoved the human soldiers in their way aside. Thaya pushed herself off the wall and stepped to Khy's side, Fireshot raised. She fired it before a single Nuakki could raise its weapon. Fire engulfed the man on the left, and he fell to the floor screaming. The other two halted and stared at the falling ash—all that remained of their comrade.

For a human, this might have instilled fear; for a Nuakki it instilled fearless vengeance. They surged forwards, Khy leaping to meet them. Sword clashed against horn and the blade was cut into two. Khy didn't stop and speared his horn straight through the warrior's chest.

Thaya couldn't stare; the other Nuakki was upon her. Too close to raise and aim her Fireshot, she rolled to dodge under the sweeping sword and grabbed the blade fallen in the ash. Spinning low, her sword connected with flesh, biting deep into the Nuakki's exposed calf. Howling, he fell to one knee and lashed his sword behind him. The tip caught Thaya's shoulder, grazing it. She hardly felt the sting, or her own hot blood trickle, as she sunk her blade between his ribs. The warrior shuddered and fell into the dirt, her sword embedded in his back.

Thaya stood, shaking all over.

Khy looked monstrous, a unicorn covered in blood, nostrils flared, sides heaving. He touched her bloody shoulder with his horn. The sudden searing pain made her wince, but when he pulled away, the wound had stopped bleeding.

"Get on!" he ordered and bent down.

She didn't need to be told twice and swung on to his back.

"You can use a sword," he stated, leaping towards the cliffs over the Nuakki bodies.

"No." Thaya shook her head, barely able to breathe through the adrenaline coursing through her.

"Yes," Khy insisted. But it wasn't true, she had never lifted a sword in her life.

"I got lucky," she said, daring to glance back at the one she had killed, but he was lost between the throng of Nuakki and humans. *I've killed them, and I don't like it, I don't!*

"They would have killed you had you not. It wasn't luck. You should have a sword."

"I have this," she lifted her Fireshot.

"Get a sword as well." Khy was adamant.

They made it to the mine's entrance and she slipped off his back.

"I won't leave you." Thaya shook her head.

"You must, your friends are inside and I'd do the same. I'll guard the entrance as best I can. The Nuakki aren't interested in us at this moment."

She couldn't stay with Khy *and* free Amwa. She stared into the blackness. "Amwa."

Anxiousness rippled across Khy's shoulders as she stepped away from him.

"I'll be quick," she assured him.

He nodded once and turned back to watch the battle. Out here, he'd be in more danger than she. She licked her lips, there'd be no Nuakki inside, they'd all be fighting now. She hurried once more into the darkness.

33

NOW WE ARE FREE

THAYA LIFTED HER PALM AND FOCUSED WITHIN THE CENTRE OF her body until warmth grew there.

Grinning, she let the warm Soulfire spread from her solar plexus up and along her arm and into her palm where golden light appeared. *That came faster than before, I'm getting the hang of it!* But she felt wearier after too.

She stepped forward only to trip, too intent upon her palm of light to see the loose rock.

"Ouch!" Catching herself against the wall she grabbed her stubbed toe and waited for the pain to pass.

The rock that had tripped her up gleamed in the Soulfire light. Her eyes widened. *Gold? Of course! That's what the Nuakki kill and enslave for. Gold, or their supposed theft of it, is why people are dying outside this moment!* She picked up the fist-sized rock and forced it into her pocket, nearly ripping the fabric as it was so large. Why they wanted gold, she'd have to think about later.

Looking back into the darkness she saw there were several tunnels leading in all directions, and in this mine, she had no idea where she was going. She hurried down the first on her right, but it led to a dead end. Backtracking, she took the next, which also led nowhere. She sighed and went back to the main tunnel and took the left fork. It went on further than the others and the sounds of battle faded behind her.

At an intersection, she paused to listen.

Beyond her heartbeat pounding in her ears, she heard distant, muffled voices. *That tunnel on the left!* She hurried down it only to reach another dead end.

"Damn it!" She backtracked to the intersection straight into the path of a wolf.

She screamed and flinched, but the wolf nuzzled her leg. "Teo!" Thaya clasped her hands over her racing heart.

Tess appeared moments later and then she was hugging two tail-wagging, cheek-licking canines. Teo yipped and pranced away, asking her to follow.

"Lead the way!"

Thaya had trouble keeping up with the wolves as they bounded through the tunnels. Dull light appeared ahead, and she hurried faster. Voices came, hushed, but clearer than before, and staleness touched the air. It wasn't human to live underground like a rat. Thaya scowled.

The wolves ran towards the light, but Thaya slowed. What if there was a Nuakki there, like when Osuman had been waiting? *Osuman waited only for me, and in that he's unlike the other Nuakki. He had become obsessed with me.* She tried not to think about the shock on his face when she'd used her Soulfire. *I used it to kill, and it's wrong!*

The wolves would surely warn her of danger, but when they reached the entrance by the lantern light, they stood there waiting and wagging their tails. The hushed voices had ceased.

Tess barked as she approached.

"You found them!" Thaya laughed and ruffled the wolf's mane.

She stared through the iron bars at the dirty, skinny people dressed in their awful rough tunics and rope belts. Scores of fearful faces looked up at her; men, women, children, old, young, and everything in between. The cavern curved round to the left, so there were many more people she couldn't see. She had to remind herself to breathe, and when she did there was a lump in her throat. No one moved, no one spoke. Some of them *could* speak, she'd heard them earlier so at least she could communicate with them.

She gripped the bars but was unable to open the gate. There was no Nuakki device to open it, but surely it could be moved manually too? Arendor could open any door. She moved towards the lock and handle and placed her hand over it. Closing her eyes, she focused on her Soulfire and also on the lock.

A strange thing occurred when she did this. She found herself looking inside the actual lock itself as if she were a tiny ant lost inside it. She gasped and opened her eyes. Was that part of the Soulfire ability?

Other gasps mirrored hers and people pointed at her glowing hand. She smiled. *Now I'm the source of wonder.* Her glowing hand no longer hurt now the brand was gone. Always, she'd been awed at Arendor and his magic, now she knew how it felt. Using magic was starting to become more natural.

She closed her eyes and stared into the complex mechanism of cogs and levers and tiny copper wires surrounding her. Seeing the inside didn't help at all, she didn't know what anything did. But as her hand grew warm against it and she willed for it to unlock, the mechanism inside grew warm and began to glow. Soon it was almost hot and that's when a spark occurred. The entire mechanism began to move and click, a whole mechanical world coming to life around her. The door shifted under her palm and she opened her eyes to see it slide open. She felt dizzy and suddenly exhausted, needing to lean against the wall to catch her breath. Using magic had consequences, she was learning.

The people stared in awe and slowly got onto their feet. A man stepped forward, his shaven head still bearing bloody cuts from the hands of his rough hairdresser. He looked from her to the dark tunnel beyond and rubbed the stubble on his chin.

Thaya nodded in encouragement. "Go on, it's safe. The Nuakki aren't here, they're busy."

His eyes were so wide, she wondered if he believed her, but when the others clustered behind him a flicker of a smile curved his lips. A girl pressed in front of him, her blue eyes gawping beneath a sooty forehead. She pointed to the wall behind her and several feet back in the tunnel, Thaya saw a ledge high up and almost out of reach.

Thaya frowned, wedged her foot on a lower indent and strained to reach up to the ledge. Her hand grabbed something small and she stepped down to inspect a similar small black device that Osuman had used to close the door. After all that fiddling trying to unlock the door, the girl could have pointed to the device sooner. Her withering smile at the child turned into a grin and she ruffled her inch of golden hair and chuckled, but the girl jumped at the sound. Laughing was forbidden, how could Thaya forget? However, the girl must have seen the light in Thaya's eyes for she dared to smile, then giggle.

Like the first snowball before the avalanche, the joyous laugh was infectious, spreading from one to the next person until the cavern that had been their eternal prison was shaking with the noise. Then, the people were running—not a panicked stampede for freedom, thanks to the pacifying effect of the Cleansing—but a calm determined escape into the darkness with her glowing palm lighting the way. They were free. Finally, they were free.

Daylight appeared ahead; beautiful, bright daylight. She stepped out into it and was immediately blinded by the sun, just as she had been in the past. She loved it.

A voice called out to her. She shielded her eyes and blinked at the young man running towards her from the mass of people streaming out of the mine, his mop of black hair bobbing. She gasped—could it be? She hadn't dared to hope he was amongst the slaves, but now she noted his familiar elongated eyes, deeply tanned skin and warm, smiling face. He had grown since she'd last seen him, but he was still lithe and boyish.

"Amwa!" she shouted, and ran at him, embracing him firmly.

Tears filled her eyes and she felt his splash on her shoulder. Neither spoke. In his arms, she noticed that the roar of battle had stilled. Gone were the screams, clashes of metal, booms of magic. Where enemies had, an hour ago, heaved against one another, now blood trickled into pools and dribbled down walls. Great scorch marks wounded the earth where Nuakki and human magic had clashed. She should have been there fighting at Khy's side, alongside Arto's knights, but when she looked at the slave-boy she knew what she had done was more important.

She touched Amwa's cheek. "You're free now, all of you."

He smiled, and looked from her to far away where the ocean crashed endlessly upon the shore, careless of the battle that had just taken place. There was the strangest look in his eyes that she would never be able to fully explain. Fear, pain, confusion. What does freedom mean to those forever enslaved? Did he even know what freedom was?

She placed a hand on her chest like he had done so many times, and said, "Thaya. I am Thaya. And I remember."

Tears filled his deep brown eyes and he smiled even deeper. "Thaya. Of course it is. It is your name."

They embraced again.

"They don't know what to do," said Amwa, indicating the slaves clustering just outside the mine. There had to be at least a hundred of them; all looking around, some hunched and fearful, others amazed to be outside without chains. All acted with a child-like innocence only a Cleansing could create. Would they get their memories back? The Vormae had proved they were still there if they could only be unlocked. Now they were free, who was going to look after them?

"That's quite a shiner."

Thaya whirled at Maggy's voice and touched the painful swelling of her cheek and eye. She wouldn't think about Osuman, not now. "They're free, Maggy," she said, her voice trembling.

"I can see, and it looks like this place is ours again, for now," Maggy smiled briefly, before a frown crossed her face. "Though I doubt we'll be left alone for long. The Nuakki have a nasty habit of returning to a fight, a bit like a bad smell that won't go away. Still, there's time but, oh, what a mess; look at all these poor wretches who need help. I think it would be wise to lead the people to a settlement far away from these mines and from the memories. Sadly, this is just one Nuakki stronghold from several. We've won this battle but not yet the war, if it can ever be won."

Thaya had a thought. "The Viewing Mirrors still exist. I don't know where they are, but they're somewhere here. You'll have to find them; perhaps they can help the people remember their past, remember what they were before this. The memories are there, they just have to be rekindled."

"Ah, the Viewing Mirrors...What you say lifts my heart." Maggy's faced creased into wrinkles. "I'll search these grounds all day and night hunting for those things taken from us."

"Sounds like a good idea," said a deep voice.

Thaya whirled around and her heart leapt at the sight of the man striding towards them pulling off his helmet. "Arto!" Following him was Khy, his indigo eyes unblinking as he looked her over, but he did not speak.

A bloody streak ran across Arto's cheekbone, and blood and dirt splattered his breastplate. He, too, was limping, but at least he was alive. She threw her arms around him and he lifted her with a chuckle. She couldn't stop what she did next—perhaps it was to wipe away the memory of Osuman, to replace the memory of his lips with a beautiful, wanted kiss—and she pressed her lips firmly against Arto's.

His eyebrows raised, but he didn't pull away, and she closed her eyes against the tears, allowing the whole world to melt away. Strong hands squeezed her shoulders as they drew apart, and her cheeks grew warm at the audience. She smiled sheepishly at him, glad to see an intrigued rather than embarrassed expression on his face and a little red growing on his own cheeks.

"I was about to add..." he winked at Thaya, but then turned serious, "we weren't successful in destroying the Nuakki. In fact, I'm surprised we did as well as we did. If they hadn't been weakened by the Vormae previously, we wouldn't have done so well. They're smarter than the Vormae and chose to retreat, many of them leaving in their ships. We couldn't stop them and are certain they'll be back, probably with legions more.

"Our orders are to recover the stolen gold, as much as we can, and leave as soon as possible. We've been given a day and night to do this, but for now, civilians and the injured must be tended to. Let's return to the ships where there's food, warmth and rest. Ma'am, you can ride with me." He nodded respectfully at Maggy.

Maggy pursed her lips and looked to where the Nuakki buildings clustered in the distance, then sighed. "All right, I could do with a hot meal. And some wine. Is there wine? But straight after, I'll be returning to salvage that which they stole."

"And you," Arto said gently to Thaya. "I saw you fight, and you fight well, but you can't just run into battle like that, you need armour!" He tapped his steel breastplate.

She laughed. "I didn't intend to fight at all. Besides I don't think metal can protect against their Pain Sticks." She chewed her lip at the memory. Armour couldn't protect against magic, but it would have spared her from the sword. Her shoulder still stung and ached. But he was right, something more than Maggy's clothes and her sailor's boots would surely be a good thing.

"There might be some leathers on the boat. I'll see what I can find," he said.

"I'd like that," she grinned at him.

Arto took them back to the ships amongst many other soldiers who were carrying the wounded.

With Arto leading, Thaya walked beside Khy and Amwa, and Maggy followed with her Spirit Wolves, preferring to walk rather than ride. *These people are my family now,* Thaya thought. Fi and Yenna and her brother's faces came into her mind and she blinked away the tears. *I won't forget you, not ever.*

With most of the remaining army on land retrieving the gold, there was floor space aboard the ships for them and all the freed slaves for the night. Hot food was served, as much as they could eat, and to Thaya it had never tasted so delicious. She slept deeply beside Khy on a bed of blankets with a contentment she had not known for a long time. Khy did not like the ship at all and he longed to be back on the earth. He drank purified water and filled himself full of sunlight on the deck.

Time passed quickly, too quickly, and the next day they were leaving.

She stood on the deck with Khy and the others, a strong wind tugging on her hair under a sky filled with white clouds.

"Please, come with us," Thaya begged her friend, the old woman, again.

"You know I—we—cannot leave this land, and I haven't yet had time to salvage anything." Maggy shook her head for the hundredth time.

Amwa agreed. "I'll stay with her too, and many others. I want to help them remember, so we'll try to find the Viewing Mirrors."

Thaya rubbed her chin. "It's my land too. Am I wrong to leave it?"

Maggy cupped her cheek with a wizened hand. "No, you're young, and you *must* leave it, my not-so-little Thaya. I wish for you to stay, but deep down I know you must not. Do what the Agaroths and Leonites tell you, for they're far wiser than humans are now. Find the Magi, be all that you can be. Besides, you know where to find me; I'll always be here. Oh, you've so many wondrous things ahead of you! The Magi will teach you Far Sight, Air Walking, and magics I haven't seen for decades. The next time we speak I'll bet it will be through a mirror or pool of water." Maggy's eyes lit up with wonder as she spoke, and she chuckled gleefully like a little girl.

Still, Thaya's heart sank at the thought of leaving her, and it took a lot of effort to draw away from their final hug.

"I'll look after her," Amwa reassured, his smile warming her like it always had.

Knowing he and Maggy would be together made her feel better. "I'll miss you too, my friend." Thaya embraced him one last time then turned to Teo and Tess. Their tails wagging incessantly, she hugged them close, unable to stop the tears any longer. Hot tongues licked them away.

"The boat is waiting, Thaya," Khy told her. He didn't speak aloud, though he would have had she earlier asked him not to scare the crew and reveal his true self. A talking horse was the last thing the battle-drained soldiers needed.

"The boat is ready," Arto echoed.

Thaya nodded and wiped away more tears as she stood. Forcing herself to smile, she watched them lower Maggy, Amwa and the wolves on the small, rope-strung platform down to the raft boat bobbing on the waves below. Thaya's eyes did not leave them as they navigated the spritely surf all the way to the shore.

Once safely landed, they turned and waved. Thaya waved back, noting how the wolves' tails wagged in response. No one walked away, not even when the last raft boat was lifted and secured on deck, and the sailors weighed anchor. Thaya gripped the railings of their rolling ship as it swung away from the long beach of golden sand. The tide was fast and the wind strong so they quickly picked up speed. She watched her friends become tiny specks in the distance, then disappear completely.

With a deep sigh, she looked up at the sky with a feeling of dread. The long cigar-shaped ships of the Nuakki or the small shiny ships of the Vormae were out there somewhere. Safety and security were mere illusions in this world.

"Safety and security are feelings that come from within," said Khy.

"So be it. Then I'll create my own safety and security with knowledge and courage." She laid a hand on his shoulder. *"Especially with you by my side."*

"You didn't want to stay, did you?" she asked aloud when she was sure no one was in earshot. Maggy wanted her to stay and so did Amwa. Arto thought she should too, but she knew she couldn't, there was something she had yet to do and it came before seeking out the Magi.

Khy tilted his head. "Not really, although I prefer land, or swimming, not standing on this creaky death-trap floating atop the water. But this moment I only want rest, clean water and pure sunshine." He was perfectly balanced on the rocking ship, which was a source of wonder to the milling crew who had never seen a horse act quite like him. All the other horses were securely tethered in the decks down below, but Khy wasn't having any of it. Besides, he needed sunshine. "I couldn't for the life of me think why you weren't considering using the portal gates, and then I saw you looking at Arto again. A good mate for you I think, there's nothing wrong there."

Thaya turned crimson and laughed in embarrassment. Deckhands glanced in her direction and she coughed as if clearing her throat. Thankfully, Khy didn't pursue the topic, not that she could say much on it either, confused as she was about her feelings for a man she barely knew.

Thaya looked back at the disappearing land. She'd miss them all deeply and there was much Maggy could teach her, too. "I'll return soon after I meet these fabled Magi, there are a good few things I could learn and should know already. Imagine it, soon I'll be able to wield more magic than you." She grinned at the thought.

"I doubt it." Khy snorted, making her grin even wider.

But before then lies an unfinished chapter in my life that I must complete. She turned her eyes east to the rising sun, then a little north to where Havendell and her old home, Brightwater, lay.

———

Thaya watched the sun setting. There were no clouds to mar the startling orange and red rays stark against the deep blue of the sea. Fire and water, forever apart and forever together.

She had never sailed on a ship before, except for that brief time with Arto, which could hardly be called sailing since they were being attacked by the Vormae. Despite those memories, she found she utterly loved being surrounded by endless ocean, it just felt so wild, so *free*. They could go anywhere they wanted and there was nothing but the wind and the tide to stop them.

The journey aboard the ship passed smoothly and without event—a peculiarity in her very strange and turbulent life, even the ocean grew remarkably calm when they lost sight of land. She found herself finally relaxing and waking well past dawn. She slept in a hammock beside Khy, not in with the horses, but in the storerooms amongst the creaking crates and barrels—she preferred it here, more for privacy than anything else, and also because Khy's height, along with his horn, made it impossible for him to stand up straight anywhere else.

To her delight, she was beginning to regain the weight she had lost. The meals, whilst simple, were plentiful and she found herself eating with a hunger she had never known. Two bowls of oats for breakfast, cakes for noon, cheese sandwiches for lunch and stew for dinner—all washed down with rum. Khy made do with a bucket of water—purified of course—and sunshine, of which there was plenty in these late days of summer.

As she had under Solia's command, Thaya helped out in the kitchen when she was needed at mealtimes, but at all other times, she was up on deck staring out to sea, watching the sunsets and the myriad stars bejewel the night sky above.

Unfortunately, being the captain, Arto was very busy, but every time they caught each other's eye—which was pleasingly frequent—he smiled, unfailingly making her blush.

She stood with Khy on the seventh evening, watching the late summer sun extinguishing its fiery rays into the cool blue ocean, and turned to the sound of approaching footsteps.

Arto smiled, the sun making his hair golden and his eyes sparkle. She looked beyond him to the commander who had taken the helm.

"You don't leave the wheel much. Are you sure you trust him?" She winked.

Arto laughed. "I'd trust Commander Bridge with my life. I came over to tell you something. I thought you'd like to know we should spy lights upon the land before morning, and with a good wind we'll dock at Havendell Harbour shortly after first light."

Thaya masked her disappointment. She'd hoped for longer with Arto, or at least some time to chat. "Oh, that's good, thank you. I hope I didn't embarrass you back there...I —" she began, but Arto cut her off.

"No, it was quite welcome, actually," he replied, his green eyes intensifying.

Thaya let out a silent sigh of relief. "Well, I mean, you might have someone else or even be married, and I rudely didn't even think of that." She'd never apologised for her actions, not that she felt sorry for what she had done, quite the opposite, she just didn't want Arto to feel bad, if he did, which he clearly didn't.

His lips narrowed, there was history there—he'd spoken before about a previous painful relationship, the cause of his losses, but he didn't elaborate and it wasn't her place to ask.

"No," he replied. "You just took me by pleasant surprise. Most women are...shyer."

Thaya grinned. "Normally I *am* shy, well, not normally, there haven't been many times. Well, there have been some, just not lots. I mean, under normal *circumstances* I'm shy. I was quite emotional after the fighting and..." Her cheeks grew hotter by the moment as her words tumbled out.

Khy's ears twitched, and he began backing away, trying to sneak off silently.

"Don't go," said Arto.

Khy paused and instantly gave himself away. Thaya froze.

"He's not actually a horse, is he?" said Arto, cutting straight to it. Amusement danced in his eyes.

"I don't know what you mean." Thaya gave a nervous laugh and pushed back an errant lock of hair from her forehead.

"What gave it away?" asked Khy, dropping the act.

Arto wrung his hands nervously and stepped back. "So I wasn't wrong...I, er, it's a good disguise, but I saw you for what you were outside the mines when I was hunting for Thaya. Maggy told me what she was doing, and I saw you standing there—even in the shadows a Saphira-elaysa shines with its own light." Arto's face lit up with wonder. "Ever since then, I've occasionally been able to see through your disguise, not always, but sometimes."

Khy tossed his head. "Not even magic can hide the truth for those who see. Then you have some magical ability, and this is good."

"Some," Arto nodded. "And, like Thaya, I can see the truth."

"Don't tell anyone else," Thaya warned.

"Your secret's not mine to tell. You can trust me." Arto closed his fist and laid it against his chest.

"All right, I'll trust you," said Thaya softly.

"Care to tell me the missing bits of your story?" Arto tried to smile, but his eyes flicked nervously back to Khy.

Thaya took a deep breath. This was their last day, or rather night, together and there were several hours until bedtime. Maggy was the only human that knew everything about her. She needed another human to understand her, if understanding were possible, and so she told Arto everything that had happened to her, from finding the strange scroll in the Old Temple, to Arendor the Agaroth saving her life, to her memory of touching the little Saphira-elaysa that was Khy.

Arto listened with an enthralled look upon his face as she took him to different worlds and into enormous crafts drifting far out there in the Cosmos. His face became stony when she spoke about Osuman, and he touched the faint bruise on her cheek tenderly. She loved him for believing her and not being sceptical, but then, he *had* been abducted by the Vormae alongside her, so he knew what this world suffered.

Thaya had trouble explaining her soul connection to Khy. "You see, there had always been this great hole in my life, something missing, something empty, and now I know why. Since that day we touched, my soul has been twinned with Khy's, and his with mine, for good or ill. What the future holds, we don't know." Thaya sighed. She looked up at the night sky. There was no moon tonight and the stars were more numerous than ever. Khy had long since gone to bed down below and she remained alone on deck with Arto, and a handful of crew keeping the ship on track.

"But I'm tired of me, let's talk about you. Are you happy being a knight?"

"Yes, happier being a knight than a captain of a merchant ship—although right now I find myself doing two jobs and being paid only for one. Without a sword, my hands felt empty, clumsy even, if you can imagine that. My place at this baron's side? Well, I don't think I'll be there for long. He's a greedy impatient man, a big, over-bloated fish in a small pond. I need a larger pond and a greater leader."

"A King's man," said Thaya.

He looked at her sharply, "Perhaps. You're as perceptive as the Saphira-elaysa. Maybe one day you'll turn into one." He chuckled and pressed her forehead where a horn might sprout.

Thaya laughed and raised her eyebrows, "After all I've seen, anything's possible. You know there's one last thing I left out. Hmm, I don't know if I should tell you..." Should she mention the time she saw him on Earth? She chewed her lip, only half believing herself what she had seen.

"You can't *not* say it now," said Arto.

"I suppose not...It's, again, tricky to explain, but I saw you, your future you, in the future, of course. Bah, it's hard to describe, but remember this Earth I talked about? Urtha in the future only all the magic's gone? I know it's crazy, even I can't understand it—hopefully, the Magi can—but it was you in a sort of posh tavern. You were subtly different in minor ways, but nevertheless, it was you, and you *recognised* me."

"How is that possible?" Arto frowned.

Thaya shrugged. "I told Arendor, and he said that the soul never dies, and it chooses to be reborn. It might sound like a cliché, but he said our lives must be intertwined strongly for us to meet again at a future point. I know I'm still me and not a future incarnation, but he said it anyway."

"Well, if that's true, then it pleases me." He lifted her hand and kissed it, his lips making her skin tingle. Ignoring the whistles of his crew, he placed his hands on the railing either side of her and pressed his lips firmly against hers. She closed her eyes, enjoying his warmth and the fuzzy desire fluttering in her belly. They parted, but only to draw breath. The intense look in his eyes made her feel enjoyably powerless between his arms.

"Goodnight, Thaya Farseeker," he said in a husky voice, his lingering gaze saying he really didn't want to go.

He walked her to the door where they reluctantly parted. She took the stairs leading down to her hammock, the sound of crew laughing and whistling fading as the door swung shut.

34

WE ARE ALL ONE

BRIGHTWATER WAS CLOSE.

In the blush morning light, Thaya held her breath as their ship pulled into Havendell Harbour. Her eyes swept the familiar streets to the green forests beyond. The old roads were still there, especially the main street winding up over the hill and into the trees beyond, but a lot of the harbour didn't match her memory. Gone were the numerous wooden jetties and the teetering fish-shacks selling mussels, winkles and cod. Scorch marks marred the pale grey walls of the warehouses, and there were still several piles of rubble heaped about the place. How many people had died? How many people had been captured? *I'd rather die than be enslaved.*

She shivered and pulled the rich ivy-coloured cloak Arto had given her closer. If she saw the Vormae again, she'd fight them with her Soulfire and her Fireshot, and with all her fearless courage.

The Harbourmaster's shouts had his workers scurrying in all directions to help dock the swaying galleon. Sailors tossed mooring lines and all manner of ropes thicker than her arm to the expectant harbour staff below, and slowly but surely the galleon was brought under firm control and secured in its dock. There was room for three of their warships, but the rest had to drop anchor at sea.

Finally, the ship stopped swaying. She hoped to find relief in that, but she found herself swaying anyway meaning walking in a straight line didn't come easily. A week at sea and she'd forgotten how to live on land.

She watched the soldiers disembark along the frighteningly narrow gangplank, easily marching in a straight line all the way to land. The horses followed next, certainly less convinced by the whole thing, and then the ship's crew hauled empty barrels and carts across from their storage in the decks below.

Thaya hung back and hunted the milling sailors for Arto. She couldn't leave without saying goodbye. There he was on the quarterdeck, giving orders to three crewmen and pointing to the bow. He was still very busy. It didn't look like he'd have any free time now either, so with a sigh, she waved when he looked in her direction and followed Khy's rump and the line of barrel-carrying sailors.

Moments later large hands grabbed her and spun her around.

Arto grinned. "Not going to say goodbye?" He pulled her off the gangplank and took her to one side.

Khy turned, his ears flicking back and forth; the telltale sign he was intrigued. The unicorn winked at her, then respectfully carried on to land.

"I was going to but, uh, you're busy and I didn't want to get in the way." She smiled and ended up fluttering her eyelashes girlishly.

"Never in the way. I didn't say it last night, but after

you...*ran away* all those months ago, I thought about you far too often. It concerned me."

He pulled her closer and she dared to wrap her arms around him, wanting to feel a human man's arms around her rather than a Nuakki's. She liked the prickle of his stubble against her forehead, and that he smelled totally different, natural in a way a Nuakki male could never smell. Arto wrapped his arm around her, his other hand stroking her neck tenderly. Osuman had tried to be tender, but it had always felt so wrong.

"Your...*horse*...is waiting for you," said Arto huskily when they drew apart.

"How...*when* will I see you again?" said Thaya, staring up into his green eyes.

"At the Loji Magi. You'll be there some time if you go, and you should. As chance would have it, the baron has me on an unusual assignment there after this campaign, a delivery or collection of some sort. I'd prefer to travel with you, to protect you, but I cannot join you yet. You'd do well to hire a sword or protector. I don't like the thought of you travelling alone. But then you do have a very special *horse*."

Thaya didn't like the thought of travelling with anyone other than Khy. "If such an opportunity arises, I'll take it, but my horse and I are well-armed. After I've finished in Havendell, I'll be heading straight there. Perhaps I'll even travel through your baron's lands."

"Do that, and I'll have the guards watch out for you," he said, lifting her left palm with its white spiral. He stroked it gently and then kissed it. She fancied he was soothing away her memories of the Nuakki. "I'll write to you, Thaya Farseeker, if such letters can ever find you. And should you wish to write to me, address it to Artorren Eversea."

Thaya smiled. "Would that be, Sir Artorren Eversea?"

He gave a sad smile. "Perhaps once, but no more. A new me has emerged from the ashes of my former self...and my fortune." He chuckled.

An awkward silence passed, then he pulled her close again and pressed his lips to hers. Her stomach fluttered and she felt dizzy in his arms, the heat of his body igniting fires she hadn't felt before, not even with Eddo.

Far too soon he let her go, their hands parting as they each went their own way.

In a busy port and without a harness or saddle for Khy—she dreaded asking him to wear one—Thaya decided they'd look less conspicuous if she sat on his back. 'Ride' would be the wrong word, she was quite clearly a passenger when she was on his back, and she merely had the option of *suggesting* where to go.

He never minded carrying her, and often it was he who suggested it, but she always felt awkward. She felt the same now as she pulled herself onto his back which was not so easy to do when there were no stirrups. As soon as Khy felt nobody was looking, he bent to allow her access.

"Ouch!" Something solid dug painfully into her thigh as she slipped her leg over his back. She sat up and inched it out of her pocket only to whip her cloak over it before anybody saw.

"What are you doing?" whispered Khy.

An old man leaning heavily on a walking stick looked at them and frowned.

"Don't speak here," she hissed. "I forgot about the gold! I picked it up in the mines. There's a goldsmith here, or there was. Perhaps we can mint it and change a portion into silver and copper. I've got no coin upon me at all!"

Khy nodded. Using her mind, she directed him through the busy fish market. He snorted and flared his nostrils at the stench, lifting his head high, trying to find clear air.

"Try to be more horse-like," she hissed as people eyed them curiously.

"You need a saddle and reins, Miss, or that one's gonna prance right through me livelihood," shouted a fishmonger, tutting and shaking his head.

Not accustomed to making way for humans, and keen to get out of the stench, Khy barged—gently, as he saw it—through the crowd. A young man fell back with a scowl that softened when he looked up at her. "That mount's too much for you, young Miss," he grumbled.

Thaya nodded and forced a smile. They made it through to the other side where both breathed more easily. There were fewer people here, so she quickened the pace.

"Take the road up the hill, then the first right. Let's get out of here as soon as we can."

It was difficult trying to speak without moving her lips, but then, all girls talked to their horses, didn't they? Still, she caught peculiar looks from the early morning shoppers. She smiled and nodded at them—and so did Khy, to her dismay —and had to control herself from nudging him like a horse to walk faster. He snorted, just like a horse, and decided to walk faster in his own time. Was he having fun? It seemed like he was. Well, she wasn't. This was all quite embarrassing.

Thaya stared at the flattened scorched earth where once a row of shops had stood, including the goldsmith's. "The Vormae did a good job," she muttered.

They continued up the hill and along the High Street.

Past the Old Bakery, a brand new shining sign swayed in the breeze.

"Golder's Gold," she read aloud. There were no other new signs. *No surprise a Goldsmith's was the first establishment to reopen,* she thought, *they were the richest merchants in any town.*

She dismounted Khy nearby. "I won't be long, and for god's sake, don't talk or smile or nod to anyone!"

Khy looked at her, eyes wide, ears pricked forward, nothing but the picture of innocence. She prayed no one could see his shining horn like she could.

She whirled away into the shop, a bell announcing her entrance. It was dark and stuffy inside, and an extremely short, stocky man with thick round glasses appeared through the door. The light shone off his large, mostly bald head that was encircled by a strip of wispy white hair which ran down to his sideburns and filled out his beard. He peered over his glasses at her. "How can I help you, Miss?"

Thaya had never seen such a short person before. Could he be a dwarf from the North Mountains? It didn't feel right to ask him why he was short so she replied, "Yes please, can you mint this?"

Her hands paused in her pockets. What would it look like her bringing in a huge ingot of gold? *If he IS a dwarf, they're said to live in mountains made of gold.* Well, it was no use carrying around a heavy rock, so she plonked the fist-sized ingot on the table.

His eyes lit up hungrily and he lifted the metal, inspecting it closely and sniffing it with gusto.

"Hmmmm, yes, Lonohassan gold, it's good to see it again, though I don't want to know the blood, tears and sweat that it cost you to get." He winked at her. "A soldier passed by here earlier with a similar beauty, so I'll be cutting you the same deal. Ten per cent?"

Thaya had no idea and shook and nodded her head ignorantly, "Yep, sounds good."

"It will take me half an hour," he said, then disappeared through the swinging back door.

Thaya folded her arms and turned to peer out of the thick bulls-eye glass windows. There was suspicious movement beyond the distorted glass; it looked like an old woman swathed in rags was stroking Khy's nose and laying something around his neck. Thaya's heart jumped into her throat and she ran out the door.

"There, there, my pretty," crooned the old woman, her plump bottom wobbling and shimmying under the hundred or so scarves and belts and sequinned cords draped around it. Thaya noted the sequinned scarf inching around Khy's neck—the unicorn was enjoying the petting far too much to notice! His eyes were wide, and ears forward as he inspected this peculiar woman.

"He's not for sale!" Thaya barked and pushed herself between them.

The old woman fell back with a squawk. Her mass of grey waves cascaded over boulder-like breasts and hung like a frozen waterfall around her waist. Jewelled silver rings adorned her fingers and her eyes sparkled like new copper coins. Everything about the woman screamed 'witch' and this made Thaya even more worried.

"Ahhh, and here she is, the fabled one who can tame Saphira-elaysa!" shrieked the old woman, causing passers-by to stare.

"Dear gods, shush!" hissed Thaya stuffing her finger against her lips.

The old witch chuckled delightfully, enjoying the spectacle. "I saw one once from a mile away, but that was three decades ago. I'll never be able to miss one again. Oh happy days, the Creator's alive!"

She wafted her hand and tried to shush her, but it had no effect on the witch. Thaya glared at Khy for allowing this to happen, but he was too enthralled in the woman to notice.

"Listen, kind lady," Thaya tried another tactic and leant in close.

The witch hushed and bent close, keen to be a confidant.

"If you look after him for ten minutes, I'll give you a copper piece."

"Ohh," she screeched, looking up at the sky with glee and clutching her fists to her chest. She bent back to Thaya, "One whole silver, and no spells will be cast."

Thaya huffed, but the witch opened one eye wide and winked.

"All right, all right," Thaya sighed. Whatever it took to get her gold and out of here. She turned back to the gold-smiths, shooting Khy a look. He could deal with it himself now.

She stepped back inside and welcomed the quiet gloom.

"Ahh, Miss, I didn't quite believe you'd run off," said the dwarf and coughed to clear his throat. "This is the lightest way for you to carry it, here you are; forty gold, forty silver, and one hundred coppers. He placed three small sack-cloth pouches on the table. "Minus ten per cent for me." He smiled and rubbed his hands together, thinking it a good deal for them both.

Thaya nodded, too rushed to haggle, though five gold for the whole process seemed like a lot. She quickly counted each bag as he pencilled out a receipt and passed her a carbon copy.

"Thank you, Miss."

"Thank you, er..."

"Master Derrie Copperbrook Golders," he said for her, smiling deeply so that his whiskers rose up to his eyes. She shook his huge but stubby hand and winced at his strong grip, then began stuffing the coins about her person.

"I hope you've got a sword," he said, shaking his head. "All manner of thieves and cut-throats abound on the roads and don't think they won't check your boots. They'll kill you first and ask questions later. Finding a boon like that? Well, you'll have just made their day."

He was right, and she stepped out of the shop far richer and far more nervous than just half an hour ago. She felt as if everyone who looked at her could see the gold she carried as she hurried over to Khy.

"There you are!" She stuffed a silver coin into the witch's hand and swung up onto Khy's back, keen to be gone.

The witch bit the coin suspiciously then her eyes lit up, "Ooo, it's real and fresh and shiny. No curses for you today, Missy, I'll even send some luck your way."

"Thanks," said Thaya a little sourly, and tried to urge Khy on by shoving her hips forward rather than kicking him. He didn't get the message, however, and stood still. "Go right?" she tried and grinned foolishly at the witch who raised an eyebrow.

Khy nodded and began walking.

"Oh, your scarf!" said Thaya, and tried to unravel the cheap blue lace from his neck.

"Keep it," said the witch. "A gift, for him." She winked again and turned away, holding her silver coin up into the sunlight and giggling.

"Okay, whatever," Thaya sighed and flicked at the flimsy material hoping it wasn't cursed. "Take the next right and head to the trees at the top of the hill. Let's get out of here."

She tried to relax as the trees approached and Havendell Harbour receded into the background. She had weapons, magic and Khy. Any ruffian stupid to attack? Well, that would be his or her fault. But still, perhaps she could find a safe hole to bury her money, it was everything that she owned.

"Did you talk to her?" Thaya asked.

"No, she knew me for what I was straight away. Any who can use magic or have seen us before will see through the disguise."

Thaya didn't like that one bit.

The Temple of Light loomed beyond the trees, its pointy steeples spiking up to tear at the sky. Thankfully the main road wound left away from it so they wouldn't have to pass by directly. Three grim-faced Illumined Acolytes dressed in their sand-coloured robes with black collars strode towards them, causing cold sweat to clam between her shoulders.

Khy swivelled his ears to the side, which she was beginning to learn meant he was wary. The stone-faced people, two men and a woman, heads-shaven, hands-clasped in front of them, didn't even blink as they glared at her. Servants of the gods... What exactly was in their temple? Only the initiated were allowed inside and everything that they did was kept very secret. Perhaps there was an alien preaching their sermons, Thaya chuckled inwardly then shivered at the thought. The Acolytes of Light were secretive in their undertakings but loud in their preachings and violent in their punishments.

Khy quickened the pace of his own accord and she was glad when the Acolytes did not follow them but carried on the road into town where they would ear-bash the innocent public.

They walked the long road towards Brightwater, meeting only merchants and farmers who, in the main, greeted them pleasantly. Nothing happened of any consequence, though she couldn't shift the memory of the Shades hunting her.

She slipped off Khy's back and allowed herself to relax as they trailed the country roads in the warm sunshine. Lunch was a pasty Arto had stuffed into her pack the night before and Khy enjoyed himself in the Brightwater Stream.

Butterflies danced in the air, birds tweeted in the trees, flowers nodded in the breeze amongst the rich and fertile green grasses. This was Havendell, far from the struggles and strife of the world beyond.

"Blissfully ignorant," she said to herself, fingering a perfect daisy, *and I wish I was still, sometimes. No, I can't come back. The world is calling to me, and dare I even say that the Great Spirit is calling to me? There's a long journey ahead of me.*

Three hours later, they crossed the stream over the quaint little bridge, and familiar thatched roofs poked above the trees. The homely, black-beamed cottages of Brightwater emerged from the forest.

A lump formed in Thaya's throat and she realised she had stopped walking. Khy looked at her inquisitively. Her eyes settled on the people working the fields and the children throwing a ball for a dog. One of them was the rascal Tayne, her brother's son. In the middle of the field with a hoe, was that Fi arching his back and Yenna pulling weeds?

"They're all here, Khy," she said, unshed tears wobbling her vision. "I feared the Shades or the Vormae had...but look, they're all here alive and well."

Khy looked from the people back to Thaya. "Go to them, speak with them," he said gently. "I'll wait here."

He nodded encouragingly, but Thaya felt more afraid now than she had at the hands of the Vormae.

Step by step she made her way to the fence enclosing the field in which they worked. Dear Yenna and Fi, they looked the same as when she had left, old but upright and strong, like all the people of Havendell.

"Are you all right, Miss?" asked Fi, frowning at her.

Thaya realised she was staring and crying and hastily wiped the tears from her cheeks. "Oh yes, I'm sorry, I..."

"Here's an apple if you're hungry, we've hundreds of them already!" said Yenna, a kindly smile on her face as she pulled a bright green apple out of her apron pocket.

"Thank you." Thaya took it and stared at it, struggling against a tide of emotions. She looked into the woman's eyes, but there was no recognition there, nothing at all. "I'm sorry. I'm a little emotional these days." What else could she say?

"It's all right, lovely." The older woman squeezed her arm and thankfully didn't ask for an explanation.

"Thank you," Thaya repeated, smiling and raising the apple.

"Pleasure," said Yenna.

When she turned away, Thaya quickly eased out a gold coin from its pouch and let it fall over the fence right next to a potato plant.

It took all of her will to tear herself away, and when she looked across the meadows her breath caught in her throat and she nearly dropped her apple. There, standing at the edge of the trees watching her stood Khy in the exact same position and poise as the Saphira-elaysa she'd seen in that vision so very long ago. Khy was her home, and seeing him soothed her aching heart. She walked towards him, her shoulders drooping a little less with each step.

She didn't say anything and Khy didn't ask as they made their way north along the road past the village, but she still fought to hold onto herself against the overwhelming emotions.

When the village was lost to the trees, she finally spoke, blinking through the blur of unshed tears. "They don't remember me, just like when I didn't remember them or even myself. It's good in a way, I suppose, it's just...there's something not right about not having your memories, things lost and forgotten that shouldn't have been. I guess I was never really a part of them or from here, and now I cannot stay, so I'll try to make peace with that. I'm just pleased they're well and happy, and I can say goodbye and close this chapter of my life."

"We're both adrift from our roots," said Khy, and she knew he was feeling everything she felt, which was why she didn't need to explain anything.

"Without you beside me, I'm truly adrift," she said, laying a hand on his shoulder.

They came to the jumble of ancient stones that in some ways had been her awakening point in life. "Lonohassan stone." She touched the pale yellow rock, feeling the same sense of awe fill her. "They brought it all this way trying to escape from the Nuakki. So many mysteries make sense to me now."

"Knowledge is power."

Thaya jumped at the man's voice and stared at Arendor walking towards her through the swaying grasses, an unusually wide grin on his face. "It's good to see you again, Thayannon Farseeker. Greetings, Khy-Ellumenah-Ahrieon Saphira-elaysa." He bowed deeply to the unicorn then straightened. "I think you should have this, Thaya." He waved a familiar golden tube in his hands.

"The scroll! Where did you find it?"

"It was decaying down there so I collected it and preserved it. You don't want artefacts such as these falling into the Acolytes hands and being destroyed by the Fallen Ones. This is proof of what happened. You found it, and so it belongs to you now. Consider yourself a Keeper of Knowledge."

She took the scroll and tucked it into her belt. "I shall do as you say, as always, my friend."

She hugged him and he hesitated, never easy with affection but never shunning it either.

"You have become stronger, your powers are growing," he nodded approvingly.

"I'm doing as everyone suggests, I'm going to the Magi."

"Then you are wise, and I give you my blessing. I see you still have my ring and the Fireshot, I'm impressed they've lasted this long. I came only to return to you that which should not be forgotten. I knew you would return here so I left a marker to alert me to your presence. Perhaps your Magi can teach you how to do such simple but useful things. For now, I leave you, but reach for me if you are in need."

"Thank you. I hope to visit Arothia once more sometime soon," said Thaya.

"You will always be welcome, Farseeker." Arendor bowed and stepped back, a thick grey mist rising around him. It engulfed him then vanished, leaving only the indented grass to prove he was ever there.

In silence, Thaya and Khy followed the road towards the towering White Mountains. The dirt track quickly became rugged and the grass thinned to rock.

With the summer now at its end, the snow had long since melted making it the perfect time to travel through the mountain passes. Thaya and Khy left the last of the trees behind and stepped onto the steep scree track leading up through the rock face. She didn't know how far it was to the Magi and their conclaves, only that it was a long, long way east.

A sense of urgency spurred her on. Autumn marched close and the passes wouldn't remain free of snow forever. If she found a portal, would she dare to use it? It seemed she was destined to. The track was steep, and she breathed heavily, sweat covering her face already. Without a portal, it would take a long time to get there at this rate. She just hoped she could clear the mountains before the snow came.

"Phew," she huffed and paused on the corner of a switchback.

Khy didn't appear to be out of breath at all, and his face was expressionless though she felt a certain boredom emanating from him.

Ignoring it, she looked out from the wall of grey that had dominated her vision for the last hour and gazed back down the way they had come.

"Wow."

Far below, the entire land that was called Havendell languished before her, bathed in golden sunshine. She could see everything; the white-tipped mountains ringing it on all sides but one, the rich green hills and valleys inter-laced with white rivers and small crystal lakes, and finally the sparkling Emerald Ocean far to her right. She strained to see any ships in the harbour, hoping to spy Arto's, but it was far too far away.

The view took her breath away, almost bringing tears to her eyes at Urtha's splendour. Would she ever find a place more beautiful than this? Possibly. The world, the cosmos, was a remarkably large place. Her gaze lifted from the land up to the deep, endless blue sky. There were so many worlds, so many peoples, her place was out there, and home was wherever she and Khy went. She belonged nowhere, and she belonged everywhere. They had both been enslaved and, now unshackled, the world lay waiting before them.

She smiled and laid a hand on Khy's shoulder. Nothing could compare to the sense of utter freedom that filled her.

"We're free, forever," she said.

Khy twirled his horn, sharing her feeling.

With a sharp inhale she truly understood the meaning of the scroll's final words. The exiled Lonohassans were trying to remind people of something, and she felt it keenly now as she stood beside Khy. *My twinned soul and I are two parts of one whole. We always have been, and so, too, are we also connected with Urtha, other beings, and all in the Cosmos. It can be no other way. None exist in isolation. The light itself unites us, and what is done to one is done to all. Even the darkness was once part of the light, I remember this truth deep within me.*

Her palms grew warm with Soulfire and Khy's horn shimmered with golden-silver light. "You and I are one. We Are All One," she whispered.

***

To be continued...

A FARSEEKER NOVEL

GATEWALKER

JOANNA STARR

ALSO BY JOANNA STARR

Joanna Starr also writes classic High Epic Fantasy under her pen-name, Araya Evermore, author of the bestselling series, *The Goddess Prophecies.*

THE GODDESS PROPHECIES

by Araya Evermore

Goddess Awakening ~ A Prequel

When darkness falls, a heroine will rise.

The Dread Dragons came with the dawn. On dark wings of death they slaughtered every seer and turned their sacred lands to ruin...

Night Goddess ~ Book 1

A world plunging into darkness. An exiled Dragon Lord struggling with his destiny. A young woman terrified of an ancient prophecy she has set in motion.

He came through the Dark Rift hunting for those who had escaped his wrath. Unchecked, his evil spread. Now, the world hangs on a knife-edge and all seems destined to fall. But when the dark moon rises, a goddess awakens, and nothing can stop the prophecy unfolding...

The Fall of Celene ~ Book 2

Impossible Odds, Terrifying Powers

"My name is Issa and I am hunted. I hold a power that I neither understand nor can barely control..."

The battle for Maioria has begun. Issa faces a deadly enemy as the Immortal Lord's attention turns fully in her direction. Nothing will stand in Baelthrom's way—he must destroy this new power that grows with the rising dark moon...

Storm Holt ~ Book 3

Would you sell your soul to save the world?

The Storm Holt... The ultimate Wizard's Reckoning, where all who enter must face their greatest demons. No woman has entered and survived since the Ancients split the magic apart eons ago. Plagued by demons and visions of a strange white spear, Issa must take the Reckoning to find her answers and fight for her soul to prove her worth to the most powerful magic wielders upon Maioria...

Demon Spear ~ Book 4

Demons. Death. Deliverance.

All these Issa must face as darkness strikes into the heart of their last stronghold. Greater demons are rising from the Pit, Carvon is brutally attacked, and a horrifying murder forces Issa and her companions to flee. But despite the devastating loss, she must keep her oath to the Shadow Demons and alone reclaim the spear that can save them all...

Dragons of the Dawn Bringer ~ Book 5

An Exiled King. A Broken Dream. A Sword Forged for Forever.

Issa can trust no one. Her closest allies betray her and nobody is as they seem. When a Dromoorai captures her and a black vortex to another dimension rips into her room, she realises the attacks will never stop and there is far worse than Baelthrom reaching for her out of the Dark Rift...

War of the Raven Queen ~ Book 6

"Be the light unto the darkness...Be the last light in a falling world."

They had both been chosen: he to save another race; she to save her own from what he had become. Now, both must enter Oblivion and therein decide the fate of all...

BOOKS BY JOANNA STARR

Farseeker

Enlightened. Enslaved. Erased.

Earth, 50,000 years ago before the magic vanished. Invaded by aliens posing as gods, advanced civilisations crumbled. Now, these powerful off-worlders war for control of the planet, and the people who remain no longer remember what they once were. Seduced then enslaved, humanity has fallen...

Gatewalker (A Farseeker Novel)

Coming Soon...

STARTER LIBRARY

If you would like to read more about Thaya and the worlds of *Farseeker*, I've gathered together exciting extra and deleted scenes not included in the main story. I'm also giving away my bestselling Epic Fantasy novel, *Night Goddess,* and the prequel, *Goddess Awakening,* written by my pen, Araya Evermore, exclusively to subscribers.

To receive this epic free starter library, please go to my website and join my mailing list. As a subscriber, you'll also be the first to hear about my latest novels, and lots more exclusive content.

FACEBOOK GROUP

JOIN A FRIENDLY GROUP OF FANTASY BOOK LOVERS.

Starr & Evermore's Raven Guild has been created for fans of the books to chat, share fantasy art, debate storylines, and meet other fantasy readers. You can also ask me anything about the novels.

The Guild is where you'll *first* hear about giveaways, discounts, new books and previews. It's a friendly, fun place to be and you're most welcome to join!

Go to:
www.facebook.com/groups/starrandevermore/
And click "Join Group" to join.

ABOUT THE AUTHOR

 Joanna Starr is an award-winning author, a half-elf, and creator of the best-selling epic fantasy series, *The Goddess Prophecies,* written by her pen, Araya Evermore. She has been exploring other worlds and writing fantasy stories ever since she came to Planet Earth. Finding herself in a world in which she didn't quite fit, escaping into fantasy novels gave her the magic and wonder she craved. Despite majoring in Philosophy & Religion, then Computer Science, she left her career in The City to return to her first love; writing Epic Fantasy.

Originally from the West Country, she's been travelling the world since 2011, and has been on the road so long she no longer comes from any place in particular. So far, she's resided in the Caribbean, United States, Canada, Australia, New Zealand, Spain, Andorra and Malta. Despite loving forests and mountains, she's actually a sea-based creature and currently resides by the ocean in Ireland.

Aside from writing, she spends time working, talking to trees, swimming with fish, gaming, and playing with swords.

Connect with Joanna online:
www.joannastarr.com
author@joannastarr.com

amazon.com/author/joannastarr

bookbub.com/profile/joanna-starr

facebook.com/JoannaStarrAuthor

LEAVE A REVIEW

If you enjoyed this book, I'd be honoured if you could leave a quick review for other fantasy and sci-fi lovers (it can be as long or as short as you like) on the book's Amazon page.

Thank You!

Made in the USA
Coppell, TX
13 November 2020

41320957R00288